THE ROYAL FAMILY
Loyalty Brings Royalty

Don Michael

ACKNOWLEDGEMENTS

First of all, I would like to thank God for blessing me with the experiences, creativity, and a second chance at life to be able to produce this work of art. I want to give a big shout-out to two gentleman who aided in the recreation of myself throughout my federal tour.

Lawrence Sample "LA", my brother… Thank you for the life lessons you taught me, you've had a MAJOR impact in my life and for that, I will be forever grateful. I'm working on a few things and I'll have some things in motion before you touch down, so your transition back into society will be even smoother.

Norman Talley, you're truly a stand-up guy, always smiling and kept a positive outlook, no matter what was going on around us. Love ya, can't wait until you hit the streets.

Shout-out to the RICH BOYZ twins.

Shavonya Coleman, you have been a Godsend. You've done an excellent job editing my book. For anyone who needs editing work done, you can find her on Facebook!

Shout-out to everybody from my hood… too many names to mention. Grand River/Schoolcraft area! 722!!

To all the men and women incarcerated across the U.S., hold ya head up, there is light at the end of the tunnel. To J.M., you played a huge role in the reconciliation with my youngest son. Love ya…

CHAPTER ONE

MARCH 1995

"Dolla! It's on you, nigga!" Rell screamed as he saw the car full of girls pull up on the block.

"I'm on it!" Dolla said, coming from the backyard where a dice game was taking place.

"What y'all need?" Dolla approached the four girls in the car.

"Damn, you just gon' cut into us like that? No, 'hi'? Not even a, 'what up, doe'? Where yo manners at, boy?" The pretty redbone fired off from the backseat of the car.

"Oh shit, my fault… what up, doe? What y'all tryin' to get?" Dolla asked.

"That's more like it. I know you gotta get ya money and all, but you should always be polite to the ladies," the redbone chick snapped at Dolla with as much sass as she could muster.

"Damn! I said my bad. Cut a nigga some slack. What's up with yo girl?" Dolla asked, looking towards the driver. Before she could respond, the redbone interrupted.

"My name is Savannah and we came all the way from the eastside to fuck with y'all, so show us some love."

"Ok, ok… shit," Dolla said with his hands up, now smiling. "I can respect y'all comin' from the other side of town… Plus, you come through on the regular, so I'm gonna give y'all deals every time you come by.

"Give us four of them fat bags," the driver said, handing Dolla two $20 bills.

Dolla reached in his pocket and pulled out six dime bags of some fire-ass weed and placed them in the driver's hand.

"That's for y'all. I know gas ain't cheap, so I'm gonna always make it worth your while to come through the craft."

"Damn! These bags big as hell. Good lookin'," the passenger said with a big-ass smile on her face. "We gon' strictly fuck with you… What they call you?"

"My name is Dolla. I'm out here 24/7, so y'all gon' see me. If not, holla at my nigga, Rell." He pointed to Rell, who was busy serving five different custos with a look of frustration on his face.

"Oh shit, my manz look mad as hell. Let me give 'em a hand. I'll holla at y'all."

Dolla stepped to walk away but turned back around, "Bye, Sa-vann-aah," he called with a sly smirk on his face. Savannah rolled her eyes as the girls pulled off.

"Damn, dawg. You over there rappin' with them hoes, and I'm scrambling tryin' to serve all these muthafuckin' custos, nigga," Rell complained. "I served ten different custos while you was on your 'Don Juan' shit. But I ain't trippin'. Just give me half of what I just sold in bags and I'll give you half of the money from the sales I just made."

Rell was a real nigga like that. Never on no greedy or snake shit, always one hundred with his homies. Rell, whose government name was Jerell Thomas, was a no-nonsense, by-the-book type of dude. Even at a young age, (he and Dolla were fourteen at the time), he was somewhat wise beyond his years. Very territorial, NO ONE could come close to their block and sell anything if they weren't from over there. If someone tried, (which a few people did), Rell would bust a nigga head and send them on their way. He would not hesitate or wait. If someone was T-rollin, (sneaking and serving custos on the block), Rell would handle it right then and there, with or without help.

Rell was a big boy for his age. Short, stocky, and good with his hands. He was brown-skinned with short wavy hair. Shortly after his thirteenth birthday, he dropped out of school and picked up a sack and started hustling for Dre, the neighborhood pound man, selling weed. Rell didn't see any reason for going to school. "I ain't getting paid for sittin' in that bitch, so fuck it," is what he would always say. From what he saw, all the older people who went to school and college were living fucked-up lives and struggling to pay their bills, so he saw no reason for going. He made the decision that he would become a heavyweight in the drug game and live like the rappers and sports players on T.V. one day.

Rell didn't have a big family, so there were no older people in his household to keep him off the streets and out of trouble. Rell's mother was young and a party girl at the time she gave birth to him, so she left him with her mother shortly after he was born. Never called or stopped by to check on him, never sent money. Nothing. It was as if she fell off the face of the earth. His father was a dope fiend, strung out on heroine. Rell's father was a part of his life, even though he was a fiend, up until just after Rell's seventh birthday.

One day, Rell and Dolla were walking through the alley coming from the store around the corner when up ahead, they saw someone sitting on the ground in the alley with their back against the wall of the neighborhood dry cleaners… his shoulder leaning against the dumpster. Now, this was normal in the hood because there were a lot of bums, winos, and dope fiends in the neighborhood. They would always get high off their product of choice in the alleyways all over the hood. Rell and Dolla used to call them "zombies".

As they approached the man, they realized it was Rell's father.

"Man, this nigga don't stop. He always fucked up," Rell blurted, almost as if he were talking to himself.

"Damn, that is yo old dude. Let's get him out the alley," Dolla suggested.

"Fuck it! Just leave him," Rell replied, but continued to approach his father.

"Oh shit!"

They were now up close, and Rell was the first to notice that something was very wrong with his father. Dolla wasn't paying attention at first, but after Rell screamed, he turned back and saw the same thing Rell saw. Rell's father's eyes were open but they were ice blue with dried up blood coming out of the corners. Vomit mixed with blood was all over his clothes and his head was tilted sideways, leaning up against the dumpster. Still stuck in his arm was a dirty syringe. Dolla and Rell tried shaking him but quickly realized that he was already gone.

"No, no, noooo!! Rell's screams echoed through the alleyway as tears streamed down his face. "Wake up, Daddy. Wake up!"

Dolla stood frozen, eyes and mouth wide open, in an obvious state of shock. He tried to speak, but no words or sounds escaped his mouth.

"Help me drag him around the corner to the house!" Rell yelled in a state of panic.

Dolla, snapping back to reality, helped Rell tug and pull the body, but they were unable to move him very far.

"Man, if Hammer was here, he could help us, but his daddy won't let him out of the house," Dolla said in a panic.

"Let's go get my grandma, she'll help us," Rell suggested.

The boys quickly sped out of the alley and ran up the block to Rell's grandma's house, which was right in the middle of the block. Even though the boys were running top speed, everything seemed to be moving in slow motion.

"Nana! Nana! Daddy dead in the alley! Help us get him!" Rell was screaming between breaths.

"Child, y'all slow down and catch y'all breath! I can barely understand you! It look like you about to pass out!" Rell's grandmother was dark-skinned, short and round with long black hair that she always kept in a long ponytail.

"Daddy's in the alley and he's dead!" Rell cried. This time his grandmother heard him loud and clear.

"Oh, Lord! Are y'all sure??" she asked.

"Yeah, Grandma Cill," (her name was Pricilla.) "We think he's dead," Dolla said. "We tried to pull him from the alley, but he was too heavy for us."

"Shoot! Let me call an ambulance." She quickly grabbed the phone and dialed 911.

"Hello? Please send an ambulance to the corner of Schoolcraft and Mettetal. I believe my grandson's father is dead in the alley."

"We're sending one right away, ma'am," Dolla heard the operator say through the phone.

Rell's grandmother slammed the phone down on the receiver. "Let's go to the alley and wait on the ambulance," she said as they all headed out the door.

It took damn near an hour before the ambulance arrived. Once they got there, the paramedics pronounced Rell's father dead on the scene. They placed his lifeless body in the ambulance and told Grandma Cill they were taking him to the coroner to be examined for the cause of death, even though it was already evident he died from a drug overdose.

The boys and Grandma Cill walked around the corner. "Man, this messed up. I'm going home to lay down. I'll holla at you tomorrow bro," Dolla said and hugged Rell and Grandma Cill.

"I'm sorry about your dad. I'll be here whenever you need me," he said, then walked in the front door of his house which was three doors before Rell's house.

Once Rell and Grandma Cill got in the house, they both sat on the couch.

"What we gonna do now?" She was now holding him in her arms as he looked up at his grandmother with tears.

"We gonna keep living, child. That's what we gonna do. Your father would want it that way. Even though he was on drugs, he was still a strong man, and you gotta be strong too, baby…"

A week and a half later, a funeral was held for Jerell Thomas, Sr. People from all over the neighborhood came to pay their respects. Even ones who Rell had seen throughout the neighborhood who he didn't even realize knew his father were there. There wasn't a dry eye in the church. Dolla was there, so was his sister and aunt. Hammer couldn't make it. His pops wouldn't let him go.

After the burial, the boys never spoke about it again, except for filling Hammer in on the details of how they found Rell's father in the alleyway… and the funeral.

Dolla also had family woes as well. His father was a major figure in the drug trade throughout the eighties before being indicted on drug charges and a string of murders all over the west side of Detroit. The feds charged him with the RICO Kingpin Act. He took it to trial and lost. As a result, he was sentenced to life in federal prison without the possibility of parole. Dolla's father, whose name was Dante Jones, left the streets with a few beefs that were not taken care of. As a result of that, Dolla's mother was kidnapped shortly after his incarceration. The men who kidnapped her demanded $500,000, and in return, they would set her free.

Money was not an issue. Dolla's dad was a millionaire a few times over. And even after his incarceration, the feds repossessing cars, jewelry, homes and a nice amount of cash, the man still had money in the streets. His father knew his time was running out, so he began stuffing cash into a large walk-in safe behind a wall in the basement of Dolla's auntie's house.

When word got back to Auntie Darline that her sister, (Dolla's mother), had been kidnapped, she immediately took half a million dollars from the safe for the ransom money and gave it to her boyfriend, James, who was also in business with Dolla's father. Darline's mind was playing tricks on her. She was somewhat suspicious of James, thinking he may have something to do with her sister's kidnapping. She trusted no one. But still, she reluctantly gave in and waited for sister to return.

Hours turned to days, and after a week went by, Darline considered going to the cops, even though the kidnappers demanded no police involvement. If they so much as thought the police were or would be involved, they would kill her sister without hesitation.

I knew this muthafucka James was involved... No sooner than the thought entered her mind, the phone rang. "Shit, it's about time."

"Hello? Yes, is this Darline Martin... I'm speaking with?" She was met with a deep voiced on the other end of the line.

"Yes, it is. I've been expecting your call," Darline answered, assuming it was one of the kidnappers.

"Um, ma'am. I don't know who you were expecting, but my name is Officer Davis, and I'm calling on behalf of your sister, Denise Martin. We um, found her in an abandoned house on the east side of the city. Along with her we found -"

"Oh, God! Is she alright? When can I pick her up? Is she at the station?" Darline bombarded before the officer could finish his sentence.

"Well, ma'am. As I was saying, we found her in an abandoned house on the eastside, and it appears she died from several stab wounds and a single gunshot to the head. Along with her was a man whom we haven't been able to identify at this time. Do you have any idea who could have wanted to do this to her?"

Darline was reeling with disbelief. Between sobs, she managed to say "no," although she knew her sister was kidnapped and murdered because of the drug wars Dante was into before he left the streets.

"She has… had… a son." Reality was slowly beginning to seep in. "He's with me right now. How am I supposed to tell him this?" The words came but she wasn't really sure who she was talking to.

"Well, ma'am. There are counselors that I can recommend you to for the child. Meanwhile, we need for you to come the coroner's office downtown to sign some papers and possibly help identify the gentleman she was with… if possible."

"Yes, I can be there in the morning," Darline responded, still in a state of shock.

"Okay. Sounds good, Ms. Martin. I will meet you there around nine in the morning. I am very sorry for your loss."

Darline didn't reply. She just hung up the phone.

"Dammit!!" She cursed to herself. "All this shit is Dantae's fault! Now my sister AND my man are both dead!"

She felt bad about thinking that James had something to do with her sister's kidnapping. The man only wanted to help but lost his life in the process. They never intended on returning her sister. They killed her and James and took the money too.

The next day when Darline went to the coroner's office, she left Dolla with Grandma Cill. Her heart fell into her stomach when she saw her sister laid out on that table. There was a sheet covering her body, so she couldn't see the stab wounds. She had been shot in the back of the head, so Darline couldn't see that either. It looked as if she were asleep.

When she saw James, tears began rolling down her face as if her eyes were faucets. The man had been shot in the face, nothing left but a gaping hole where his face used to be. The only way she knew it was him was from the tattoo on his neck which said "loyalty".

"Ms. Martin, do you know this man?" Officer Davis asked.

"I'm sorry, but I don't recognize him." Despite her reply, Officer Davis had a strong feeling that she in fact did.

"Not to sound harsh, but may I ask what made you cry even harder after taking a look at this gentleman?"

"Listen, I said I don't know him. My mind is racing a hundred miles a minute. I'm just taken aback by all of this. Now, if you'll excuse me, I have to go make funeral plans for my sister."

"I understand. Here, take my card and don't hesitate to call me if you need anything. If I get a breakthrough in this case, I'll call you, Ms. Martin," Officer Davis said, now eyeing her suspiciously.

"Thank you, and if I hear anything, I'll be in touch with you as well, Officer Davis."

As she pulled out of the parking lot, so many questions were going through her mind. *How will I tell Darin about his parents? Will the kidnappers come looking for me?*

Once she arrived home, she was mentally worn out. After picking Dolla up from Grandma Cill's, she brought him home and prepared dinner. Darline never thought something like this would happen to her sister. Denise may have been romantically involved with a drug dealer, but Dante was a good man and a provider for Denise and Dolla. Denise worked as a clerk downtown at the county building. She made good money. She and Dante had a huge house in a community called North Rosedale Park. Black politicians, judges, doctors, lawyers and a few major drug dealers lived in this area.

Darline had made two promises to herself. First, she was going to raise Dolla as if he was her son, and second, she vowed to herself, never to have anything to do with do drugs and not to associate with anyone involved with drugs. *Fuck that shit. Ain't no man or anybody else worth what comes with the game,* she thought to herself.

Darline was a dime piece just like her sister Denise was. Tall, dark-skinned, hourglass-shaped with light brown, almond-shaped eyes. The only difference between her and her sister was that Denise had a slightly lighter skin complexion and she wore long hair while Darline wore her hair cut short.

Time passed, and Dolla's mother was buried. Darline explained the situation as best as she could to Dolla. She knew that he was hurt, but he seemed to keep it bottled up inside.

"If you ever want to talk about it, I'm here for you, baby," Darline would assure him. She had no problems raising Dolla. After all, she still had a nice chunk of money that his father had left behind. Once a year, she would take him to see his father who was locked up in Victorville, which was in California. She kept Dolla well fed and he stayed with the latest clothes, shoes, and video games… more than enough for one child. Dolla had a good heart. He would share his shoes with his best friends, Hammer and Rell. At first, Darline would get mad at him for this, but soon she realized that Hammer and Rell were not as privileged as he was, so she backed off the subject.

Years began to pass and now Dolla was beginning to come into himself. Even though he was only fourteen, the boy was damn near six feet tall, dark-skinned with the same light brown eyes his mother had.

"Who is them hoes anyway?" Rell asked. "I been seeing 'em come through for a minute now. Which one you mackin' on? Shit, next time they come through, call me over and put me on one of them bitches!" he rambled on.

The fact of the matter was, the boys were only fourteen, but they were already fucking, drinking, and smoking.

"You think Hammer gon' be able to come outside today?" Rell asked.

"I hope so. That nigga ain't been out all week. His peeps be holdin' his ass hostage for real!" Dolla said.

No sooner than Dolla finished his statement, the boys looked up to see Hammer walking up the street. "There go that fool right there!" Dolla exclaimed.

"You sure?" Rell asked.

"Hell yeah! That's his El Debarge-lookin' ass!" They both busted out laughing.

It was him alright. Tall, lanky, high-yellow complexion and long curly hair. Hammer was a straight-up pretty boy. On the outside looking in, a person would mistake him for being soft, but he had some of the best hand skills in the neighborhood. Nobody their age could fuck with him. NOBODY.

Hammer was hustling with Dolla and Rell, and the three of them were working for Dre, but sometimes his parents would keep him in the house for weeks at a time. They used to stay on his ass.

"Hammer, what up, my nigga?" Rell yelled as they exchanged dap.

"What up, doe, my niggaz… what's crackin'?"

"Damn, nigga. I see they finally let yo ass out the house," Dolla said.

"Yeah, y'all know my pops be trippin'… Roll up. I'll match y'all. I ain't smoked in a minute," Hammer said.

"Alright, bet. We ain't got no blunts though. We can slide up to Bennie's," Rell said. "We need some squares and a forty too." Just as they turned around to walk to the store, some custos came walking up the block.

"I got 'em y'all," Hammer said as he proceeded to serve the dudes that came from around the corner.

"Yo, Dennis! If you see some custos come through, tell 'em we'll be back in about ten minutes. I'll look out for you when we get back," Dolla yelled to the man across the street who was sitting on his front porch.

"I got you. Just bring me some squares back," Dennis yelled back to the boys.

Dennis was a cool-ass nigga… always on the porch drinking and kicking it. Whenever it was slow on the block, the boys would post up on his porch and smoke weed and listen to him talk about back when he was younger, hustlin' just like they were doing. Whenever the police would roll through, Dennis was always the first one to see them. "HOOK DOWN!" he would yell out.

When the boys made it to the liquor store, they saw a neighborhood fiend named Krissy standing out front.

"Krissy, what up doe? We need a favor… Go in the store and grab us two forties, a box of blunts, and two packs of squares. I'll give you five dollars for looking out."

"Bet! I need that. Good lookin' out, Dolla." She took the $25 from him and walked inside Benny's Liquor.

"Dawg, I bet that bitch would suck five dicks for five dollars," Hammer said. They all busted out laughing.

"What, you wanna find out? Let me find out you like dope fiend pussy!" Rell teased.

"Fuck naw, nigga. I'm a pimp fa real!" Hammer said, pounding his chest. The boys were laughing and talking shit to each other when Krissy came walking out the store.

"Here y'all go," she handed the boys the bags. "Now can I get that five dollars?"

"Get the fuck outta here!" Dolla yelled. "It should be at least six dollars in change. You can keep that."

"I was just playin', damn," Krissy smiled, showing the few yellow teeth she had left in her mouth.

"Good lookin'," the boys all said at the same time.

As they were crossing the street, Krissy yelled out to them, "If y'all need anything - and I mean anything, I ain't hard to find!"

The boys didn't even look back, they just kept walking back to the block.

As soon as they got back, there were five different custos waiting on them.

"Hammer, go ahead and get yo serve on. We gon' fall back for the day," Rell said. "You ain't been out all week, so we know you need that paper."

"Fa sho!" Hammer said as he ran up to the custos and began serving them.

"Man, when y'all left, at least ten more people came through. Not even the ones that stayed and waited on y'all," Dennis said. "Y'all lil niggaz got this block bangin'!"

The boys walked across the street and posted up on the porch with Dennis.

"Here you go, O.G.," Rell said as he reached in the bag and pulled out a pack of cigarettes, tossing them to Dennis. "You know we appreciate you, Dennis. You always lookin' out for us," Dolla said.

"Ain't nothin'. Y'all lil niggaz know I got y'all," Dennis replied.

"Nigga, bless the bottle, so we can crack open one of them brews," Hammer said. "Rell, split open a blunt while I break one of these bags down."

"The bags so muthafuckin' fat, we gon' get two fat-ass blunts outta one of them bitches," Dolla said.

The boys blessed the bottle and Dolla cracked the top off. Before he could take a swig, Dennis said, "Pour some of that shit in my cup before y'all get to hittin' that bitch from the neck."

Dennis held out an empty jelly jar that he used to drink his liquor out of. Dolla filled his glass up and after that, Dennis took a long swig of the beer and let out a loud-ass burp.

"Damn, nigga. I bet they heard that shit around the corner," Rell laughed.

Dennis and the boys sat on the porch drinking, smoking weed, and talking shit while Hammer steady served custos in between.

"Damn, it's almost five o'clock. Y'all know that nigga Dre gon' be pullin' up in a minute. Let's get his paper together," Dolla said.

Every day, Dre would pull up around five and collect his money and drop off $2,500 in dime bags to Dolla and Rell. They would split up the bags between the three of them and push the sack off. About twenty minutes later, Dre was coming down the block, driving a 1996 Chevy Tahoe with the sounds banging, setting off anti-theft alarms on the cars parked on the street.

"Here he comes," Hammer said, speaking the obvious.

"Shit, you can hear that nigga coming from two blocks away," Rell said.

Dre pulled up to the curb with a bad-ass, brown-skinned chick in the passenger seat. Dre was a short brown-skinned nigga with a big-ass stomach and long braids. He was definitely getting money. He had three more blocks around the westside banging just like that one, and he also sold ounces of crack here and there for $600 a pop.

Dre turned down the music and let the passenger side window down.

"What up doe, niggaz? Rell, jump in the back and holla at me!"

As soon as he cracked the window, all you could smell was the strong odor of hydro in the air.

As Rell climbed into the back seat of the truck, Dolla yelled out, "Yo Dre, can you give us some of that dro you smokin' on?"

Dre looked him up and down and replied, "I might." Rell counted out $2,250 and handed it to Dre. While Dre was double counting the money, Rell told them they still had $250 in bags left.

"Bet," Dre said, as he stuffed the money in his pocket. He reached into the glove compartment and pulled out a Ziploc bag filled with dime bags of weed and tossed it in the back to Rell.

"That's $2,500 right there, lil homie. Y'all keep $250 out of that," Dre said.

Dre was paying them $50 off every five hundred dollars' worth of weed they sold.

"Y'all wanna keep that two-fifty in bags from the last sack or y'all want the two-fifty in cash right now and y'all give me $2500?" Dre asked.

"We'll take the cash," Rell said.

Dre reached in his pocket and pulled out five $50 bills and gave them to Rell.

"Yo Dre, can you give us a little bit of that dro you got?" Rell asked.

"Yeah, I got you."

Dre asked the girl to go in her purse and give Rell some hydro. When she opened her purse, the smell of hydro literally hit Rell in the face. She pinched off a nice sized stalk out of the bag, which looked like it was an ounce worth and handed it to Rell.

"Here you go, baby," she said, as she placed the weed in his hand.

"Damn, you got any sisters?" Rell asked. Dre and the girl busted out laughing.

"I see you got a mannish one on your hands," she replied.

Dre just shrugged his shoulders. "Alright, lil homie. I gotta make moves," he said. "I'll get at y'all tomorrow."

Rell hopped out the back of the truck and walked up to Hammer and Dolla with the $2,500 sack under his shirt and the stalk of hydro in his hand.

"Come on, y'all. Let's separate this shit into three sacks. We can smoke and drink the last forty while we do it."

"Bet," Dolla and Hammer said at the same time. Dre was still parked on the curb, rolling up a blunt so Dolla walked to the passenger side of the truck.

"Yo, Dre. I got some new custos coming thru and they lovin' this shit."

Dre stopped rolling up the blunt and handed it to the girl. He just looked at Dolla with a smug expression on his face and said, "that's what's up," and stomped on the gas pedal and smashed out.

Dre would always act funny towards Dolla. He knew Dolla's father before he got locked up and deep down, he was envious of Dolla. Dre knew that Mettetal was banging because of Dolla and the respect Dolla got from being Dante's son. He always knew it was only a matter of time before Dolla would eventually take over the block and many more blocks, just as his father did. He wanted to cut Dolla off so bad but if he did, he knew that he wouldn't get any money from that block anymore. Mettetal put at least fifteen thousand in Dre's pocket every week like clockwork. Hell, he even thought about killing Dolla, but he knew that would do more harm than good. Dolla rarely ever left the hood, so he knew if he killed Dolla, it would have to be in the hood and that would make shit hot.

A fourteen-year-old kid murdered would bring so much police around, it would fuck Dre's money up and a lot of other hustlers in the hood too. But more important than that, Dolla's father would find out his son was rolling for Dre and that would sign Dre's death certificate. So, it ended up being a "can't live with him, can't live without him" type of situation.

Rell, Hammer, and Dennis were in the garage separating the weed into three different sacks.

"Yo, y'all roll that shit up yet?" Dolla asked walking through the garage.

Three young guys were walking down the block and saw Dolla walk into Dennis's backyard. As soon as they got in front of Dennis's house, they yelled, "Yo, Dolla... y'all niggaz on?"

"Yeah! Hammer, go ahead and serve 'em."

"I'm on it," Hammer said as he jumped out the chair and ran up front.

"Yo, Dolla. Including the $250 from the last sack, I separated the bags into three, $950 sacks. Here's yours," Rell handed Dolla his sack.

"Oh, yeah. Here's your cut from the last sack." He gave Dolla $100, kept one hundred for himself, and him and Dolla decided to give Hammer fifty, even though he didn't help pitch off the last sack.

Hammer came back just as they were about to fire up the hydro blunt.

"Rell, put some fire on that muthafucka, and crack that other forty open! Y'all lil niggaz bullshittin'!" Dennis said.

Rell fired up the blunt and took three heavy pulls of the hydro smoke into his lungs. He immediately started coughing and gagging. He was coughing so hard tears flowed from his eyes. He handed Dennis the blunt and quickly grabbed the forty by the neck and hit it hard.

Dolla, Dennis, and Hammer were laughing their asses off.

"Fuck y'all!" Rell yelled, but he was laughing too.

"Man, y'all young punks got virgin lungs! Let me show y'all how to hit this shit," Dennis said.

After taking a few pulls, he was coughing and choking just like Rell did. "Man, this shit is strong!" Dennis said.

"Guess yo old ass got virgin lungs too!" Dolla said and they all busted out laughing.

They finished the blunt and the beer - high as hell. The hydro weed was much stronger than the reggies (regular weed) they were used to smoking. Customers were coming left and right. Rell and Dolla let Hammer do his thing and he was getting his sack off quick. Dennis went into the house to lay down, so the boys just posted up on his front porch.

"Yo, if we had some of that hydro to sell, we would make a killing," Dolla said.

"Hell yeah, we would make twice as much as we making now," Hammer said.

"Nigga, what?! We would make WAY more than we making now because it would be our OWN sack. We could just buy some weight of that shit and sell Dre's sack and our own sack of hydro!" Rell said.

"Hell yeah! I'm gon' holla at Dre about that shit tomorrow," Dolla said.

The boys were still high as hell and started wrestling. Dolla, Hammer, and Rell moved in the streets like grown men. Except for the look of youth on their faces, one would never know in reality, they were just kids. They would sometimes get high and play tag, wrestle and have huge water fights in the spring and summer with other kids from the neighborhood. In the winter, the snowball fights were waged as stages of war. In the midst of all the drug dealing, they still managed to experience somewhat of a normal childhood.

Rell was about to put Hammer in a full nelson when Hammer screamed to the top of his lungs.

"Ahhhh!" Rell immediately let go of his friend, noticing that he was really in pain and wasn't joking.

"Shit, my fault bro! I didn't mean to- …"

"Naw. It ain't you, fam," Hammer said, lifting up his shirt.

Rell and Dolla both let out a collective "daamn" as they looked at Hammer's back, revealing a big-ass knot with bruises all around it.

"Man… what happened, Hammer?" Dolla asked, obviously concerned.

Hammer snatched his shirt back down. "My pops be trippin', man. I'm tired of his shit fa real, dawg," Hammer said.

"He know you hustlin' or somethin'?" Rell asked.

"Naw, man. He just be snappin' over the smallest shit."

None of the boys' families knew they were hustling. Dolla's aunt was a receptionist at a hospital. She was working odd hours. Her schedule was always changing and Dolla's older sister, Chantel, was in college in Chicago. Rell's grandmother was always at home. Sometimes she would be sitting outside on her enclosed porch, listening to the radio and she would see the boys running to and from cars all day.

"What y'all be doing running up to them cars like that?" Grandma Cill would ask.

"We ain't doin' nothin', Nana. Just people sliding through," Rell would say.

Grandma Cill wasn't stupid either. She knew the boys were up to something, but she never thought it was drugs because none of the people they dealt with looked like crackheads. Hammer's mother didn't work. She'd had a stroke, so she would just stay at home. Hammer's father worked twelve-hour shifts as a manager at a steel plant. His father had a drinking problem. Whenever he was at home, all he did was drink and yell about this or that. People on the block suspected he abused Hammer's mother, Karen. She rarely came out of the house. And whenever some of the ladies on the block would invite her to play cards, she would always say "I can't."

One day last summer, everybody was outside. It was one of the hottest days of the year. Out of nowhere, Hammer's mother came charging out of the house screaming, "get away from me! Don't touch me!" Hammer's dad had caught her before she made it out the front yard and slammed her on the ground, then picked her up and carried her into the house. Whenever neighbors did see Hammer's mother, she didn't have any bruises on her face, so people just thought they were the type of people that kept to themselves. No one paid them any mind.

Time passed, and it was about nine o'clock in the evening.

"I gotta go. I'll holla at y'all tomorrow," Hammer said as he dapped his homies.

He gave Dolla and Rell his sack and the money from the sales of the day. "It's only $150 left in bags. I'm supposed to go to school in the morning, but if I don't, I'll be out here early," he said.

"Alright, my nigga. Stay up!" Dolla and Rell yelled as Hammer walked to the house.

"I'm bout to bounce too, bro," Dolla said to Rell. "I'll see you when I get out."

"Alright, fam. Tomorrow," Rell said.

Dolla walked down the street to his house.

Man, I don't know why them niggaz fuck wit that school shit, Rell thought to himself as he walked to Dennis's house. Rell would stay out on the block serving until about twelve or one o' clock in the morning, then go home and go sleep. He knew his grandmother went to bed at about nine o' clock at night, so she didn't know what time he came in. He would always leave his bedroom window open so he could crawl in and hop straight in the bed without waking her. The next day, he would wake up at about seven thirty, take a shower, eat something, and head out the door like he was going to school. His grandmother never knew he wasn't in school. Rell knew a guy – the nerdy type. He would pay the boy to make him up a report card around the time they were supposed to be issued.

When he got to Dennis's house, the door was open. He could see Dennis sitting on the couch in the living room watching T.V.

"Yo, Dennis!" Rell yelled as he walked through the front door.

"Nigga, you betta knock next time before you walk up in my shit! I almost jumped out this chair and shot yo ass!" Dennis said. He had a smile on his face, but Rell could tell he was dead serious.

"Aye, you feel like postin' up wit me for a couple hours?" Rell asked.

"Don't I always watch yo back, lil homie?" Dennis asked.

"True dat. Let's post up on the porch and fire up this blunt I got," Rell said.

"Alright, here I come now," Dennis grabbed the sawed-off shotgun and sat in the chair with it tucked under his shirt. Dennis was in his middle thirties, but he could easily pass for twenty-three or twenty-four. Tall, brown-skinned, medium build, and sported a mini tapered afro. He used to work at the Chrysler plant for ten years, but they offered him a buyout of seventy-five grand, so he took it. The house he lived in was his mother's until she passed in 1990. The house was paid off, so all he had to do was keep up the taxes and pay the utilities. He also received $75,000 from a life insurance policy his mother had. Dennis bought a Cadillac and now he just kicked back at the house smoking, drinking, and fucking females between the ages of eighteen and thirty years old.

"Dig, young dawg. Let me drop some game on you right quick," Dennis said in between puffing on the blunt. "You know I ain't got no problem watchin' yo back or nothin', but it's time for y'all lil niggaz to get strapped. Y'all been out here hustlin' for about a year now and y'all doin' real good. Hell, y'all doin' a lot better than a lot of grown folks. Trust me when I say this, whenever you doin' good, you get put up under the scope, a lotta eyes be on you. It's other niggaz that will try to take what you got… You understand? I can't be around y'all twenty-four seven, it's time for y'all to get some burners," he said, referencing guns.

"I know a guy who can get y'all straight, so get y'all some money together and I'll holla at my man for y'all."

"How much we gonna need?" Rell asked.

"Give me $400 and I'll make somethin' happen for y'all."

"Thanks, Dennis. You always lookin' out for us," Rell said.

"It ain't shit… y'all my lil homies. Now it's time for y'all to look out for yourselves."

Rell and Dennis sat up talking shit while Rell served custos until midnight.

"I'm about to go to the crib. I'm thru for the day. Good lookin' out, D. I'll get at you tomorrow," Rell said.

"Alright then. I'm bout to call one of my freaks over here for a late-night session, I'll holla at you tomorrow."

Rell crossed the street and climbed through the bedroom window. While he was laying in bed, he thought about what Dennis told him earlier. *That nigga, D right. It's time for us to strap up so these niggaz won't think we slippin',* Rell thought to himself…

CHAPTER TWO

Smack! Smack!

"Bitch, you think I'm playing with you?!"

Smack!

Hammer woke up groggy, still half-asleep, thinking he was dreaming when he heard his father yelling and screaming at the top of his lungs.

Smack!

"Bitch, don't run from me!"

That and the sound of breaking glass let him know that he wasn't dreaming. He was wide awake.

Hammer's mother ran in the basement and locked the door behind her.

"You better open up this muthafuckin' door, Karen!"

Now, Hammer's father was screaming. He could tell his father was drunk because his speech was slurred.

"I'm tired of your shit, Mike! I'm taking our son and I'm leaving yo ass!" Karen was yelling from behind the locked door.

"Bitch, you ain't goin' nowhere!" Hammer's father yelled, kicking the door in sync with his words.

"Okay, you don't wanna open this door?"

Hammer's father took off running upstairs to his and Karen's bedroom. He ran right past Hammer and straight into the bedroom, opened the closet door, reached up on the top shelf, and pulled a small silver case down. He opened the case and pulled out a thirty-eight revolver and stormed out the bedroom heading back downstairs.

Hammer was standing in the hallway when his father came out of the room with the gun in his hand.

"What you bout to do with that?? You better not hurt my momma!" Hammer screamed, attempting to block his father's path.

"Boy, move the *FUCK* outta my way!"

Hammer didn't listen. Instead, he grabbed his father's leg and pulled as hard as he could. His father, caught off guard, stumbled and almost fell.

"You little muthafucka!"

Smack!

Hammer's father smacked the shit out of him, then pushed him into his room. Hammer flew through the doorway, hitting his side on the corner of a wooden dresser.

"You come outta this room and I'm gonna fuck you up!" His father took off downstairs towards the basement.

Ugh! Hammer was curled up on the floor, clutching his side. It felt as if someone had sucked the air out of his lungs. He wanted to yell to his mother, "watch out, Daddy got a gun!" but he couldn't make a sound. Every breath he took, he could feel a sharp pain. Rolling back and forth on the floor, Hammer was helpless. All he could do was hear his father yelling and screaming downstairs.

"Bitch, I'm telling you now, if you don't open this goddamn door, I'm gonna shoot it open! You got until I count to three. One… Two…" Hammer's mom was on the basement floor, balled up… clutching her knees and crying.

"Please God, take this man out of my life…. I can't take this anymore!" She said softly between tears.

Boom!

Boom!

Hammer's dad shot the doorknob and the lock completely off. He ran down the basement stairs and grabbed a fistful of his wife's hair, dragging her up the stairs.

"You see what you made me do? You see what you made me do?? You see?"

"Aghh! You hurting me, Mike!" Hammer's mother yelled.

Hammer heard the gunshots. He tried to get up, but he was in too much pain. He knew that his dad didn't kill his mom because he could hear her screaming. Even though he was in pain, he made it to his bed.

He could hear his parents coming up the stairs.

"All this shit is your fault, Karen! If you would just do what the fuck I tell you to do, we wouldn't be fighting all the time!" Karen didn't even respond.

They made it up the stairs and Hammer's father looked in his door and then turned to Karen.

"Baby, clean yourself up, I need you tonight."

She knew what that meant. He wanted to have sex and if she objected, it would result in another beating. She got in the shower and got herself together. When she made it to the bedroom, Hammer's father was lying in the bed naked, with his dick in his hand. She cut the light off and climbed into bed with him.

"Come over here and suck me good, momma," he said, grabbing her head and easing her to the tip of his dick.

As soon as he entered her mouth he moaned, "Ooohh that's my girl." He rammed all nine of his inches into her mouth fast and hard.

"Guggh!" She was gagging but wasn't missing a beat. She bobbed up and down in rhythm with his fast and hard pumps… tears falling down her face.

Then, out of nowhere, he snatched his dick out of her mouth.

"Turn over," he said as he flipped her on her stomach and forcefully arched her back, so her ass was up in the air.

"Mmmmm," he moaned in pleasure as he entered in and out of her from the back.

"Ahhh!" Karen winced from the pain. The man was fucking her so hard, it felt like her pussy was on fire. "You're hurting me!"

Hearing that only made him fuck her harder and faster.

"Oh shit, I'm about to cum!" he yelled, snatching his dick out of her pussy and ejaculating on her back.

"Damn, you got some good-ass pussy, woman!" He said in between breaths. He collapsed next to her and ten minutes later, he was asleep.

Karen felt violated. She laid there naked, sore all over. She felt as if she was trapped like a caged animal. In her mind, the only way she saw escaping this man was death, and she knew that could happen at any moment the way he would drink and beat on her. She curled up in a ball and cried herself to sleep.

Hammer had heard everything. He sat there on his bed, dried tears on his face… eyes bloodshot red. He was tired of his father's shit. Tired of him beating his mother, tired of the man beating on him, the continuous physical and mental abuse, he was sick of it.

He's gotta go, Hammer was thinking to himself. *I'm gonna kill 'em! I'm gonna kill 'em tonight!!*

He looked around his room and saw a baseball bat laying up against the wall.

I'm gonna beat his ass to death!... But what if he wakes up and take the bat from me? Hammer scratched that idea.

Then he looked on the dresser. All that was on there was an empty plate with a butter knife and a fork on it.

"That's it! I'm gonna stab his ass!" Hammer said out loud.

Hammer went to stand up and the pain he felt by his ribs felt even worse.

"Shit!" he cursed under his breath.

His side felt a little better when he hunched himself over, so he just stayed in that position. He made his way over to the dresser and grabbed the fork off the plate. Then he headed to his parents' bedroom.

The door was wide open. Still hunched over with the fork clutched in his right hand, he stood in the doorway, watching his parents sleep. Hammer's father was snoring loudly while his mother was curled up at the end of the bed dozing. Fear suddenly gripped Hammer, he started to have second thoughts.

Fuck it, he said to himself.

Just as he was about to walk out, he noticed something. The glowing sights of his father's gun on the nightstand next to their bed caught his eye. He tiptoed over to the nightstand, laid the fork down, and picked up the revolver. Suddenly, his side wasn't hurting at the moment. In actuality, it was still hurting, but the adrenaline rushing through him temporarily blocked the pain. He took a few steps backwards, looking at his father laying on his stomach snoring.

"Say goodbye, muthafucka," Hammer whispered as he raised the gun with both hands and pointed it at his father.

At that very moment, it seemed as if everything was moving in slow motion. His childhood was flashing before his eyes. All the beatings... all the abuse... swirling around in his mind.... And then....

POW!

Hammer's father body shook violently. The recoil from the gun made Hammer almost drop it. His mother jumped up out of her sleep.

"What the…"

POW!

POW!

She saw the silhouette of her son in the darkness. With each shot, the flash from the barrel illuminated the blank expression on Hammer's face.

"No, baby. Please stop!" Karen yelled.

POW!

Hammer shot his father again. There were now four gaping holes in the man's back. Blood was everywhere. All over the bed. On Hammer. On his mother. On the wall behind the bed.

Hammer's father let out an animalistic groan. *Urrgghh...* Now gurgling on his own blood as he eventually let out his final breath.

Click!

Click!

Click!

The gun was empty, but Hammer was still pulling the trigger. His father was dead, murdered at the hands of his own creation.

Karen ran to her only child.

"Oh, God no!!" She was holding Hammer, crying and shaking so violently, one would have thought she was the one shot. She let Hammer go then crawled over to his father.

"This is all your fault!!" she repeated over and over, leaning over his lifeless body and hitting him with her fist. She didn't even notice Hammer walk out of the room and down the stairs.

Once downstairs, he picked up the phone and dialed 911.

"911, what is your emergency?"

"Yeah, I just shot my dad and I think he's dead. The address is 14578 Mettetal," then he hung up the phone.

Now, one thing about the police in the hood, they always took a long time to make it to the crime scene. This particular night, they were on the scene in less than ten minutes.

BANG!

They kicked in the door and swarmed the place.

Karen was still upstairs, and the police found Hammer in the living room sitting on the couch, with the gun still in his hand.

"DROP THE GUN!!! DROP THE GUN NOW!!!!"

The police had Hammer surrounded with their guns drawn.

His mother came running downstairs with two policemen following behind her.

"Please put the gun down, baby!!" she pleaded.

She walked towards the couch and one of the policemen tried to stop her, but she snatched away.

"Michael, give me that goddamn gun now!" Hammer looked up at his mother and handed her the gun.

The police rushed him immediately and slammed him to the ground and cuffed him.

"Don't hurt him!! He was only trying to protect me!" his mother yelled.

They took Hammer outside and placed him in the back of a police car. As soon as they walked out the front door, the scene looked like something out of the movies. Police cars were everywhere on the block. Neighbors were standing outside in their night clothes being nosey, trying to figure out what was going on. Hammer looked to the left and saw all the neighbors. In the midst of the small crowd that was gathered outside, he could see his two friends Rell and Dolla. He even saw Dennis standing outside too. A few minutes later, a coroner's van and a crime scene vehicle pulled up. At the same time, two police officers got in the car with Hammer and they drove off.

The cops took him to the second precinct on Grand River and Schafer, which was about ten minutes away from his house. They fingerprinted him then placed him in a single-man cell on the felony side of the precinct. The cell was cold and reeked of piss and mildew. It was almost four in the morning and everyone was asleep in their cells. Hammer sat on the wooden slab that was supposed to be considered a bed. He tried to lay down, but the pain in his side was hurting more than it was before he shot his father. It seemed as if the pain came rushing out of nowhere once the adrenaline from killing his father wore off.

Then out of nowhere, Hammer started to silently cry. He wasn't crying from the pain he was in, nor was he crying because he was in jail. Hammer was crying tears of joy. He knew his mother was safe, no more beatings for her or him. No more living trapped in the house like a prisoner. He and his mother were free now. Even though he was locked up in a cell, for the first time in a long time, Hammer felt free.

A few hours later, an officer came and got Hammer out of his cell. She took him into a small room and told him to have a seat. She told him that with his permission, she wanted to know what happened. Hammer told the officer about the constant beatings, his father's drinking problem, and how his father used to keep him and his mother locked in the house for weeks at a time. By the time he was finished telling the officer about the beatings and the abuse, it seemed as if the woman was about to start crying.

She immediately felt sorry for the young man and his mother. "Are you hungry, Michael? Would you like something to eat?" the officer asked.

"Yes, please," Hammer replied.

The officer left out of the room to go get Hammer something to eat. When she returned, she had two bologna and cheese sandwiches and two boxed juices for him.

"Here you go… Oh gosh, are you okay?"

She noticed Hammer slumped in his seat, wincing in pain.

"My side hurts bad," Hammer said.

"Let me take a look." The officer lifted Hammer's shirt and examined the boy's swollen and bruised side. She noticed a huge knot and a bruise on his back.

"It hurts every time I breathe," Hammer said.

"Oh, Lord. We're gonna have to get you to a hospital."

Moments later, two male officers entered the room and placed cuffs around Hammer's wrists and ankles, then transported him to a hospital.

Handcuffed to the hospital bed, the doctors told him that he had two broken ribs. The doctor took some of Hammer's blood, then wrapped his side up with bandages. There were two policemen outside the door. One of them stepped in and told Hammer that his mother came by the station but was informed that she couldn't visit him until tomorrow.

Two hours later, Hammer was transported from the hospital to the Lincoln Hall of Justice, better known as Wayne County Juvenile

Detention Center. Once he arrived, it took about two hours to process him. They housed him in block five south.

Once in his cell, he crawled onto his cot and was asleep within five minutes. Hammer missed breakfast. He slept all the way until lunch. That night was the best sleep he'd had that he could remember.

For the first few hours of the day, it was slow on the block. Dolla and Rell would see cars coming down the street that they knew were customers, but once the drivers saw the police on the corner, they would turn in the opposite direction. The boys didn't care either, they were stunned from the situation that happened with their friend.

Sitting on Dennis's porch, the three of them tried to put together what had transpired. They saw Hammer in the back of the police car, they saw his mother yelling and screaming, they saw a coroner van, and they saw the police bring someone from out of the house zipped up in a body bag on a stretcher. Seeing that made everything clear; Hammer murdered his father.

"Damn, I can't believe this shit. I would have never thought some shit like this would happen," Rell said.

"Yeah," Dolla agreed. "I wonder what pushed him over the edge like that."

"Hold on a minute. Y'all niggaz serious right now?" Dennis asked. "I know y'all smarter than that. Y'all be runnin' up and down the block, slangin' all day and y'all still don't watch y'all surroundings?"

Dolla and Rell just looked at each other puzzled.

"Man, I saw this shit coming a long time ago. The niggaz pops was beating the shit outta him! That's why his pops wouldn't let the lil nigga out the house sometimes. The man was beating on his moms too! And she's a good woman! I've known Karen for a long time, and she was loyal to that dude. That shit over with now, the bitch-ass nigga got what he deserved. I never did respect a nigga who could just sit up and beat up on a woman all day. That nigga was a straight-up coward," Dennis ranted.

"Damn, this shit is fucked up. So, what you think the hook gon' do with Hammer?" Dolla asked, referring to the police.

"Shit, I don't know for sure. It could play out a few ways. Depending on how it happened, they could say it was self-defense and release him. They could keep him until he turns eighteen then let him out, or they could keep him until he's eighteen and send him to state prison until he turns twenty-one. Worst-case scenario, they could charge him as an adult and give him life in prison."

"Life in prison? Damn, not my nigga," Rell said. "Maybe they'll give him the self-defense thing."

"Only time will tell, only time will tell," Dennis shook his head.

Business finally picked up around two in the afternoon. People were coming left and right, copping the fat-ass dime bags.

"Yo, Dolla. We gon' holla at Dre about that hydro shit?" Rell asked.

"Yeah, when he pull up on us today, we'll crack on him about that shit. You think he'll sell us some weight of that shit?" Rell asked.

"I don't see why not, especially if we got the money up front," Dolla said.

"Oh yeah, almost forgot… When I was posted last night, me and Dennis was kickin' it and he said it's about time we get some burners."

Dolla thought about what Rell just said to him. Deep down, he knew Rell was right. They were both young niggaz in the game doing better than most men.

"Alright then… How much we gon' need and where we gon' get some guns from?" Dolla asked.

"He told me all we gotta do is come up with $400 and he got us," Rell said.

"Alright then. We'll holla at him in a few days."

Around five thirty that evening, Dre came flying down the block with the sounds banging as usual. This time, no one was with him, so Dolla opened up the passenger door and hopped in.

"What up doe, Dre?"

"How we lookin'?" Dre asked dryly.

"Shit, we had a little situation last night and we couldn't move like we wanted to this morning."

"Fuck you mean, y'all had a little 'situation'?!" Dre asked, knowing that when "situations" happened, that usually meant police were involved.

Dolla went on to explain how Hammer killed his father last night and how the police were coming and going until about two o' clock in the afternoon.

"Damn, that shit crazy…" Dre calmed down a little after finding out what happened. "Well, how much you got for me?" he asked.

"Right now, we got $1,250 in cash, and the rest in bags."

"Alright. I'll tell you what, Dolla. Give me the twelve-fifty and call me about nine o' clock, and I'll swing by and hit y'all with another sack. If y'all done by nine, I'll pay you for this sack right here. I think I'm gonna put somebody else over here wit y'all since it looks like Hammer ain't comin' back no time soon."

"Naw, we straight on that. Me and Rell can handle this shit over here," Dolla said.

"Is you askin' me or tellin' me?" Dre shot back at Dolla with a menacing stare.

"All I'm saying is me and Rell been holdin' this shit down for a year now. Even wit Hammer gone, we got this shit under control. Sometimes, Hammer couldn't come out for weeks at a time. Plus, we got burners, so we ain't worried about no drama," Dolla added.

"Alright then. Fuck it. Y'all niggaz say y'all can hold it down. Hold shit down then. I'm bout to smash out, call me – "

"Oh, one more thing," Dolla cut in. "Me and Rell was wondering if we could buy some weight of that dro you had the other day and we can sell it as a little side hustle for ourselves."

"Let me get this straight. I just took a loss and y'all askin' me about coppin' some dro for y'all selves?? Maaan, hop out my shit. Call me at nine, we'll talk about that shit some other time," Dre snapped.

"Dolla gave Dre the $1,250 and hopped out the truck.

"What that nigga say about the dro?" Rell asked.

"Man, he talkin' bout he just took a loss today, holla at him some other time…" Dolla said.

"On some real shit, I don't think he want us to have our own shit, Dolla. Dre think we supposed to roll for him forever," Rell said.

"Oh yeah, and when I was in the truck wit him, that nigga was talkin' bout putting somebody else over here wit us and I was like, 'hell naw!' This *our* muthafuckin' block, Rell! We the ones who got this shit bangin' like this, not that nigga, Dre!"

Dolla and Rell were heated. They knew Dre was trying to keep them under him. Dre didn't want the boys to get too big.

"Dolla, what up? What you wanna do? I'm tired of that nigga, Dre. I say we tell him we ain't fuckin' wit 'em no more and he need to kick rocks," Rell suggested.

At first, Dolla didn't say nothing. He thought about what the outcome would be if they just simply told Dre that they wasn't fuckin' with him no more. First off, they would need a connect to cop their weed from. Second, Dolla knew that Dre wouldn't just walk away.

"Dig, we gonna have to get a plug lined up on the weed first. Then, we gonna have to smoke that nigga. To him, we just some lil niggaz. He ain't just gonna let us move him up off the block. So ain't no use talkin' to him. We gotta get them burners first, then put the play down on his ass," Dolla explained.

"How much you got saved up?"

"Shit, I got about three thousand stacked up," Rell said.

"Alright bet, we gon' get them burners tomorrow, then we gonna line up a plug. After that, we gonna blow that bitch-ass nigga into outer space. You game, nigga?" Dolla asked.

"Fa sho," Rell said.

The boys spent the rest of the day slangin' and putting together the move they was gonna put down on Dre. Before Dolla turned in at his usual time, the boys went over to Dennis's house and smoked a few blunts and told him about their plans.

"D, you think you could get those burners for us tomorrow?" Rell asked.

"As long as y'all got the money. Put it in my hands and I'll holla at my dawg for y'all," Dennis said.

"Hey, you know where we can get some weed too?" Rell asked, hoping their friend could help them out.

"I know a nigga. Just let me know when y'all ready."

"Bet," Dolla said.

Time was passing, and it was time for Dolla to go in the house. "Yo, I gotta head home, y'all. I missed school today, so I gotta go tomorrow. Rell, walk me to the crib and I'm gon' hit you wit my half on the burners."

"Let's go," Rell said.

"Alright, D. I'll holla at you tomorrow. Thanks for lookin' out for us," Dolla said.

"Man, don't trip. I got y'all," Dennis said.

"Yo, D. I'mma shoot down the street to Dolla's house right quick, I'll be right back," Rell said.

CHAPTER THREE

Hammer's mom waited patiently in the visiting area of the detention center for her son. A few moments later, he walked in and sat across the table from his mother.

"Hey, baby. How they treating you in there?"

"It's cool," Hammer said nonchalantly. "Momma, you alright out there?"

"I'm okay, son. I just wish you were home with me. Your dad had some life insurance. It's not much, but it should keep the bills paid until I can find a part-time job. I've been feeling a lot better since the doctor prescribed me some new blood pressure pills. As long as I keep taking those, I'll be fine."

"Have you heard from my friends, Rell and Darin?" Hammer asked.

"Yeah, they stopped by the other day asking about you. They gave me $100 to put on your books. I gave it to the clerk downstairs, so it should be on there by now. They also said to write them when you get a chance…" She paused. "Everybody misses you, Michael. All the neighbors on the block stop by and ask about you all the time."

Hammer and his mom had been talking for about an hour when the R.A. walked over.

"Scott, visit's over. Let's go." Hammer and his mom hugged and before he could turn to walk away, his mother started crying.

"Michael, I love you. You're all I got. I need you to stay strong and I'll be waiting for you to come home."

"I love you too, Momma." Hammer turned away and walked out of the visiting room with the R.A...

About a week passed and Hammer's first court date was taking place.

"Michael, my name is Victor Nelson and I'll be your lawyer for this case. The prosecutor wants to charge you with murder in the first degree for the shooting of your father. But I've looked over your case, and I'm pretty sure I can get the judge to knock it down to manslaughter."

"How much time is my son looking at?" Karen asked with the deepest concern.

"Well, Mrs. Scott... technically, they can keep your son in the juvenile system until he's eighteen, then move him to a state prison and hold him there until he turns twenty-one. But under the circumstances of the deceased abusing you and my client, I think I can convince the judge to release him into your custody when he turns eighteen."

Hammer was thirteen at the time, but he would be turning fourteen in six months.

"Please, Mr. Nelson. Do whatever you can to get my son home to me as soon as possible."

"Ma'am, I assure you that I will do everything I can."

The court proceedings began, and Hammer's lawyer argued his client's case, painting a picture of the events taking place in the home setting and the psychological effects that it could have on a thirteen-year-old child.

"Your Honor, I ask that my client only be charged with manslaughter."

The judge sat back in his chair and stared at the child sitting before him charged with such a violent crime. Needing more time to think, he called a short recess and requested that the attorneys join him in his chambers.

"All rise for the Honorable Judge Harris. Court is now in session." Once the judge sat in his chair, the bailiff told the people they could be seated, and court resumed.

"Looking over this case, I have come to the decision to charge Michael Scott with first degree manslaughter. Mr. Scott, how do you plead?"

Hammer had to clear his throat before he spoke. It felt like he had a frog in his throat.

"Guilty, Your Honor," Hammer responded. You could hear the nervousness in his voice.

"Very well then. Sentencing will take place two months from today. Court is dismissed," the judge said as he slammed his gavel.

Hammer shook his lawyer's hand then turned around and looked at his mother who was sitting in the row behind him. He smiled and mouthed the words, "I love you," to her, and Karen responded by saying she loved him too. Hammer was then taken to the holding tank and waited with other juvenile offenders until it was time to transfer them back to the detention facility.

Two weeks had passed since Rell and Dolla decided to kill Dre. The boys were ready to handle it a week prior, but Dennis said it would be best if they waited and stacked some more paper. They had a little over five thousand a piece so far. They felt like the time was at hand to do the hit.

Dolla and Rell gave Dennis the money for the guns and he looked out for them as promised. Rell had a nine-millimeter sixteen shot Glock and Dolla had a twenty-one shot P80 9 Ruger. Dennis took the boys to an abandoned apartment building on Greenfield and Fenkell where they'd practice shooting. Dennis even showed them how to take the guns apart and clean them.

Dolla's birthday was coming up and he wanted to have a big party, but they decided to get Dre out of the way first. The weekend was here and Dolla could stay out late, so the boys were on Dennis's porch, drinking a forty and smoking. It had been a busy day for them. Now that the day was almost over, they had time to put together a plan.

"We need to make dawg disappear quick," Rell said. "I'm tired of dealing wit his fat ass.

"Me too," Dolla agreed, blowing smoke out of his nose. "We just gotta make sure we do this shit right, ya feel me?"

"Whatever y'all do and wherever y'all do it, it can't be on this block. Y'all gotta lead that nigga away from here. And when it does happen, y'all gotta be prepared to switch shit up. The whole hood gon' be on fire behind that shit," Dennis said, passing the blunt to Rell.

The three of them just sat on the porch smoking blunt after blunt, talking until about one in the morning.

The next day, the boys were up early. Every Saturday morning, they would cut Grandma Cill's and Ms. Scott's grass. It seemed like every ten minutes, a customer came walking or riding up the block. They had only been working for three hours and sold $500 in bags already. As soon as they finished Ms. Scott's yard, they pushed the lawnmower into Dolla's auntie's garage. When they were coming out of the backyard, Dolla spotted a grey Dodge Shadow coming down the block. He looked closer as the car approached and noticed that it was the girls from the eastside who came through a few weeks ago.

As they pulled over to the side, Dolla and Rell stood there staring at them. The driver blew the horn yelled, "Y'all gonna look out for us or y'all gonna just stand there lookin' stupid?"

Before Dolla could take one step toward them, Rell shot over to the girls like a bat outta hell.

"What up doe, ladies? What can I do for y'all? I remember y'all from a few weeks ago, and I didn't get a chance to introduce myself. My name is Rell."

One thing about Rell was that he was a confident guy. He had no shame in his game.

"Well, if you got the same shit as Dolla, then we fuckin' wit you," the driver said.

She was a little older than the other girls. The way her and Rell were eying each other, you could tell they were feeling each other. While Rell and the driver were conversing, Dolla walked around the car where Savannah was sitting in the backseat by herself. Dolla reached in the car and unlocked the door and sat down next to her.

"What up, Savannah?" Dolla asked with a big smile on his face. "It's good to see you again."

"Hello, Dolla," Savannah replied, attempting to act like she was irritated.

"Damn girl, you ain't miss me?"

"Boy, please…" she shot back at him.

The girl in the front passenger seat glared at Savannah. "Girl, would you stop it? Dolla, right before we pulled up, she was just talking about how fine you was."

"Bitch, shut up!" Savannah yelled at her friend.

"Oh, yeah?? Dig that," Dolla said, his smile even wider than before.

Savannah didn't say anything. She was blushing. That alone spoke volumes.

"Hey, y'all. Check it… Me and my nigga Rell's birthday comin' up. We gonna be havin' a party next weekend. Y'all wanna come?"

"Where at?" The driver asked, cutting Rell off in the middle of his conversation. "Y'all gonna have weed and drinks?" It was easy to see that the driver was the fastest and most outspoken out of the trio.

"Hell, yeah! We gonna have all that shit on deck!" Rell said. "Y'all just make sure y'all show up. The party's gonna start at six. We gonna have it right here on the block at my big homie house."

Rell pointed to Dennis's house.

"How can we get in touch wit y'all?" Dolla asked, hoping Savannah suggested they exchange phone numbers.

"Don't worry, we'll be there," the driver said.

"Damn, baby. I didn't get your name," Rell said to the driver.

"My name is Carrie, and this is my girl Starr," she pointed to her friend in the passenger seat. "And y'all know my girl Savannah in the back."

"We sho'll do, but I hope I can get to know her better," Dolla said without taking his eyes off her.

Savannah just smiled.

"Well, we gotta go," Carrie said. "Next Saturday, right?" she asked, handing Rell a $20 bill.

"Right!" Rell said, handing her four dime bags.

"Ok then, Rell. We gettin' off to a good start," Carrie chimed in, winking at Rell.

"Alright, see y'all next week," Dolla said, hopping out of the back seat.

"Y'all be careful," Savannah said to Dolla.

"*DAMN!* I'm gonna fuck the shit outta that bitch Carrie, watch!" Rell yelled as soon as they pulled off. Dolla didn't say anything but on the inside, he was all smiles.

Vrrrrrr! Vrrrrrr!

Dre's cell phone was vibrating from an incoming call. He didn't notice, he was too busy hitting a sexy little light-skinned chick from the back.

"Ohhhh… yeah baby. Fuck me!!!" The girl was screaming as Dre continued drilling her juice box in a steady rhythmic pace.

His cell phone began to vibrate again. This time, he felt it in his pocket because his pants were down to his ankles.

Whoever it is gonna have to wait until I get my nut off…

Shortly after that, his beeper went off.

That got Dre's attention because he knew people paged him in the midst of an emergency.

"Fuck!" he yelled, snatching his dick out of the girl without warning.

"Baby, what you doin'? I was just about to cum," the girl whined.

"I gotta take this call," he said to her, realizing the number on his pager came from a payphone on the corner of Schoolcraft and Mettetal.

What the fuck goin' on over there now? he thought as he dialed the number on the screen. After the third ring, someone picked up the phone.

"Dre, is that you?" Dolla asked.

"Yeah, it's me. What the fuck is goin' on?" Dre asked.

Dolla went on to explain to Dre that the narcs were all over the block flicking people and how a narc car pulled up, four-officers deep and jumped out chasing the boys.

"Damn, dawg! What the fuck y'all little niggaz doin' over there to make shit hot?" Dre screamed into the phone.

"We ain't doin' nothin', Dre! Just servin' custos."

"Shit, it's gotta be something! The hook don't just pop up out of nowhere flicking niggaz! Y'all probably served to an undercover or something!!"

"Naw, Dre. We been serving the same muthafuckas. Ain't nobody new been comin' thru," Dolla insisted.

"Well, it ain't shit I can do about that now. Meet me on the block at eight tonight," Dre demanded.

"Naw, the block too hot. Ain't no tellin' if them muthafuckas somewhere posted up watchin' shit. Just meet us at the school park on Longacre," Dolla suggested.

"Bet. Y'all lil niggaz be there at 8:00 sharp," Dre barked into the phone.

Without waiting for a response, Dre hung up the phone. "These dumb-ass lil niggaz," he said out loud, sitting on the edge of the bed.

"What's wrong, baby?" the girl asked, massaging Dre's shoulders from behind him.

"I don't speak my business to nobody," Dre said, even though the girl was sitting on the bed listening to the conversation the entire time.

"Well, let me see if I can do something to make you feel better," the girl said as she reached around and pulled his dick out of his boxers, shifting her head into his lap...

Dre pulled up to the park with his sound system banging. He saw the boys coming out of the park, walking up to the truck. Dolla was about to open the passenger side door when he noticed a female figure sitting in the seat through the tinted window. *Damn! Who the fuck is this bitch with him?*

"Fuck it," he said out loud as he opened the back door and slid in the truck.

Rell climbed in after Dolla and shut the door. Rell was sitting behind the sexy-ass, light-skinned bitch and Dolla was sitting behind Dre. Rell could tell from the bulge on Dre's waistline he was strapped. The boys also noticed a black duffel bag in the trunk space behind them. Dre turned the music down a little bit, but the bass was still booming through the speakers.

"Now, tell me what the fuck is goin' on," Dre said.

Rell began to run down everything that happened earlier that day.

"Shit, the hook still ridin' up and down the block right now," Dolla cut in saying.

"Oh yeah? I just rode past the block and I didn't see no muthafuckin' hook nowhere," Dre said matter-of-factly.

"They was out there when we left," Dolla said defensively.

"Where my money at?" Dre asked.

"Yo shit right here," Dolla said, pulling out the bookbag and unzipping it.

"Aye yo, Dre. Look," Rell said.

Dre turned around to look at Rell, not realizing Dolla just pulled out a pistol from the bookbag. Dolla reached around the opposite side of Dre's headrest with the gun.

Pop!

The gun went off, sending blood and brain matter flying at Rell and the girl in the front seat.

"*Ahhhhhhh!*" the girl screamed, fumbling for the door handle. But before she could open it, Rell shot her in the side of the face.

Pop! Pop!

The second shot hit the girl in the side of the head, taking her out of existence. Dre lay slumped on the steering wheel but oddly, the horn wasn't going off. The only thing that could be heard was the music blasting out of the speakers.

"C'mon. Let's go, nigga!" Rell yelled as he was about to hop out the truck.

"Hold on!" Dolla said. "Grab that muthafuckin' duffle bag out the back!"

Dolla raised Dre's bloody shirt and grabbed his strap, then fumbled through his pants pockets and found a small wad of cash. Rell had reached in the back and grabbed the duffle bag.

"You ready, nigga?" he yelled.

Dolla snatched the hoodies out of the bookbag he had then threw one to Rell. The boys quickly put the hoodies on and Dolla threw the guns into the bookbag and put it on. They quickly exited the truck using their shirtsleeves to open the doors and wiped off the handles on the outside of the back doors too.

The boys took off running through the park headed towards the school. They had two bikes parked on the side of the building. Once they reached the bikes, they jumped on and shot off.

Minutes seemed like hours before the boys made it back to the block. Dennis was holding it down while they were gone. After serving a custo, he looked up and saw the boys flying around the corner on their bikes. He also noticed the black duffle bag Rell had on his shoulder.

"Put the bikes in the garage and y'all niggaz go in the house," Dennis commanded.

Once the boys got in the house, they felt relieved. They were glad it was over. With Dre out of the picture, they knew that they were going to make some real paper.

"Hell yeah, nigga! You was on point!" Rell walked over to Dolla and dapped him.

"It had to be done, ya feel me? Bitch-ass nigga left us no choice," Dolla said. "I just feel bad ol' girl was there."

"Yeah well, she was at the wrong place at the wrong time. We just couldn't let her walk away from that shit," Rell said. "It is what it is."

"Wait a minute… A bitch was there too?" Dennis asked.

Dolla and Rell filled Dennis in on the details on how the hit went down. On the inside, Dennis was proud of the little niggaz. They showed the characteristics of becoming bosses someday as long as they continued to play their cards right.

"Dig, I'm gonna need them pistols y'all got," Dennis said.

"But why?" the boys asked looking confused.

"Listen, y'all can't keep them guns, they gotta go. I'll grab some more for y'all tomorrow. Y'all don't wanna risk getting caught with those with them fresh bodies on them."

The boys nodded their heads in agreement with the game Dennis was putting them up on.

You see, Dennis was Dolla and Rell at one point in his life; he was out there getting money, but when he got the job at Chrysler, he kinda fell back. His best friend got killed and Dennis ended up killing the niggaz responsible. Working at Chrysler, he was making good money. Plus, the workers there were getting high off cocaine and crack. Some smoked weed, so all while he was working there, he was slanging to the employees too. Once he took the cash buyout, he just kicked back and enjoyed life, but the streets had been in his blood since day one.

"What's in the bag y'all got?" Dennis asked.

Dolla and Rell almost forgot about the bag. Their adrenaline was still pumping from the hit they'd just pulled off. Rell grabbed the bag and unzipped it.

"Damn!" He couldn't believe what he was looking at.

"What is it, nigga?" Dolla asked as him and Dennis moved in closer to get a look.

Rell began emptying the contents of the bag onto the floor. All in all, there was five pounds of some of the greenest reggies the boys ever seen, a large scale, and they counted exactly $12,000 in cash in big and small bills.

"Damn! We just hit a major lick!" Dolla exclaimed, grinning from ear to ear. "Oh shit, I almost forgot!" Dolla reached into the bookbag and pulled out a bloody bankroll.

"Where did you find that?" Rell asked.

"I got this off that nigga too," Dolla said nonchalantly, as if he had done this many times before.

He grabbed the bookbag he was carrying the hoodies in and opened it up, pulling out the gun he took from Dre. It was a 45 Colt.

"Damn, that's a big-ass burner," Rell said.

"Here," Dolla handed the gun to Dennis. The forty-five looked brand new.

"You can have it, D."

"Naw, Dolla. As bad as I want it, this one gotta go too," he said. "Ain't no tellin' who this pistol is registered to."

"Well, when you get rid of it, see if you can trade it in for something else for yourself," Dolla insisted. He counted forty-five $100 bills from the money he grabbed from Dre's pocket.

"We about to eat out here for real now!" Rell said, rubbing his hands together.

Dolla counted out two grand and gave it to Dennis. "Thanks for everything, big bro."

"No doubt, I got y'all," Dennis said, stuffing the cash in his pocket.

Killing Dre was a power move for the boys. Not only did they now have the block to themselves, they had an extra five pounds and $14,500 to start off on their own. Things were looking good for the boys indeed. They split the cash and weed between the two of them.

"Yo, let's go out back and smoke something," Rell suggested.

"Damn, I'm gonna have to run to the store and get some blunts," Dennis said. "Y'all just chill here until I get back."

"Aye, bring some squares back too, D," Dolla said.

As soon as Dennis stepped outside, he saw two police cars flying down Schoolcraft with their lights flashing, sirens blaring.

"Check it… y'all just stay in the house. If some custos come on the block, don't serve them. Y'all need to stay off the streets tonight. I'm gonna go to the gas station by the school and see if that's where the hook is headed," Dennis said.

Dolla and Rell watched Dennis pull out of the driveway from the window as he headed to the gas station. They were nervous after hearing the police sirens. As soon Dennis turned the corner, a customer came rolling down the block, driving slow and looking to see if anyone was outside. Once the customer realized no one was out, he drove off.

"Damn, I hope this nigga D hurry up and get back. I need to smoke. My nerves is bad," Dolla said.

"Don't even trip, my nigga. We straight. We didn't leave no prints behind and nobody saw us," Rell said.

About ten minutes later, Dennis was pulling into the driveway. Once inside, they sat at the table and rolled a few blunts. Rell fired up the first one and asked Dennis what he saw when he went to the gas station.

"The hook had the whole street blocked off. I couldn't see much, but I did see Dre's truck. They had the doors wide open and they was all in that bitch," Dennis described the scene.

"Look, the shit is over and done wit. Just make sure y'all don't speak a word of this to no one. After what happened, y'all gotta change shit up too. The whole hood gon' be on fire for a minute. If they find out he's a dope boy, the hook is gonna start raiding all the known drug spots in this area, tryin' to press niggaz for information. Tomorrow, y'all need to go to the phone store and get y'all some pagers. Hand out the numbers to custos and have them meet y'all at the corner store or something. Y'all gonna have to be strapped up too. By tomorrow sometime, I'll have some burners for y'all," Dennis instructed.

Dennis, Rell, and Dolla sat around a few more hours smoking and planning for the next day. After that, Dolla and Rell left, taking their money and weed with them. Before they left, they took off the hoodies and left the duffle bag and bookbag with Dennis.

Afterwards, Dennis went into the backyard and put the clothes and bags in the grill and set them on fire. Tomorrow, Dolla and Rell would get rid of the shoes and underclothes they had on that day as well.

Once at home, Dolla lay in bed, replaying the day's events over and over in his head. He thought about his friend, Hammer. *Is this what Hammer felt like after killing his dad?* But the crazy thing about it was, Dolla didn't feel a thing. He spent the rest of the night laying in bed, knowing that this was a major turning-point for him and his homies. Meanwhile, Rell was asleep with a smile on his face, happy that his dreams of becoming a boss in the drug game were finally taking form.

The next day, he and Dolla hooked up early so they could get their day started. First, the boys got rid of the clothes they had on the night before. Then they went to the gas station to get some baggies because they had to bag up some weed for the day. Once they were back on the block, they quickly bagged up two pounds in dime bags at Dennis's house. Dennis agreed to hold the block down for a few hours while they took care of business.

The boys caught the bus to Northland Mall to do a little shopping and grab some pagers from the phone store. They both spent about $1,600 on shoes, clothes and their pagers. They grabbed up a few pairs of Jordans, some Adidas', and a gang of clothes. Once they were finished shopping, they stopped in the barber shop that was inside the mall and got haircuts. After that, they left the mall and waited on the bus.

While at the bus stop, the boys began planning Dolla's birthday party. Once they arrived on the block, they quickly dropped off their bags and ran to Dennis's house. As soon as they arrived, they began calculating numbers on pieces of paper. The block was doin' numbers! Within a few hours, $700 had already been made and they still had the rest of the day to go.

Dennis fell back and let the boys do their thing. They were handing out their pager numbers to the customers, telling them to page them from the corner store and put the number of bags they wanted in the pager and the boys would meet them at the store. This way, the block would have less traffic, if any, and wouldn't alert the police. After a few weeks, they would return things back to normal.

The boys were moving the sack off as they usually did, but later on in the day, the custos that were pulling up began telling them to be careful because the hook was riding through the hood.

"Y'all ain't noticed all the hook that's been around this bitch today? Man, some shit must have happened around here," one of their regular custos was saying while Rell was serving them.

"Shit, I don't know what's goin' on around here," Rell said, acting like he didn't have a clue as to why the police was in the area so strong.

Dennis said he had to go handle something and told the boys he would be back a little later. Hours passed, and the sun was going down. The weekends were always busy, and this weekend wasn't any different. Dennis got back around nine-thirty that night. Once he got in the house, about twenty minutes later, he was hanging outside the door, flagging the boys to come inside.

"Let me holla at y'all for a minute," he said with a fat-ass blunt hanging from his mouth.

The boys ran down to the house. Once they were inside, they sat on the couch. Dennis fired up the blunt he had, took three strong pulls then passed it to Dolla.

"I gotta show y'all something," Dennis said, then walked down the hallway toward his bedroom. Once he came back, he had a blanket wrapped up with something inside.

"What's that?" Rell asked. No sooner than Rell asked the question, Dennis placed the blanket on the floor and unfolded it.

"Damn!" the boys both said at the same time. Inside the blanket were two baby Glock fortys and an SKS.

"These ours?" Dolla asked, picking up one of the Glocks.

"Of course. I gotta make sure my lil homies strapped up. Ain't no tellin' who Dre told he was comin' to see y'all before y'all smoked him. Y'all gotta keep y'all eyes open out here, for real," Dennis instructed.

"What the fuck is this big-ass gun?" Rell asked picking it up.

"That right there is called a SKS, but niggaz on the streets call it a 'K' or a "choppa". It shoots thirty rounds a clip and it came wit two."

"Why they call it a 'choppa'?" Dolla asked.

"Well, they call it that because the bullets used go through damn near anything. Houses, cars, bulletproof vests… so y'all gotta be careful wit this one. Once I show y'all how to use it, y'all gonna be dangerous. When niggaz see a choppa come out, they hit the deck!" Dennis laughed. "Tomorrow, I'll take y'all to the spot we shoot at and show you how to move wit this bitch."

Within three days, the boys were low on weed. Now, they needed a new plug. Once again, Dennis came through for them, introducing them to a new connect. The weed was ok, but it wasn't like Dre's shit.

The weekend rolled around, and it was Dolla's birthday. The boys were dressed in Adidas track suits. Dolla had on a black and white one with the black and white Concords and Rell had on red and white one with red and white Concords.

It was a busy day as usual. The boys were running back and forth, meeting custos up at the store. It seemed like as soon as they would leave the store and get halfway down the block, one of their pagers was going off.

Dennis was running around getting liquor, beer, and blunts. He picked up two of his girls to cook for the party. As the day went on, Dolla and Rell were slanging and calling people they knew from the neighborhood and from the school Dolla went to, letting them know where the party was gonna be. They were also letting customers know at five o'clock, they were shutting down and would be back in business the next morning.

The party started around six that evening. There were people Dolla and Rell knew from the neighborhood and from school as well. There was plenty of weed and drinks to go around for the night. Even those who didn't smoke or drink were having a good time. By eight, the party was off the chain. There were females everywhere and they were all scoping Dolla and Rell, hoping that the boys would pick one of them out to be their girlfriends.

There was so much weed smoke in the air that anyone who didn't smoke was sure to catch a contact high. The two girls Dennis brought over cooked a bunch of chicken wings and there was plenty of Kool-Aid, pop, water, and chips.

"Aye, Dolla. You think them chicks from the eastside gon' come thru?" Rell asked. Rell was already tipsy and had danced with several girls. He was having a ball.

"Shit, I don't know," Dolla said, shrugging his shoulders.

Deep down, he hoped they would show up too. He was standing in the corner of the room, smoking a blunt with some of the homies he knew from school and his hood. There were a few bitches Dolla had his eye on, and he decided he wasn't going to spend his birthday sitting on his ass waiting for some girl when it was pussy all around him.

Crystal and Kayla were from around the corner and came to the party. Both of them knew Rell and Dolla for a long time, and they also knew that the boys were getting money. They swore that before the night was over, they were going to be Dolla and Rell's girlfriends. Kayla was short and dark-skinned with long hair and a big booty. Crystal was average height, brown-skinned with a nice ass and round plump breasts.

"Rell, call your boy over here. I want to give him a birthday dance," Crystal said.

"Alright, hold on a second." He had a handful of Kayla's juicy ass in one hand and a cup of Remy V.S.O.P. in the other.

"Yo, Dolla! Let me holla at you for a minute, bro!" Rell yelled from across the room.

Dolla made his way over to Rell and the two girls.

"What up doe, Crystal and Kayla?" he said, hugging the two girls. "Y'all enjoying the party?"

"Yeah, this shit off the hook," Kayla said, as she was hitting a blunt and taking a sip of the liquor she had in her cup.

Dolla noticed that the girls looked good. Looking at Crystal's nice round ass made his dick hard instantly.

"Y'all ain't gon' wish a nigga happy birthday?" Dolla asked, with his arms in the air.

"Happy birthday!" Kayla yelled with a big smile on her face.

R & B music was blasting out of the speakers. Guys were slow dancing with girls. Rell was grinding up on Kayla.

"Let me give you one of your birthday gifts," Crystal whispered in Dolla's ear. She grabbed his hand and led him into the middle of the room. "Wait right here," she said, then disappeared into the crowd.

Seconds later she emerged with a chair in her hand.

"Sit," she said in a commanding but seductive tone.

Once Dolla sat down, she began dancing for him. She was sitting on his lap, grinding him like a professional stripper.

"Do you like?" she purred in his ears with her arms wrapped around his shoulders.

"Uh-huh," Dolla moaned, as he sat his cup down and palmed her ass with both hands. Her ass was as soft as marshmallows…

Carrie and Savannah pulled up across the street from Dennis's house. They could tell that the party was jumping because the front door was open, and you could hear the music blasting from outside.

Once the girls walked through the front door, the weed smoke literally hit them in the face. People were everywhere - all along the walls and dancing in the middle of the room.

"Where is these niggaz at?" Carrie asked Savannah. "You see them?"

"Naw," Savannah said as she and Carrie held hands, making their way through the crowd.

Crystal was on her hands and knees, popping her ass in a slow seductive rhythm. Dolla was ready to hop out of the chair and fuck her right there on the floor. Caught up in the moment, he didn't even notice Carrie and Savannah standing by watching the show.

"Oh shit! What up doe, Carrie? Savannah?" Rell said, walking up to them with his arms open. "We thought y'all wasn't gonna make it," he smiled, hugging the girls.

When Dolla looked up and saw Carrie and Savannah, for a second, he thought he was about to throw up. When he made eye contact with Savannah, she had a look in her eye that could kill. Rell led the two girls off to get something to drink and roll up a blunt.

Dolla's dick was rock hard from watching Crystal slow grind and bounce her ass, but as soon as he saw Savannah standing there with her arms folded and staring at him with the, "you-just-fucked-up-your-chance" look on her face, he immediately went limp.

After the song went off, he thanked Crystal and told her he would be right back and headed in the direction of where Rell took off with the girls.

Once he made his way through the crowd, he saw Rell standing next to Carrie talking, and Savannah was sitting on the couch with a glass of champagne, smoking a blunt.

"What up, Savannah?" Dolla said, easing on the couch next to her.

"You tell me," she said before hitting the blunt.

"I'm glad you could make it to my party. I thought you wasn't goin' to show up."

"Well, from what I see, you wouldn't have noticed if I was here or not with your girl dancing for you and everything…" Sarcasm dripped from her voice.

"Wait a minute. That ain't my girl. That's just a friend I grew up wit," Dolla said in a serious tone. "She was just dancing for me because it's my birthday."

"Tell me anything," Savannah said dryly.

"Naw, I ain't gon' tell you anything. I'm gon' tell you the truth, and truth is, I'm tryin' to get to know you. Fuck her. Why don't you tell me a little about yourself?"

Hmmm... that was a good one. "Well, as you know, I'm from the eastside. My parents work at Chrysler, and I go to Burbank Middle School."

"Your parents still together? Damn!" Dolla said, as if that type of thing was unheard of.

"Yes, they're still married."

"What do you want to be when you grow up?" Dolla continued.

"I want to be a lawyer someday. That's my dream," she replied. "Now why don't you tell me a little about yourself, starting with your real name," Savannah asked.

"My real name is Darin Jones. I've been coming on this block off and on my whole life, but I'm not from here. I was born in a neighborhood called North Rosedale Park."

"Wait a minute. You're from North Rosedale? My daddy goes to church and one of his best friends is a doctor and he lives over there! You gotta be rich to live in that neighborhood!" Savannah said, surprised that he was from there.

"Yeah, my parents WERE rich. My father was a drug dealer."

"He was? What happened to him?" she asked with concern.

"The FBI locked him up, accusing him of doin' all types of shit and he ended up getting life in prison. But once a year, my aunt takes me to see him. That's who I live with now."

"Where's your mom at?" Savannah asked.

Dolla took the blunt from his ear and lit it. Taking a strong hit, he inhaled and exhaled the smoke out of his nose.

"Well, people say my dad had a lot of beef out here in the streets before he left, and people wanted to kill him. But by my father being locked up, they couldn't get to him, so they kidnapped my mom. Sometime later, they found her body in an empty house… Bitch-ass niggaz killed my momma," Dolla said as he downed the remainder of Remy V.S.O.P. that was in his cup.

Savannah didn't know what to say. A part of her wanted to reach out and hug him and assure him that everything was gonna be alright. Her eyes teared up and it looked as if she was about to cry.

"Damn, I'm so sorry… That's terrible," she managed to say, even with her hand over her mouth. "Did the police ever find out who did it?"

"Nope, but one day I will and, when I find out, I'm gon' kill them muthafuckas myself," Dolla said with confidence. For a second, there was silence between the two of them.

"Hey, where's yo girl, Carrie and Rell at?"

"They was just standing next to us a minute ago," Dolla said, changing the subject.

"Maybe they dancing or somewhere getting' to know each other too," Savannah said. "I think my girl likes him…"

"Ummm…" Rell moaned in pleasure, biting his bottom lip. He was getting some of the best head he ever had in his young lifetime. Carrie was slowly moving up and down the shaft of his rock-hard dick and gently massaging his balls. Sucking dick would make Carrie's pussy wet. It turned her on watching guys squirm and moan helplessly.

"Damn, baby. I'm finna bust," Rell said as he began releasing his hot load into Carrie's mouth. Once Carrie realized he was cumming, she took as much of him into her mouth as she could and swallowed every bit.

Once Rell was finished, she lifted her head and arrogantly whispered, "You like that?"

"With a big smile on his face, Rell replied, "Would you marry me?"

They both busted out laughing. "Next time I see you, I'm gonna let you see how good this kitty is," Carrie said with a devilish grin on her face.

Savannah was beginning to feel a little tipsy from the four glasses of wine she'd drank. That, with the combination of two blunts had her feeling like she was in the clouds.

"Hey, if it's okay with you, I would love if you would join me on the dance floor," Dolla said to Savannah.

What the hell... she thought. She was feeling good at the moment, and after having a long conversation with him, she looked at Dolla in a different light.

"Okay, as long as you can control yourself," she said, placing her hand in his.

"I don't know if I can, but I'll try," he said, leading the way to the dance floor.

Savannah wrapped her arms around his neck and Dolla wrapped his arms around her waist. For two songs straight, they said nothing. As they were dancing, it seemed as if they were making a connection spiritually. Dolla had to fight the urge to slide his hands down to her ass. *Better just play it safe tonight*, he thought to himself.

Neither he nor Savannah noticed Crystal and Kayla staring at them, envious of Savannah getting close to Dolla.

"Do you see this bitch?" Kayla said to her friend.

"Don't even trip, girl. Soon, she'll be gone, and I'll have him later on tonight," Crystal said.

Crystal and Kayla both stayed around the corner on St. Mary's. Kayla was spending the night at Crystal's house and Crystal's mother worked as a bus driver for the city. She had to work the late shift from ten until six a.m., so the girls could stay out late.

"Aww shit, look at my girl!" Carrie said, watching her and Dolla dance.

Savannah turned and saw Carrie and Rell looking and blushed.

"Girl, where you been at?" she asked.

"Me and Rell went outside and kicked it for a minute," Carrie said, looking at Rell who was standing tall with his chest out and his head held high.

"Nigga, what's up wit you?" Dolla asked, eyeing Rell suspiciously.

"I'm good," Rell said, a slight grin on his face.

"Damn, it's almost 11:00," Savannah said, glancing at her watch.

"We gotta be heading back towards the way then," Carrie said.

"Well, let us walk y'all to the car," Dolla said.

As they walked the girls to the car, Dolla reached out and grabbed Savannah's hand. "I'm glad you came to the party. That was the greatest gift for me."

"I'm glad I came too. I really had a good time," Savannah admitted.

Carrie had already got in the car and started it up. "C'mon, we gotta go, bitch!" Carrie yelled.

Before Savannah could say or do anything, Dolla grabbed her and hugged her tight. To his surprise, she hugged just as tight, if not tighter. Slightly leaning away, they stared into each other's eyes. Their heads moved in closer to one another as if they were about to kiss.

Honk! Honk!

"C'mon, Savannah. Damn! We already late!" Carrie yelled.

Snapping out of the trance she was in, Savannah eased back and got into the car.

"Oh, wait," Dolla said, reaching into his pocket. He ran up to the window and gave the girls three bags of weed and gave Savannah his pager number. "Page me as soon as you can," he said.

"Awww, that's sweet of you. Thanks!" Carrie said. Savannah didn't say a word. The big-ass smile on her face and her blushing red cheeks said it all.

"Alright, we'll see y'all later. Rell, don't forget what I said," Carrie said, then pulled off.

Dolla and Rell turned and headed back into the house to party. After a few drinks, blunts, and hours, the party was coming to an end. All the guests thanked the boys and wished Dolla a happy birthday before leaving.

"Do y'all mind if we hang around a little while longer?" Crystal asked. "We ain't got shit to do, plus we wanna smoke and drink a little more."

"Shit, that's cool with us," Rell said. "Yo, Dolla. Match me a blunt."

"Alright, bet," Dolla said.

He walked down the hallway towards Dennis's room. He could hear music coming from out of the room.

"Yo, Dennis. You wanna hit this blunt?" Dolla asked, but there was no response.

"Yo, Dennis. You…"

He noticed the door was cracked. Peeking through the crack, Dolla couldn't believe what he saw. The two girls that cooked for the party were in the room with Dennis. One was sucking the shit out of his dick, and the other was sitting on his face, and she was sucking his dick too!

Damn, this nigga D is a player, Dolla thought to himself as he walked back to where Rell and the girls were.

"That nigga D ain't smokin'? Rell asked.

"Hell naw. That nigga busy right now. C'mon, y'all. Let's go to the basement," Dolla said, as he picked up a half-full fifth of Remy V.S.O.P.

The basement was plushed out. It had a leather sectional sofa, big screen TV, pool table, dart board, and a king size bed. There was also a microwave and a mini-fridge full of beer. The four of them smoked three blunts and finished off the fifth of Remy.

"Now, before me and my girl leave, let me give you the OTHER half of your birthday gift," Crystal said, as she made her way to the middle of the room.

Dancing to the music, she began removing her clothes piece by piece. First, her shirt. Then her pants, followed by her matching bra and panties. Dolla, Rell, and Kayla sat there watching as she seductively danced naked, looking Dolla dead in his eyes. She didn't care that Rell and Kayla were watching as well.

Dolla's dick felt like it was about to bust right out of his pants. Crystal's sexy body, plus the combination of weed and liquor had him ready to fuck her right in front of Rell and Kayla. Meanwhile, while Crystal was dancing, Rell was getting horny too and began caressing Kayla's thigh. Before long, he had two of his fingers inside of her.

Fuck the bullshit, Dolla thought to himself. Just as he was about to get up and take Crystal to the bed, she leaned over and reached in Dolla's pants and pulled his dick out, placing him inside of her mouth.

It seemed as if Dolla lost control of himself as his head fell backwards, resting on the back of the sectional as he looked up at the ceiling. A few minutes later, Crystal snatched his dick out of her mouth and began riding him like a racehorse. Dolla quickly snapped out of the trance he was in and lifted Crystal up off him.

"Damn, baby. What's wrong?" Crystal asked, taken by surprise.

"Hold on for a second," Dolla said as he reached in his pocket and pulled out a condom.

He quickly tore it open and put it on, not noticing the disappointing look on Crystal's face. He did notice Rell on the other side of the couch with Kayla bent over hitting her from the back.

Dolla's dick got even harder, looking at Kayla's big round chocolate ass waving back and forth as Rell pounded away. He grabbed Crystal and she sat back on top of him and began riding him reverse cowgirl style. After about fifteen minutes, Dolla couldn't take anymore. He exploded into the condom and Crystal came at the same time.

"Damn, I needed that," Dolla said, almost out breath.

"Yeah, well guess what? Me and Kayla don't have to go home until about five in the morning, so there's plenty of time to have some more fun," Crystal said, kissing him on his neck.

"Hey, y'all got some more weed? I wanna smoke," Kayla asked from the other side of the room sitting next to Rell.

"Does the Detroit River got water in it?" Rell asked arrogantly. "You ain't said nothin' but a word." Rell reached in his pocket and pulled out five dime bags. "We gon' be smokin' all night. It's my niggaz birthday!"

They opened the box and rolled five monster-sized blunts. Two blunts into the session, the boys noticed the girls sleeping and went to the mini fridge to grab two beers. They stood by the pool table smoking a blunt and talking about the party.

"The party was off the hook!" Rell said, passing the blunt to Dolla.

"Yeah it was, bro. I was surprised Savannah and Carrie showed up. They was lookin' fine as hell."

"Yeah, it seem like you and ol' girl connected. When I looked up, y'all was dancing together, lookin' like a couple that had been together for ten years or somethin'," Rell laughed.

"While you laughing, I saw you ducked off in the corner with Carrie all caked up and shit!" Dolla said before taking a long drag from the blunt.

"Carrie got a good head on her shoulders, nigga… in more ways than one," Rell said, with a sly grin on his face. He told Dolla about Carrie's good head skills.

"Damn, nigga. It's like it was *your* birthday!" Dolla said, laughing. "My nigga, I saw you drillin' Kayla from the back too, she got a fat ass! How is the pussy?" Dolla asked.

"Shit, I was gonna ask you the same shit about Crystal," Rell said. "Dig, I got an idea."

"What up?" Dolla asked.

"Let's cut off the lights and I'll go over to Crystal and you go over by Kayla and we fuck the shit outta 'em," he suggested.

"Bet, I'm wit that!" Dolla said, rubbing his hands together.

They cut off the lights. Rell walked over to Crystal and Dolla walked over to Kayla. The boys ended up fucking the both of them that night. Once they were finished, it was about four in the morning. They all sat around for the next hour, smoking and talking… then the girls left.

Dolla and Rell laughed to themselves, thinking about how they both fucked Crystal and Kayla. But what they didn't realize was that when they were putting the plan together, the girls heard everything. They didn't care though. They both knew that Rell and Dolla were on the come-up, and they figured that fucking them would put them at the top of the list with the boys, and that was perfectly fine with them.

CHAPTER FOUR

Business went on for the next few weeks, smooth as ever. The hood calmed down from the double homicide and instead of meeting the custos at the store, they switched back to serving them as they walked or would drive down the block.

One day while the boys were on the block hustling, Ms. Scott called them over to her house. She told them that Hammer had written them a letter and handed it to them. They thanked her and gave her $100 to put on his books. They also told her that they would be checking on her, and if she needed anything to let them know. She thanked the boys and they left, headed back to Dennis's house with the letter. Once they made it back down the street, they opened the letter to read it.

My niggaz,

What up, doe? What's crackin' wit y'all? Everything straight? As for me, I'm just chillin', tryin' to stay out the way. These muthafuckas gave me five years for that shit I did. But I ain't trippin' tho. That dude had to go for real. I was tired of him beatin' on me and my moms. I just be in this bitch playing basketball, workin' out here and there. It's some cool-ass niggaz I met since I been down too. They ain't fam like y'all, but they help the time pass. I had to beat a nigga ass too last week. Nigga thought he could take something from me, so I had to fuck him up right quick and let him know shit is real. Dolla, I know your birthday just passed, and I'm sick I had to miss it. I know you and that wild ass-nigga Rell was foolin' that day! Yo, if y'all niggaz can, I need y'all to tear my moms off somethin' from time to time. The last time I talked to her, she said that she out there strugglin', trying to keep the bills paid and shit. Don't worry about me, I'm straight. Just try to look out for my O.G. Y'all niggaz already know it ain't nothin' but love. If y'all can, send me some pictures of some hoes or some magazines. Write back A.S.A.P and let me know what's poppin' out there! Y'all be safe!

Hammer

It felt good to finally hear from their friend. They had mixed emotions after finding out he had to stay locked up until he turned eighteen, but they were laughing when he told them how he had to whoop a nigga's ass. They both knew how Hammer got down when it came to fighting, so they could imagine the ass-whoppin' he put on the dude that stole from him.

Later on that night, the boys wrote Hammer a letter and told him what was going on and some of the changes that had taken place since he'd been locked up… (in so many words of course) and put it in the mail the next day.

Days were passing, and the block was steady pumping. The summer was approaching soon, and the boys knew that business would pick up even more. With the responsibility of copping the pounds, bagging them up, and posting up on the block pushing the sacks off, the boys were wearing thin. Even Dennis saw it and suggested they hire a worker.

At first, Dolla and Rell felt there was no reason to put somebody else on the block.

"I'm sayin', D. We been runnin' this bitch without no outside help, so why change shit up?" Rell asked.

"Well for one, y'all niggaz ain't workers no more. Y'all some young bosses. If some shit was to go down, and eventually it will, y'all have to be out here to make sure shit straight. If y'all go to jail, who gonna run the block? Who gonna cop from the plug? Y'all money would STOP. Y'all got a new position, and it's time for y'all to play it. Get a nigga, pay him, and y'all play the background and watch from a distance," Dennis said.

"I just feel like bringin' another person might bring bullshit too," Dolla said.

"Listen to me, lil homies. Bullshit gonna come regardless. It's all in the way you handle it when it comes. Y'all barely been in the game for a year, and y'all done had to smoke a nigga. And don't think shit gonna stop there either. If y'all plan on doin' this shit all the way, y'all gonna have to learn to plan ahead and master the art of change. Do y'all really think this block gonna do numbers like this forever? Y'all gonna eventually have to open up other spots if y'all plan on lasting on these streets," Dennis said.

Dolla and Rell listened, knowing that what Dennis said made perfect sense. It was time to fall back and put a new face on the block… But who? They thought about it while smoking a blunt. All of a sudden, someone came to Rell's mind who he thought would be perfect for the job.

"I think I got somebody in mind to hold shit down," Rell said.

"Who?" Dolla asked.

"That nigga Rick from off Woodmont," Rell said.

"Who the fuck is Rick from off Woodmont?" Dolla asked.

"The fat-ass nigga we always see at the store turning in bottles and shit."

"Oh yeah, I know who you talkin' bout. But what makes you think he'll wanna fuck wit us though?" Dolla asked.

"Shit, look at him, bro! That nigga ain't got shit. Plus, I know for a fact he smoke weed. I know that nigga will roll for us," Rell said with confidence. "He always up at the store, so we'll catch him up there and let him know the deal."

"Naw, we gonna *talk* to him first and see where his mind at. We can't put a nigga down wit us if he ain't got no common sense," Dolla said.

"Yeah, true dat," Rell agreed.

The next day rolled around and Rell had already been up to the store four times looking for Rick, but had no luck running into him.

"Damn, any other day this nigga would be glued to the liquor store. Now that we lookin' for him, he ain't nowhere to be found," Rell said frustrated.

"Shit, he'll turn up sooner or later," Dolla said.

It was now almost four that afternoon, and the block was doing numbers. Both Dolla and Rell were tired from the combination of running back and forth, serving custos and smoking blunts. Dennis was right, it was time for a change.

"Rell, why don't you run back up to the store and see if dawg up there?" Dolla said.

"Alright. You gonna be straight while I'm gone?" Rell asked, knowing that it was the busiest time of the day.

"Yeah, I'll be able to hold the block down. Just grab that nigga and come right back," Dolla said.

Rell took off and headed up to the liquor store. Just as luck would have it, he spotted Rick walking into the store with a garbage bag full of bottles. Once Rell made it inside the store, he heard Rick arguing with Jerry, the Arab man who ran the store.

"C'mon, Jerry. Let me slide just this one time," Rick asked desperately. With all the money I spend with y'all, I should be good for it."

"What money you spend!? If anything, we spend money with you taking all those bottles you bring in! Five dollars is the limit for one day and you have already brought in $10 worth of bottles. Now you have more! The bottle room is filled up, I can't take any more bottles from you today. Take them somewhere else!" Jerry said in a heavy Arabic accent.

"Fuck!" Rick cursed. He was headed for the door with his bag of bottles when Rell cut off his path.

"Hold on, big dawg. Can I holla at you for a minute?"

"About what?" Rick asked, slightly annoyed.

"First off, how much you got in bottles in that bag?" Rell asked.

What the fuck do you care? Rick was thinking to himself.

"Five dollars," he mumbled.

"I'll buy them from you," Rell said, reaching in his pocket pulling out a fat-ass wad of cash. "Here you go," he said, handing Rick a $10 bill and taking the bottles from his hand.

"Damn, good lookin'!" Rick said, stuffing the money in his pocket.

"You drink?" Rell asked, sitting the bag of bottles in the corner.

"Yeah, I drink brew," Rick said.

"I'll grab us up some forty's and some blunts. I wanna holla at you about some money shit. You got some time on your hands?"

"I ain't doin' shit, we can kick it," Rick said. An older man walked into the store and headed towards the coolers filled with beers.

"Yo, my man. Can you grab us up a few fortys?" Rell asked the man. The man looked at Rell and Rick, noticing how young they were.

"I don't know about that. How old are you kids?"

"I'll pay you ten dollars," Rell said.

"In that case, what kind of beer y'all want?" the man asked smiling, revealing a mouth full of yellow teeth.

Rell smiled and chuckled, shaking his head. *The power of a dolla...* he thought to himself.

"Grab us up two forties of O.E. and a box of blunts with three cups." He handed the man $20 bill.

Rell and Rick were headed towards the door to wait on the man outside when Jerry yelled out from behind the counter, "Ricky, take your bottles with you!"

Before Rick could respond, Rell said, "He straight… you can keep 'em," and the boys walked out the door.

A few minutes later, the man came out of the store with a plastic bag containing the beers and the box of blunts and handed them to Rell.

"Good lookin'," Rell said, grabbing the bag. "C'mon Rick, let's be out."

"Where we goin'?" Rick asked.

"We headed over to my block to kick it. It ain't far from here," Rell said.

They cut through the alley for three blocks and as soon as the hit Mettetal, Rell could see Dolla scrambling between three different cars, serving custos.

Once Dolla served them all, he looked up and saw Rell and Rick headed his way.

Damn, that's a big-ass boy, Dolla thought to himself, looking at Rick. He had to weigh at least two hundred pounds. He was dark-skinned with the biggest afro Dolla had ever seen.

Once Rick and Rell met up with Dolla, Rell introduced the two. "This that nigga, Rick, I was tellin' you about," he said.

"What up, doe? Everybody call me 'Dolla,'" he said, extending his hand.

"Sup wit ya? My name Rick," he replied as they dapped each other.

"C'mon, let's kick it on the porch," Dolla suggested, walking towards Dennis's porch.

As soon as they all sat down, Dolla lit up a cigarette. "Tell us a little about yourself," he said.

"Well, as you know, my name Rick. I stay over on Woodmont. Me, my momma, and my sister moved over here from Joy Road a few months ago after my brother was killed.

"What school you go to?" Rell interjected.

"Shit, I ain't been to school in a while. I stopped going after what happened to my brother."

"What happened to your brother, if you don't mind me askin'?" Dolla inquired.

"My brother used to hit licks. One time, he robbed a liquor store and when he was comin' out, the hook saw him ski-masked up and jumping in his car. They gave chase and had him trapped on a dead-end street. My brother had already did five years in the joint before that and he always used to say that he would never let the police catch him again. So, he hopped out of the car and started shooting at the hook. He ended up killing one of 'em, but the other officer killed him."

"Damn, that's fucked up," Rell said, splitting open a blunt.

They sat on the porch getting to know each other, smoking and drinking forties. All the while in between the conversation, Dolla and Rell were taking turns serving the custos.

"You ever hustled before?" Dolla asked Rick.

"I've sold weed here and there, but nothin' serious though," Rick answered.

"So, what do you do to make money?" Rell asked him.

"Shit, I try to cut people's grass here and there, and I collect bottles and turn them in," he admitted shamefully.

"Well, as you can see, we sell weed over here and we lookin' for somebody to hold shit down for us… You think you would be interested?" Dolla asked him, point blank.

"Hell yeah!" Rick had a big smile plastered on his face. "I heard about some niggaz sellin' weed over here, I just didn't know it was y'all. I'd love to fuck wit y'all."

"Okay, then. It's settled. You'll start tomorrow morning. We'll pay you $200 a day," Rell said.

"Two hundred?! Damn, I could help my momma out and get fresh as hell!" Rick said excited, looking at his raggedy clothes he had on.

"Here, take this," Dolla said, reaching on his hip and giving Rick his pager. "We'll page you in the morning, so be listening out for us. The pager number is on the back. Tomorrow we'll show you how to move and put a sack in your hand. You gon' have to work at night too, but we gotta get you strapped up first."

"I got a .25 at the house. It was my brother's. I don't keep it on me, but while I'm rollin' for y'all, I'll have it wit me," Rick said.

"That's what's up, cause you gonna need it," Rell said. "Listen, we takin' a chance on fuckin' wit you. All we ask for is loyalty and we'll give you the same in return," Dolla said firmly.

"Man, I appreciate it, and I'm gon' hold shit down fo real. You'll see," Rick said with the utmost sincerity in his voice.

"I hope so, fam. I hope so…. Oh yeah, we gonna need to know where you live too. Don't take this the wrong way, but if you cross us, I'm gon' deal wit ya," Rell said, showing Rick his Glock .40.

"I won't. I just wanna be part of the team," Rick replied.

Early the next morning, Dolla went to the payphone to page Rick. As soon as Dolla was walking up the street, he saw Rick coming from the alley. *Damn, that was quick. This nigga ready to work*, Dolla thought to himself.

Rell and Dolla put a sack in his hand and then sat back and watched as Rick served the custos. At first, the customers were a little reluctant to fuck with him because they didn't know who he was, but after noticing Dolla and Rell on the porch, they knew Rick was straight.

As the day went on, Dolla and Rell didn't do anything but watch Rick move the bag and hand him a fresh sack whenever he ran out. He caught on pretty quick. He loved the fact that he was making fast money and he wanted to show Dolla and Rell he could hold shit down.

"For a big nigga, he sure can move quick," Rell said to Dolla, watching Rick push the sack off.

"Yeah, I think he's gonna make the cut," Dolla said, standing in Dennis's driveway, dumping the inside of a swisher into a garbage can.

"We startin' to move up now. By the time Hammer get out, we'll be bosses fa real," Rell said, breaking down some weed.

"We definitely movin' in the right direction. All we need now is a better plug with cheaper prices and better quality," Dolla agreed. "Don't get me wrong, Dennis's manz is straight, but he can barely keep up wit what we be wantin' to cop."

Rell didn't say anything. He just nodded his head in agreement because he knew what Dolla was saying was the truth. They called Rick over to the porch to smoke with them. Dennis had left earlier that morning, but as soon as the boys were about to light the blunt, they saw Dennis coming down the street in his Cadillac.

He pulled into the driveway and got out the car.

"Sup, niggaz?" Dennis asked, walking up on the porch and dapping the boys.

"D, this our manz, Rick. He gon' be holdin' shit down for us. Rick, this the big homie, D." Dolla said, introducing the two. "

"What's happenin', young hustla?" Dennis said as he dapped Rick.

The four of them sat on the porch, kicking it. In between that, customers were pulling up and Rick was on that shit. The boy had drive in him and Dennis, Rell, and Dolla could see it. With Rick on the team, Rell and Dolla could focus on other things, like finding a new plug for example.

Another two weeks went by and everything was going smooth. Rick was holding the block down. He got himself a new wardrobe and was able to throw his mom a couple dollars. She was a raging alcoholic and once she noticed Rick was making money, she didn't give a fuck what he was doing to get it, as long as he kept it coming. She loved her son without a doubt, and she didn't want him to end up like his brother. "I'm not gonna tell you how to get your money, Ricky. Please, just be careful. I wouldn't know what to do if I lost you," she would always say.

While Rick was handling his business, Dolla and Rell were busy trying to find a new connect. Through Dennis, they met three different people, but it was either the prices were too high, or the product wasn't good.

"We better off just fuckin' wit the plug we got now," Rell said, as they were driving. Dennis and Dolla both nodded in agreement.

They drove to the mall and Dolla got another phone and him and Rell grabbed a few outfits and stopped to eat in the food court.

"We should go back to the pager store and grab them two phones we saw," Rell said.

"I got something even better for y'all," Dennis said, stuffing a handful of french fries into his mouth.

"Like what?" Dolla asked.

"Burnout phones. We'll stop by my homie's house on the way back to the hood and grab them up."

"Damn, D! You the muthafuckin' man," Rell said.

"I know, Dennis said arrogantly."

While eating, the three of them talked shit to each other and tried to holla at different girls as they passed by them. After eating, they swung by Dennis's people's house and the boys paid for three burnout phones for $800 each. From there, they headed back to the hood. They had to bag up a few pounds and wanted to check on Rick and make sure he was okay.

Once they made it back to the block, the boys gave Rick his phone and they went to drop off their clothes they'd bought from the mall. Dolla made it back to Dennis's house before Rell, so he grabbed the scale and weighed up a half a pound and then began bagging up three-gram dimes.

Rell walked in the door shortly after Dolla got started.

"That nigga Hammer wrote us," Rell said, holding up the letter in his hand.

"Open that shit then, nigga," Dolla said before getting out the chair and heading toward the kitchen to wash his hands.

Once he came back to the table, Rell opened the letter up and they began to read it:

My niggaz,

What up? It was good to hear from y'all in that letter you sent me. From what I'm hearing, shit changing out there. Thanks for that money y'all sent to me. My moms said y'all be tearin' her off some paper too and I appreciate that, for real. School about to be out. What y'all niggaz got planned for the summer? Shit, I forgot. Dolla the only one who go to school. It's summertime every day for that nigga, Rell! Time is movin'. Niggaz gon' look up and see me home soon. I can't wait! Make sure y'all got some hoes lined up for me too! My moms said she got some pics y'all took out there, good lookin'. Now if I can get her to send them to me, I'll be straight! Like I said in the last letter, I done came across some real niggaz. I remember y'all tellin' me Dre wasn't around no more. I met a dude in here, he'll be home next week. His name is Pedro and I think he can help y'all find somethin' y'all lookin' for out there. He was havin' a few problems in here and I straightened shit out for him, so he owes me one. I gave him the 4-1-1 on where y'all at, so as soon as he get out, he gonna be comin' to holla at y'all. From what the nigga be tellin' me, y'all won't be disappointed. They about to put on a movie so I'm gon' have to cut this letter short. One luv, be safe out there,

Hammer

After reading the letter, the boys were trying to figure out what Hammer meant about Pedro.

"Shit, we already got a worker, so we straight," Rell said.

"Yeah, he don't know about Rick yet. If and when this dude Pedro come around, we'll let him know," Dolla said. "What we really need is a connect..."

Over the past few weeks, Dolla and Savannah talked on the phone every day. Neither she nor Carrie had been around since the party and Savannah said it was because she had to buckle down on her studies. The summer was approaching fast and she wanted to be on top of things so she could graduate with honors and enjoy herself with no worries. Dolla had been asking her when they could meet up and go out on a date every day for the past week, and finally she gave in.

"Ok, Dolla. Maybe we can catch a movie or something. I'll see what Carrie has planned this weekend and if she's not busy, we'll come holla at y'all.

"Well do me a favor. Make sure she's not busy, 'cause I wanna see you," Dolla said in a commanding but humorous tone. "Carrie's always busy, let you tell it."

More than you know… Savannah thought to herself.

The weekend finally rolled around and Rell and Dolla were getting ready for the date they had planned with Savannah and Carrie. They made sure they had more than enough weed bagged up and left it at Dennis's house, ready to distribute whenever Rick ran out during the day. Dennis said he had no plans for the day, so he didn't mind holding the sacks and giving them to Rick when needed.

The girls arrived at about four o' clock in the afternoon. They looked good. Carrie had on a sundress that was so short until, if the wind blew too hard, her goodies would be exposed. By the way, her ass was jiggling until it was easy to see that she was wearing a thong - if anything at all.

Savannah was wearing a tight black halter top and a pair of tight black leggings that capitalized on her curvaceous frame. She also had on a pair of six-inch heels and her hair was pinned up in a bun. Dolla and Rell just stood there with their mouths open when the girls got out of the car. The smell of the perfume only enhanced their sexy aura.

The boys were also fresh dressed. Dolla had on a grey GUESS jacket and pants outfit with a white tee on and a pair of crisp grey Air Force Ones. Rell had on a black GUESS outfit with a white tee and a pair of black and white Air Force Ones. They exchanged hugs with the girls, complementing each other on their gear game.

"Can we smoke something before we go to the show?" Carrie asked.

"We already on it," Rell said as he reached in his jacket pocket and pulled out a blunt he had already rolled. They called Rick over to the car and introduced him to the girls and the five of them leaned on Carrie's car and smoked the blunt. Once the blunt was gone, they got in the car and were getting ready to pull off.

"Yo, Rick. You straight?" Dolla asked.

"Yeah. I'm good, bro," Rick replied.

"Be safe. We'll see you in a few hours. If you need us, just call one of our phones.

"Fa sho, I'm definitely gon' be safe," Rick said as he pulled up the side of his shirt, exposing the small caliber handgun he had.

Once they pulled off, they stopped at the liquor store before heading to the movies.

"We gotta wait til somebody pull up and ask them to cop some drank for us," Rell said.

"Gimmie the money, I'll get it," Carrie said with her hand out. Dolla and Rell had a confused look on their faces, but they reached in their pockets and pulled out knots of cash. Savannah already knew what Carrie was up to, it didn't surprise her at all.

After everybody told Carrie what they wanted, she got out of the car and pranced into the store. A few minutes later, she came out with a bag containing the liquor and a small plastic bag full of ice.

"Who did you find to get the drinks that quick?" Dolla asked.

"I bought it myself," Carrie said matter-of-factly. "I got a fake I.D.," she said, holding it in her hand and waving it in the air.

"Damn, girl! You gon' have to hook me and my manz up wit some of those!" Rell said.

They decided to go to Norwest Theater, which was in the hood on Grand River and Longacre, right across the street from where they killed Dre and the girl that was with him.

Once they pulled into the parking lot, Dolla handed Savannah his bottle of liquor. "Put this in your purse. We gonna have to sneak this shit in."

Savannah put the bottle in her purse along with two wine coolers as well. "Y'all ready?" She asked.

"Umm, me and Rell finna hit a few corners," Carrie said as she winked at Savannah. "We'll catch up with y'all."

Rell looked puzzled but didn't say anything. He thought back to the party when she gave him some bomb-ass head and figured whatever she was up to, it had to be a good thing.

"If anything come up, call me."

"I got you, my nigga," Rell said before Dolla and Savannah hopped out of the car.

Once inside the movies, Dolla grabbed two big buckets of popcorn and a few boxes of candy. They sat back and watched the movie and made small talk while drinking.

Where the fuck are we going? Rell thought to himself as he and Carrie rode down Six Mile. About ten minutes later, they were pulling into a motel across the street from the eighth precinct police station. Carrie ran into the office and paid for a short stay. Once she got the key, she called for Rell to get out the car.

Damn, she sure knows her way around the westside, Rell thought to himself.

Once inside the room, Rell rolled up a few blunts and they sat back and smoked, kicking it and drinking. Carrie got up off the bed and turned the T.V. on to the porn channel. Rell played it cool. He already knew what time it was.

"I'll be right back, I gotta use the bathroom," Carrie said. While she was in the bathroom, Rell was watching a guy hit a big booty bitch from the back on T.V. He was beginning to get aroused, picturing himself inside Carrie the same way the guy was with the girl on T.V.

When Carrie came out of the bathroom, she had nothing on. Her body glistened from the baby oil she had on. "Remember when I told you I was gonna let you see what this pussy was like?" Carrie asked in a seductive tone. She crawled towards Rell on the bed then sat on top of him. He started sucking on her nipples and at the same time, began to feel his manhood rise.

Carrie slowly got up off Rell then laid next to him with her legs spread wide open. Without hesitation, Rell got up and placed his head between her caramel-complected thighs. Rell had never eaten pussy before. He had always assumed that was for suckers, but once he saw her pretty pink center, it was as if he had no control over his movements. It felt like he was having an out of body experience.

Her juices began running down her thighs and covered Rell's face as he darted his tongue in and out of her, rotating it in a circular motion on her pearl.

"Ooohh baby, don't stop!" was all Carrie managed to say before her body began jerking violently.

"Damn! I'm cumming!" she screamed in pleasure. Rell didn't stop. Carrie was having an orgasm. She was horny as hell and she also knew she was turning Rell out, which made her even more horny. Rell was rock hard and ready to enter her.

"Grab a condom out of my purse," Carrie said, trying to catch her breath.

Rell leaned over and grabbed the condom, tore open the wrapper and quickly put it on as if it would vanish in thin air if he didn't move fast enough. Then he spread open her legs and he dove into her wetness.

"Uggghh…" Rell moaned as he moved in and out of her juice box. Carrie was loving every minute of it, digging her nails in his back, sucking on his neck. Rell then flipped her onto her stomach and entered her from behind. Carrie was moaning and biting the pillow at the same time. Rell pounded Carrie from the back. Minutes later, his whole body locked up. He was cumming…

Dolla and Savannah meanwhile, were enjoying themselves. During the movie, they talked about all types of stuff. Once it was over, they walked out the theater holding hands. When they got to the parking lot, they saw Carrie and Rell parked on the far end of the lot. As they approached the car, they saw them chilling with their seats reclined. Rell had one of his legs hanging out of the window like he didn't have a care in the world. Dolla and Savannah could see and smell the potent chronic smoke escaping from the car windows.

"Damn, y'all smokin' good. Let us smoke wit y'all," Dolla said, as he and Savannah got in the car.

"Girl, fire this one up," Carrie said, handing Savannah a blunt and a lighter.

"How was the movie?" Rell asked.

"It was straight. What y'all end up gettin' into?" Dolla asked.

"Shit, just hit a few corners and kicked it," Carrie said.

"Hey, can we get something to eat? I'm starving!" Savannah said before coughing from hitting the blunt.

"It's whatever y'all wanna do, baby," Dolla said patting her on the back.

Rell and Carrie were hungry too. They had worked up an appetite from all the fucking they did at the room. They drove to the Coney Island restaurant on Grand River and Schafer. They all had the munchies, but their eyes were bigger than their stomachs. They ordered about $40 worth of food - wing dings, chili cheese fries, chili dogs, milkshakes, slices of cake... You name it, they ordered it. While eating they took turns playing the arcade games.

The girls dropped Dolla and Rell off on the block. Before parting ways, they all said goodbye to each other. Right when Dolla was about to turn to walk away after giving Savannah a hug, she grabbed him and kissed him on the lips, catching him off guard. Her lips were so soft, and he could taste the strawberry lip gloss she was wearing. A few seconds felt like an eternity as their tongues collided.

"Call me tomorrow," she said, after pulling away.

"Man, see if they got any more friends," Rick said after they pulled off.

"I got you, but trust and believe, bitches gonna be throwing pussy at you soon enough," Rell said.

A week passed by and the boys still had no luck in finding a new plug. Dennis did everything he could, but eventually ran out of resources. Not saying the plug they had was all bad, it was just that they knew things could be better. The plug they had just simply couldn't keep up. Dolla and Rell could only get five pounds at a time and they would try to re-up when they were down to their last two pounds, but the guy would take FOREVER. By the time the plug did get to them, they would be down to their very last, if not completely out.

Dolla and Rell were sitting in Dennis's garage with the garage door open chilling, when Rick walked up.

"Aye, it's some lil nigga out front askin' for y'all. Want me to send him back here?" Rick asked.

"Yeah, that's cool bro," Dolla said.

Rick walked back up front and a few seconds later, a short frail looking guy approached them.

"Who the fuck is this?" Rell said out loud, gripping his pistol under his shirt.

"What up, my man? We know you?" Dolla said, breaking the ice.

"I'm looking for Rell and Dolla," the boy said. He spoke with a slight accent and with his skin complexion and slick black hair, one could tell he was of Hispanic descent.

"What you need, nigga?" Rell said with a smug look on his face, still gripping his pistol.

"My name is Pedro. I was locked up with your friend, Hammer. He said you guys needed some help."

Rell and Dolla turned and looked at each other, thinking the same thing. *Why would that nigga Hammer send a weak-ass lookin' nigga over here to try to roll for us?*

"Uh, we straight for now, fam. We already got somebody workin' for us," Dolla said trying his best not to bust out laughing.

"Oh no, I don't sell drugs my friend," Pedro said, laughing a little. "Hammer told me you guys needed a PLUG."

The word *plug* caught the boys' attention, now they were all ears.

"Yeah, he told you right. But how can you help us if you don't sell drugs?" Rell asked.

"My uncle. He's in the business and I know he can provide you with what you're looking for. I usually don't introduce people to my uncle, but Hammer looked out for me while I was locked up. I'm grateful for that. He told me that you two were his brothers and y'all needed a plug, so I figured I would return a favor to Hammer by introducing y'all to my uncle," Pedro said.

"Ok, how can we get in touch with him?" Dolla asked. Pedro reached in his pocket and handed Dolla a business card.

"Angel's Funeral Home," was on the card with a number on the bottom. "His number is on the other side, call him when you're ready. I must go now. It was a pleasure meeting the two of you. Maybe we'll meet again," Pedro said.

"Maybe so… Maybe so," Rell said. Pedro turned around and left the same way he came.

CHAPTER FIVE

"Lockdown! The gym is closed. Return to your cell blocks!" the fat white R.A. said. The inmates weren't even in the gym for ten minutes and a fight had broke out.

Once back on his cell block, Hammer laid across his bunk and read a magazine. June was approaching, and Hammer had been locked up a little over three months. Yet, he was already imagining what he would be doing once he was released.

Sometimes at night while he was sleeping, he would have dreams about the night he killed his father. The judge had ordered him to see a psychologist while incarcerated, but in reality, it was hurting him more than it was helping him. Every time Hammer would see the doctor, it would be the same procedure: talk about the night of the murder, how he was feeling about killing his father… blah, blah, blah. Hammer wanted to just put it all behind him and shut it out, but the staff and authorities kept bringing it back up. It was like peeling a scab from a wound before it fully had a chance to heal, over and over again.

I wonder if Pedro got at Dolla and Rell, he thought to himself.

Hammer knew that if what Pedro was saying about his uncle was true, Dolla and Rell could make a lot of money. Hammer gained respect from the other inmates quickly. It seemed like everybody in the detention center fucked with him. Six Mile niggaz, Seven Mile niggaz, Dexter and Linwood niggaz, Brightmoor niggaz… everybody fucked with him. Even eastside niggaz had love for him too, and that's rare because in Detroit, eastside and westside niggaz usually stayed beefin'.

Hammer was glad he had dudes like Dolla and Rell in his corner. They made sure his mom needed for nothing. He couldn't wait to get back out there and get money with his homies.

"Fuck this shit," he grunted as he got up from his bed. He hated thinking too much, so he went into the dayroom area and watched a little T.V., then played dominoes for a few hours.

The day flew by and it was time to lock down for the night. The inmates stepped into their cells and staff went door to door, locking each one. Hammer's bunkie got sent to the disciplinary block for fighting with staff, so Hammer had the cell to himself and he couldn't stand it. He tried to lay down and go to sleep, but he couldn't. As he lay on the bunk, he couldn't shake the images of his father in his head.

He got up and went to the sink to splash some cold water on his face. Once he was done, he reached for his towel to wipe his face off. Looking in the mirror, he instantly became angry. He didn't like what he saw, which was his father's face. He was a spitting image of his father and it made him sick to his stomach. The only difference was that Hammer had long hair and his father had worn his short.

"I hate you, muthafucka! I'm glad I killed yo bitch ass!" Hammer yelled, staring at the mirror. Tears began to fall down his face as he reached under the sink and grabbed the razorblade he had hidden, just in case he had to cut some niggaz.

"I'm nothin' like you! Nothin'!" He yelled, clutching the razor…

"Hello?" A woman answered the phone.

"Yeah, can I speak to Gordo?" Dolla asked.

"May I ask who's calling?" the woman asked.

"Yeah, tell him it's Dolla."

"Hold on one second," the woman said.

"How can I help you?" a man said with a strong Spanish accent.

"What up, doe? My name is Dolla. Your nephew, Pedro, gave me your number and said you could help me out. I'm looking for a plug on some…"

Click…

The phone went dead.

"What the fuck?" Dolla said. "I know this nigga didn't just hang up on me. Fuck 'em." Dolla hit the end button on his phone.

"What happened?" Rell asked.

"Bitch-ass nigga hung up on me. I knew that lil muthafucka Pedro was on some bullshit," Dolla said.

"You talkin' bout that funny-lookin' boy who came through here the other day?" Rick asked.

"Yeah, hoe-ass nigga talkin' this and that about his uncle. He was just talkin' that shit so Hammer could keep them niggaz from whopping his ass while he was locked up!" All three of them busted out laughing.

"But for real, though. I would have bet money that the boy was on some real shit though. He pulled up in a new Benz with some tinted windows on that bitch," Rick said.

"Was he drivin' that bitch?" Rell asked.

"Naw," Rick said. "But why would he even waste time comin' over here if he was just wolfin'?"

Before anyone could say anything else, Dolla's cell phone rang.

"Who the fuck is this?" he said, answering the phone.

"Don't ever call me talking like that again." It was Pedro's uncle on the other end. "Meet with me tomorrow night at the nightclub on Michigan and Cecil. Come prepared, nine o' clock." Then the man hung up the phone.

"Who was that?" Rell asked.

"It was that nigga, Gordo. He wants to meet with us tomorrow night," Dolla said.

"Bet! We bout to come up now!" Rell said, rubbing his hands together.

"We'll see, bro. We'll see," Dolla said skeptically.

Dennis spent most of the early part of the day out taking care of some business. When he finally arrived home, he saw Rell, Dolla, and Rick sitting on the porch. Whenever Dennis would have to leave, he would unlock his garage so the boys could have a place to chill. They needed some advice on what to do and they knew they could count on Dennis to point them in the right direction.

Walking up on the porch, Dennis could tell the boys were in deep thought.

"It look like y'all sittin' here tryin' to come up wit a master plan. What up?" Dennis asked. Dolla and Rell told him about Pedro and his uncle and that he wanted to meet them tomorrow. Dennis didn't say a word while they were talking. He just sat and listened with an emotionless expression on his face.

After they were done, Dennis leaned back in his chair and rubbed his chin as he formulated a solution to their problem. Dennis had always been a quick thinker.

"He didn't give y'all a name to ask for or anything like that?" Dennis asked.

The boys all shook their heads no.

"Ok, this what we gonna do. I'll drive y'all to the club to meet with him. I know where that particular club is at. It's in southwest Detroit. I've been there a few times. He told y'all to bring money, so obviously the product will either be there or somewhere nearby. We're gonna need someone else with a car too. Just in case this shit is a setup, we can have the money in a different car parked somewhere else. That way if niggaz is tryin' to rob y'all, they won't be able to get the money. Once we see that everything is official, THEN we'll send for the money. Only thing y'all got to do now is find somebody with another car to ride with the money."

"Let's get Carrie and Savannah to do it," Rell suggested.

"I don't think that would be a good idea," Dolla said.

"Why not? They got love for us," Rell said.

"That may be true, but when it comes to money, you never know, fam. And if shit went foul, we don't even know where they live. You feel me?"

"You right. I didn't even think about that," Rell admitted. He knew Dolla had a point there.

"Well, who can we get then? Cause I can't think of nobody else," Rell said.

"Aye, I don't mean to be in too much or nothin', but if y'all need somebody with a car, I can ask my sister to do it," Rick said.

"That would be perfect. And this is OUR business, Rick. You family. Don't ever forget that," Dolla said.

That night when he went home, Rick asked his sister if she could make the run tomorrow night.

"I don't know about that," Rita said.

At twenty-four, Rita had the body of a goddess. One look at her and a person would think she was a stripper or a call girl. Dark-skinned, just like her brother, with short hair and an hourglass figure. She didn't have a job. She used the gift God gave her; her looks. She wasn't a prostitute or anything like that, but she only fucked with older men who had money. She had a judge, doctor, and an owner of a successful chain of restaurants. Whatever she wanted, they gave her. Cars, clothes… you name it. One of them even offered to buy her a home. She had seriously considered it but declined.

Rita wanted a house, but she wanted to buy it on her own. Whenever she did, she would move her mother in with her. She wanted to move her mom to a nice neighborhood someday. She only had one small problem. She liked to drink.

"What's in it for me?" Rita asked.

"I'll pay you," Rick said, slightly annoyed.

"Well one thing for sure, money always makes Rita move!" she said. Where we gotta go?

Dolla, Rell, and Dennis were ready to meet Gordo at the club. The three of them were strapped up and between Rell and Dolla, they had $25,000 in a duffle bag. They also had two large scales ready to weigh their product. Dolla was going to ride with Dennis and meet with Gordo, and Rell was going to ride with Rita and the money. All they were waiting on was for Rita to pull up.

"Yo, Rick. You sure she comin', bro?" Rell asked.

"Yeah, she'll be here. I told her I was gonna pay her, and she ain't gon' miss no money."

"Don't worry about it. We got her," Dolla said.

Ten minutes later, Rita was pulling up in her brand-new Chevy Caviler. She parked and hopped out of the car quickly, catching the boys by surprise. They expected her to be some fat girl, but she was the total opposite. Dennis, Rell and Dolla's mouths literally fell to the ground.

"Y'all ready, bro?" Rita asked, walking around the front of the car. She stumbled slightly and almost fell, but quickly regained her balance. Rick just shook his head. He knew the moment she stumbled that she had been drinking. *How come she just can't ease up off the bottle for a minute?* He thought to himself.

"You alright, sis?" Rick asked sternly.

"I'm fine. Just help me put these bags in the trunk," Rita said.

One of her sugar daddies had taken her shopping earlier that day. She popped the trunk open and she and Rick put the bags in the trunk. Even from a side view, a guy could tell Rita had a fat ass. She bent over a little harder when putting the bags in the trunk because she knew Dolla, Rell, and Dennis were watching. She smiled to herself, knowing that they were watching. Rita loved the attention men would give her.

"Okay, I'm ready. Let's go," she said to Rick.

"Naw, I gotta post up here. My man, Rell, gonna ride with you and you gonna follow Dolla and Dennis," Rick said.

Dennis and Rita locked eyes for a second. She liked what she saw, but he wasn't her usual type. She only fucked with niggaz that was paid, and most of them were older in age. She quickly tried to calculate Dennis's net worth and she assumed it wasn't very much. True enough, he had a new Cadillac and his house looked nice, but she knew he didn't have money like the guys she was currently dating. *Maybe I'll make an exception for this one*, she thought to herself.

"Dolla and Rell went in the house and grabbed the money and the scales and went back outside.

"Let's go," Dolla said, as he hopped in Dennis's car.

"Follow us," Dennis said to Rita. Rick dapped Rell then walked over to Dennis's car.

"Y'all be careful," he said, as he reached in the car and dapped them.

"Fo sho. You too," Dolla said. "We'll be right back." They pulled off the block and headed to southwest Detroit.

They were almost at the club. As they were driving down Michigan Avenue, Dennis just so happened to look in his rear-view mirror and noticed that Rita was swerving a little bit.

"Man, I wonder what's up wit ol' girl. She swervin' like a muthafucka," Dennis said. Looking through the side door mirror, Dolla noticed it too. He quickly pulled out his cell phone and called Rell.

"Baby girl, you alright?" Rell asked Rita.

"Yeah, I'm good. Just a little sleepy," Rita said, her words slurring slightly from the alcohol she had been drinking earlier.

"I'll buy you a pop or something cold to wake you up once we get to where we going. But for now, I need you to hold it together. I got a lot of money on me. Plus, I'm strapped. We don't need no hook fuckin' wit us," Rell said.

Rita knew Rell was right. She just nodded her head in agreement and cracked her window so some air could flow through the car. *Maybe this will help*, she said to herself.

Rell's phone rang. He knew it had to be Dolla, so he answered it quickly.

"What up, bro?"

"Man, what up wit ol' girl?" Dolla asked. "She swervin' like a muthafucka!"

"I know, I know. I just put her up on game about that shit. She say she's a little sleepy," Rell said.

"Tell her to wake the fuck up! We can't afford to get flicked," Dolla said.

"I'm already on it," Rell said as he hung up the phone.

A few minutes later, they were less than a block away from the club and could see the place lit up. Cars were entering and leaving the parking lot. Dolla's adrenaline was rushing. His heart was beating so hard, it felt like it was about to come out of his chest - not from fear, but from excitement.

Rell could see them entering the parking lot.

"Pull up in that liquor store parking lot across the street," Rell told Rita. Dennis had already told the boys about the liquor store and suggested that Rell and Rita park there before they left the hood.

"You see anybody?" Dennis asked, as they pulled in the parking lot.

"Hell naw. Let me call him," Dolla said, as he was looking around the parking lot. The lot was full and there were guys going in and coming out of the club.

After three rings, Gordo picked up.

"Step out of the car," he said, then hung up the phone.

Dolla opened the car door and stepped out.

"I'm watchin' yo back, lil bro. Go handle your business," Dennis said before Dolla shut the car door.

He didn't know which way to go. Once he was standing in front of Dennis's car, he started looking around and noticed a black SUV with tinted windows flashing its headlights.

Ain't no turnin' back now, Dolla said to himself, as he calmed his nerves and headed in the direction of the black truck. As soon as he made his way to the passenger side, a Mexican guy opened the door and got out.

"Come with me," he said as they headed towards the entrance of the club.

"Umm, I'm not old enough to go in there," Dolla said to the man.

"Don't worry, you're with me," the man said as they walked through the front door.

Once inside, Dolla couldn't believe his eyes. He watched in amazement, walking through the club, looking at all the naked girls around him. There was a stage in the middle of the club and two poles on each end. As the loud music boomed through the speakers, there was a female who was completely naked, dancing seductively as guys cheered her on, throwing fistfuls of cash onto the stage at her. Everywhere he looked he saw bad bitches. Guys were getting lap dances, and he could have sworn he saw a female giving a guy some head under one of the tables.

They made their way through the club and stood in front of a door in the back.

"Step inside," the man said to Dolla, as he opened the door.

Once Dolla stepped inside, he felt as if he just entered the gates of heaven as he saw all types of half-naked women walking around. Black women, White women, and Hispanic women… they were all over the place. Some were sitting at the counter, counting money they made for the night, and others were changing outfits, getting ready to go into the club area. A few were even sniffing lines of powder cocaine. A short redbone chick was walking in their direction when the man stopped her in her tracks.

"Keshia, I need you to check my man out for me," he said, looking in the direction of Dolla.

"Ok, José. Follow me," the girl said to Dolla. There was a bathroom at the end of the room, and Dolla followed her inside.

"Ok, hunn. Take your clothes off for me," the girl said.

At first, Dolla was wondering what the fuck was going on. He was supposed to be meeting the plug, but instead he was in the bathroom with a bitch who was asking him to take his clothes off.

"For what??" he asked.

"So I can make sure you ain't wearin' no wire for the hook," she said sarcastically, assuming that he should already know the drill.

"Oh, shit. My fault," Dolla said, as he began taking off his clothes.

Once he stripped down to his boxers, he just stood there and stared at Keshia.

"I'm gonna need you to take those off too," she said with a serious look on her face.

Dolla, slightly embarrassed, took off his boxers and handed them to Keshia. Her cheeks turned red as she blushed when she saw Dolla's manhood.

"You look pretty young. How old are you?" she asked.

"I'm fifteen," Dolla replied, putting as much bass in his voice as he could.

"Wow, you're packin' more than some of these grown men in here," she said with a grin on her face.

"Thanks," Dolla said with confidence."

Keisha searched his clothes and shoes very quickly and thoroughly. She even took the clip out of his gun and inspected it to make sure there were no wires hiding anywhere whatsoever.

"Ok, you can get dressed now. You're clean," she said before she walked out of the bathroom.

"He's clean, José," Keisha said, heading towards the club area.

"Thank you, baby," José said before reaching out and slapping her on the ass.

Dolla finished getting dressed, then stepped out of the bathroom where José was waiting on him. They made their way through the club and back out to the parking lot where the black truck was parked. José opened the back door and told Dolla to get in. Then he climbed in the passenger seat of the truck. Once inside the truck, he saw two men sitting in the third row behind him. José sat on the passenger side. The driver had tattoos all over his body, including his head and face, and there was a heavy-set older man with salt-and-pepper-colored hair and a long goatee dressed in an expensive-looking suit with a diamond ring and a diamond watch on his wrist.

"Hello, my friend. I am Gordo," he said, as he extended his hand to Dolla.

"They call me Dolla," and he reached out and shook Gordo's hand.

"Before we spoke, I had my assistant check you for wires. Can't trust nobody nowadays, eh?"

Dolla didn't say anything. He just nodded his head.

"What can I do for you, Mr. Dolla?" Gordo asked.

"What you got?" Dolla asked.

Gordo chuckled a little bit before answering. "I have everything, Dolla. Heroin, weed, cocaine… What is it that YOU need?"

"Oh, I need weed. How much do you charge per pound?"

"It all depends on how many you get, my friend. How much do you have to spend?"

"$25,000," Dolla said nonchalantly.

"Okay, for twenty-five, I will give you forty pounds," Gordo said.

Gordo didn't say it, but he was impressed that a boy his age had that much money. Between Dolla and Rell, they had saved a little over forty thousand a piece.

"Can I get it now?" Dolla asked.

"Sure. As long as you have the money with you, that won't be a problem," Gordo said. "My associates will take you to the product and once there, you can make the exchange. Now, if you'll excuse me, I have other business matters to take care of. It was nice meeting you, Dolla, and I look forward to doing business with you again."

And just like that, the driver got out and opened Gordo's door and he stepped out and walked into the club.

"Follow us," the driver said before he hopped back in the truck.

As Rita pranced out of the liquor store, all eyes were on her. The parking lot was filled up with customers running in and out of the store. Just as she was about to crack open the soda she bought, someone grabbed her arm.

"Excuse me, miss," the man politely said, but with an aura of authority in his voice. When she turned around, she almost got sick to her stomach. The two police officers seemed to have appeared out of nowhere. The sight of them made her sober instantly.

"Yes, how can I help you, officer?" she said, with a slight tremble in her voice.

Rell had his seat leaned back, staring into space, thinking about the power play him and Dolla was about to receive. *We finna blow up now*, he thought to himself, realizing that his dream of becoming a big-time drug dealer was coming true. He just so happened to glance in the sideview mirror, and what he saw put him on alert.

"Oh, shit!!" he said, as he saw the police talking to Rita. *What the fuck the hook want?* He quickly scanned the parking lot and noticed they were parked four cars over. *If it even look like they about to come to the car I'm gonna break*, he decided, as reached in the backseat and grabbed the bag full of money.

Rell's phone rang, and it caught him off guard. He nearly jumped out of his skin.

"Yeah?" Rell said, answering the phone.

"Everything good?" Dolla asked, as he got in the car with Dennis.

"Yeah, you ready?" Rell asked.

"Yeah, just follow us. We about to pull out the lot in a second," Dolla said.

"Alright. We on it," Rell said, then hung up the phone.

Damn! I gotta do somethin' to get the hook off her. Rell's mind was racing.

"So, can I get your number or do I gotta give you a ticket for parking in a handicapped spot?" one of the officers asked, flirting with Rita.

"Yo, sis! We gotta go! Mama just called and said the baby got a fever! We gotta take him to the hospital!" Rell said, leaning out the passenger door. Rita quickly caught on to the distraction Rell was trying to throw at the hook.

"Oh my God! I gotta go see about my baby!" she said, heading toward the car before the police officer could even respond. She got in the car and let out a sigh of relief.

"Whew! Good lookin'! Bitch-ass nigga wanna try to get my number. I can't stand the hook!" Rita had a lot of hate inside her towards the police after they murdered her brother, and she didn't mind letting it be known.

"Aye, let's get outta here. They ready to go," Rell said, talking about Dolla and Dennis.

Rita started the car and pulled out of the parking lot. As soon as they did, they saw Dolla and Dennis pulling out of the club, following a black Suburban. Rita and Rell quickly caught up with them, and about five minutes later, they were pulling up to a house on Junction and Magnolia Street. They all parked behind each other and Dolla was out of the car before anyone else.

All of a sudden, something strange happened. Two of the men in the truck quickly jumped out with AK forty 47s pointed at Rita and Rell.

"Who the fuck are they?" one of the men yelled out. Rell quickly whipped out his pistol and got out of the car.

"Wait a minute!!" Dolla yelled at the two men. "They have the money! I didn't want to keep it with me because it was our first-time meeting and I wanted to make sure shit was straight!"

The men slowly lowered their weapons. Rell stood ready for anything with his pistol in his hand and Dennis sat in the car with his strap in his lap as well. Everyone was on alert now. Rita damn near pissed on herself when she saw the two men emerge from the truck with large assault rifles.

"Yo, Rell! Bring me the bag!" Dolla said. Rell reached in the car and grabbed the bag with the money and the scales and handed it over to Dolla. Once the driver saw Rell hand Dolla the bag, he stepped out of the truck.

"This way, Dolla," he said as he started walking up to a dimly-lit house. Dolla headed up to the house right behind the driver.

"You straight, bro?" Rell asked, still a little paranoid.

"I'm good, fam. I'll be right back," Dolla said over his shoulder, then disappeared onto the side of the house.

Once inside, Dolla felt a little more comfortable when he saw an older Spanish woman and three little kids running around. Dolla and the driver walked into a dark bedroom and when the man turned on the light, he walked over to the closet and swung the door open. The room had a light scent of marijuana, but once the closet door opened, the piney scent of weed seemed to suck the air out of the room.

"Damn!" Dolla said when he saw all the trash bags full of weed in large Ziploc bags.

"Here's the money. All twenty-five grand of it," Dolla said, removing the two scales from the bag before handing it to the man.

"I'll count the money and you can grab the weed," he replied to Dolla. "The Ziploc bags weigh eleven grams. Altogether with the bag, it will come up to four hundred and sixty per pound," the driver added, as he dumped the money on the bed and began quickly counting.

Ten minutes later seemed like hours as Rita, Rell, and Dennis patiently waited outside. Rell was standing outside next to Dennis's car while Dennis had his window rolled down talking with Rell.

"What the fuck is taking so long?" Rell said. His neck was on swivel mode as he kept looking left and right, watching his surroundings. Dolla came walking from the side of the house with the duffle bag on his shoulder. He was also carrying a black trash bag. Dennis reached down and hit the trunk release button and the trunk popped open. Dolla walked right past Rell and put the bags in the trunk and closed it shut.

"We good?" Rell asked.

"Yeah. Now let's get the hell outta here," Dolla replied. Dolla got in the car with Dennis and Rell got in the car with Rita and they all pulled off simultaneously.

They made it back to the block around eleven thirty. Rick was down the street taking care of a customer when he saw them pull up into Dennis's driveway. He served the custo and quickly made his way down the street to Dennis's house.

When Rick walked up on the porch, he saw that the front door was open and knocked. Rell came to the front door, smoking a cigarette.

"What up, bro?" he said, dapping Rick. "You wanna hit this square?"

"Yeah, good lookin'," Rick said, as he stepped into the house and grabbed the square from Rell and took a drag.

Rick didn't even have to ask how things went. He saw a pound on the table along with three blunts already rolled up.

"Damn! This shit green as hell!" Rick said, picking up a large bud and smelling it.

"Fire up one of them blunts," Dolla said. Rick grabbed one of the blunts and sparked up. He hit it a few times and passed it to Rell. It was some of the strongest reggies he had smoked in a long time. Rell was very satisfied.

"Man, we bout to eat for real now!" he exclaimed before handing the blunt to Dolla. Dolla had hit the weed and automatically knew it was strong before he took a pull. He yelled over to Dennis, who was in the corner talking to Rita.

Dennis walked over and grabbed the blunt and took four quick pulls from the blunt.

"This shit some fire," he said before walking back over to Rita. Rita was tired from the day's events and was ready to go. She wrote down her number on a piece of paper and handed it to Dennis.

"Call me," she said to Dennis. Then she winked and headed towards the front door. Before she walked out the door, she stopped in front of Rick and stuck her hand out. Just as Rick was about to go in his pocket, Rell stopped him.

"I got it," he said and handed her four $100 bills. Her eyes lit up when she saw how much Rell was giving her. She wasn't expecting that much.

"Thanks!" she said, as she grabbed the money and stuffed it in her pocket. "If y'all ever need me again, let me know!" Rita said.

"Bet. Just make sure you don't be swerving all over the road next time," Rell said laughing, but serious at the same time.

Rick, Rell, Dolla, and Dennis sat at the table and fired up another blunt.

"My sister was swervin' all over the road tonight?" Rick asked Rell.

"Yeah, she was a little bit. But she said she was tired," Rell replied.

"That's bullshit. I could tell she had been drinking before y'all left, but I didn't think she was that drunk," Rick said, disappointed in his big sister.

"Damn, that's fucked up," Dolla said.

Dennis didn't say anything, but on the inside, he was disgusted. He was feeling her a little bit too. One thing Dennis couldn't stand was an alcoholic woman. A long time ago, he was in a relationship with a girl who drank all the time. She had gotten pregnant with Dennis's child and he was proud to know he would be a father soon. There was just one problem; she couldn't stop drinking. Dennis tried everything to get her to stop, but she never did. It seemed like the more he expressed his concern about her drinking, the more rebellious she became, and she would drink even more. As a result, she ended up having a miscarriage. Dennis was crushed from the loss. He left her and vowed to never fuck with a woman who constantly drank all the time. Rita was a bad-ass bitch no doubt, but he made up his mind at that very moment that he would not call or date her.

Dolla and Rell were satisfied with the weed they got from Gordo. After spending $25,000, the boys had $30,000 a piece left. They were going to make an additional $35,800 profit off of the forty pounds, and that was after deducting the $25,000 to cop the weed. Things were looking up now. They made an agreement that they would put something to the side for Hammer until he came home, and they would continue to look out for his mom while he was locked up.

They finished up selling the last couple of pounds they got from Dennis's homeboy and two days later, they dropped the product that they got from Gordo on the block. The custos loved the new batch the boys had, and people were coming back constantly. It took only three weeks to get rid of all forty pounds and the boys were ready to see Gordo again. Dennis would take them to re-up, and they would give him anywhere between three to five thousand every time. The boys had a lot of love for Dennis and they wanted to hit him off well for all the game he had given them.

CHAPTER SIX

The summertime had rolled around and Dolla barely graduated middle school. Rell was so happy that he was finally making some real money. One day, he took $10,000 in small and large bills and gave it to his grandmother. He loved his grandmother dearly, and he always swore to himself that once he became large in the game that he would take care of her.

"Boy, where did you get this damn money from?" Grandma Cill asked. Rell knew that this conversation was going to come around sooner or later. He sat down and explained to her how he had been hustling for over a year now and that he was saving all his money.

"I didn't raise you to sell drugs. You know better than that, Jerell." She was disappointed in him and he knew it, but he felt better telling her the truth than lying or keeping it a secret. If something bad was to happen, he would he would want her to know what he was into from him and not from anyone else. He loved her with everything he had inside him. She was the mother and father he never had. God only knows where he would be without her.

He told her that he wouldn't be doing it forever, only until he could get a good job or until he had enough to start a business. But deep down, he knew that he didn't plan on stopping. He was going to hustle until there was no more hustlin' left.

The block was banging harder than ever before. There were days when Dolla and Rell would have to post up with Rick just to keep traffic running smooth. There was beginning to be too much activity on the block. Dennis was the first to really take notice, and one night, he decided to let the boys know it was time for a change.

"I think it's time for y'all to switch shit up," Dennis said.

"What you mean? Everything is runnin' smooth," Dolla said.

"Grandma always used to say, 'if it ain't broke, don't fix it,'" Rell said.

"And your grandmother is right, but when it comes to the game, sometimes change is good," Dennis said.

Dolla, Rell, and Rick all looked a little confused. They didn't understand where Dennis was coming from.

"You see, business is picking up. Y'all have a lot of different faces comin' and goin' all hours of the day, runnin' to this car and that car, servin' muthafuckas right out in the open. Kids be outside playing and they see what's goin on. All it's gonna take is for one or two of them to tell their parents and they're gonna take offense to it. Next thing you know, you're the bad guy. They won't see the neighborhood kid when they look at you anymore. They'll see a drug dealer, the guy who runs up and down the street sellin' shit in front of their kids. Shit like that can cause problems for y'all. Someone might want to call the police."

Now what Dennis was saying began to make perfect sense.

"Maybe we should tell the custos to page us from the store and we meet them like we used to," Rell suggested.

"Yeah, I think that would be best," Dolla agreed.

"I'm cool with that," Rick said. "Anything to keep shit low-key, I'm wit it."

"That's straight for now, but I got an even better idea than that," Dennis said. "It's time for y'all to get a spot, a house where y'all can hustle behind closed doors. It don't get no more discreet than that."

"But how we gonna do that?" Dolla asked. "We too young to get a house, nobody is gonna want to fuck wit us. And where we gonna go? Nobody fucks wit us over here cause this our block."

"If we gotta take this shit somewhere else, we might have to lay some niggaz down," Rell said.

"Don't trip, I'm already one step ahead of y'all. The corner house across the street from Hammer's mom is for rent. It's been empty for a while now. Let me see what I can do," Dennis said.

The boys switched up and had the custos meeting them at the store, and a week later, one of Dennis's girlfriends met up with the landlord who was renting the house out. The landlord was an older white guy who looked to be in his late fifties, early sixties. The house was his parents', and the man grew up there in the late fifties. Sometime in the late sixties, Blacks moved into the neighborhood, and all the Whites packed up and moved out. His parents owned the house and rented it out to families. Once they passed away, he inherited it and rented it out too.

He showed the young lady around but couldn't take his eyes off of her juicy ass. She noticed. In fact, that's what she wanted. Dennis told her to dress as sexy as possible, but still maintain a somewhat classy look. The business suit that she was wearing was well above the knees - the perfect look for the mission. She told the landlord that she worked at a law firm downtown and she definitely looked the part.

"I'll take it. I'm prepared to pay the deposit and first month's rent today," she said.

"Okay, that's great! I'll just need you to sign some papers for me and I need a copy of your I.D. and we'll be all set," the landlord said. The young lady began to explain to the landlord how she lost everything in a house fire and that she was sleeping at a shady motel. She broke into tears, explaining how she was scared at night and how she just wanted to be somewhere safe. She could have won an Oscar, the way she put on her act. The man felt so bad for her, he told her she could move in right away if she wanted to.

"It's okay, I understand. Whenever you do get your I.D., just call me and we'll make a copy of it then." To be honest, the man could care less about an I.D. Once he saw the wad of cash she had on her, that's all the identification he needed. She gave him seventeen hundred, and he gave her copies of the paperwork and the keys.

"My account number is on the bottom of the last page. Rent is due the first of each month. All you have to do is go to the bank and wire the rent money to my account. Keep the receipt for your records."

"Thank you so much," the young lady said, and gave the man a hug.

"You're quite welcome. If there's any problems, if you come across anything in the house that needs repairing, don't hesitate to call me," he said.

The man got in his car and pulled off. He was happier than the woman was. Times were tight for people in the inner city, and he couldn't keep the house occupied. He had to start paying the taxes out of his pocket. On top of that, the neighborhood was getting worse, and he feared that someone would end up vandalizing the house if it stayed empty too long.

Once she saw the landlord pull off and was out of sight, she jumped in her car and headed down the street to Dennis's house. She tapped lightly on the door and Dennis let her in.

"It's all taken care of, baby," she said dangling the keys in her hand.

"Thanks, and this is for you," he handed her $300. "Go get yourself something nice."

She sat the keys on the table and placed the money in her purse. "I appreciate that, but I want my OTHER payment for my services," she purred seductively. Dennis lifted her off her feet and carried her off into his bedroom…

Dolla, Rick, and Rell had been running back and forth from the store to the block all day. It seemed like as soon as they got back on the block, one of their pagers would be going off. They decided to take shifts just posting up at the store with a sack for a few hours before switching up with each other. The day turned into midnight and they decided to shut down. Serving the custos was indeed a better way of handling business, but it had the boys running back and forth constantly throughout the day.

Wore out from the day's work, they went over to Dennis's house to smoke and kick it for a while.

"Damn, y'all niggaz look like y'all been workin' a twelve-hour shift at the plant!" Dennis said, noticing that the boys looked tired. They didn't seem to find the joke Dennis made funny at all.

"We just ready to smoke and relax," Rell said, plopping onto the couch. Dolla and Rick fell on the couch next to Rell.

"Yo, D. You feel like rollin' up?" Rick asked.

"C'mon, y'all. Bring that shit wit ya, we got business on the floor," Dennis said.

"What type of business?? That shit can't wait til tomorrow?" Dolla asked. Dennis shot a look at Dolla that let him know that it wasn't nothing else to discuss on the matter.

"Let's go," is all he said and headed for the door. The boys looked at each other and reluctantly got up and followed behind Dennis. Soon as they got outside, Dennis locked the door and took off walking down the street. Rell wanted to ask where they were headed but decided against it. He could sense that something was bothering Dennis. Once they got to the corner, Dennis stopped and turned around and faced the boys.

"This way," Dennis said, heading into the alley. Out of nowhere, Dennis cut over to the side door of the corner house.

What the fuck is he doing? Dolla thought to himself. Dennis pulled out the keys, unlocked the door, and stepped inside. The boys followed him inside. Now it had hit Dolla what was going on.

"This the crib you was talkin' bout makin' a spot?" Dolla asked. Dennis stared at all three of the boys before speaking.

"Dig, I got a lot of love for y'all niggaz. I try to put y'all up on as much game as I can. I'm not quite old enough to be y'all father, but I DO look at y'all as my little brothers. I want y'all to be as successful and safe as possible. Whatever I tell y'all, it's so y'all can be the best at it as y'all can be. Don't ever take anything personal or get in y'all feelings. When it comes to business, know this: Business NEVER stops! You can be tired, sick… that shit don't matter. The three of y'all should be able to run things with ease. I try to be there for y'all as much as I can, and all I ask for in return is respect. When I told y'all it was business on the floor earlier, and y'all was actin' like y'all was too tired, that shit kinda pissed me off, man. Whenever y'all need to cop, I'm there. When y'all needed some burners, I was there. New spot, here I am. I took time out of my personal schedule to make sure y'all had a safe place to roll. When I said we had business, it could have meant anything. Somebody could have been trying to kill me or I could have needed y'all for something, and niggaz ask me can it wait til tomorrow cause they tired!?"

Neither Dolla, Rell, or Rick could look Dennis in the eye. They knew that everything that he just said made perfect sense. The man went out of his way time and time again for them, seeking nothing in return… the true meaning of having love for someone.

"You know what, I didn't look at it that way. Just know that we appreciate everything you do for us," Rell said.

"And I hope you know that if anybody was to even as much as spit in your direction, we'll gun a nigga down wit no questions asked," Dolla said sincerely.

"I know I just started hustlin' wit y'all, but let it be known that I got y'all back, and I got a lotta respect for you, D," Rick said.

"I fucks wit y'all the long way, and I know y'all got love for me too. Just tighten up, alright?" Dennis had a smile on his face now. He felt like he went a little too far yelling at the boys like that, but he knew it was for the best.

They all dispersed around the house in different directions, looking around. The house was nice-looking, not raggedy and tore-up like a lot of other spots in the city. It had a full basement, two bedrooms on the first floor, and one big bedroom on the second floor. The kitchen was a decent size and the garage sat in the alley.

"Damn, a nigga could live in here for real!" Rell said, impressed with the house.

"This y'all shit, a place of business. The lights will be on for another month, then y'all gonna have to find somebody to put the lights on in their name. The rent is seven hundred a month, and it is due on the first. Bring the money to me and I'll send the payment off. Remember, this is a BUSINESS. It's not good to have anybody in here that ain't a part of y'all money circle. That goes for bitches too. If y'all got a bitch y'all wanna fuck, take her someone else or bring her to my crib. A lot of money is going to come in and out of these doors and you don't want anybody be able to calculate how much y'all makin'. Keep the house clean and presentable. You gotta respect the neighbors. Don't play music too loud. Try not to be posted in the front yard, instead kick it in the back. It's a lot of shit y'all gonna need for the house, so starting tomorrow, I'll shoot y'all around to get some of the stuff y'all need," Dennis instructed.

"Good lookin' out, D. Man, I don't know what we would do without you," Dolla said.

"Now, it's just one more thing we gotta do," Dennis said.

"What's that?" Rell asked.

"Roll a muthafuckin' blunt and bless this house!"

"We about to bless this bitch two or three times!" Rick said, pulling out some weed.

The next day, Dennis and Dolla headed out to grab some stuff for the house. Rick and Rell stayed back and were telling all the custos to start coming to the new spot. The first stop was the lock and door shop right around the corner. Dolla paid for two security doors and bars for the front and back of the house. The installation specialist would be over the next day to hook everything up. The next stop was to the thrift store. Dolla bought two couches, a dining room set, three mattresses, dishware, a refrigerator, and a stove. From there, they stopped at a hardware store and picked up some hinges, screws, two-by-fours, nails, and some chicken wire. When they were leaving the store, Savannah called.

"What up, sexy?" Dolla said.

"Nothin'. What you doin'?"

"Right now, I'm doin' some shopping, but I'm getting ready to head back to the block."

"You want some company?" she asked.

"As long as you the company, I'm wit it," Dolla said.

"Boy, you silly. Me and Carrie about to leave in a minute."

"Bet, I'll see you then," Dolla said, then hung up the phone.

Once back on the block, Dolla, Rick, and Rell carried the hardware supplies into the house and Dennis went to get some tools from his garage. Once Dennis made it back to the spot, the boys grabbed the tools and got to work. They nailed the chicken wire on all the windows in the back of the house, just in case somebody tried to firebomb it. Then, they took all the hinges they bought and nailed them on each side of the front and side doors. During business hours, they would slide two-by-fours through the hinges across the doors. That way, in case of a raid, it would take more time for the police to knock the doors down.

Just as they were finishing up, Savannah and Carrie pulled up.

"What y'all doing over here?" Carrie asked as they were getting out of the car.

"Just hookin' up our store," Rell said.

"Store?" Savannah asked, confused about what Rell was talking about.

"This our spot now, baby," Dolla said, grabbing Savannah and holding her in his arms.

"Can we see the place?" Carrie asked.

"C'mon," Rell said, as he led Carrie into the front door. Dolla and Savannah walked in behind them. Rick was in the kitchen rolling up a blunt when the four of them walked in. The girls spoke to Rick, then continued walking through the house, looking around.

"Damn, this is a nice house. We gonna have some fun in here," Carrie said playfully, elbowing Rell in his side.

"I wish, but this ain't the place for that. Anything could happen at any time, and we don't want nothin' to happen to y'all," Rell said referring to Carrie and Savannah.

"Awww!" Carrie said pouting. Rell was beginning to grow on her.

"Don't trip. There are other places we can go," Rell replied with a sly grin on his face.

"When y'all gonna get some furniture and stuff?" Savannah asked, noticing that there wasn't even a chair in the house.

"Oh, I took care of that this morning," Dolla said. "They will be delivering the furniture sometime today. All we need now is a T.V. and a radio."

"Y'all tryin' to get it today?" Carrie asked. "We'll take y'all."

"Bet!" Rell said. "Aye, Rick. We bout to get a T.V. and some other shit. Can you hold it down til we get back?"

"That's what I'm here for," Rick replied.

Rell ran down the street to get some money while Carrie and Savannah waited in the car. By the time Rell came back, Dolla had already rolled up two blunts for the road. Rell hopped in the passenger seat next to Carrie and they pulled out. They smoked one of the blunts on the way and by the time they got to the mall, they were high as hell. They stopped in the electronics store and bought two nineteen-inch T.V.s, a video game system, a few games, and a radio. They told the clerk that they had some more shopping to do, so the clerk let them leave the stuff they just bought until they were finished shopping.

They went to the music store and bought some cassette tapes to listen to. They were all hungry, so they got something to eat in the food court. Once they were finished eating, Dolla and Rell surprised the girls and told them they could grab some things if they wanted to. Carrie and Savannah ended up buying a few outfits and some shoes, courtesy of the boys.

Before they left, they doubled back to the electronics store and grabbed the stuff they bought. The boys' hands were full, so Carrie and Savannah helped them carry some of the stuff back to the car. They lit the other blunt and headed back to the block.

When they pulled up, they saw a delivery truck parked in front of the spot.

"That must be the furniture," Rell said.

Rick was serving customers in front of the house. He was letting people know to come to the house from now on starting the next day. They wanted the house fully secure before they started hustling from out of there.

Dolla and Rell took the stuff they bought from the mall into the house and went back outside with the girls. They kicked it for a while and business began to pick up as the day went by. Dolla and Rell had to help Rick take care of the custos coming back and forth.

"Aye, it look like y'all real busy right now, so we about to dip and let y'all take care of y'all business," Savannah said. Dolla didn't want her to leave, but she was right. There was too much going on at the time.

"Alright then. Call me later," Dolla said, sticking his head in the car and kissing her lightly on the cheek. Rell walked over to the driver side and did the same.

They spent the rest of the day getting the house ready for the next day. Rick was glad to be part of a winning team. In less than two months, he managed to save close to $10,000. Before that, he was turning in bottles and cutting grass for a living. He was able to help his mom out, and she never asked questions about where the money was coming from. His life did a complete three-sixty turn around, and he wasn't going back to being broke, no matter what. He was even fucking a few hoes from the neighborhood. When he first moved into the hood, girls wouldn't pay him any attention. Now, he was literally having to peel them off his dick.

"Can y'all hold it down for a second? I gotta run up the street right quick," Rick said.

"We got you, my nigga. Everything good?" Rell asked.

"Yeah, I'll be right back," Rick said, handing his sack to Rell.

About twenty minutes later, Rick was coming through the alley carrying two bags. It was getting dark, and the sun was going down, but people were still coming to buy weed with no sign of things slowing down. Dolla was talking to a car full of girls, and Rell was sitting on the porch when Rick walked up.

"What's in the bags?" Rell asked. Rick pulled out three bottles of Moët and a pint of Remy V.S.O.P. and a box of blunts.

"Damn, it's yo birthday or something?" Rell asked, laughing.

"Naw, it's a celebration! I just wanted to thank y'all for giving me a chance and bringing me into this family. I ain't never had niggaz show me love like y'all do. I appreciate it, and I'm ridin' wit y'all niggaz until my muthafuckin' casket drop," Rick said, meaning every word.

Rell yelled form the front porch to Dolla. "Yo, come grab a bottle. It's a celebration, nigga!" Rell popped the cork on one of the bottles at the same time.

"Damn, can we celebrate with y'all?" the girl in the backseat asked.

"Why not?" Dolla said. The girls pulled over and parked, then they got out of the car and walked in the house behind Dolla. Rick put a rap tape in the radio and music filled the house. Rell was busy rolling up blunt after blunt. Dolla was on the couch talking to the girls.

The party was going well. They sat at the table playing spades and talking shit. Customers were calling their phones and the boys took turns serving them. They were low on drinks, so Rell went to the store to get some more. He came back with more bottles.

"This round's on me!" he yelled, sitting the drinks on the table.

Everybody in the house was feeling good and buzzing from the weed and liquor.

"Hey! Let's play strip poker!" the tall dark-skinned girl suggested.

"That's what's up, but I don't know how to play," Rick said.

"Don't worry, I'll teach you," she said and winked.

Come to find out, Dolla and Rell didn't know how to play either. The girls were kicking their asses. They had the three of them down to their boxers.

"We ain't gonna win this shit," Rell said, and folded his hand. "We getting our ass beat."

"Tell y'all what. We'll even the score then," the mixed girl said.

The next thing you know, the three girls stripped off their clothes and were only wearing their bra and panties.

"Now how am I supposed to concentrate on the game? It's gonna be hard as hell!" Rick said.

"What's hard as hell?" the tall dark-skinned girl asked. She definitely wasn't referring to the game.

"Hey, let's play truth or dare!" the brown-skinned girl suggested, looking directly at Dolla.

"I'm down for it," Dolla said. The game started with a little kissing, then it progressed to touching. Dolla kinda felt bad about what he was doing. The weed and alcohol were playing tricks on him. One part of him was saying, *don't do it*, but the other half was saying, *fuck that shit, it's not like y'all in a relationship, you ain't even got the pussy yet!* Plus, someone had tried to call him twice and he knew it was Savannah, so he didn't answer.

Rell had bought some condoms when he went to the store earlier. He already knew what time it was once the girls came into the house. Rell figured now was the time to turn it up a notch. He took the box of condoms out of his pocket and tossed them on the table.

"Damn! That's how you feel?" the mixed girl asked, grinning from ear to ear. Rell grabbed one of the condoms and grabbed the mixed girl by the hand.

"Let me holla at you for a minute," he said to her, heading to one of the bedrooms. That move alone set the stage for Rick and Dolla. Rick grabbed the dark-skinned girl and grabbed a condom off the table and went to the second bedroom. *Fuck it*, Dolla said to himself and fucked the brown-skinned girl on the couch.

After the girls left, the boys rolled up a blunt and talked about how each one of the girls were in the bed.

"Now that's the way to start up a spot!" Rell said, laughing.

"Aye, what was them hoes names? I need to see that chocolate thang again!" Rick said. Rick had a thing for tall girls.

"You know what? I don't know, I never asked!" Dolla said. The three of them busted out laughing.

The next day, the security doors and the bars for the windows were installed. Custos were coming left and right to the new spot. They would come to the side door facing the alley to get served. The boys had the SKS assault rifle in the spot, plus the three of them had their pistols. Whenever someone would come to the door, all three of them would be standing in the doorway with their guns in hand. One of them would be holding the SKS for customers to see. That way, if anybody was thinking of robbing the spot, they would definitely think twice after seeing the firepower that was on deck. Customers having to come through the alley to get to the side door helped hide the amount of traffic that was coming and going.

Dolla left the spot to go to the store and get some cigarettes and some blunts. Once he got there, he saw dope fiend Krissy jumping out of a raggedy-ass car. Dolla could see that the driver was an old man who looked to be in his sixties. *Must be one of her tricks*, Dolla thought to himself.

Once Krissy saw Dolla, she walked over to speak to him.

"Dolla, I need some money. Can you help me out, baby?" she asked.

"Shit, you just jumped out that old man's car. It look like you just made some money," Dolla said.

"That couple of dollars ain't about nothin'," Krissy said. The thought of the boys needing somebody to put the electric and gas in their name for the spot came to Dolla's mind. He decided to seize the opportunity.

"I got a way for you to make some money if you can help me out."

"Anything," Krissy said, twirling her nappy-ass weave, trying her best to look sexy.

"Listen, I got a house and I need you to put the electric and gas bill in your name. I'll give you $50 right now and I'll give you $50 every month for yourself every time the bill is due."

"Ok, give me the address to the house and I'll call the light company," Krissy said.

"Shit, you can do that right now from my cell phone." Dolla reached in his pocket and handed her the phone. She dialed the number to the light company and within twenty minutes, the lights were switched over into her name.

"The light bill will come in the mail, honey," Krissy said to Dolla. Dolla reached in his pocket and handed her six $10 bills.

"Here you go. And there's a tip for you," Dolla said, referring to the extra $10.

"Thanks!" Krissy's eyes lit up while she stuffed the bills in her pocket as if they would fly away if she didn't hurry. "Anytime you need me, I'll be around!" Krissy said, then took off down Grand River, most likely headed to a crack house.

Once back at the spot, Dolla let Rell and Rick know that the light bill situation was taken care of. The three of them were handling things better than most grown men, and Dennis was impressed. Every day, he would come over to the spot and chill out with the boys, smoking weed and talking shit. Dolla, Rick, and Rell came up with the shifts they would work running the spot. The first three days of the week, Dolla and Rick would be there in the morning and Rell would be there sometime in the afternoon. Dolla would be able to leave and take care of any business necessary, and Rick and Rell would hold the spot down. Around midnight, Rick would leave, and Dolla and Rell would stay the night, serving the custos. The next three days was the same, except Rick would spend the night instead of Dolla. Then, the last day of the week, Dolla and Rell would give Rick the day off and the two would hold it down while Rick worked the night shift with Rell. Even though Rick would be off that day, he would be chilling at the spot anyway, kicking it with Dolla and Rell unless he had a bitch to fuck or if he wanted to do some shopping and chill with his mom.

Business usually ended at about two a.m., sometimes three on the weekends. They never left the house without someone there, and they always made sure neither one of them was by themselves at night.

Dolla wanted to work the night shift all seven days, but he didn't want Aunt Darline to become suspicious of his whereabouts during the late-night hours. Deep down, he knew the truth would come out eventually, and he knew it would break his aunt's heart. He loved her to death for raising him after his mother was killed, and he would be forever grateful for that, but hustling and the streets was in his blood.

CHAPTER SEVEN

Savannah's birthday was coming up and she wanted to throw a huge birthday bash. Dolla suggested that they get a few hotel rooms, that way she could invite all her friends. It had been a while since they had seen each other, but they talked on the phone on a regular basis. Dolla wanted Savannah to have the best birthday ever, and he was gonna spend enough money to make sure she did.

Everything was going good with the spot. It seemed like since they opened up, they were making more money than they were slanging off the hip. They were able to make more serves at night, which helped increase the day's take. Rick and Dolla were at the spot, and they ran out of weed early in the morning. Customers were still coming, and Rick would tell them to come back in twenty minutes. Once they saw the block was clear, Dolla told Rick he would be right back. He had to run down the street to get a sack from Dennis's house. They didn't want any custos to see them running from the spot to Dennis's house because that was where they would bag up and keep the sacks at.

"Go ahead. I'm gonna run up to the store right quick, I'll meet you back here," Rick said. He went to the store and grabbed a pack of cigarettes. While walking through the alley, he stopped and lit up a square. He didn't notice the guy walking behind him, and when he did hear something, it was too late. Out of nowhere, Rick felt cold steel up against the back of his head.

"If you even think about movin', I'll blow yo muthafuckin' head off," the man with the gun said.

"What the…?"

"Shut the fuck up!" the man said before Rick could finish talking. With his free hand, the man reached in Rick's pocket and pulled out $700 and about $200 in dime bags. He also found Rick's pistol and took that too.

"What you doin' wit this, shootin' squirrels or somethin'?" the man laughed as he stuck Rick's pistol in his pocket. After taking Rick's money and pistol, the man didn't even bother taking Rick's pager or phone.

"Now get the fuck on fo' I smoke yo' bitch-ass, nigga," the man said. Rick started walking and without turning around said, "I hope that shit is worth yo' muthafuckin' life, nigga."

"What?!" the man said before letting off a round.

Pop!

The bullet pushed Rick forward as it entered his shoulder.

"Fuck!" Rick yelled in pain as he grabbed his shoulder and took off running. The man thought about finishing Rick off but changed his mind.

Fuck 'em. Nigga didn't see me, and I got 'em for what he had, the man thought to himself and took off running in the other direction.

Dolla was at Dennis's house picking up a sack when he heard a gunshot.

"Aye, did y'all hear that?" Dolla asked Rell and Dennis.

"Yeah, sounded like somebody let off a shot," Dennis said.

"That shit sounded close too," Rell said.

"Oh shit, Rick said he was going to the store, I hope…" Dolla didn't even finish speaking. The three of them left the house and took off running towards the spot. They were a few houses down from the spot, and there was Rick, running out of the alley, holding his shoulder.

"It look like that nigga been hit!" Rell said as he upped his strap. Dolla did the same, pulling out his pistol and cocking it.

"Rick, what up, bro? You straight?" Dolla yelled out. Rick turned and saw Dolla, Dennis, and Rell running in his direction.

"What the fuck happened?" Dennis asked. The three of them had their pistols out, ready to hit anything moving.

"Bitch-ass nigga robbed me in the alley then shot me in my shoulder!" Rick said out of breath from running and wincing from the pain of the gunshot wound.

"Did you get a chance to see that nigga?" Dolla asked.

"Naw, he crept up on me from behind," Rick replied.

"Let me get this nigga to a hospital. Wait right here, I'm gonna grab the car," Dennis said. Dolla and Rell took off running up the alley to see if they saw anyone who might look out of place, but they didn't see anyone. They turned around and headed back to the spot.

"Look!" Dolla said, pointing to some specs of blood on the ground. "This is where Rick must have been shot at."

Once they got back to the spot, they spent the day hustling and trying to figure out who could have shot their friend. They didn't have any enemies, but they knew that by them being so young and making a lot of money, people were bound to become envious of them. They thought hard but couldn't come up with anyone in particular who might wanna bring drama their way.

"Maybe it was just a random lick," Rell said.

Later on in the evening, Dennis and Rick made it back to the block. The nine-millimeter bullet went in and out of his shoulder, so all they had to do at the hospital was clean the wound to prevent it from being infected, then gave him a prescription for some painkillers and sent him on his way. The doctors said it would fully heal in about a month, but they wanted him to come back in two weeks to clean it again and make sure the wound was healing properly.

Dennis, Rell, Rick, and Dolla sat at the spot, smoking and trying to figure out who had the balls to fuck with them.

"Somebody was probably watchin' us," Rick said.

"Naw, because if he was watchin' y'all, he would have known Dolla had left and tried to force you in the house, most likely," Dennis said.

"Man, I can't come up wit shit," Dolla said.

"Oh yeah, I'm gonna pay y'all back the money he took from me too," Rick said. "I got it at my mom's crib."

"What?!" Rell said, somewhat insulted. "Nigga, we don't give a fuck about no punk-ass weed and a few hundred dollars. You family! Yo life is more important. We gon' get money regardless!"

"Rell is right. You family. Plus, whatever losses we take, we take 'em together," Dolla said. "Just keep y'all ears to the street, and I'll do the same. Something will turn up. It always does when shit like this happens," Dennis said.

Everything went back to normal when about two weeks later, Crystal came over to the spot to cop some weed. The boys hadn't seen her since Dolla's birthday party.

"I heard about y'all spot. Everybody sayin' y'all got some flames, so I had to come check y'all out. Gimme two of 'em," she said, handing Dolla a $20 bill.

"This the best shit in the hood right here, and we the only ones who got it," Dolla said arrogantly, as he handed Crystal two bags of weed.

Crystal looked at the weed. Then she opened the bag and smelled it. "This look like the same weed a nigga got that be at the gas station on Schoolcraft and Greenfield," she said.

"Oh, yeah?" Dolla asked. Dolla knew for a fact they were the only ones in the hood who had that particular grade of weed. This guy Crystal was talking about had to be the one who robbed and shot Rick. "What time he be up there?" Dolla asked.

"For the last two days I ran into him around this time of day," Crystal said.

"Oh, ok then. You been alright though?"

"Yeah, but I'll be better if I could get up wit you later on, tonight," she said.

Dolla wasn't thinking about getting no pussy at the moment. Only thing Dolla wanted was revenge for what happened to Rick. "Shit, just get at me. You know where I'm at," he said, spinning her off.

After Crystal left, Dolla shut the side door and walked into the living room.

"I think I know who shot you, bro!" he said to Rick who was playing the game.

"Who?" Rick asked, jumping up and tossing the video game controller on the floor. Dolla told him about what Crystal said about the guy who was posted up at the gas station.

"Let's go!" Rick said before picking up the SKS. He was ready to put some bullets into the dude.

"Hold on, bro. First, we gotta get you another pistol. Then before we holla at ol' boy, I want to see what kind of weed niggaz got at the other two spots in the hood. If they weed different than ours, which I'm almost sure it is, then without question, that's the nigga who robbed you," Dolla said.

"Well let's get on that shit now, cause ain't no telling how long this nigga gon' be around if it's him," Rick said.

Dolla got on the phone and called Rell and told him to get Dennis and come through. Ten minutes later, Rell and Dennis walked through the side door of the spot. Dolla told them about the conversation he had with Crystal.

"That's gotta be him! I'mma kill his ass for fuckin' wit my manz!" Rell said, growing more and more angry by the minute.

"Good lookin', but I got this one, bro," Rick said. "I'm gonna stank his ass where he stand."

"Hey, Dennis. Do you think you can get Rick another pistol by tomorrow?" Dolla asked.

"I don't see why not. I'll holla at my man when I leave from here," Dennis said.

"Before you leave, do you think you could swing by the other two spots in the hood and buy some weed from them? I just wanna make sure we don't end up hittin' the wrong nigga."

"I'm gonna head that way now, and I'll bring back the weed from the other spots."

"Bet. We'll be here," Dolla said.

Dennis left to get some weed from the other two spots and was back on the block thirty minutes later.

"One thing I can tell you is that they weed ain't nothing like y'all shit," Dennis said, tossing the two dime bags on the table.

"Yeah, they definitely ain't our shit," Rell said, looking at the brown and dark green weed inside the bags.

"Dolla, come with me right quick," Dennis said, heading for the door.

"Where we goin'?" Dolla asked.

"To the gas station this nigga be at and try to find him."

The gas station on Schoolcraft and Greenfield was always jumping. Most of the hustlers in the hood would go there to gas up their old schools and whips. It seemed like at any time of the day, one could pull up and find a bad-ass bitch pumping her gas or paying for something inside the station. They sold movies, music, even white tee's and bootleg clothing. And hustlers could get their baggies to put their drug of choice in. They had all types of different sizes and colors.

Black was posted up with the weed he'd got from a nigga he robbed two weeks ago. The dude he stuck up had a few hundred dollars in cash on him and a few hundred in weed. The weed was some of the greenest reggies he had seen in a while, and that shit smoked good as hell. Once he decided to post up at the gas station with the weed two days ago, he damn near sold out without even trying. Selling drugs wasn't his thing. Stick ups was his hustle.

Growing up, Black would constantly get bullied, and things were taken from him on a daily basis. He had always been scrawny and frail, and he couldn't fight his way out of a wet paper bag. But when he picked up his first pistol at the age of thirteen, he quickly realized the power it possessed and the fear it would put in someone's heart. From that moment, he never put it down. He stayed on Schoolcraft and Lauder between Greenfield and Hubbell. He robbed a lot of people on his side of the hood and killed several niggas in the process. Bitches, niggas, preachers... he didn't give a fuck. If you looked like you had it, he would take it from you. And if you resisted, he wouldn't hesitate to put some bullets in your ass. Black had been robbing people for over eight years. Now at twenty-one years old, he didn't plan on stopping.

He was down to his last six bags and he wanted to re-up. He wanted to try hustling and sticking niggaz up at the same time. There was just one problem. He didn't have a plug to cop from. He knew a few niggaz with some weight, but they didn't trust him as far as they could throw him.

Black lit up a cigarette and laughed to himself as he blew the smoke out of his nostrils. *Me hustling... I ain't even got a goddamn pager,* he said to himself. He just didn't have that hustler's swag. He wasn't a people person. The way he knew how to communicate with someone was by mostly sticking a gun in their face.

"My man, you know where some trees at?" the young dude asked Black.

"Yeah, what you trying to get?" Black asked.

"I got twenty dollars," the boy said, handing Black the money. Black reached in his pocket and grabbed two dime bags and gave them to the boy.

"Damn!" These bags big as hell! And they look like some greens! I know a lot of people who would fuck wit you. You always up here?"

"Yeah, just get at me," Black said.

The boy walked away and jumped in the passenger seat of a new Cadillac.

"Damn, I might have to rob that lil nigga," Black thought to himself.

"D, that's gotta be him!" Dolla said, hopping in the car, showing Dennis the bags. "Ain't nobody got this shit in the hood. Nobody!"

"Now that we know who it is, it's time to put the muthafuckin' play down," Dennis said.

Dennis dropped Dolla off at the spot and got some money from Rick, then headed to see his homie about some guns. Dolla told Rell and Rick about what happened at the gas station.

"How this nigga look?" Rell asked.

"He older than us, but the nigga is little as fuck," Dolla said. "I can't wait to put a plan together to kill the nigga who robbed Rick."

A knock on the side door snapped them out of their thoughts. It was Reggie, one of their childhood friends.

"Let me get one," Reggie said, handing Rell a $10 bill. Rell looked behind Reggie and saw a tan-colored Chevy Malibu parked with the engine running.

"Damn Regg, that you?" Rell asked, admiring the clean old school.

"C'mon man, you know what I do. I tilted that bitch," Reggie said.

"That's right, I forgot. Joyriding is yo thang," Rell said laughing. Rell handed Reggie a bag then dapped him.

"I'll holla at you," Reggie said, then headed towards the car.

Outta nowhere, an idea came to Rell.

"Reggie, hold up!" Rell said, stepping out of the house. "What you gon' do wit that?" he asked, referring to the stolen car.

"Shit, I'm gon' ride this bitch till the wheels fall off, ya feel me?" Reggie said.

"You wanna sell it?" Rell asked, knowing that money was the key to most doors in life.

"What you wanna give me for it?"

"I got two hundred for you right now," Rell said. Reggie didn't have to think twice about the offer. He could steal a car in less than sixty seconds, so getting another stolie was easy for him.

"Bet," Reggie said.

Rell reached in his pocket and gave Reggie ten $20 bills.

"You ain't steal this muthafucka from this hood, did you?" Rell asked him.

"Naw, bro. I got it from my cousin's hood. He stay on Chicago and Terry," Reggie said.

Rell opened the driver door and hopped in. Reggie was standing outside the car.

"The screwdriver that's in the ignition is the key. That's how you cut it off and start it up."

"What you plan on doin' wit it?" Reggie asked.

Damn! This lil nigga askin' too many goddamn questions, Rell thought to himself.

"I'm gon' have my dawg retag this bitch," Rell told him.

"That's what's up. I'll holla at you," Reggie said before taking off down the alley.

Rell got out of the car and opened up the garage, then hopped back in the car and backed it into the garage. He walked back into the spot and Dolla and Rick were smoking.

"I know how we can hit that hoe-ass nigga that robbed you," Rell said to Rick.

"How?" Both Rick and Dolla asked at the same time.

"Let me hit the blunt first and I'll tell y'all," Rell said, grabbing the blunt from Rick.

Black was back at the gas station posted with a sack. He had sold out of the weed he had yesterday and finally came across a guy that would sell him an ounce for $100. The weed wasn't as potent as the weed he got from the lick he hit a few days ago, but it was selling. The only reason he chose to re-up is because it kept him from spending his own money to smoke, and there was always the possibility of coming across a customer who could be a good lick if the opportunity presented itself.

Black was thinking about what hood he was gonna go to stick somebody up that night when he saw the young boy from yesterday walking towards him.

"What up, doe?" the boy said once he reached Black.

"What up, nigga? What you need?" Black said with a tone as if he was selling crack to a fiend.

"How much you got?" the boy asked.

"Man, what you need?" Black asked, becoming irritated.

"I want everything you got on you, fam," the young nigga said.

"Oh, that's gon' be $150. You got that?" Black asked arrogantly, knowing that the boy didn't have that much money.

"I'll take it," the boy said, pulling out a handful or small bills.

The sight of the money threw Black off balance for a second. He contemplated on just snatching the cash out of his hand and taking off running, but then he thought about the long-term end of the situation.

This lil nigga got money. Ain't no telling what his people got, he thought to himself, remembering that the last time he saw him, he was with someone in a brand-new Cadillac.

I'll just wait a little while longer and gain his trust, then we'll meet somewhere else on my terms. Black was a grimy-ass nigga who didn't give a fuck about anyone but himself.

He took the money from the boy and handed him the whole sack and gave him $10 back.

"Good lookin', bro!" the boy, said happy that he got a deal.

Naw, you can thank me next time, Black thought to himself.

"It ain't nothin'. You my lil homie," Black said to the boy. "I'll holla at you tomorrow."

"Alright, bet," Black said, as the boy turned around and walked off.

With Black selling out, there was no reason for him to be standing up at the gas station, so he decided to go home for a minute.

Rell and Rick were parked on Schoolcraft and Winthrop, watching Dolla buy the weed from the guy who robbed and shot Rick. They knew once Dolla bought Black out that Black would eventually leave from the gas station and they could catch him slipping somewhere where there was less traffic and no security cameras around.

Dennis was holding down the spot for them, so once Dolla bought the weed from Black, he took off walking, headed back to Mettetal. They saw Black leaving the gas station.

"You ready, bro?" Rell said, looking over at Rick. This would be the first time that Rick would "put in work," killing someone, and his adrenaline was rushing, stomach full of butterflies. Rick didn't say anything, he just nodded.

Rell started up the car and they pulled off. Black was walking down the street, mapping out his plans for the night. Almost every night, he would creep out and look for a lick, and sometimes if someone was slipping during the day, he would stick them up too. Whenever he would have a good day, he would take the next one off and trick with one of the neighborhood dope fiend whores. He was deep in his own thoughts… didn't even notice the tan Malibu following him.

Black turned off Schoolcraft and made a right on Lauder, which was the block he stayed on. By the time he was halfway on the block, the car that was following him jumped the curb and struck him, sending Black into the air, then crashing to the pavement hard. He was still conscious, and tried to push himself up, but instantly felt pain shooting through his arms. When he looked, he saw a bone protruding from his arm and realized it was broken.

"*Fuck!*" Black yelled out in pain.

Rick jumped out of the car and walked up to Black. He kneeled down towards him.

"Remember me, muthafucka? Huh?"

Black didn't know who the guy was, he just stared at Rick, trying to figure out what was going on.

"Answer, me nigga!" Rick said, kicking Black in the ribs. He kicked him a few more times then pulled out his pistol. "I'm the nigga you robbed a few weeks ago and you shot me in my shoulder. Remember that?" Rick asked.

Black was curled up in a ball from the pain he was in, but when Rick said who he was, he knew it was over for him.

"Fuck you!" Black managed to mumble. All the shiesty and grimy shit Black ever did in his young life had finally come back to haunt him.

"Like I said before, I hope that shit was worth yo life," Rick said.

The six shots from the thirty-eight entered Black's body and face, enveloping him into the darkness.

After turning a few corners, Rell pulled up into the driveway of an abandoned house. Once in the backyard, he and Rick quickly got out of the stolen car. Rick opened the back door and grabbed the gas can and emptied the gas out on the inside and the outside of the car. Rell opened the driver door and lit a cigarette, tossing it into the car. The two of them walked off, headed back to the block.

Savannah's birthday was the weekend coming up, and Dolla was helping her get things ready for the party. He paid for two double bedrooms that were connected by two large doors. They were furnished with a refrigerator, stove, microwave and a jacuzzi. Carrie had already taken the money and reserved the rooms for the weekend with her fake I.D. The rooms were located in the suburbs of Southfield.

Carrie and Savannah had done some shopping and bought their outfits for the weekend. They also grabbed some swimsuits so they could swim in the hotel pool. The girls were excited. Savannah wanted her 15th birthday party to be special - one to remember.

Dolla, Rick, and Rell were looking forward to the party as well. With everything that was going on with them, they couldn't wait to kick back and enjoy a stress-free weekend. Dennis knew that the boys had a lot going on, so he volunteered to hold down the spot for the weekend while they got a chance to enjoy themselves. The hood had been a little hot lately, so it would be good for the boys to get away for a few days.

The weekend rolled around, and Carrie dropped Savannah off at the room, then went to pick up Dolla, Rell, and Rick. After she picked them up, they headed to the hotel. Once they got there, Dolla immediately walked up to Savannah and hugged her and gave her a passionate kiss.

"Hey, I missed you," Dolla said, noticing her beauty. Her hair was down to her shoulders in curls, and even though she was just wearing a white tee and some tight red velour pants that were hugging her lower area just right, she was glowing. At that very moment, she looked more beautiful than Dolla had ever seen.

"Hey y'all," Savannah said, speaking to Rick and Rell. She was still blushing from the kiss Dolla just laid on her lips. They both spoke back, and they noticed her beauty too.

Damn. My nigga got him one, Rell said to himself, proud of his homie.

Once they got settled in, they took the complimentary champagne from the jacuzzi and popped the cork. Everyone filled their glasses and toasted to Savannah's birthday. The rest of the people Savannah invited were on the way, but they didn't have any drinks or blunts.

"Girl, I gotta find a liquor store around here and grab up the drinks," Carrie said, ready to get the party started. "Rell, will you ride with me?"

"I'll ride with you anywhere, baby," Rell said. Dolla and Rick gave them some money along with a list of stuff they wanted from the store. Rell and Carrie walked out the door, but Carrie went next door and pulled out a key and walked in the room.

"C'mon," Carrie said, whispering as if they were being watched.

"But I thought..." Rell stopped mid-sentence. It dawned on him what Carrie was up to, so he quickly walked in the door and shut it behind him.

"We only got time for a quickie," Carrie said as she began unbuckling Rell's pants.

Savannah's guest began arriving, and the party was slowly getting started. She invited some of her friends from school and a few of her boy cousins. Her cousins, Dolla, and Rick immediately hit it off, even though most of the time, eastside and westside niggaz didn't get along.

Her cousins could tell Dolla and Rick were getting money and they gave Savannah the nod of approval.

Twig and Psycho were trying to set their mark on the eastside in the drug game. Her other cousin, Drew, was a star basketball player at Burbank Middle School. The small group was even on the boy/girl ratio, so no one would be sticking out like a third wheel at the party. Carrie and Rell made it back and had two cases of beer and ten bottles of different liquor. They also bought a carton of cigarettes and two large boxes of blunts. They grabbed a bunch of snacks and munchies, so no one would be drinking and smoking on an empty stomach.

"Damn! What took y'all so long?" Savannah asked.

"Yeah, we thought we was gonna have to put some work out here in Southfield!" Rick said.

"We had to find a store, and it was busy as hell in there." Carrie said. In reality, the store was right down the street, less than two blocks away. Carrie and Rell's little "quickie" lasted a little longer than they both had planned.

Bottles were popped and blunts were rolled up. Within minutes, everyone's cup was filled up with top-shelf liquor, and weed smoke filled the air. They had the air conditioner on low and they put wet towels under the hotel room door to keep the smell of weed from escaping from the rooms. Carrie had opened the double doors that separated the two rooms, so more space was available for everyone to move around comfortably.

The music was blasting through the speakers and the boys were shooting dice while the girls watched, secretly choosing which boys they liked among themselves. Dolla stung niggaz in the dice game, breaking it up. The winnings were a little over $200, and Dolla walked over to Savannah, placing the money in her hand.

"That's just one of your gifts," he said, and lightly kissed her hand.

"Happy birthday, girl!" Savannah's friend, Rena said. Everyone else screamed "happy birthday!" in unison and threw the remaining liquor in their cups in the air.

"Ahhh! Not on my hair, y'all!" Savannah shrieked as the liquor rained from the sky. But she didn't really care, she was enjoying every moment. Carrie had brought along a camera and began taking pictures.

"This weekend is gonna be one to remember," Carrie said, taking pictures of everyone. She took pictures of the boys. The girls struck a mean pose for the camera. Then, she took a picture of Savannah and Dolla dancing together. She had Rick take a picture of her and Rell.

"I bought plenty of film," Carrie whispered to Rell, as Rick was busy snapping shots.

Savannah's cousin, Drew, was a weed smoker and he drank occasionally, but tonight he had a little too much to drink. Savannah went to use the bathroom and found Drew leaning over the toilet, puking his guts out.

"You alright, cuz?" Savannah asked.

"Yeah, I'm good," Drew said before heaving more of the food inside of his stomach into the toilet.

Savannah couldn't help herself. Feeling a good buzz, she felt a little silly and ran and got the camera from Carrie. She went back to the bathroom and started taking pictures of Drew bent over the toilet.

"C'mon, cuz!" Drew said, sticking one hand out, trying to prevent her from getting a good shot. Savannah took off running out the bathroom once he got ahold of a bar of soap and threw it at her.

The night was ending, and slow music was setting the mood for the guys and girls to choose and pair up to dance. Slowly, one after another, they began making their selections and danced to the music. Twig was dancing with Lisa, a slim, short redbone with red hair. Psycho was dancing with Rena, caramel complexion and thick in the right places. Drew had sobered up from all the throwing up he did earlier and was dancing with Kristen, light-skinned and slightly plump, but she was beautiful. Rick had paired up with Victoria, who was tall and slim with grey eyes. There was something about tall girls that drove Rick wild.

Rell and Carrie were all over each other. The chemistry between them seemed to grow stronger each time they encountered each other physically.

Dolla was leaning up against the wall and Savannah had her back to him while slow grinding to the music. Savannah's ass was so soft in those velour sweats, if felt like a pillow. Dolla's dick was standing at full attention, and she could feel it pressing against her backside. He was buzzing hard and he had to control his animal instinct. He wanted to grab her and carry her to the bed and fuck her to sleep, but he cared about her so, he didn't put any pressure on her whatsoever. But when the time came for them to explore each other sexually, he made up his mind that the experience would be so intense that she wouldn't be able to get enough.

The night had ended with everybody passing out in both of the rooms. People were on the floor, the couches - anywhere there was space, someone was sleeping.

Rell and Carrie slept in the bed in one room and Dolla and Savannah slept in the bed in the other room. Dolla would awaken to sounds of someone in the bathroom fucking. He would block it out and doze back off. But later on, he would wake up and hear moaning again.

Lucky muthafuckas, he mumbled, putting the pillow over his head to drown out the moans and groans coming from the bathroom. Savannah heard noises too and it made her horny as hell. She was ready to give in to temptation. *Be patient, now's not the time,* she said to herself.

The next day, everyone took turns jumping in the shower and getting dressed. After everyone was dressed for the day, they went to the hotel dining hall and helped themselves to the free breakfast. After that, they went back to the rooms and changed into their swimwear and went to the pool. They played Marco Polo, had diving contests, and even had a cannonball contest. After that, they went back to the room and had a smoke out. They smoked a little over a half ounce and they all were high out of their minds.

After a while, the munchies kicked in and they were all hungry.

"Hey, it's an all-you-can-eat place about two blocks from here. Let's go there!" Carrie suggested.

"I'm down for that. I'm so hungry, my stomach is talkin' to me," Lisa said.

They left the room and headed to the restaurant. Come to find out, the restaurant was about four blocks from the room and by the time they made it there, they were all starving. Rell, Twig, Dolla, Drew, Psycho, and Rick split the charges, and everyone grabbed a plate and rushed to the buffet. They had seafood, Italian, Chinese, and American food.

Everyone was stuffing their faces when out of nowhere, a waitress walked up to their table with a cake and a number fifteen candle in it.

"This is for the birthday girl, Savannah," the waitress said. Then other waitresses approached the table, clapping their hands and singing "happy birthday". Dolla, Rell, and everyone else joined in. Savannah was speechless. The cake caught her by surprise.

"Make a wish!" Rena yelled. Savannah closed her eyes, made a wish, and blew out her candle.

"Who did this?" she asked, referring to the cake. Everyone was throwing up their hands and shaking their heads. When she looked at Dolla, he was just sitting with a devious grin on his face.

"You!" Savannah screamed, playfully punching him in the shoulder.

"What good is a birthday without a cake?" Dolla said, throwing his hands in the air. Dolla cut a slice of the cake and handed it to Savannah.

"Awww!" everybody at the table said teasingly.

"Knock that shit off!" Dolla yelled. slightly embarrassed.

After eating, they all headed back to the room. Savannah's cousins had driven there. Twig and Psycho had a base rental (a crackheads van), so they loaded up everybody and headed back to the eastside.

"Carrie, can you shoot me back to the block? I wanna get back to the spot and hold shit down," Rick asked. Before Rick left, they rolled up a blunt and smoked while reminiscing about the party.

"You sure you don't wanna stay, bro?" Dolla asked.

"Naw, I'm gonna go ahead. That way if Dennis got some shit to do, he can break away and take care of it," Rick said.

Dolla and Rick dapped each other and Rell, Carrie, and Rick left to drop him off on the block.

Savannah was sitting on the couch watching T.V. and Dolla was rolling up another blunt.

"Dolla, can you bring me one of those bottles of champagne?" she asked. Dolla grabbed a bottle and took it over to her.

"Here you go."

"There's a movie about to come on. Watch it with me, baby," Savannah said, patting the empty spot on the couch. Dolla popped some popcorn and grabbed a half-full fifth of Remy V.S.O.P. and the blunt and an ashtray and sat down. They sat back and watched the movie, smoking a blunt.

Halfway through the blunt, Dolla jumped up from the couch.

"What is it, baby?" Savannah asked.

"I almost forgot something," Dolla said, as he rambled through a bag.

Savannah didn't pay it any mind. She turned her attention back to the movie. Dolla snuck behind Savannah, who was still sitting on the couch and wrapped his arms around her.

"Happy birthday, baby. It's just a lil something." At first, Savannah didn't know what Dolla was talking about, but when she looked down in her lap where Dolla's hands were, she noticed a black velvet box.

"What's this, baby?" she asked, turning around and looking at Dolla.

"Open it up and see," he said and took a step backwards. When she opened the box, there were two smaller boxes and a card inside. When she opened the first box, she was speechless. She saw the diamond earrings glistening in the light and she felt as if she was about to cry.

"Dolla... I..."

"Open the other one," he whispered.

She opened the box and shrieked at the sight of the fourteen-carat gold chain and a gold heart-shaped charm. She opened the card and read it aloud.

Happy birthday! I am grateful to have someone like you in my life. You're a good-hearted person and may you have many more blessed birthdays. Loyalty brings royalty!! Dolla.

She got up and wrapped her arms around Dolla.

"That's the sweetest thing anyone has ever done for me. You didn't have to do this."

"It's nothin'," Dolla replied nonchalantly.

She stood on her tiptoes and kissed him softly on the lips. They sat back down and watched T.V. and had a few more drinks. Savannah was tipsy and feeling warm inside as she laid her head on Dolla's shoulder.

"I'm ready," she said calmly.

"Huh?" Dolla asked. He was high and drunk and didn't understand what she was saying. She lifted her head up from his shoulder and looked him in the eyes.

"I'm ready…for you," she said, placing one of his hands in her lap.

Dolla couldn't believe his ears, he damn near fell off the couch. He had been waiting patiently for this moment.

"Are you sure?" he asked her, but she didn't answer. The look in her eyes said it all. They began kissing each other passionately as their tongues darted in and out of each other's mouths. Dolla wanted to take it slow with her. Rell had found out through Carrie that Savannah was a virgin and Rell told Dolla. Rell had also told Dolla that he had ate Carrie's pussy a few times and gave him pointers on how to do it correctly when the time came. Now was that time.

He moved to her neck, kissing her while gently fondling her breasts. Her nipples were standing at full attention once he reached her plump melons. He was circling around her nipples with his tongue, teasing her, then he began sucking them.

"Mmmmm," Savannah moaned, biting her lower lip. He slowly moved down her stomach and then removed her boy shorts and the pink panties she was wearing. Her juices were already flowing before he even began to tickle her pink pearl with his tongue. Strategically, he moved his tongue at a fast pace. Then he would slow down, heightening the stimulation. His actions were sending a tingling sensation throughout her body, then she suddenly began convulsing. She gasped as she began to cum all over Dolla's face and in his mouth.

When she was finished, Dolla lifted his head up and her juices were all over his face. His manhood was swelling, and it felt like his rod was about to bust through his jeans. He carried her over to the bed, laid her down gently, then reached over into the nightstand drawer and pulled out a condom.

He quickly got undressed and slid the condom on. Savannah looked in awe; she knew he was well endowed, but the sight of his long wide rod made her even more moist than she was in between her thighs.

Dolla grabbed her legs and placed them on his shoulder, then he began to enter her slowly… inch by inch. About halfway inside her, he noticed her slightly wincing in pain and she was clinching his wrists tight, so he decided not to go in any deeper. Instead, he started moving in and out without exiting her completely.

At first, it was very painful. But after a short while, it started feeling good to her.

"Deeper," she moaned in a husky tone. Dolla eased all ten inches inside her. Slowly, he moved in and out of her, carefully calculating each stroke. A few minutes later, she was cumming again. This time when Savannah came, it made Dolla do the same. He jerked. Then his body locked up as he released his load into the condom. Dolla collapsed onto the bed next to her and they fell asleep in each other's arms.

Rell and Carrie made it back to the room after dropping Rick off on the block. They knocked on the door but didn't get an answer.

"Maybe they went for a walk or something," Rell said. They opened the door to their room and as soon as they walked in, Carrie went straight to the double doors that separated the rooms. She gently pushed them open.

"Ooooh" she gasped, placing her hand over her mouth. Savannah had told her that she was going to have sex with Dolla, but Carrie thought she wouldn't go through with it.

"What up?" Rell asked, walking over to where Carrie was standing, noticing the expression on her face.

"Look," Carrie said, stepping to the side so Rell could get a good view. Rell peeked into the room and saw them asleep in each other's arms.

"Ok, they sleep, so what?"

"No. Look, fool!" Carrie said, pointing to the empty condom wrapper on the floor next to the bed.

"My muthafuckin' nigga," Rell mumbled to himself and cracked a smile. Carrie pulled the doors shut and looked at Rell.

"Our turn," Carrie said, curving her lips into a smile.

"You ain't gotta tell me twice," Rell said as they made a B-line to the bed.

Dolla and Savannah woke up a few hours later and showered together. After getting dressed, Dolla walked over to the window and saw Carrie's car parked outside.

"I wonder how long they been back from dropping Rick off," Dolla said to Savannah.

She got up from the couch and knocked on the double doors before turning the lock and walked into Carrie's room. Carrie and Rell were sitting on the edge of the bed smoking a blunt.

"Girl, let me hit that," Savannah said, walking over and taking the blunt from Carrie's hand. Dolla grabbed a bottle of champagne and walked into the room with his hands in the air.

"The party ain't over wit yet!" he said before popping the cork.

Each of them filled their glasses and Dolla and Rell began to roll up blunts. Savannah ran next door and grabbed the gifts Dolla bought her to show Carrie.

"Damn, so this is what it took to finally get that pussy of yours wet, huh?" Carrie said, looking at the diamond earrings.

"Bitch, please!" Savannah said, laughing.

They spent the day smoking and drinking and listening to music. The night came, and the couples retreated to their own rooms. It had been a weekend to remember, indeed.

"Did you enjoy your weekend?" Dolla asked Savannah.

"Yes, I did. It was better than I expected it to be…. Dolla, can I ask you something?"

"Yeah, what up?"

"What are your plans for the future?" Dolla had never thought about that.

"Hmmm, that's a good question. I never really took the time to sit down and think about that type of shit, you feel me?"

"Well, promise me that you WILL take the time out to think about the future, ok?" Savannah said.

"I promise you that I will. What about you?" Dolla asked.

"Well, once I finish high school, I plan on going to college to get my degree in criminal law."

"You gonna be the hook?!" Dolla asked.

"No, silly. I'm gonna be a criminal defense attorney," Savannah said.

"Whew! I thought I was sleeping wit the enemy for a second!" Dolla joked.

"I'm gonna be the one who can save your ass if you get caught up in some bullshit!" Savannah said, pointing her finger at him.

They smoked another blunt and had a few more drinks before heading off to bed. Dolla plopped on the bed and was getting ready to go to sleep when Savannah climbed on top of him.

"Uh-uh. You ain't bout to get off that easy," she said, pulling his shirt up over his head.

"I was hoping that I wasn't," Dolla said with a huge grin on his face. He tried to get up, but Savannah pushed him back down.

"Let me do this," she said. She kissed him from the chest down to his stomach and unbuckled his belt. Pulling his pants down, she could clearly see that his dick was standing tall. She reached into the slit of his boxers and pulled his large muscle out. She wrapped her soft lips around the tip and then began bobbing up and down the shaft of his muscle, slowly trying not to hurt him with her teeth. This was her first time sucking dick; Carrie had been showing her how to do it with a popsicle for about a week now.

She got a kick out of seeing Dolla moan and squirm and curl his toes. Dolla couldn't take it anymore. He sat up and grabbed a condom and opened it up with lightning speed. He put the condom on, then pulled her on top of him. Her pussy was already wet and once he slid inside of her, she began slowly moving up and down on his manhood.

"Damn, baby. This shit feel good as hell," Dolla said, gripping her ass in the palm of his hands. Savannah couldn't even make a sound. It felt so good to her, all she could do is bite her bottom lip. She released her joy juice all in Dolla's lap.

When she was done cumming, Dolla turned her over on her stomach and entered her from behind. Savannah couldn't take it anymore. She was shaking like she was having a seizure. But in reality, she was experiencing her first orgasm. Looking down and seeing her soft yellow ass ripple back and forth like waves in the water was too much for Dolla. It brought him to his climax shortly after Savannah's orgasm…

They were up early and slightly hung over from the night before. They quickly showered and dressed, then packed up their clothes. The four of them met in the parking lot and jumped in the car and drove around to the front of the hotel to drop off the room keys. While Carrie took the keys to the office, Rell rolled up another blunt for the road.

Savannah had enjoyed her birthday. She did and got everything she wanted, plus a little more. Carrie had a good time too. She was happy for her friend. *She's with a guy she really likes and he gettin' money and don't mind spending it, and she finally lost her virginity. Good girl,* Carrie thought to herself.

Dolla, Rick, and Rell had a good time as well. They got a chance to have some fun and get away from the stress that sometimes comes with the game, but now it was time to get back to the money.

They arrived on the block refreshed and ready to take on whatever the world brought their way. They kissed the girls and said their goodbyes, then walked to the side door and stepped into the spot.

"What's crackin', my niggaz?" Rick asked, dapping them as they stepped in the house. Weed smoke filled the air and rap music was blasting out of the stereo speakers.

"Y'all missed Dennis, he just left. He said he'll be back later."

"How's business been?" Dolla asked.

"Man, this bitch been bangin'! We already up about five hundred more than usual at this time of day. One of the other spots must have gotten hit or something!" Rick said.

But it wasn't that. They had the best product on that side of town, and word was spreading. Word on the street was, "Them Schoolcraft and Mettetal niggaz getting money."

CHAPTER EIGHT

May 2000

Over the years, things had gotten even better for Dolla, Rell, and Rick. They were now nineteen years old and had gotten their driver's licenses. They also had a set of fake IDs from a customer who worked at the Secretary of State. Savannah graduated from Denby High School and received a scholarship to go to Michigan State University in Lansing to study law. She was staying on campus because that allowed her to focus on her studies. That, and the fact that her mother and father were arguing all the time about her mother's drinking problem and the city's crime rate, was souring.

People were getting killed left and right and she worried about Dolla and the boys all the time.

"Don't worry about me. Worry bout them muthafuckin' books," is what Dolla would always say whenever she brought up the subject in conversation. Their relationship was going well, even though Savannah was an hour away from the city. They talked every day and Dolla would commute to Lansing every other weekend to spend time with her. He gave her whatever she asked for, and a lot of the times, she didn't even have to ask.

He was fucking other girls, but Savannah was the only one he cared for. Other girls, he would only fuck two or three times, then pass them on to his homies or just wouldn't call them anymore. Once Savannah was finished with college, Dolla planned to invest in something legit to get out of the game. Then he was going to marry her.

Carrie wasn't in school, but she left with Savannah and ended up falling in love with the star quarterback of the football team. On the inside, Rell was a little hurt, but he quickly got over it. There were so many females coming and going, he stayed in some pussy like tampons.

Rick was doing good too. He had a lil nigga on Joy Road hustling a sack for him and he was still holding the spot down on Mettetal. Rick and Rell were in a friendly competition over who could fuck the most girls. They were fucking girls from all over the west side.

The boys were riding clean too. Dolla had a money-green 1986 Monte Carlo SS with a tan ragtop, sitting on some twenty-inch gold Daytons. Rell had a black 1986 Cutlass Supreme with glass t-tops and some twenty-inch chrome Daytons. Rick was driving a cocaine-white 1984 two-door Chevy Malibu on some twenty-inch blades. All three of them had low profile Pirelli tires, so the rims looked even bigger, and they got their sound systems installed at Mammoth Sounds on Grand River and Greenfield Avenue.

Dolla's auntie finally found out he was selling drugs. She was disappointed in him and felt as if he should know better after what the drug game did to his parents. She stuck to her promise she made to herself many years ago.

"Darin, I love you and you're the son I never had, but as long as you continue to sell drugs, I cannot be a part of your life. I will be there for you if you ever decide to walk away from the streets, but until then, I can't associate with you," she said.

It broke Dolla's heart to hear those words, but he respected the decision she made. She had lost a sister, brother-in-law, and a boyfriend to the drug game, and she didn't want any parts of what comes along with hustling.

It seemed like the years had flown by, and now it was finally time for Hammer to be released from the juvenile detention center. It was Wednesday, and Hammer was getting released that Friday, which meant the boys had two days to plan for his surprise welcome home party.

They had already called Club D.E.T. on Schoolcraft and Greenfield and reserved the party for Saturday. Hammer also said he wanted an old school box Caprice, so they bought him a 1985 powder-blue, two-door Caprice with tinted windows and some twenties on the feet of the car. They also had sounds installed in his car and they had to pick it up today from Mammoth. They were gonna park it in his mother's garage and surprise him when he touched down.

Friday came, and Hammer's mother was at the detention center bright and early in the morning. The R.A.s woke Hammer at five in the morning, and it took a few hours to process him before he was released. At eight a.m., May 9, 2000, Hammer was released back into the world as a free man.

He left the street at the age of thirteen, nothing but a child. Now, he was eighteen, considered a grown man in society. This was the best day of Hammer's young life. He ran into his mother's arms and picked her up while hugging her at the same time. To him, it looked like his mom didn't age one bit. She still looked the same from when he left the streets five years ago.

Karen took a step back and looked at her son. Hammer had gained about thirty pounds in muscle mass and had a deep cut down the side of his face. He still had long hair. But looking deeper, she could tell that the years of incarceration had hardened her son.

"C'mon, let's go," she said, wrapping his hand into hers. Once they reached the car, he could tell that his mom was doing pretty well for herself. She had a brand new 2000 Toyota Corolla and was well-dressed.

"So, how's your health been?" Hammer asked sincerely.

"I've been fine. As long as I keep taking the medicine the doctors prescribed for me, I'll be okay."

"Where are you working at?"

"Right now, I work as a receptionist at a dentist office downtown. It's part time for now. I've only been there a month. I got the job through a temp agency, so there's no telling how long the job will last. Thank God for Darin and Jerell. They have been looking out for me on a regular basis since you have been gone."

Hammer smiled at the thought of his best friends holding his mom down for all those years. He was thankful to have some loyal niggaz on his side because one thing for sure, loyalty was hard to find in the streets.

They stopped at a restaurant and ordered something to eat. While eating, they talked and laughed, catching up with the time they were apart. Hammer loved his mother more than anything in the world. He was glad he killed his father for abusing her, and if he had to for his mother, he would kill again.

After they were finished eating, they headed home. Once Hammer arrived in the hood, he noticed a few things had changed. There were a few new stores and some of the old ones were gone. When he and his mom turned the corner on Schoolcraft and onto the block, Dolla, Rick, Rell, and Dennis were standing in front of the spot, which was directly across the street from his mother's house.

The car barely came to a complete stop and Hammer was already out, running across the street.

"What up doe, niggaz?" he yelled as he embraced them one by one.

"This the homie, Rick, we was tellin' you about in the letter," Rell said, placing his hand on Rick's shoulder. "He's one of us. Family."

"What up, bro? Dolla and Rell always used to tell me stories about y'all growing up," Rick said, giving Hammer dap.

"They told me a lot about you too. Glad to have you in the family," "Hammer replied.

"Who live here now?" Hammer asked, wondering whose house he was standing in front of.

"This our shit, nigga. We got a spot now," Dolla said.

"Ok, then! That's wuz up." He noticed the fleet of old schools parked on the block.

"Those y'all cars over there?" Hammer asked.

"Nigga, what you think?" Rell said, assuming Hammer should already know what time it was.

"Yo, Dennis. I know that's gotta be yo shit right there," Hammer said, pointing to a navy-blue Cadillac DTS.

"You already know, lil homie," Dennis said.

"I see you done put some weight on. You still good with yo hands, nigga?" Dolla asked.

"C'mon, man. Niggaz couldn't fuck wit me in there," Hammer said.

"What the fuck happened to yo face, fam?" Rell asked.

"Some bullshit," Hammer said, rubbing the long scar on his face.

"Yo, Hammer. Do the honors," Rick said, handing him a blunt. Hammer had smoked a few paper joints here and there that other inmates would smuggle into the detention center after receiving visits, but when he lit the blunt and took a pull, he immediately started chocking. They all broke out laughing at him.

"You got virgin lungs, boy!" Dennis said, patting him on the back.

"Let's go in the house for a second," Dolla said, walking up on the porch.

"Dennis, you bout to take care of dat?"

"Yeah, I'll be right back," Dennis said.

Once the boys were in the house. They all sat at the dining room table. Dolla walked in the back and emerged from the hallway holding a half gallon of Remy V.S.O.P.

"I'll get some cups," Rell said and went in the kitchen. At the same time, someone was knocking at the side door.

"And I'll get the door," Rick said.

After serving the custos, Rick made his way back to the dining room table to join the fellas and saw four glasses of Cognac sitting on the table.

"I want to make a toast, to family…Loyalty brings royalty!" Dolla said, raising his glass in the air.

"LOYALTY BRINGS ROYALTY!" Rick, Hammer, and Rell said at the same time, raising their glasses in the air.

They downed the first shot and Dolla filled up their glasses again.

"Man, we glad you came through wit that connect for us," Rell said to Hammer.

"By the way, what ever happened to that nigga, Dre?" Hammer Asked.

They filled him in on how they killed him and the bitch that was with him.

"Damn, y'all niggaz been putting in work, huh?"

"It's all part of the game," Dolla said before downing his shot.

"Let me get another shot of that shit," Hammer said, reaching for the bottle.

"Naw, not yet. We got some business to handle," Rell said.

There was a knock at the side door and Rick went to answer it. When he opened the door, it was Dennis along with three customers standing behind him. Rick served the three custos and then let Dennis in the house.

"Y'all ready?" Dennis asked the boys.

"Yeah. C'mon, y'all. We gotta go handle some shit," Dolla said.

"Aye, y'all got my sizes?" Rick asked as Rell, Dolla, Dennis, and Hammer headed out the door.

"We got you, my nigga," Rell said before stepping out the door.

They walked across the street, but instead of walking towards the cars, they walked into the alley and stopped at Hammer's mother's garage.

"Open the door," Rell said to Hammer. Hammer lifted the garage door, and what he saw made his jaw hit the floor.

"Damn! This all me?" Hammer asked, walking into the garage and checking out the two-door Caprice on twenty-inch rims.

"Yeah, that's all you," Dolla said.

"Catch!" Dennis said, throwing the keys to Hammer.

Hammer opened the car door and sat in the driver's seat. He looked around at the white leather and sky-blue lining interior, then fell back into the seat. Everything seemed to be moving so fast: just a few hours ago, he was in jail. Now, he was free and had a dope-ass ride. He put the key in the ignition and started the car. The sounds were turned up and at first, it scared the shit outta him. He turned the music down out of respect for his mom being in the house.

"Once you get that shit out yo trunk, the speakers gon' bang even harder," Rick said.

Hammer got out of the car and walked around to the back. He popped the trunk open and saw a black garbage bag.

"What the?" Hammer said, picking up the bag up.

"Open it up and see, nigga!" Dolla yelled.

Hammer opened the bag and instantly became lightheaded when he saw all $100 bills.

"Damn! How much is this?" he asked.

"Nigga, count the shit and find out!" Dennis said.

Hammer sat the bag on top of the trunk and started counting the money. It was separated into $1,000 bundles and Hammer counted fifty of them.

"Shit, niggaz gettin' money like this?? I ain't never seen this much money in my life!"

"Well, now you have. Go put that shit up in the house so we can go and take care of this business," Rell said.

Hammer had a strange look on his face.

"Nigga, what's wrong wit you?" Dolla asked.

"It's been a long time since I been back in that house… Last time I was in there…" Hammer's voice drifted off as the night he killed his father began to replay in his mind.

"Man, fuck that shit, nigga! You did what you had to do. Now shit over wit. That shit was for the better! Now go put that shit up so we can bounce!" Rell said, snapping Hammer back into reality.

"You right, bro. You right," Hammer said dappin' Rell then giving him a hug.

Deep down, he knew his friend was telling him the truth; the shit had to be done. He paid his dues, and now was the time to put it all behind him.

"I'll be right back."

Rell smiled as he watched Hammer leave the garage and run in the house. His homie was back, and he knew shit was about to take off now. He knew that Hammer would go hard, and with him back on the streets, the team would be unstoppable.

Hammer came back outside with $1,000 in his pocket and he was ready to go.

"Let's go. I'm ridin' with you," Dennis said to Hammer.

Rell and Dolla jumped in Rell's Cutlass and waited for Hammer to pull out the garage. Once he pulled out onto the street, Rell pulled out behind him. Hammer would sneak and drive his father's car sometimes before he got locked up, so he wasn't a stranger to driving. He was a little shaky at first, but after he turned a few corners, he had his seat leaned back and the sounds banging.

They stopped at the T-shirt store on Six Mile and picked up the shirts they had the store customize for them. After that, they went to the mall and picked up some black Air Force Ones. Then they headed back to the hood and turned corner after corner. Running into old friends, Hammer, Dennis, Rell, and Dolla would pull over and kick it.

"Heeeee's baaaaack!!!" Rell would yell out whenever they pulled up. All the girls in the hood were going crazy when they saw Hammer. He was ready to take one of them back to the spot and fuck the shit outta 'em. It had been so long since he got some pussy, and he was ready to beat some up. But the boys assured him that later on that night, he would be knee deep in a bitch.

When they got back to the block, they let Hammer get familiar with the custos by serving them as they came to the door. The night came, and the boys got dressed up for the surprise party for Hammer. Hammer thought they were going to a room to fuck with some hoes; He had no idea what they had in store for him. Dennis volunteered to hold the spot down until the morning. The boys wanted to shut the spot down and take Dennis with them, but he declined.

"Y'all gotta keep getting this money while it's comin'," Dennis said.

They jumped in their cars and followed each other to the liquor store. They loaded up on liquor and blunts for the party. By the time the party was over, the liquor stores would be closed, so they wanted to stay one step ahead of things.

On the way out, Dolla heard somebody calling his name. It was dope fiend, Krissy.

"Dolla, I need you one time," she said, as she was trying to stop her hands from shaking. She couldn't stand still, and it looked as if she was chewing on her inner jaw. She was feenin', and Dolla could tell.

"What up? I don't gotta pay you for the lights til the weekend. I'm busy right now," Dolla said, as he opened up his car door.

"I know, I know. Can you pay me in advance, please?? I really need it."

"If I do that, then you gonna be in bad shape next week. Niggaz ain't trickin' wit you or somethin'?" Dolla asked.

"It's been slow today. Please help me out," Krissy pleaded.

"Alright man, goddamn!" Dolla said, reaching into his pocket. "Here, take this." He handed her three $20 bills.

"That's $10 extra, now I gotta go. I'll holla at you later."

"Wait! There's one more thing I need to holla at you about," Krissy said, walking closer to the car.

"Man, what is it now?" Dolla asked, looking up at the roof of his car. His body language clearly spoke volumes, and it showed that he was becoming irritated.

"You wanna rent my house in Brightmoor? I know all the people who get high. It's a lot of money over there, baby," Krissy said.

Dolla paused and thought about the offer. The boys could use the extra money, now that Hammer was home. Even though they'd never sold cocaine before, he had the plug to get it. "You gotta keep getting the money while it's comin' in," Dennis had said before they left the spot, and the words were ringing in Dolla's mind right now.

"Meet me at the spot tomorrow," Dolla said.

"I'll be there bright and early," Krissy said before turning on her heels and walking away.

What the fuck we pullin' up in here for? Hammer thought to himself, as he followed behind Dolla, Rick, and Rell pulling into club D.E.T. on Schoolcraft and Greenfield. The parking lot was packed with cars, but surprisingly, there were four V.I.P. parking spots available. They all parked and got out of their cars. The four of them were dressed in the same outfit: black Air Force Ones, black shorts, and black T-shirts with the letters "S.C.B." (Schoolcraft Boyz) in white print on the front of their shirts.

"Man, what's up with the hoes at the room? I'm tryin' to fuck something!" Hammer said.

It had been years since he even saw some pussy and right now, he was ready to drill into a bitch.

"Don't trip, we got this," Rick said, as they walked through the doors.

"Schoolcraft in this bitch! 100 years!" Rell yelled, as they stepped in the club.

Immediately, all eyes in the place were on the boys. Once everyone saw Hammer, the place erupted in cheers and applause.

"Welcome home to my main man, Hammer! Schoolcraft's finest! It's been a long time!" The DJ announced on the microphone.

People were coming to speak to him left and right. Some he remembered and some he had never seen before in his life, but they knew him through word on the streets. There was a throne-like chair sitting on the stage. The club manager made the stage a special V.I.P. section surrounded by red velvet rope. People could only enter the section if Hammer allowed them to. There was a waitress that was specifically assigned to tend to that area.

The club was packed wall to wall, and the ratio was two women to one man, so all the men in the club had plenty of females to choose from. The party was jumping, and drinks flowed like water. Hammer was sitting back, blowing blunt after blunt with Rell, Dolla, and Rick. He felt as if he was on top of the world, as if he was a king. Only the baddest chicks were let behind the ropes to chill with the boys.

As the music pumped through the speakers, girls were shaking their asses like professional dancers. As the party was winding down, Hammer had two women literally glued to him. Once the party was over, Dolla, Rick, Rell, and Hammer left the club with five girls in two different cars following them. They drove to a motel on Grand River and Telegraph and got two rooms next to each other with double beds in each room. After a few blunts and a few drinks, the fucking and sucking commenced. Dolla and Rick were in one room and Rell and Hammer were in the room next door.

One of the girls Hammer was with was eating another girl's pussy and the one who was getting her pussy ate was sucking Hammer's dick a hundred miles an hour. Hammer came quick, but the girl was sucking him off so good that his dick stayed hard. He took turns on the two girls, then the next thing he knew Dolla, Rell, and Rick were waking him up, telling him it was checkout time.

They made it to the block around twelve thirty that afternoon, and Dennis had told Dolla that Krissy had came through looking for him twice already.

"What the fuck that bitch want? Light bill ain't gotta get paid til the weekend," Rell said.

Dolla told the boys about the business offer she made.

"She talkin' bout it's a lotta money to be made in that hood. Y'all niggaz wit it?" Dolla asked.

"Hell yeah!" Rick answered without hesitation.

Krissy popped up at the spot about an hour later and they sat down and talked and came to an agreement. They would have to give her two ounces of crack each month. Krissy had met an old man and she was moving in with him, but she would still be coming to the house throughout the week. She knew all the smokers in that hood, and she also knew how to cook cocaine into crack.

"Dolla, do you think you could put my nephew on? He's a good boy. He just needs a little push, that's all.

"Yeah, we can do that," Dolla said.

In actuality, that was a perfect set up. Dolla knew that Brightmoor was a gold mine, but he also knew that it was one of the most territorial hoods on the westside. When it came to the crack game, niggaz was not playing from that way. If you weren't from around there and you called yourself trying to "set up shop," niggaz was coming, and they would be coming to kill.

Her nephew would be the front man. He'd get one more guy from that hood and slap him in the spot and let it roll until the wheels fall off. Dolla felt like Hammer would fit in perfect over there as well. All he had to do was start fucking a female from that hood and he could open up all types of doors for the team. Now all Dolla had to do was holla at Gordo for the work and everything could begin to move from there.

"I'm gonna come and check the spot out tomorrow. Tell your nephew to be there so I can meet him."

"Alright, Dolla. It's gonna pay off in the long run, honey, you'll see," Krissy said with confidence.

"I know, I know," Dolla said, walking Krissy to the side door. "Here, take this," Dolla reached in his pocket and gave her $20.

"Thank you", Krissy said sincerely. "You're a good man, Dolla. A lot of people try to treat me like shit because I get high, but you're the only one that treats me like a human being, with respect. I want you to know that if there's anything I can do for you, I will."

"It ain't nothin', you good people's and I fuck wit you. We gon' eat together," Dolla said.

"Eating ain't the word, honey. Y'all gonna get rich!" Krissy said. Then she took off up the alley.

The next day, Hammer and Dolla met Krissy and her nephew on Fenkell and Blackstone. When they turned onto the block, they were surprised to see that there were only about ten houses standing on there. The other houses were either burned down or completely torn down, leaving nothing behind but a grassy lot.

"Damn, this block is fucked up," Hammer said as he was scoping out the desolate area. Truth is, the whole Brightmoor community was like that. Block after block, few homes were still standing. Most houses were either abandoned or burned down. It used to be a predominately White area, but when crack cocaine moved in during the late 80s, along came the violence with it. Blacks began to move in and take over the neighborhood, turning it into the hub for drug activity. From the late 80s throughout the 90s, turf wars literally ran the neighborhood into the ground. What Hammer and Dolla saw now was the end result of those drug wars.

"But you know what? This is a good thing for us, bro. By there being so much space around the spot, we'll be able to see everything going on around us. It will be damn near impossible for the hook or anybody to hit the spot without us seeing them first," Dolla said.

They pulled up across the street from the house and got out of the car. On the outside, the house was in bad shape. Over half the aluminum siding was missing and three out of eight windows were boarded up. Once they stepped inside, it didn't look any better than the outside. Paint was peeling off the walls, the carpet was stained badly, and there was a faint scent of piss and mildew throughout the three-bedroom, one floor house.

"This a spot for real," Hammer said.

"Hey y'all," Krissy said sitting on the couch. "What y'all think?" she asked them.

"The place definitely need some work done to it, but we gon' make it do what it do," Dolla said with confidence.

"Gary should be here in a minute. I sent him to the store to get some cigarettes."

"Who's Gary?" Hammer asked.

"My nephew I was tellin' y'all about," Krissy said.

Hammer and Dolla both lit up cigarettes and looked around the house, trying to assess the costs it would take to get the spot ready. About five minutes later, Gary came walking in the door.

"Gary, these are the guys I was tellin' you about. They gonna flood the hood with that A-1 shit," Krissy said.

"What up, doe?" Gary said, exchanging dap with Dolla and Hammer. Dolla and Hammer introduced themselves and they sat down and rolled a blunt and began to talk business. Gary was perfect for the job. Standing just under six feet tall, he was a big husky guy. Light brown complexion with a bald head gave him an intimidating look. He had the build of a football player or a bouncer.

Gary had lived in Brightmoor all twenty years of his life. He knew who was who, and how shit moved in the area, so he ran down the whole layout of the neighborhood to Dolla and Rell. He knew all the fiends too. His mother got high, along with his Aunt Krissy, so it was always around growing up. He had been selling dope since he was twelve and he was pretty good at it. The only problem was that guys from his neighborhood saw that he had the potential to become major and they would do everything they could to hold him back over the years. They would sell him weak dope, and guys with weight would never sell him anything over an ounce.

Brightmoor was all Gary ever knew. He almost never ventured out of the area, and because of that, he didn't have too many plugs to cop cocaine from. Gary had a two-year-old daughter, and whatever profits he would make, he would have to end up spending to help out with her, so he was always stuck in one spot, never able to re-up bigger than before… But that was about to change.

Dolla, Hammer, and Gary hopped in Dolla's car, and they took a ride through the neighborhood. In Dolla and Hammer's hood, the crime rate was on the rise, but in Brightmoor shit was outta control. The neighborhood was rough, and it seemed like there were stuffed animal and deflated balloon memorials on every corner.

As they turned corner after corner, Gary would point out different spots, and told them a little about each person who controlled them. He also was able to tell them who would be a potential threat as well. Gary wasn't really worried about the stick-up niggaz because he grew up with them, and they wouldn't mess with anything he had a hand in.

They pulled up back to the house on Blackstone and assured Gary that the shop would be open in less than a week. Gary got out of the car, and Dolla and Hammer headed back to Mettetal. There was only one thing left to do: get some money together and call Gordo. Once back on the block, Dolla, Rell, Rick, and Hammer put together a plan that would end up being a serious power move for them.

The next day, they got their money together, and Dolla was ready to pay Gordo a visit. Rick put $20,000 into the pot, leaving him with only $2,000 left to his name. He didn't mind because he knew that it would pay off in the long run. Hammer put up $20,000, and Dolla and Rell put $30,000, giving them a total of $100,000 to spend with Gordo.

Dolla loaded the money in his car and was ready to go and see the plug. Rick would be tailing him, driving his sister's car. There was no way Dolla would risk bringing the bricks back in his car. It was too flashy. He made a mental note to invest in a low-key vehicle, something like a minivan. Rick would be the one to bring the bricks back to the hood in his sister's car.

Dolla and Rick got in their cars and pulled out of the alley and turned on Grand River, headed for Southwest Detroit. When they crossed Greenfield, Dolla noticed the hook was a few cars behind him and was closing in fast. *Fuck 'em,* he thought to himself. He hadn't violated any traffic laws, plus his license was valid, so he wasn't tripping at all.

The police pulled up on the side of Rick and told him to switch lanes. Once he switched lanes, they jumped behind Dolla.

"Damn! What the fuck these bitches want?" Dolla yelled, turning off the busy main street, pulling into a driveway.

He backed out and parked on the street facing the hook. The two officers stepped out of their squad vehicle. One of them stood back a distance with his weapon pointed in the direction of Dolla's car, and the other officer approached with his hand on his weapon, but it remained in his holster.

Dolla had already had his window cracked and his driver's license ready.

"Turn the engine off and let me see your muthafuckin' hands!" the officer yelled to the top of his lungs.

Dolla did as he was told, and the officer walked up and snatched open the car door.

"Step out of the car," the officer said firmly.

"But I have..."

"Step outta the muthafuckin' car with your hands up!" the short and stocky officer yelled, cutting Dolla off mid-sentence.

He knew he was going to jail because he had a pistol on his waist, but he had a gut feeling that something wasn't right with these two officers.

"Any drugs or weapons on you, Dolla?" the officer asked, patting him down.

Dolla? How the fuck this nigga know my name? Are they really cops? Dolla thought to himself.

The officer felt the gun on Dolla's waist, and with his free hand, he quickly grabbed his pistol out of the holster.

"Turn around and put your hands behind your back!" the officer ordered.

Dolla turned around and the officer cuffed him.

"Fuck! They about to take this nigga to jail!" Rick said before punching the steering wheel. He could see the hook putting handcuffs on his homie, and all he could do was sit back and watch helplessly. For a second, he thought about driving over there and taking his chances by shooting at the hook, but he quickly changed his mind.

"Can't be getting into a shootout with the hook in broad daylight," he said out loud. "I guess I'm gonna have to follow him to the station and try to see what they do wit him."

The officer had thrown Dolla's pistol onto the driver's seat of Dolla's car, and when he searched through his pockets, he found $5,000 and a quarter ounce of weed. When the officer saw the money, his eyes lit up as if he'd hit the jackpot. He then began to look around to make sure there were no bystanders watching. When he saw the coast was clear, he stuffed the money into his uniform pocket.

"Dirty muthafucka," Dolla mumbled.

"Ok, Dolla. Let me explain to you what rights you have. You got a nice little operation jumpin' off on Mettetal. Your name has been ringing bells in the streets. You have the right to hustle, and by all means hustle. I have the right to collect five thousand from you each month from this day forward. If you refuse to pay your monthly tax, I have the right to shut your shit down and plant something on you to put your ass in prison for a long time. Do you understand?" the officer said, standing face-to-face with Dolla.

"You got that," Dolla said, clenching his jaw down on his teeth.

"The name's Miller," the officer said. Then he reached into Dolla's car and pulled out Dolla's gun.

"Ten-millimeter Smith and Wesson, huh? You have good taste." Then the officer took the clip out and threw it as hard and far as he could down the street, then threw Dolla's gun back into the car.

"I'll be seeing you around," officer Miller said, uncuffing Dolla.

"Now get yo' bitch ass outta here before I change my mind and put a case on yo' ass, nigga."

"Dolla got in the car and the officers pulled out from behind him. They drove past, looking at Dolla with stoic expressions on their faces.

How in the fuck did the hook get onto me? Dolla asked himself as he watched the crooked officers pull off.

Them taking the $5,000 didn't really bother him. He was just glad the officer didn't locate the button to the stash spot Dolla had installed by the neighborhood collision shop which contained the $100,000 in cash.

Dolla's phone was ringing and Rick's number flashed across the screen.

"Yo," Dolla answered.

"Man! What the fuck was that all about, bro? You straight?" Rick asked.

"Yeah, we'll talk about it later. Let's just get to Gordo. We already runnin' behind," Dolla said, then hung up the phone.

Dolla started the car and drove down the street to pick up his clip Officer Miller had tossed. He turned around and pulled out onto Grand River. Rick pulled out behind him from the other side of the street and they cautiously drove to meet with Gordo.

Dolla pulled into the club parking lot and Rick pulled into the liquor store down the street and waited for the call. By now, most of the doormen and security knew who Dolla was, and they let him in with no questions asked. Dolla looked around the club and spotted Gordo at a table with two big bodyguards on each side of him. Gordo had a bottle of Don Julio tequila and two glasses sitting on the table. Dolla shook hands with him and sat across the table from him.

"Have a drink with me," Gordo said, filling the shot glasses. The two toasted glasses, then downed the shots.

"What took you so long? I've been expecting you," Gordo asked.

"I got pulled over by the hook. Nothing serious though," Dolla said.

"They just gave you a ticket?" Gordo asked.

"No. They let me go, but the crooked muthafuckas took some money from me."

"Really? I have some connections in the police department. Did you happen to get their names?" Gordo asked.

"One of them said his name was Officer Miller."

"Which precinct is it?" Gordo asked.

"It's the second precinct," Dolla said.

"Okay, I will look into it. You won't have any problems like that again, I assure you," Gordo said sincerely.

They sat and made small talk for a few minutes, then they got down to business.

"So, what can I do for you?" Gordo asked.

Dolla had just copped fifty pounds of weed two weeks ago and unless it had been a good month, Gordo didn't expect him to be re-copping so fast.

"Um, I ran into another business opportunity, and I was wondering how much a brick would cost me."

"One brick?" Gordo asked.

"No, no… Actually, I have one hundred thousand to spend."

A hundred, huh? This young man is moving, Gordo thought to himself, putting numbers together in his head.

"If you'll excuse me for a moment," Gordo said, leaving the table.

A few minutes later, Gordo returned to the table and sat down.

"This is what's going to happen. I will give you ten kilos for $16,000 each. Being that you only have $100,000, I will take that, and you will owe me sixty thousand. The cocaine you will receive has not been touched, it's clean. You will make a lot of money very fast, and you might also gain enemies just as fast. Do you have enough fire power?" Gordo asked.

Dolla thought about the question Gordo had just asked him and decided to walk through the door of opportunity Gordo had just opened.

"I could use some extra burners," Dolla said.

"Good, I will take care of it for you. You will be getting a call from one of my associates tomorrow with a meeting place."

One of the bodyguards' phone rang. He answered it, then handed the phone to Gordo. Gordo placed the phone to his ear, listened, then hung up without saying a word.

"Your order is ready. These two gentlemen will take you to the product, "Gordo said.

"Thanks," Dolla said, and shook Gordo's hand.

"I don't know how I could ever be able to repay you for helping me get on my feet," Dolla added.

"Don't worry. But one day, I shall ask you for a favor," Gordo said.

"Whatever I can do for you, let me know," Dolla replied.

"Dolla, it is your time, and never forget, *el tiempo es dinero*," Gordo said.

"What does that mean?" Dolla asked with a confused look on his face.

"It means 'time is money,' my friend, time is money..."

"You right about that, Gordo. Adios," Dolla said and walked out the door with the two bodyguards.

Gordo poured a shot of Don Julio and swallowed it quicker than he poured it. He poured another one, then raised his glass in the direction of a man sitting on the other side of the club. The man had a glass and raised and raised his also to Gordo.

"Thanks, Officer Miller," Gordo said downing the shot.

Gordo had Officer Miller from the second precinct on his payroll. He was one of many. Gordo had sent Officer Miller to pull Dolla over earlier that day. He liked Dolla and didn't wish any harm to him, but he had to display the power he possessed, putting Dolla in a position where he would owe Gordo a huge favor someday. It was business, nothing personal.

Once Dolla was in the car, he grabbed his cell phone and called Rick, instructing him to get ready to move out. Rick saw Dolla pulling out of the club parking lot behind a white Audi and started the car and pulled out of the store trailing behind them. They pulled up to the house on Junction and Magnolia, and Dolla pressed the release button to the stash spot. The side panel on the car door popped open and Dolla grabbed the black trash bag full of money and followed the two men in the house.

Once inside, neither of the men spoke to each other. They walked past the old lady and the kids and headed straight to the bedroom. The men pulled out two large scales and a bag containing ten kilos of powder cocaine. Dolla cut on the scale and weighed each kilo. The Ziploc bag itself weighed sixteen grams and with the brick inside, it weighed out at one thousand twenty-four grams.

After weighing all ten bricks, Dolla placed them back inside the bag and waited for the men to finish counting the money. After counting the money, the men put it back inside the bag, then placed the bag inside of the bedroom closet.

"Vamanos!" one of the men said, and they headed towards the door.

Dolla didn't understand what the man had said, but judging from their body language, he could tell that it was time to go.

After exiting the house, Dolla walked over to Rick's car and opened the back door and threw the bag inside.

"Be careful. I'll be right behind you," Dolla said.

Rick waited for Dolla to get into his car. He said a silent prayer, started the car, and pulled off. Rick had roughly close to one million dollars in street value of drugs in the car. He knew if he was to get caught, he may never see the streets again, so he drove cautiously and stayed alert all the way back to the hood. They took the bricks to Dennis's house and kept them there until they got things set up on Blackstone.

At the spot, Dolla told the crew about the encounter he had with the crooked cops.

"Damn. Somebody had to be speaking our names to them muthafuckas," Rell said.

"Then again, our spot be bangin' harder than any weed spot in the hood. I mean, even a blind nigga can see we eatin'. Plus, we ain't been raided yet," Rick said.

Hammer had gone to the store before Dolla and Rick arrived and returned with a fifth of Hennessy and a case of beer.

"This a celebration. Y'all niggaz my family. Loyalty brings royalty!" Hammer said, holding the fifth of Hennessy high in the air.

He opened the fifth and everyone poured a cup.

Dolla stood up and said, "we are royalty. May we maintain a bond that cannot be broken, not by police, not by a bitch, and not by no niggaz. We are The Royal Family, the best of the fuckin' best! Royal Family!" Dolla yelled to the top of his lungs.

"Royal Family!" all of them shouted in unison, then they downed their shots.

They spent the rest of the night getting fucked up and talking about what they were gonna do with their newfound wealth that was sure to come.

The next day, they had the security doors and bars installed at the spot on Blackstone. Gary got two fiends to paint the inside of the house. The fiends also pulled up the carpet and waxed the hardwood floors. They got the furniture and most of the items for the house from the same thrift store they got the stuff for the spot on Mettetal. The furniture arrived and once it was arranged, it didn't look or smell like the same house.

They decided to leave the outside as it was. They didn't want the house to stand out, but to blend in with the rest of the houses on the block. Krissy arrived later that afternoon and Dolla, Hammer, and Gary were waiting on her. Neither of the boys knew how to cook cocaine into crack. Krissy was secretly one of the best cooks around. She used to cook for some of the kingpins back in the eighties. Cooking all those kilos of dope made her curious, and that is how she started smoking crack.

Dolla ran outside and grabbed the brick from the stash spot in his car and ran back into the house. He handed the brick to Krissy and she just stood there with a smile on her face, shaking her head.

"What?" Dolla asked.

"Where is your scale, honey? I got a glass pot that will only be able to cook about four and a half ounces at a time." Krissy explained.

"Oh shit, my fault… Aye, Hammer. Grab that scale out of the trunk for me!" Dolla said, tossing Hammer the car keys.

Hammer ran to the car and grabbed the scale and ran back inside the house. He gave the scale to Krissy, and she sat it down on the counter and weighed four and a half ounces and put it in a separate bag. Then she put a pot of water on the stove and turned it on. She reached into the top cabinet and grabbed a large glass pot. She had a black grocery bag and pulled out a few boxes of baking soda and some mannitol. Gary, Hammer, and Dolla were literally so close up on her, she could feel their breath on her skin.

"Can I get some space, *please*?? SHIT!" Krissy snapped.

The boys backed off and watched her from a distance. They didn't like the smell from the fumes coming out of the pot.

"That shit making me dizzy," Gary said.

They stepped out of the kitchen and just stood in the doorway and watched her. It took a little over an hour to cook up the whole kilo.

"Dolla, come over here," Krissy said, signaling him with her hand.

Dolla walked over to the counter where the chunks of dope were sitting on top of paper towels.

"Weigh your shit up," she said, then took a step backwards and lit up a cigarette.

When he was done weighing the dope, it turned out that with her culinary skills, she had turned the kilo of cocaine into sixty ounces of crack cocaine.

"Damn! This almost two bricks right here!" Dolla exclaimed.

"Yeah, I do this shit," Krissy said arrogantly with one hand on her hip. "But listen up. Y'all gon' have the best dope in this hood. Trust and believe niggaz gon' get in they feelings about that, ESPECIALLY once they find out y'all ain't from around here. Whenever shit looks like it's about to get ugly, y'all gotta crush a muthafucka real quick, you hear me? This shit is not weed. Niggaz KILL for this," Krissy said in a serious tone.

"Anybody fuck wit us, they goin' in the dirt," Hammer said.

The boys grabbed a long full body mirror that was hanging up in one of the closets and cleaned it off. They laid it across the table in the living room. Hammer took Dolla's car and ran up to the gas station for a box of razor blades, rubber gloves, and as many boxes of sandwich bags he could get his hands on.

"Can I get a box of blunts too?" Hammer asked the Arab man behind the bulletproof glass.

"No problem," the man said with a smirk on his face. He knew from the items Hammer was purchasing that he sold drugs for a living.

"You must have a lot of shit to cut up, huh my friend?" The Arab man asked.

"Something like that," Hammer said, surprised that the he cut into him like that.

He paid for the items and quickly raced back to the spot.

Once Hammer got back to the house, Dolla weighed out twelve ounces, then broke it down into four ounces each and handed four ounces to Hammer and Gary.

"Ummm, can I get paid for my services, please?" Krissy asked.

"Oh shit, I almost forgot." Dolla ran back into the kitchen and weighed up an ounce and gave it to Krissy.

"Here you go. You get that every time you cook a brick for us," Dolla said.

Krissy was so excited, she started sweating.

"Bet. I got you, Dolla," Krissy said, wrapping the ounce up, sticking it in her pocket.

Dolla went back in the living room with Hammer and Gary to cut some dope up, and Krissy went into the one of the bedrooms.

Not bad for an hour and a half days work, Krissy thought to herself. She would get an ounce each time she cooked for them, plus $60 a month for having the electric bill in her name for the spot on Mettetal. *Keep this up and I might not have to sell pussy anymore.*

At that moment, she decided that she would make sure that the boys ran through bricks like underwear, but when you had coke that strong, it wasn't gonna be hard at all. She reached in her bra and pulled out her glass stem. She took a razor and cut a small chunk off the ounce and sat it inside the stem and lit it.

Dolla, Gary, and Hammer were chopping away at the chunks of crack, cutting them into dime rocks. The back bedroom door flew open and Krissy came speed walking down the hallway into the living room. Her eyes were wide open, and they looked like quarter-dollar coins.

"This, this shit *good*!" She could barely talk straight. "I'm gonna brin… bring y'all buis - business right now!" she said and flew out the front door.

It didn't take long because fifteen minutes later, there was a knock on the door.

"Who dat!?" Gary yelled, jumping up and walking towards the door.

Hammer followed behind him. Gary looked through the peephole and saw a frail older man.

"Oh, shit. That's that nigga, Ten Speed." He opened the door and Ten Speed already had two $10 bills in his hand.

"Let me get two of 'em," he said in a raspy tone.

Gary reached for the money and Ten Speed pulled back, moving the money from his reach.

"I cut a lotta grass for this. Make sure it's the same shit Krissy got," he said.

Gary snatched the money out of his hand and came back with two dimes and placed them in Ten Speed's hand.

"If it's good, I'll be back, and I'll send more people," he said.

"Well I guess I'll see you later then," Gary said and closed the door.

"Why they call ol' boy Ten Speed?" Dolla asked Gary once him and Hammer were done serving the custo.

"Because he ride all over the hood all day on a old-ass Ten Speed with a lawnmower tied to the seat of the bike," Gary said, laughing at the same time. "He cuts most of the people's grass in the hood… the ones who still have grass left. A long time ago, he had a successful landscaping company, but he started getting high and smoked that shit all up."

Dolla's cell phone rang. It was a number he didn't recognize.

"What up," he said through the receiver.

"There is a brown minivan parked on West Warren and Scotten Street. Go pick it up. The license plate number is DLT-1094."

"I'm gonna send one of my homies," Dolla said.

The man didn't respond. He just hung up. Dolla quickly dialed Rell's number.

"What's crackin', my nigga? Shit smooth?" Rell asked. He was glad that they graduated to the crack game. He knew there was a lot of money to be made.

"Everything good. Listen, I need you to go swoop something up real quick," Dolla said.

"Shit, I got you, my nigga. Where the shit at?" Rell asked.

Dolla gave him the info and the name of the street.

"Brown van. Plate number DLT-1094. I got you," Rell said reciting back the info to Dolla.

"You got somebody to run you over there right quick?" Dolla asked.

"I'll just get one of the custos to shoot me over there," Rell said.

"Alright, bet. Don't take all day though. Get on it as quick as you can," Dolla said.

"I'm on it. Y'all niggaz be safe over there."

"Alright, y'all too," Dolla said then hung up.

About ten minutes later, Candy came over to get some weed. She was about five years older than the boys but had known them for years. She stayed two blocks over on Mansfield street. She was fucking with a nigga named Block who stayed on Winthrop. They'd just had a baby girl, and they had been copping weed from Rell and Dolla for a long time.

"Candy, what up? How's the baby?" Rell asked.

"She doin' good. She wit her grandma right now. Me and Block about to go to a movie or something," she said.

"Aye, can y'all do me a favor?"

"It all depends. What you need us to do?" Candy asked.

"Nothing major. I just need y'all to drop me off on Warren and Scotten. I'll give y'all $35," Rell said.

She stood there tapping her thigh, pondering the offer. "Alright, me and Block will shoot you over there. Can you pay us in weed though?"

"I got you," Rell said, grabbing up four dime bags and a blunt.

"Rick, can you hold it down for a minute. I gotta go pick somethin' up right quick."

"Yeah, I got this," Rick said.

"Alright, bet. I'll holla at you in a minute."

Rell left out with Candy and they got in the car with Block.

"Baby, we gon' drop Rell off on Warren and Scotten. You know how to get there?" Candy asked.

"Yeah, one of my homies just moved over that way. Rell, what up doe, nigga?" Block asked.

"Shit, can we smoke on the way?" Rell asked.

"Roll that shit up," Block replied.

Rell gave Candy three dime bags and $5. With the extra bag he had, he took half of it and rolled up a fat-ass blunt. Rell fired it up and they pulled off.

Once they got to Warren and Scotten, Block asked which way to turn.

"Right or left, fam?"

Rell wasn't sure, but he didn't want them to know. "Right," Rell said, going with his first mind.

Once they made a right on Scotten, Rell was looking for the brown minivan.

"How far down?" Block asked.

"Just keep going, I think it's the next block," Rell said, seeing that there wasn't a brown van on the first block.

On the second block, there was no sign of the van either.

If it's not on the next block, I'm just gonna have them let me out, Rell thought to himself.

It wasn't until they crossed over to the third block that he saw the brown minivan parked on the left side of the street.

That's gotta be it right there. The van was facing them, so Rell couldn't see the license plate.

"Pull up next to that van," he said, pointing to it.

Block pulled up on the other side of the street and parked.

"You sho you gon' be straight right here?" Block asked, scoping out the shady area.

"Yeah, I'm strapped. I wish a nigga would," Rell said. "Alright y'all, I'm out." He dapped Block and Candy.

"Boy, be careful out here!" Candy said as Rell got out of the car.

Rell walked around to the back of the van and looked at the license plate.

"This is it. DLT-1094."

The windows were tinted, so he couldn't see what was inside. The only windows that weren't tinted were the driver and passenger windows and the windshield. Block and Candy sat there as they watched Rell looking at the plate, then trying to look through the tinted windows.

"Is he about to steal that van?" Candy asked Block.

"Baby, have you paid attention to what that lil nigga ridin' in the hood?" Block asked, reminding her of Rell's black Cutlass on twenty-inch rims. "Them lil niggaz getting money."

Rell didn't see a key anywhere, so he just walked to the driver side door and opened it. He climbed in. It was then he noticed that the keys were in the ignition. He turned the key forward and the van started right up. He looked over at Block and Candy and threw up the peace sign, letting them know he was straight. They blew the horn and pulled off. Rell noticed that the gas tank was full, so he wouldn't have to make any stops. He could shoot straight to the hood from Scotten street.

He threw the gear in drive and before he pulled off, he wanted to straighten up the rear-view mirror. When he did, what he saw startled the shit out of him.

"What the fuck?" Rell said when he saw all the weapons piled up in the back of the van.

The back-row seats had been removed. All Rell could see was all types of pistols, different types of shotguns, and assault rifles of all makes and models, and box after box of ammunition.

"This some mob type shit for real," Rell said as he pulled off.

Once he was on the road headed back to the hood, he pulled out his phone and called Dolla while he was sitting at a red light.

"You straight?" Dolla asked Rell.

"Yeah, we good, bro. I'll see you later," Rell said, and hung up the phone.

CHAPTER NINE

The spot on Blackstone was boomin' hard. They made their first sale at about three thirty in the afternoon and by eight o' clock that night, they had made a little over three thousand. Krissy was dropkicking fiends left and right to the spot. Out of the brick and the extra twenty-four ounces, they cut up $76,000 in dime rocks, not even counting the ounce they gave to Krissy, which they could have cut up about fourteen hundred more dollars.

Dolla and Hammer were completely taken aback by the enormous profit they'd made from just one brick alone. Dolla would be able to pay Gordo back from the first brick and still break even with the $16,000 left over. It was like they'd gotten ten extra kilos for free. On top of that, the crack house was only open for five hours, and they already had generated $500 more than what they made in a whole day from the weed spot on Mettetal.

It was at this moment Dolla understood why his dad sold cocaine. The money a person could make was astronomical, but there was a catch; If a nigga got caught, the hook would put you UNDER the jail. Everything a person does has rules that must be followed. With this particular hustle, if you broke the rules, it could cost you your life in more ways than one. Sometimes even your loved ones could get caught up as well. This game was not for the weak or faint of heart.

Dolla stayed the night at the house on Blackstone along with Hammer and Gary. Fiends were coming at all hours of the night, and the three of them barely got any sleep.

The next morning, Dolla went to the neighborhood Coney Island and grabbed up some breakfast for the three of them and headed back to the spot. Once he got back, they sat at the table and ate while Dolla was laying the game plan down.

"Hammer, I want you to run this spot. Make sure you get ahold of a little bitch in this hood to fuck wit yo pretty boy ass, that way we can keep most of the day's work stashed at the bitch house."

"You already know I'm on top of that. Fuckin' bitches is one of my specialties," Hammer said.

"Gary, we gonna need somebody else over here too. You got anybody in mind?" Dolla asked.

"Yeah, my lil homie, E-baby, a real nigga. He'll fit right in," Gary said.

"Ok, cool. Bring him thru tomorrow. This what we gonna do. We'll pay you eight hundred a day, my nigga. You fuckin' wit us now, we family, The Royal Family. You'll meet the others soon enough. We a mothafuckin' movement, and we stand firm on loyalty. I got a lot of love for your Aunt Krissy, and she said you a solid nigga. We don't play that snake shit. We lay niggaz down for that. Keep it one hundred wit us and we'll do the same wit you. We all the same, ain't nobody better than the next, so if anyone of us violate, that person can get it. You feel me?" Dolla asked after giving Gary the lowdown about the crew.

Gary nodded his head, fully understanding where Dolla was coming from and what he meant.

"As for that nigga, E-baby, you gonna be responsible for whatever he does, so keep that in mind, fam," Hammer said.

"Fa sho. Gary, you feel like takin' my car and runnin' to the store and getting a bottle and some blunts?" Dolla asked.

"Yeah, I can do that."

"Bet. Bring back a fifth of whatever you like to drink, some red cups, and a pack of squares." Dolla tossed him the car keys and gave him a $50 bill.

"I'll be right back," Gary said as he walked out of the door. As soon as he swung the door open, three fiends were walking up.

"Yo! You got three out here!" Gary said.

When Hammer was finished serving the custos, Dolla passed the square he was smoking to Hammer.

"What you think about him?" Dolla asked Hammer.

"From what I see, the nigga down and he wanna eat. I don't get a bad vibe from him," Hammer said.

Gary knocked on the door and Hammer let him in.

"We gotta get some spare keys made," Hammer said.

"There's a place up on Fenkell and Burt Road that copies keys," Gary said.

"We'll hit that bitch in the morning then," Hammer said.

"What's in the bag?" Dolla asked Gary.

Gary pulled out a fifth of tequila eighteen hundred. They blessed the bottle then filled their cups up halfway.

"Loyalty brings royalty!" Hammer said, raising his cup. Dolla and Gary followed suit.

After a few shots, Dolla and Hammer told Gary to hold it down for a little while so Dolla could take Hammer back on Mettetal to get his car. Once they got on Mettetal, they parked in front of Hammer's house and walked across the street to the spot. When they got in the house, Rick, Rell, and Dennis had three blunts in rotation and were drinking on some Hennessy.

"What up, doe?" Dennis asked, dapping both Dolla and Hammer. He heard about them opening the spot on Blackstone and was happy for them.

"Niggaz movin' up in the world, huh?" Dennis asked.

"Yeah, shit movin' like a mothafucka over there too," Hammer said.

Dolla and Hammer told Rick, Rell, and Dennis how the spot already pulled in three thousand in the first five hours.

"Damn! That's more than we make in a day over here!" Rick said, surprised at the numbers Blackstone had did in a short amount of time.

"The van is parked in the garage if you wanna go take a look," Rell said to Dolla.

"Damn, I almost forgot about that shit." Dolla got up and walked out the side door and opened the garage. Once inside, he slid open the sliding door on the minivan and he was somewhat stunned when he saw the array of weapons.

Damn. That nigga, Gordo, came through for real. It's gotta be at least thirty-five to forty different burners in here, he said to himself, looking through the pile.

"We gotta get somewhere to put this shit. We don't wanna just leave it sitting here in the garage. The hook come thru and find all this shit, it's all over wit," Rell said to Dolla after stepping into the garage.

"Yeah, you right. We'll figure somethin' out. Maybe we can keep them at Dennis's house for a while until we can find a permanent spot to put them." Dolla said.

Dolla and Rell walked back inside the spot as Hammer was on his way out.

"I'm bout to head to Blackstone. I'll holla at y'all niggaz," Hammer said, dapping them.

"Be careful over there and call us if you need something," Rick said.

"You know it. See y'all later," Hammer said, then walked out the door.

"Man, it's been a long day," Dolla said, pouring a cup of Hennessy. He slammed the first shot, then poured another and lit a cigarette.

"Dolla, you know the lil nigga I been' tellin you about that be shakin' a bag for me over on Joy Road?" Rick asked.

"Yeah, what about him?"

"Well, I been kickin' it wit 'em, and he be tellin' me how the yae be bangin' over there," Rick said, referring to crack.

"I think we should put some shit down over there too. Spread some shit around, you feel me?"

"I was thinking about that shit the other day. I had been meaning to crack on you about that shit," Dolla said.

"Wit all them bricks y'all got, it would definitely be a good move for y'all. It's about time y'all put some young niggaz over there too, that way y'all can be able to move around freely and monitor y'all spots and be able to watch the neighborhood itself surrounding the spots." Dennis suggested.

"That's why I got love for you, D. Since we was little niggaz, you always gave us the blueprint on how to move in these streets," Rell said.

"I knew the hustle was in y'all blood way back when y'all was snotty-nosed lil niggaz, sellin' nickel bags off the hip. Now look where y'all at," Dennis said.

"I know, and this shit right here is just the beginning, Dolla said."

That conversation had taken place a little over a month prior. Dolla took Rick up on opening on Joy Road. They had a weed spot and a crack spot inside of an apartment building on Joy road and Greenfield. The spots were directly across the hall from each other. The landlord was a slumlord and most of the tenants in the building were either on drugs or just unemployed, waiting on a check every first of the month. The tenants in this building seemed to have given up on life and accepted the current situation they were stuck in. The landlord knew that Rick and his crew were selling drugs out of the building and he didn't care. He just charged them an extra $150 a month in rent for each apartment. He even put some fake lease papers together for them to make shit look legit in case someone came snooping around and asking questions.

Nickel bags was the choice of that hood, and Dolla and the boys filled the order. They let the nigga who was selling weed off the hip for Rick run both the spots. The dope spot was doing close to $5,000 a day, and the weed spot was doing around $1,200 a day. In return, the crew paid T-mac $1,000 a day. T-mac was about five feet four inches with cocoa-brown skin and weighed about 130 pounds, soaking wet. As a result of that, T-mac developed the "little man complex." He had a hot temper and always felt like he had something to prove to the world and to those around him. He had an older brother named J-rock who was finishing up a ten-year sentence for conspiracy to sell a kilo of cocaine. At one point in time, J-rock had Joy Road on lock between Greenfield and Schafer, which was about two miles of territory. He also had a strong team who called themselves "Exit Nine Incorporated". But after J-rock caught his case, the team fell apart with most of them either getting locked up or killed. J-rock had plans to once again, take control of his neighborhood and rebuild the empire he had once as soon as he was released from federal custody. T-mac ended up bringing his childhood friend, Monster, to help him run the spots.

Monster and T-mac were a hell of a combination. Where T-mac lacked in size and strength, Monster had that hands down. The both of them were seventeen, but Monster looked like a grown-ass man. He got the name because of his size and because he was ugly as fuck. He was a big solid guy with hands the size of bricks, and they felt like bricks too if you were one of the unlucky ones to get hit with one of his punches. He was so black, he almost looked purple and one of his eyes was crooked.

Monster would hold down the weed spot while T-mac would run back and forth between the two spots. They had an older dope fiend named Bo running the door of the crack spot. Surprisingly, Bo was somewhat trustworthy, but that was only because of the fear he had of Monster and T-mac. Everyone had love for T-mac's older brother, so when niggaz saw T-mac hustling out of the apartments, none of the other neighborhood hustlers had a problem with it. Monster was getting

$500 a day, and he was elated about it. He spent most of his money on clothes and tricking with some of the girls who would come to buy weed. He'd never had so much pussy in his life.

As for the spot on Mettetal, the crew ended up hiring two sixteen-year-old boys named Quick and Bruce who were once custos, but Dolla and Rell saw something in them that reminded them of how they were when they were at that age. Quick was tall with a medium build, light-skinned with braids. He had an athletic build and put you in the mind of a young basketball player. Bruce was light-skinned as well with a slim, lean frame with long braids and green eyes. They were very responsible and mature for their age and Dolla, Rell, Hammer, and Rick all took a liking to the two young hustlers in training. Plus, Dennis would stop by to check on them throughout the day and drop game on them. The crew paid them $1,200 every week. Everything seemed to take off almost overnight. Each one of the spots was doing numbers, but the spot on Blackstone was banging out of control. They were running through a brick-and-a- half a week with ease, and as the saying goes, more money, more problems…

The spot had been banging all day. Hammer, E-baby, and Gary had been running around like chickens with their heads cut off. Hammer had met a girl named Victoria who stayed around the corner on Westbrook, but she stayed on the other side of Fenkell. She was a sexy-ass redbone with short hair, and she had the body of a goddess. She worked in a bar on Fenkell and Telegraph as a waitress, plus she was getting Section 8, so her rent was extremely low. Hammer would hide the work and a few guns at her house, and she didn't mind, as long as he spent a little time with her and fucked her good.

Hammer had a spare key to the house and had to run there three times already today. Things seemed to finally slow down for about three hours. Hammer, E-baby, and Gary were playing the video game and smoking blunts, so they really didn't notice how fast time was passing.

"Y'all niggaz want a shot?" Gary asked Hammer and E-baby who were still playing the game.

"Yeah. Bring two shots back with you," E-baby hollered back, never taking his eyes off the T.V.

Gary walked over to the table and filled three cups with liquor and carried them over to where E-baby and Hammer were sitting. Gary handed them their cups and he just so happened to look out of the front window.

"What the fuck?!" Gary yelled throwing his drink down on the floor.

"What up?" Hammer said, jumping up and reaching for his pistol on his waist at the same time.

E-baby was on his feet as well and ran to the window where Hammer and Gary stood. What they saw was a young nigga who had to be no older than seventeen years old, standing across the street serving fiends. What pissed them off even more was that a fiend was approaching the spot, but the young nigga called him across the street.

"Hold on! I know that bitch-ass nigga! That's Vick and he works in Trigga's spot!" E-baby said. "We used to steal cars together back in the day."

Trigga had a crack house four blocks over that had been banging for years but had only been raided once. He was one of the dudes Gary had warned Hammer about being a potential threat. Before Hammer or Gary could even get a chance to react, E-baby shot out the front door and ran across the street to where Vick was standing.

"Nigga, what up? You want some…"

Bink!

Bink-bink!

E-baby hit Vick with three quick but stinging blows to the head, causing him to stumble backwards and stopping him from finishing his sentence. E-baby stood on the tip of his toes and swung a wild right hook that connected with Vick's jaw, dropping him to the ground. E-baby moved quickly, putting hands and feet all over Vick. The two were the same age, but Vick was bigger and taller. But that didn't stop him from putting Vick on his ass.

Hammer and Gary just stood back and watched E-baby work. He basically stomped the boy unconscious, then reached in his pocket and took his sack and his money from him.

"This our shit now, you bitch-ass nigga!" E-baby yelled, then kicked him in the face one more time and spit on him.

To be so small, E-baby was good with his hands.

This little nigga a beast, Hammer thought to himself. Two fiends were standing by watching the whole time.

"Here you go, fam," E-baby said, then tried to hand the money and the sack to Hammer.

"Naw, my nigga. That's all you. You earned it," Hammer said, patting E-baby on the back. "Listen up. Don't ever let nobody outside these doors tell y'all we out 'cause we'll never be out!" Hammer said to the two fiends.

"E-baby, let me see that sack." E-baby tossed the sack to Hammer.

"Catch," Hammer said to the tall skinny fiend, throwing him the sack of stones E-baby took from Vick.

"This shit ain't nothin' compared to our product, but consider it a gift," Gary added. Both the fiends' eyes lit up as if they'd hit the lottery, and in a sense they did - the crack lottery.

"Thanks, mellow," the tall fiend said to Hammer.

"Don't thank me. Thank my lil nigga, E-baby," Hammer informed the fiend.

"Thanks, young gangster," the other fiend said to E-baby.

"It ain't shit," E-baby replied.

"We'll be back to holla at y'all," the two fiends said, then walked off.

E-baby was a solid young dude. He stood about five feet eight inches, with a very slim frame, but his body was extremely cut with lean muscle. He had very soft and wavy hair, which was somewhat unusual for a typical black man. He was dark-skinned, but the texture of his hair would make one swear he was mixed with another race. E-baby grew up in Brightmoor just like Gary and was raised by his grandfather.

E-baby's birth given name was Edward, and he never knew his parents. His grandfather did the best he could raising him, but with his poor health and living off a social security check, he could only do so much for the boy. With his grandfather's bad health, he just couldn't keep up with E-baby so, he was free to run wild in the streets. All E-baby needed was some structure and guidance, and now that he was with Dolla and the rest of the crew, he would receive just that.

Hammer, Gary, and E-baby turned and walked back in the spot, leaving Vick on the ground moaning in pain.

Three days had passed since that incident and the spot was banging as usual. The day was turning into the evening and the sun was beginning to set, but it was still hot outside. E-baby had been with his girlfriend all day and when he called Hammer and Gary to let them know he was on his way to the spot, they asked him to stop by the liquor store and grab a bottle and some blunts and a few packs of squares. Once E-baby got to the spot, he lit up a square and put the bottle of liquor in the freezer.

"Let's roll up. I need to smoke something," E-baby said.

"Yeah, I bet, after being caked up and laying in pussy all day long, I would have to smoke too," Gary said laughing.

"Nigga, I don't say shit when you be pullin' yo' little disappearing acts wit yo' baby momma," E-baby shot back at Gary.

Hammer even had to laugh at that one. Hammer grabbed a few blunts and walked into the kitchen and began splitting them open over the trash can. Gary and E-baby were in the living room kicking it.

"Yo, Hammer. Grab the drink out the freezer and bring some cups wit you!" Gary yelled from the living room while serving a custo.

"Y'all niggaz gotta come get y'all shit. I got my hands full rollin' up these blunts!" Hammer yelled back to Gary.

Gary wanted to leave the security gate locked and the front door cracked to let some fresh air circulate through the house but changed his mind and turned on the box fan instead. Gary and E-baby walked into the kitchen and Gary grabbed the liquor out of the freezer.

"Grab some cups," Gary said to E-baby.

"Grab me one too," Hammer said. "I'm almost finished rollin'…

Rat! Tat! Tat! Tat!

Rat! Tat! Tat! Tat! Tat!

Gunfire erupted, shattering the glass in the front windows of the spot.

"What the fuck!" Hammer, Gary, and E-baby squatted down and pulled out their pistols. E-baby's pistol was on the dining room table, so he was a sitting duck for the moment.

"Shit! I need my burner!" E-baby yelled over the gunfire in a crouched position. "I'm bout to try to grab it off the table!"

Hammer grabbed him by the arm. "Fuck that! If them muthafuckas comin' in, they gon' have to find us! All these bullets flying thru this bitch, you won't make it to yo burner. Just sit tight!"

Hammer was yelling so his voice could be heard over the gunshots. What was only about two minutes felt like an hour. They heard tires screeching, and the gunshots stopped. They got up and ran to the living room with their guns drawn. Dust particles were floating in the air all over the living room. The entire area was riddled with bullet holes. By E-baby putting that bottle in the freezer and not on the table, along with Hammer rolling blunts in the kitchen and the perfect timing of E-baby and Gary's thirst saved their lives; If it hadn't been for those reasons, the three of them would have been dead.

E-baby grabbed his gun off the table and without even speaking, the boys split up in different directions, looking through the windows around the house to make sure nobody was lurking around. Once they saw the coast was clear, they walked outside. Gun shells littered the entire front of the house.

"I'll grab a broom and start sweeping all the glass and shit up," Gary said and went in the house to get the broom and dustpan.

Hammer bent down and picked up one of the shell casings. "The bottom of the shell had the numbers 7.62 on the bottom.

"These niggaz was shootin' AK's at us," he said with disgust and dropped the shell back on the ground.

They knew who was behind this. It could only be one person, and that was Trigga.

"Them niggaz is fuckin' dead," Hammer said, growing angrier by the second.

Gary was cleaning up, and E-baby went over to help him. Hammer pulled out his cell phone and began making calls. Dolla was at the apartment on Joy Road, dropping off some work and kicking it with Monster and T-mac when his phone rang.

"What, up bro?" Dolla asked when he answered.

"You need to get over here A.S.A.P," Hammer said.

"Why? What's up?" Dolla asked.

"Just get over here now. I don't wanna talk about it over the phone," Hammer said, then hung up.

Soon as Dolla hung up, he headed for the door.

"Aye, I gotta take care of something. I'll holla at y'all later," Dolla said, then walked out the door.

Eight Mile Road had a strip of topless dancing nightclubs that stretched out about a mile long on the west side of Detroit. Rell was at Tiger's, a club that he hit on a regular basis. He was in the V.I.P. booth getting his dick sucked by Lexi, one of the baddest bitches in the club. Her head and neck were moving as fast as a chicken pecking feed. Rell's phone started vibrating. He slid his hand into his pocket and pulled out his phone, checking the caller I.D. to see who it was. Grandma Cill had been sick for the last few days and he wanted to make sure she wasn't trying to reach him.

Once he saw it was Hammer, he figured that it wasn't important.

I'll call that nigga back when I'm finished, he thought to himself, as he sat the phone down next to him. He was just about to cum when his phone went off again, which threw him off from reaching a climax.

"Fuck!" he said out loud and glanced over at his phone without stopping the dancer from performing her oral services.

He saw Hammer's number again and this time, his sixth sense told him something wasn't right and to answer. He answered, thinking maybe one of the spots got raided, but when he heard the tone of Hammer's voice, he knew it was something else. Hammer could hear the music booming in the background where Rell was.

"We need you on Blackstone RIGHT NOW!!" Hammer yelled through the receiver.

"I'll be there in fifteen minutes," Rell said.

"Hurry up! Some shit on the floor!" Hammer said, then hung up.

Rell hit the end button on his phone and pushed Lexi's face to the side.

"What's wrong, baby?" Lexi asked, worried that she wasn't satisfying Rell with her lip service.

All the strippers knew Rell and they also knew that he was getting money and she didn't want to be on bad terms with him.

"Nothin'. I gotta go," Rell said, jumping up and fixing his pants.

He reached in his pocket and grabbed a $100 bill and threw it on the couch and stormed out of the club at a high rate of speed.

Once outside, he waited impatiently for the valet attendant to bring him his car. Once the attendant pulled up with his car, he came flying in the attendant's direction. The attendant was worried that Rell was gonna put hands on him and flinched, but Rell handed him a $20 bill.

"Thanks, Rell," the attendant said nervously and accepted the money in his shaking hands.

Rell jumped in the car and slammed the gear into drive and pulled out of the parking lot like a bat outta hell…

Rick, his mother, and his sister were at a seafood restaurant on Telegraph Road. Rick had followed them there in his car. He wanted to drive them to the restaurant himself, but his mom didn't want to ride in his car.

"That damn thing is noisy, and your radio be on too loud," his mother said, so she and his sister, Rita, drove in her car instead. Once they made it to the restaurant, they had to wait a few minutes before they were seated. After making it to their table, they sat down and looked at the menu selection and placed their orders. While waiting for their food, they had a few drinks and enjoyed some appetizers while talking. Rick's phone started ringing, and he excused himself from the table to take the call.

"Hammer. What up doe, nigga?" Rick asked.

"Shit, we got something on the floor. Everybody on they way. We at the Blackstone crib," Hammer said.

"Shit, I'm out with my moms and sister at this restaurant right now. Can it wait til I'm done?" Rick asked.

"Naw fam, it's urgent. You feel me?" Hammer expressed the seriousness of the situation from the tone of his voice.

"Alright, I'm on my way, bro," Rick said, then hung up the phone.

What the fuck goin' on? Rick thought to himself.

He slowly walked back to the table, trying not to look troubled from the phone call he'd just got.

"Hey, y'all. I'm sorry, but I gotta go."

"Why? We just got our food," his mother asked.

"I know, I know. But Dolla's car broke down and he's stuck on the freeway. I gotta go pick him up. But we gotta wait on the tow truck first," Rick said, coming up with a quick lie off the top of his head.

"Oh, wow," his mother said, slightly disappointed. She didn't want him to go, but she respected and admired the loyalty he had to his friend. "Well, you better go help him out then."

"How come Dolla can't wait on the tow truck on his own and just ride back with the driver?" his sister asked.

"He ain't got no money on him," Rick said becoming irritated.

"Dolla ain't got no money??" his sister asked, sensing that Rick was on some bullshit. She knew for a fact that Dolla was hood rich. It was then that she knew her brother was lying but, his mother hadn't caught on.

"Naw, he don't got no money on him," Rick said once more, and glanced at his sister with a look that said, "mind your fucking business."

He reached in his pocket and gave his mother $300. "Here, this is for the bill."

"Boy, this is more than enough!" his mom said.

"Alright, just keep it then," Rick said, then reached over the table and kissed her on the forehead and headed for the exit.

After Hammer finished calling Dolla, Rell, and Rick, they all arrived on Blackstone in under a half hour. Hammer, Gary, and E-baby told them about Vick being posted in front of the spot, t-rollin' their custos, telling them that their spot was closed. They also told them how E-baby beat the shit outta Vick, then how all of a sudden tonight bullets come flying through the windows and the front door. They covered up the front windows with plywood.

After the shooting, they didn't see not even one police car and the fiends were steady coming like clockwork. Hammer ran over Victoria's house and grabbed two AK forty-sevens that had been converted into fully automatics and a case of ammo and brought them back to the spot on Blackstone.

We got K's too, Hammer said to himself. Weed smoke filled the air as the six of them smoked blunt after blunt, thinking of how to go about handling the situation.

"Ok, here's what we gonna do, Dolla said…

CHAPTER TEN

Trigga and his crew were posted at the spot on Burgess, hustling. It had been two days since he'd sent a few of his niggaz to shoot up the spot on Blackstone. Shit was still slow, but it was beginning to pick up a little bit. He was hoping that he'd killed them, but if not, he was pretty sure that it would make them want to close up shop. He had to do this to a few niggaz who called themselves setting up shop in his hood, and every time, niggaz would pack up and ship out.

I think I'm gonna send somebody over there to torch that bitch, he thought to himself, taking a pull from a blunt. His young niggaz he had holding down the spot were in the corner shooting dice when there was a knock on the door. The young niggaz continued to shoot dice as if they didn't hear someone knocking.

"Aye, one of y'all get the muthafuckin' door!" Trigga said. "That's probably why the numbers ain't been good for the last few days. Let me find out y'all muthafuckas putting a dice game before my money and I'm gon' put a hole in one of y'all niggaz."

The young hustlers knew Trigga meant what he said. He didn't get the name Trigga by faking. He popped that pistol, and anyone that knew him knew he was about his murder game.

Vick limped to the door and opened it. He was still fucked up from the beating he took from E-baby two days ago. He'd lied and told Trigga and the rest of the crew that the niggaz on Blackstone rushed him.

"Ten Speed, what up?" Vick asked.

"Let me get one, and my cousin want two of 'em," Ten Speed said. Vick couldn't see the guy Ten Speed was with because there was a blind spot on the porch. The man stepped into Vick's view and had a $20 bill in his hand.

"You say this yo peoples, Ten Speed?" Vick asked. He had never seen the guy before and even though he was old as hell and looked like he smoked, Vick was still somewhat leery about serving him.

"Ok, Ten Speed. But if this nigga the hook, it's gon' be yo ass, nigga," Vick said, taking money from the both of them.

"Didn't I just day he my cousin?? He straight, damn!" Ten Speed said, offended by Vick's comment. Vick raised his hand and smacked the shit out of Ten Speed.

"Watch yo muthafuckin' mouth, nigga! Don't make me fuck you up!" Vick yelled, then squared himself off like he was ready to punch Ten Speed.

"You got that," Ten Speed said, holding his cheek. His lip was busted and bleeding a little bit from the smack as well.

"Muthafuckin' right I got it, bitch-ass nigga!!" Vick said, reaching in his pocket and pulling out three $10 stones and handing them to Ten Speed. Vick was about to close the door when the old man spoke and got his attention.

"What up?" Vick asked. It looked like he was ready to smack the old man too.

"Um, I got some guns I'm tryin' to sell for the lows," the old man said.

"Oh yeah? What you got?" Vick asked.

"I got a .45 Desert Eagle and a Thompson .45 rifle with a 75-round drum and a .50 cal pistol."

Trigga could hear the old man from where he was sitting, and when he heard him say something about a .50 cal pistol, that got his attention.

"Say, old man. Where you get ahold of some shit like that from?" Trigga asked. Trigga was short and weighed at least 280 plus pounds. He was yelling from across the living room, sitting in a recliner.

"I was in the army," the old man replied.

"How much for all of 'em?" Trigga asked.

"Gimmie $400, and you can have 'em," the old man said.

Trigga knew he couldn't beat that. It was a sweet deal. Still, he tried his hand with the old man.

"Man, that's kinda steep. I just paid all my bills and all I got is a hot $350," Trigga said.

"Run it," the old man said without any hesitation.

Trigga smiled on the inside. "Works every time," he mumbled under his breath.

"I gotta go get 'em right quick. They at Ten Speed's house. I'll be back in a little bit," the old man said, and walked off the porch.

"How many of 'em was it in the house?" Dolla asked Ten Speed and Krissy's boyfriend.

"I saw five of 'em," Ten Speed said.

"Did y'all see any guns?" Hammer asked.

"Nope, not one."

"Ok. Good lookin', my man. You've done your job," Dolla said, and gave Ten Speed five dime rocks and a $50 bill.

"Thanks!!" Ten Speed said and grabbed the rocks and the money and headed out the door. He hopped on his bike and peddled off with a huge grin on his face.

"I get paid for five minutes of conversation and them Burgess niggaz get dealt with. That's killin' two birds with one stone," he said as he rode off into the night.

"E-baby, get that stolie ready. Back it in the driveway so we can load the burners up," Dolla said.

E-baby ran out the house and picked up the stolie that was parked down the street. Keith, Krissy's boyfriend, put a rock inside of his glass stem and fired up.

"Man, what the fuck you doin'? You gotta go in the back room with that stankin' shit," Rick said.

"Keith, you know better than that. These boys don't wanna smell that shit. Come with me," Krissy said.

The boys had the van loaded with the guns and were ready to roll. All of them wanted to ride. Each one of them took it personally because them Burgess niggaz put them in danger, and if you fuck with one of The Royal Family, the whole team coming for your ass.

Rell walked to the back room where Keith and Krissy were. "C'mon, let's go," he said to Keith.

Keith hopped up and walked out of the bedroom behind Rell, high as a kite. Keith and all the boys piled up in the van, and E-baby started the van. They pulled off, headed for Trigga's spot on Burgess. Once they were on Burgess, they cut off the headlights and backed into the backyard of an abandoned house directly across the street from Trigga's spot. The boys were dressed in all black and were concealed in the darkness of the night.

"Y'all niggaz ready?" Dolla asked in a low, even tone. "In and out, let's stick to the plan and crush these bitch-ass niggaz."

Rick was the first one to get out the van. Once they saw him ease into the garage of the abandoned house, Keith, Dolla, Hammer, Rell, and E-baby jumped out the van and headed across the street. Gary was in a crouched position with a Mac-ninety, peeking out from the abandoned house. Keith knocked on the door and waited with a duffle bag full of blocks of wood. He was nervous as hell, and the buzz he once had was now completely gone.

Vick opened the door, but the security gate door was locked. "What up, doe?" Vick asked, recognizing who the man was.

"I got them guns with me," Keith said, holding up the duffle bag for Vick to see.

"Hand it here," Vick said, sticking his arm through the security gate.

"Hell naw! Until I see some cash, the bag stays with me," Keith said.

Damn, this old-ass nigga up on game, Vick thought to himself. He wanted to see if the old man was stupid enough to hand him the bag, but it didn't work.

"Hold on a second," Vick said and walked away. "Trigga, that one fiend here with the guns. He outside on the porch," Vick informed Trigga.

Trigga was in the bathroom taking a shit. "Let 'em in, and if it's what he says it is pay, the man," he yelled from the bathroom.

Vick walked back to the front door and unlocked the gate. "Step in," he said, and moved to the side to let Keith enter. As soon as Keith put one foot over the threshold, Dolla, Rell, and E-baby came charging into the house from the blind spot on the porch, knocking Keith to the floor.

"*What the fuck*??" Vick yelled, startled form the ambush.

The other three guys that were shooting dice were completely caught off guard as well. Vick knew immediately shit was about to get ugly. He didn't recognize three out of the four men, but he figured they had something to do with Blackstone because E-baby was with them. Second of all, the men didn't have on any masks, which meant Vick and his team's chances of survival was slim to none.

"What the fuck y'all want?" one of the guys who was shooting dice asked.

"Yo life, muthafucka," Rell replied, as he walked up on the man and started hitting him in the mouth and the head with the butt of his shotgun. Blood was gushing from the man's mouth and the side of his head. Keith bolted out the front door and flew across the street to the van like a bat outta hell.

Vick weighed his options and realized that he wasn't gonna make it out of this alive and ran for Trigga's gun that was on the stand next to his chair. E-baby squeezed the trigger on his Mac-ten and five shots hit Vick in the back. He crashed to the ground and began dry heaving. E-baby walked over to Vick and kicked him until he rolled off his stomach and onto his back. E-baby stood over him and without saying a word, he pulled the trigger.

Fthththththattt!

A burst of automatic gunfire hit Vick in his face, ending his existence. The other three guys stood there, completely frozen. It was as if you could hear their hearts thumping one hundred miles per second in their chests. They knew that they were next.

"Wait a minute… Keith said it was five people in the house!" Hammer said.

As soon as Hammer said that, they heard a window break from somewhere in the house. When Trigga heard the gunshots, he damn near shitted his guts out.

"What the fuck?!!" he yelled. He immediately realized it was only one way out, and that was through the bathroom window. The only problem was that he was too fat, and it was damn near impossible for him to fit through it. He knew that if he stayed in the bathroom, he would eventually be discovered and killed, so he took his chances and took off his shirt, wrapped it around his arm, and broke out the window and began to climb through it.

"It came from over here!" E-baby yelled, as he ran to the bathroom door and tried to open it. It was locked, so he began kicking it as hard as he could.

Trigga was about halfway out the window but got stuck. He could hear someone kicking on the bathroom door and he twisted and turned as much as he could, cutting the lining of his stomach on the loose shards of glass that were still stuck in the window, trying to get out before it was too late.

Across the street, Rick and Gary noticed a fat guy trying to climb out of a window on the side of the house. The light that was on the side of Trigga's spot shined on him as he struggled to free himself from the window. Gary stepped out from behind the house and took aim, but Rick said, "I got this one G," as he raised the 2-2-3 Bushmaster rifle with the scope and put Trigga in his sights.

Rick squeezed the trigger lightly and three bullets ejected from the barrel. Trigga didn't see it coming. He felt a bullet hit his arm, then his shoulder, and then his neck. Trigga was dead as he hung motionless from the window. The bathroom door flew open and E-baby just stared at the fat-ass nigga hanging halfway out of the window. When he realized he was dead, he walked away and went into the front room with Rell, Hammer, and Dolla.

First, they searched Vick and Trigga, then they searched the other three boys for money then tied them up with bedsheets, quickly ransacking the house, looking for more money and drugs. They found what looked to be around a few thousand dollars and about four and a half ounces of crack. After the extensive search, Hammer, Rell, and Dolla shot the three boys execution style.

E-baby ran outside on the porch and signaled for Gary. Gary grabbed the large gas can and ran across the street at top speed and into the house and began pouring gasoline everywhere.

"C'mon, let's be out," Hammer said, and they headed for the door.

"Wait!" Rell said as he spotted a huge machete laying up against the wall on the other side of the of the room...

CHAPTER ELEVEN

They made it back to the spot on Blackstone safely and everybody hopped out the van except E-baby.

"I gotta get rid of this van," E-baby said.

"Alright, bet. Keith, follow E-baby in your car and bring him back here once he gets rid of the stolie. After that, your job will be done," Dolla said.

E-baby pulled off and Keith followed behind him. Dolla, Rell, Hammer, Rick, and Gary walked in the spot. Krissy was sitting on the couch smoking a cigarette. When she didn't see Keith walk in with the boys, she became worried.

"Where's Keith? Did something happen to him?" Krissy asked.

"Naw, he wit E-baby, they'll be here in a minute," Gary said.

For about ten minutes, everyone just sat in complete silence, wrapped up in their own individual thoughts. Rell grabbed the bottle of liquor from the table and poured two shots back to back. Moments later, they heard firetrucks and pretty much knew where they were headed. Keith and E-baby walked through the door and the both of them poured a shot and let out a sigh of relief.

"Y'all hear them firetrucks?" E-baby asked.

"Yeah, it sound like they sent the whole fire station through this muthafucka," Rick said.

Dolla and Hammer counted the money they took off the niggaz from the spot on Burgess. It was a little over $10,000, which was a lot more money than they thought it was. Dolla and Hammer split the money with Rick, Rell, Gary, and E-baby, and gave Keith $350 and the four and a half ounces of crack they took from the house as well.

Krissy was sitting on the couch watching T.V., but as soon as she saw Keith get that four and a half, she got up and grabbed him by the hand.

"Let's go in the back and celebrate, baby," she said to him, and they disappeared into the back bedroom.

All six of the boys began rolling up blunts and pouring drinks. They'd never got a chance to formally introduce themselves to each other. It was kinda fucked up they had to meet under these circumstances. They were all just talking and getting to know each other when E-baby noticed the news was on.

"Hold up, y'all be quiet for a minute!" E-baby said, as he tuned up the volume on the T.V. set.

This is Diana Waters from Channel Four with live breaking news. I'm reporting to you from Detroit's northwest side on Fenkell and Burgess. Firefighters received a call to respond to a fire. When they arrived, they were not prepared for what they saw. They found the house engulfed in flames and on the front lawn there appeared to be two severed heads. After the fire was distinguished, authorities also found five bodies inside the house. It appears that all five of the victims are males and were fatally shot before the fire was set. Police suspect this to be a gang-related act of retaliation, but they can't officially confirm at this time. There are no witnesses or leads as of now. Authorities are labeling this "the Burgess bloodbath," and they are hopeful that someone will step forward and provide some information that will help shed some light on this brutal act of violence.

For a second, they all continued to stare in silence at the T.V. in a daze. Dolla walked over and shut it off.

"Now, let this be a lesson and a reminder of how real the shit we into can get. Them niggaz was slippin'… too comfortable. We must not allow ourselves to be sloppy like that. Money comin' in, but our lives are more important than any amount of money. As long as we still breathin', we gon' eat. Don't speak on this shit to NOBODY, I mean nobody. Matter of fact, this will be the last time we ever speak of this night. Starting tomorrow, we gonna let Krissy run the spot during the daytime and we gonna lay low for a week or two. Gary, E-baby, y'all still gonna get paid, but y'all gonna be fuckin' with our other spots. Joy Road is doing alright, but I know those spots can be doin' a lot more. We gonna spend some time building them up so they can produce some real numbers. I love y'all like brothers and we CANNOT let anyone, or anything come between us." Dolla paused and looked at each one of them to make sure his message came through loud and clear.

"No one's gonna stop us. We gonna keep getting this money until it ain't no more." They all exchanged dap, and for the rest of the night, they sat up and drank and smoked until the sun came up.

After that night, they never had problems out of anyone in that hood. Word was out. The street niggaz knew what time it was.

"Don't fuck with them Blackstone niggaz. They killin' shit."

The next day, they took Gary and E-baby over on Mettetal and introduced them to Bruce, Quick, and the big homie, Dennis. From there, they shot over to the apartments on Joy Road and Greenfield and introduced them to T-mac, Monster, and Bo. E-baby and Monster hit it off well. He saw potential in Monster and could tell he had a heart of gold.

But when he shook hands with T-mac, he immediately got a bad vibe from him. It was like E-baby could feel some sort of malice in T-mac's heart and he thought T-mac noticed it too. The whole time they were at the apartments T-mac kept his distance from E-baby. When they left,

E-baby didn't speak on the bad vibe he got from him, but he definitely kept it locked in the back of his mind.

The next day Hammer, Rick, Dolla, Rell, and T-mac spent the whole day networking. T-mac, Dolla, and Hammer hit the streets with testers for the fiends. Rick and Rell hit the streets with weed, giving away free samples to mainly bad bitches and some of the Chaldeans and Arabs that would come from Dearborn, which was less than a mile away from the spot.

Gary, E-baby, Monster, and Bo stayed behind at the apartments and caught the new customers while brandishing high-powered rifles and semi-automatic pistols to send the message that niggaz wasn't playin' no games.

When the night came, Dolla and Hammer dropped Gary and E-baby off at the spot on Blackstone. Then they stopped in the hood on Mettetal and checked on Bruce and Quick. Dolla, Hammer, and Rell all decided to meet up at club D.E.T. on Schoolcraft and Greenfield to let off some steam and have a few drinks.

When they got there, the club was packed. Bitches were everywhere and niggaz spoke and showed their respect for the boys. Throughout the club, they moved around, fucking with the hoes and just enjoying the moment. They ended up meeting a guy named Les, who co-owned a car lot on Seven Mile and Evergreen with an Arab. They got to talking, and Les convinced them to stop by the car lot in the morning.

The next day Dolla, Rell, Hammer, and Rick came to the conclusion that it was time to step their game up and each of them grabbed up $20,000 from their savings and headed up to Les's car lot. When the boys stepped in, Les could literally smell the money on them. Les spent his downtime hitting different clubs all over the city, mainly in drug-infested neighborhoods, looking for ballers like Dolla and the rest of his crew. He'd convince them to stop by the car lot and then sell them salvage title luxury vehicles.

Knowing the hustlers couldn't spend $10,000 at a time legally, he would underwrite the sales slips and charge them monthly until the car was paid off if they didn't have the cash to pay for it in one lump sum. The catch with that was, if you were one week behind on your payments, he would send a team out to repossess the car.

What the hustlers didn't know was, Les had tracking devices installed in the cars and he would not tell them until they paid the car off. Then he would have them bring the car to the lot and remove the device. A lot of hustlers knew about Les, and they knew that if you missed that payment, he was coming for his shit and there was nowhere you could hide the car from him. A few tried, but he always would find the car. Always.

"Fellas, fellas! Good to see y'all stop by!" Les said, getting up from his chair and shaking each of the boys' hands.

"We tryin' to see what you got on deck for us," Rell said.

"Oh, we got whips for days. Come with me and we'll walk through the lot and just tell me what you like."

There were all types of different cars and trucks on the large lot... Benzes, BMWs, Jaguars, Cadillacs, old schools, Audis... you name it, chances were, it was on the lot. The boys test drove a few cars and when it was all said and done, they worked a deal with Les and would end up paying a little over $100,000 for the four cars they picked.

Les bought the salvage title cars from an auction, so he'd ended up doubling his money with ease. The cars had been in accidents previously. They had minor body damage, but they didn't have any damage to the frame or engine parts. All Les had to do was fix the panels here and there and a person would never know the true history of the car. Each of the boys put $25,000 down. Les put the paperwork together and they pulled off the lot in four new cars.

They drove to the lot in Dolla's Monte Carlo and once they purchased their new cars, Dolla left his old car and told Les he would be back to pick it up later on.

"No problem, no problem. If y'all know anybody trying to spend some money for a good car, let me know!" Les said and gave a smile and a charming wink to the boys before they left. They immediately drove down the street to a rim shop and each of them paid for rims to be installed on their cars.

A few hours later and the cars were ready. They all followed each other back to Mettetal block. Quick, Bruce, and Dennis were in the spot and saw them pull up in front. They came outside to check out their new whips.

Dolla had a 2000 black Mercedes SL 500 with twenty-inch Lexani blades. Rell had a 2000 candy-apple red Corvette on some offset Asantis. Hammer had a silver 2000 Lexus RX 300 truck on some twenty-inch Davins, and Rick had a cocaine-white 2000 7-series BMW with some twenty-inch DUB edition rims.

"Damn! Y'all niggaz bossin' up!!" Quick said, as he stood back looking at the cars all parked behind each other.

"Rell, you gotta let me stunt out in the Vette one day, fam," Bruce said, sitting in the driver's seat.

"Keep doin' what you doin', and you'll have one quicker than you think," Rell said.

Dennis was impressed, to say the least.

"I gotta upgrade now. Y'all got my Caddie lookin' like a hooptie," Dennis joked.

"You already know you can get with us whenever you ready," Hammer said, dapping Dennis.

"Who knows, maybe one day I'll take y'all up on that offer," Dennis replied.

The boys spent the rest of the day riding around and checking on the spots. Rick went to pick up Gary and E-baby to drop them off at the apartments on Joy Road and Greenfield. When Rick pulled up across the street from the spot on Blackstone and told Gary and E-baby to come outside, they came out looking up and down the street for Rick and until he blew the horn. They didn't recognize him in the white-colored Beamer.

"This bitch sick! You just copped it today?" E-baby asked.

"Yeah," Rick replied modestly. He was a little uncomfortable with all the attention the car was bringing. Don't get it twisted, heads would turn when he drove his Malibu, but not like THIS.

"You don't like the whip or something?" Gary said, noticing the modest response Rick gave.

"Naw. It ain't that, my nigga. I like it and all. I just gotta get used to it," Rick said.

"Shit, if you can't get used to it, give it to me," E-baby said, laughing and elbowing Rick in his arm.

"Stack yo paper up and both of y'all will have one too, you can bet on that," Rick said sincerely.

Right before they pulled off, Krissy opened the front door.

"Ok! I see you, baby!" she yelled to Rick.

"Thanks. You straight in there?" he asked, making sure she had enough dope for the moment.

"Yeah, but I'll need more in a few hours!" Krissy said.

"Call Hammer. He got you. I'm out," Rick said, throwing the car in drive and pulling off.

"Yo, Rick. Get on a main street as quick as you can. The hook been ridin' up and down the side streets all day fuckin' wit niggaz," Gary said.

"Yeah, shit been a little hot around this bitch," E-baby added from the backseat.

The three of them knew the hood was hot because of the work they put in over on Burgess a few days ago. The last thing any real hustler wanted was violence in the neighborhood they did business in, especially murders. That type of shit brought the police to the hood, and they'd start to snoop around and flick niggaz, hoping they catch somebody with something heavy so they could try to pump information out of people. Known spots usually got raided as well, which meant money would slow up. But there was no other option; the Burgess niggaz had violated, and they had to be dealt with.

They hit Fenkell and headed to the apartments on Joy Road. Monster saw Rick pull up in front of the apartments. He didn't know it was Rick. He thought it was a custo. Monster was holding down the weed spot while Bo and T-mac were across the hall serving rocks to the fiends. Bo and T-mac were outside on the tier of the apartment talking when Rick pulled up. When T-mac saw Rick, Gary, and E-baby get out of the car, he stopped talking, mid-conversation with Bo.

Man, these niggaz eatin' for real out here, T-mac thought to himself.

"Lookin' good, bra man!" Bo said, dapping Rick. Bo was alright. Even though he got high, he cleaned up real nice, and he was thankful for the crew giving him a chance. Most of the young niggaz looked at Bo as nothing but a crackhead from the hood, but not Dolla, Hammer, Rell, or Rick. They treated him like a man - with respect, and they were paying him more than enough to support his habit and have a few dollars left over too. Things were finally looking up for Bo.

E-baby, Rick, and Bo sat and kicked it for a minute and T-mac and Gary walked across the hall to the weed spot where Monster was. Since they hit the streets and did a little "promoting" the day before, the spots were doing a lot better already. They had some of the best dope in the hood, so the fiends were coming left and right. Monster was loving the sudden increase of the female custos. The girls liked him, they all thought he was sweet, despite his appearance.

Rick went back out to the car and popped the trunk. He went under the spare tire and grabbed a plastic grocery bag full of dope and weed and ran back upstairs. The six of them stood outside on the tier and smoked two blunts. Then Rick grabbed up the money from yesterday's take and handed them the sacks, gave them all dap, and took off.

"Call me if y'all need me. Be safe," Rick said before he got in the car.

"You too, fam!" Monster yelled.

"Man, I like them niggaz," Bo said. The rest of them nodded in agreement.

"That Beamer is nice," Monster said. "All we gotta do is stay loyal and we'll be ridin' like that too, bro," E-baby said to Monster. "Just watch."

Monster looked over and saw T-mac staring into space. "You alright, Mac?" Monster asked.

"Yeah, I'm straight," T-mac said, then walked into the weed spot and closed the door behind him...

A few weeks had passed and the first of the month rolled around. That was one of the busiest days for all of the spots. On the first, the spots would do double the numbers, and the rest of that week would bang as well. Dolla was a little wound up and tense from all the shit that had taken place in the last month. He needed to get away; clear his mind. He and Savannah stayed in touch with each other on a daily basis and usually saw each other once a month, but Dolla wasn't able to make it to Lansing to see her at all last month. Today, he was gonna let Hammer, Rick, and Rell take care of things and go out to Lansing for the weekend to spend some time with his girl.

It took about an hour to drive from Detroit to Lansing, but Dolla made it there in about forty-five minutes. Once he got to the hotel, he paid for a suite for the weekend and unpacked and jumped in the shower. When he got out, he rolled up a blunt and searched for something to wear. After he dressed, he picked up his cell phone and called Savannah.

"You here, baby?" Savannah asked, excited her man finally made it. Every time he came into town, she loved to show him off to her friends, teachers, and anyone else she associated with on the college campus.

"I can't make it, boo," Dolla said.

"Whhhyyy?!" Savannah asked in shrill voice.

"I'm just playin', Vannah. I'm here already," Dolla laughed.

"Boy! You better stop playin' with me! Where you at?" she asked.

"I'm at the room, but I'm about to be on my way to you. Be ready when I get there."

"Hurry up!" Savannah said, then she hung up the phone.

It took Dolla about twenty minutes to get to Michigan State University from the hotel. As soon as he pulled up on campus, eyes were on him as he parked the big black 500 Benz. He got out the car and made his way to the dorm where Savannah lived. There were all types of women everywhere. Black, White, Asian, Spanish, all types of flavors. Dolla had to exercise the discipline of a monk to keep from staring too hard. There were eyes everywhere, and he didn't need any of Savannah's friends running back to her saying, "I saw your man drooling over some girl." Plus, Savannah could hold her own and stand next to any of the girls on campus.

He got to her room and knocked on the door. Savannah's roommate, Mary, opened the door.

"Hey, Dolla! Good to see you!"

Mary was a white girl majoring in medicine. Every time Dolla saw her, she was upbeat and in a good mood.

"What up, Mary? How you been?" Dolla asked.

"Great! I was just leaving. Savannah's in the shower. Just relax and make yourself at home," she said and walked out the door.

"I thought I told you to be ready!" Dolla yelled and plopped on the couch. *Women,* he thought to himself then pulled out some weed and began breaking it down. "Might as well roll somethin' up while I'm waiting."

When Savannah got out the shower, she put on some scented lotion with glitter in it, dried her hair, and put it in a ponytail and walked out to the living room area where Dolla was sitting on the couch watching T.V.

"Hey, baby!" she said, hopping into his lap and kissing him. Her body was so soft and smelled so good, it gave Dolla an erection instantly. The bath robe she had on hugged the contours of her hourglass figure.

"It look like you gettin' thicker, ma," Dolla said, slapping her on the ass.

"Let me light this up," Savannah said, grabbing the blunt Dolla rolled that was wedged between the side of his head and his ear. She reached into his pants pocket to grab a lighter, and in the process of doing so, she could feel the hardness of his manhood.

She looked at Dolla and he had a grin on his face. "You a freak!" she said.

"Only for you, baby. Only for you," Dolla replied.

She lit the blunt and took a pull. She only smoked when Dolla came to visit, and when he did, she would smoke all weekend. She would just unwind and take her mind off her studies. After smoking the blunt, Savannah leaned back on the couch and let her buzz kick in.

"I needed that," she said.

Dolla couldn't keep his eyes off her juicy thighs. He placed one of his hands on her leg and began to slowly roam her body.

"You better stop playin'," Savannah said in a husky tone. Ever since she felt the stiffness of Dolla's rod when she went through his pants pocket, she was secretly in heat as well.

He began kissing her on her thighs then made his way to her love button. She was dripping wet as he placed his face between her legs and began to rotate his tongue, tasting her juices. She grabbed his head gently with both hands and leaned her head back in pleasure.

"Looks like we both gonna need a shower after this," Dolla said, after raising his head up from in between her legs. She opened her robe and pulled him on top of her and they commenced to love-making.

After they took a shower together, they got dressed and headed out. When they got to the parking lot, she stopped in her tracks when she saw the brand-new Benz.

"This is yours?" she asked.

"Yep. It was time to upgrade," Dolla said.

They got in the car and headed to the Lansing Mall. On the way to the mall, Savannah was enjoying the ride in the luxury vehicle. The Benz seemed to be floating on air while they were on the freeway. They hit a few bumps on the way and she didn't feel a thing when they ran over the small potholes.

I gotta get me one of these when I finish school, she thought to herself.

Dolla gave her $3,000 and told her to get whatever she wanted. He followed her around to different clothing and shoe stores while she bought all different types of stuff. Most niggaz didn't like going with their girlfriends shopping, but Dolla didn't mind. He got a kick out of watching her bounce around through the stores with a smile on her face. He was glad to be away from the city for the weekend. Lansing was more laid back than Detroit, and he didn't have to constantly look over his shoulder. He didn't even have to bring his pistol with him, even though he had it stashed in a hidden compartment in his car. Make no mistake about it, Lansing had some rough areas, but it wasn't like the city. Crime seemed to plague Detroit as a whole. Everywhere you went, shit was fucked up.

After shopping, they stopped at an Italian restaurant nearby the mall and grabbed a bite to eat. The waiter took their orders and Dolla also ordered a bottle of Dom Perrigan. The waiter checked Dolla's fake I.D., then he turned to Savannah. Before she even had a chance to speak, Dolla said to the waiter, "It's disrespectful to ask a woman her age," and gave the waiter a grim look. The waiter got the hint and apologized and walked away. He quickly returned with the bottle of champagne in a bucket of ice along with two crystal glasses. He popped the cork and filled each glass with the expensive champagne.

"Your food will be out shortly," he said and excused himself from the table. Dolla and Savannah toasted glasses and tasted the champagne.

"Now this is what all the hustling is for right here," Dolla said, holding the glass to the light, examining its contents.

Savannah frowned and sat her glass down on the table.

"What's wrong, baby? You don't like the champagne?" Dolla asked.

"No, it's not that," Savannah said, circling the tip of her finger around the lip of her glass.

"You wanna let me know what's goin' on then??" Dolla asked, but it sounded more like an order.

"Dolla, I love you and I'm thankful to have you in my life. I don't know what I would do without you. I want you to be the father of my children and my husband someday. Baby, you can't sell drugs forever. It's only going to end up two ways: with you either in prison or you getting killed. I want you to think about something you enjoy doing besides selling drugs and invest some money into it. You're making some good money right now, but who knows what could happen in the future. Now is the time you should be setting something up so, if things start to go bad, you'll be prepared."

Dolla didn't say anything, but deep down, he knew she was right. If he didn't start investing some of his money into something legit, he would end up just like the majority of the hustlers that came and went generations before him; washed up. He was getting used to touching large amounts of money and he needed to make sure that never changed.

"Do you hear me talking to you?" Savannah asked, snapping Dolla from his thoughts.

Dolla looked up and saw a tear roll down Savannah's cheek. "Awww, don't do that," Dolla said, getting up from his chair.

He walked over to Savannah and placed one hand under her chin and wiped the tear from her face with his free hand.

"Listen, I love you and you WILL be the mother of my children and my wife, and I give you my word that I will come up with a legitimate business plan. I'm gonna start taking steps to invest my money into something as soon as I get back to the city," Dolla said as he kissed her softly on the cheek.

What Dolla said was like music to Savannah's ears. The food arrived, and they enjoyed their meal, talking about future baby names. When they were finished eating, Dolla paid the tab and tipped the waiter handsomely. They were stuffed. The lasagna Dolla ordered tasted better than any lasagna he had ever eaten before, and Savannah had also enjoyed the chicken alfredo she ordered. The red velvet cake they had for desert topped it off.

After leaving from the restaurant, they went to the park and smoked a few blunts and then took a long walk.

"What you wanna do next?" Dolla asked. Whenever Dolla was in Lansing, he would have the most fun. Going out to the club with the fellas and stunting out was fun too, but being in Lansing, he would also get a peace of mind and relaxation as well.

"Ummmm, let's see… I know! There's a carnival in town, let's go there!" Savannah suggested.

"That's what's up. I ain't been to a carnival since I was a lil' nigga," Dolla said.

"It's about fifteen minutes from here," Savannah estimated. "Let's go now!"

By the time they made it to the carnival, their buzz from the blunts they smoked at the park was at its peak. The moment they stepped foot on the grounds they, immediately ordered some elephant ears and cotton candy. Dolla and Savannah played every game the carnival had, from basketball to knocking over the bottles to squirting water at the target until the balloon swells up and pops. They came across a game that required shooting a little red star with a BB gun, and if done in a certain amount of time and ammo, one would receive a prize. Dolla noticed two bears that were stuck together in a kissing formation by magnet that he wanted to win for Savannah.

"Step right up! Step right up! Hit the target, get a prize! One dollar!" the fat white guy said, trying to lure Dolla to the booth. Dolla stepped up and paid the man.

"This gonna be easy," Dolla said to Savannah, picking up the air-powered BB gun.

Fifteen dollars later, Dolla still had not won the prize. He damn near blew his high trying to shoot that red star.

"C'mon, baby. Let's do something else. You know these games be rigged anyway," Savannah said.

"Hold on, not yet. I think I got this thing figured out," Dolla said, refusing to give up.

He noticed that the BBs would veer to the left when shot from the gun, so he didn't aim directly at the target but slightly to the right and pulled the trigger. This time, he hit the target, erasing the red star from sight.

"I got it! I got that bitch!" Dolla said, thrusting his fist into the air.

"Winner! Winner!" the man shouted, trying to gain the attention of the others passing by the booth.

"Pick a prize!"

"Gimme them kissing bears," Dolla said, pointing.

The man reached and pulled the bears off the shelf and handed them to Dolla.

"Good lookin'," Dolla said, grabbing the bears.

Dolla's chest was poked out as if he was a hunter that went out to the forest and killed a lion and brought it back home to his family for food.

"Here you go, baby," he said, handing Savannah the bears.

"Thank you!" Savannah said. She gave Dolla a sloppy kiss on the face then stuffed her prize inside her large designer purse. After that, they must have ridden every ride in the carnival at least three times. Dolla and Savannah both felt like kids again as they ran around the park from ride to ride.

They left from the park and stopped at the liquor store. Dolla bought two bottles of Moët, a pack of cigarettes, a box of condoms, and a box of blunts. When they got back to the room, Dolla fired up the jacuzzi and rolled up a few blunts. Savannah grabbed two glasses and set them alongside the jacuzzi with the bottles of champagne. They both stripped out of their clothes and climbed into the jacuzzi. Dolla grabbed one of the bottles of Moët and popped the cork. He filled both the glasses and handed one to Savannah.

"A toast to us," Dolla said, raising his glass.

"To us," Savannah said and clicked glasses with Dolla.

She was thankful to have a guy like Dolla in her life. She loved everything about him. He was smart, confident, gangsta, and goal-oriented. Not to mention, she loved his tall, dark, slender frame. His hazel brown eyes really set it off as well.

They drank, smoked, and fucked like animals all night long until they passed out from sexual exhaustion. The next day, they didn't even leave the room. They ordered room service for breakfast and ordered pizza for dinner. They sat and watched movies, smoked, drank and made love the entire day. The old saying is true, "time flies when you're having fun."

Dolla had to get back to the city and Savannah had to get back to the campus to get ready for class which began early Monday morning. He dropped her off at the college and they reluctantly parted ways.

"Call me later and let me know you made it back safe," Savannah said.

"I will," Dolla replied and leaned over and kissed her.

She got out of the car and walked off headed for her dorm. He hated to see her go, but on the flip side of things, being apart from each other only strengthened their bond and also kept them focused on their goals for the future.

Once Dolla got back to the city, he called up Gordo. The crew needed to re-up except this time, Rick drove the same van that Gordo gave them that was full of guns. They took the van to their neighborhood collision shop and had the ceiling inside slightly lowered. When they would turn the ignition key forward, hit the brake pedal twice, and hit the windshield fluid button, the ceiling would drop, revealing a stash spot for the drugs.

After leaving from seeing Gordo, they had a hundred pounds of weed and twenty kilos of pure cocaine. They stashed the drugs at Dennis's for safe keeping. Dolla took two bricks and left from Dennis's house, headed to the spot on Blackstone.

Rick stayed behind at Dennis's house and took three pounds and broke them down into dime bags. Dolla met up with Krissy on

Blackstone and let her do her thing in the kitchen with the bricks and kicked it with E-baby and Gary in the living room, smoking blunts. Once Krissy was done, Dolla took nine ounces to the spot on Joy Road.

When he pulled up, he looked in his rear-view mirror and saw Rick pulling up behind him. They walked up to the apartments and Rick dropped off a pound and a half to Monster who was posted in the weed spot. Dolla walked over to the dope spot and Bo, Hammer, and T-mac were posted up, kicking it. He dropped off the nine ounces of crack and told Hammer to swing over on Blackstone and grab the rest of the dope and take it to Victoria's house. Hammer got up and dapped Bo and T-mac, then left headed to Blackstone.

Dolla stayed at the weed spot and kicked it with Monster. Rick left and went to the spot on Mettetal to lend Bruce and Quick a hand. Rick, Quick, and Bruce became close because Rick was at the spot with them most of the time. E-baby and Monster talked on the phone daily and hung out together whenever they had free time. Hammer, Bo, and T-mac were close, and Dolla, Gary, and Rell clicked as well. They were one big happy family.

Once a month, they would rent a limo or party bus and load as many bitches as they could and go out. Quick and Bruce were too young to get in the club, so they would take the limo and cruise around downtown until everyone else got out of the club. They would rent a few rooms for the night and would spend the night drinking, smoking, and fucking the girls they brought with them.

Dennis wasn't really into the club scene, so he would hold the spot down on Mettetal for them. Bo would hold down the apartments on Joy Road. He would have to do a lot of running back and forth between both spots, but he didn't mind. He was getting paid double, so he actually looked forward to when they would have their once-a-month outing. Krissy would post up in the spot on Blackstone.

Everything was going smooth as silk for Dolla, Hammer, Rick, and Rell. Rick and Rell both ended up moving into the apartments on Greenfield and Eaton, and they were staying across the hall from each other. They also rented an apartment in the same complex and used it as a stash house for their guns and drugs. They would leave a little something at Dennis's house too, but the majority of the drugs were in the apartment.

They personally made stash spots inside the apartment and had several hidden surveillance cameras installed as well. Only Hammer, Rell, Rick, Dolla, and Dennis knew the stash house existed. Dolla had an apartment on Seven Mile and Telegraph, and Hammer chose to stay with his mom on Mettetal. He tried to offer her the chance to move into a new house in the neighborhood of her choice, but she declined. She liked her house and didn't want to move to a different area.

The boys also bought four used minivans from Les to move around in while they were grinding throughout the day. Dennis brought up a point that it didn't look good pulling up in front of different spots with Benzes and BMWs. It only made the boys stand out. That way if anyone was watching, they wouldn't be able to tell who was the boss or who was the customer.

Dolla called Rell, Hammer, and Rick up and suggested that they get some ice from the jewelry store in Hamtrammack on the east side of the city. The four of them met at the jewelry store. When they walked in, the first thing Dolla did was talk to the owner and told him they planned to spend a large amount of money. The owner immediately closed the store and locked the front door, preventing anyone from entering while he served the boys.

All the niggaz that was getting money knew about this particular jewelry store, so did all the jack boys. The owner didn't mind buying stolen jewelry from the jack boys either. He would sell all his jewelry for the lows, and they were all certified. The boys purchased iced-out Rolex watches, platinum diamond chains, and four three-carat diamond rings, totaling just a little under $70,000. The store owner even threw in four pairs of iced-out Cartier glasses for free to show his appreciation for their business.

After leaving the jewelry store, they went to a Coney Island restaurant for a bite to eat. They sat back and stuffed their faces, talking about different girls they were fucking and different hoods they wanted to open up shop in. They were making a lot of money… so much money that they were constantly looking for different ways and things to spend it on.

"Let me holla at y'all for a minute," Dolla said, cutting them off from the conversation they were having.

"Listen, we want to keep this money comin' in and try to make a way where our money can't be taken from us. As of right now, if the hook was to catch us slippin', there's a possibility that they can take everything from us that took us years to build. Basically, what I'm saying is that we need to start washing our money through some legit business investments.

"What you got in mind?" Rick asked Dolla.

"Well, what we need to do is think about what we like. It's no secret that we like to sell shit, but just take some time to think of something you would like to sell that's legit. Instead of just blowin' our money, for the next two months, we should let it stack and then we can start to make our ideas come to life."

"That's what's up, my nigga. My momma gonna be proud of me," Hammer said.

"Shit, she already is, nigga. Trust me," Rell said.

CHAPTER TWELVE

They spent the next two months grinding hard. Gary turned the crew on to a team of niggaz from the Mo' (Brightmoor), that respected their movement. They had a spot off of Schoolcraft and Chapel, right next to the I-96 freeway. They had customers that were coming from Redford, which was a suburban neighborhood about two miles away from their spot. Their plug got knocked and they needed a new connect.

Gary introduced Dolla to the niggaz and from there, they began copping from the boys through Gary. The only catch was, the niggaz couldn't purchase the cocaine in powder form. It would already be cooked up for them. Even though Dolla had Krissy step on the dope twice, it still was a lot better than the dope the Chapel niggaz was getting from their previous plug.

They were copping two bricks a week and they were paying $23,000 per brick, which wasn't too bad. Bricks were going for twenty-eight to $30,000 at the time, so they were winning all the way around the board. Hammer also met a nigga from Joy Road between Southfield and Evergreen named Maine, who was running through a brick a week with ease.

Monster was fucking a bitch in his hood and one day they crossed paths and blew a few blunts and kicked it. Through conversation, they found out they were both in the same business. Monster would sell bricks for $25,000, pocketing the extra $2,000. Maine would also cop a few pounds of weed here and there for $1,000 a pop. Hammer would let Monster sell all the work to Maine, being that Monster introduced Hammer to Maine.

All of Dolla, Rick, Rell, and Hammer's soldiers were doing good too. Their pockets stayed on full. Through Les, E-baby copped a dawg-ass, cocaine-white 1996 Impala SS. Gary had a green Chevy Tahoe on twenty-inch rims. Monster bought a 1997 navy blue Range Rover, and Hammer helped T-mac buy a black 1999 Acura Legend. The car had low miles on it and was basically brand new. Quick bought a tan 1986 Regal on some twenty-inch chrome Daytons, and Bruce purchased a sky-blue Delta 88 sitting on some twenty-inch blades. Even Bo bought a 1996 Cadillac STS from Les.

Everybody on the team was eating, each one a boss in their own way. Dolla, Rell, Hammer, and Rick treated them all fair, even though sometimes, T-mac would complain to Monster about one thing or another. Monster would remind him of how they both were struggling before Rick put them on their feet, but the way T-mac saw it, HE put the boys on their feet.

"See, you let them niggaz take advantage of you. You never was smart. You don't know how to think. When my brother get home, he gon' show niggaz how to ball," T-mac would always say to Monster.

Monster loved his friend, but he was getting tired of T-mac talking down to him, calling him dumb and stupid. It seemed like the closer T-mac's brother got to getting released from prison and the little bit of money he was making, the more it was all going to his head.

Another month had passed and Dolla was ready to go see Savannah in Lansing, but this month things were gonna go a little different. A few weeks prior, Dolla wrote his father and told him that he wanted to visit him and that he wanted to bring his girlfriend and introduce her to him.

Dolla had Savannah fill out a visitor form and she mailed it to the prison. It took a week and a half for the authorities to approve her application.

Dolla picked up Savannah and they stopped at a supermarket and grabbed a few items for their short trip. Dolla's father was housed in USP Allenwood, a high-security prison located in White Deer, Pennsylvania. Coming from Michigan, it was about a six-and-a-half-hour drive. Dolla left from Detroit, headed to Lansing at about 7:00 a.m. and made it in about an hour. They left from Savannah's dorm at about 9:30 a.m. and made it to the prison a little after 5:00 that evening.

When they pulled up and parked in the parking lot, the heavily gated prison and all the barbed wire surrounding it instantly intimidated Savannah, sending a chill down her spine. The both of them used eyedrops to clear the redness from their eyes from the blunt they'd smoked a half hour prior to their arrival. Dolla sprayed on some cologne and Savannah lightly sprayed on some perfume so no one would smell any smoke on their clothes.

They both got out of the car and Dolla lit up a cigarette as the two of them walked hand-in-hand to the front entrance of the prison. Dolla was a little nervous. It had been a few years since the last time he'd seen his father. He was at Schuykill FCI, which was about two hours away from Allenwood USP about three years ago, but his father kept getting into fights and threatening staff. As a result, he kept losing his visitation privileges and was transferred to a United States Penitentiary.

Before they were able to enter the visitation area, they were thoroughly searched by officers and had to walk through metal detectors. Once inside, they sat down and waited for Dolla's father, Dante' Jones, to be called to the area. The visitation area was packed with people visiting their incarcerated loved ones. Women, children, and men of all ages and different nationalities were there to show support and spend a little time with their loved ones who were on lockdown.

After about ten minutes of waiting, Dante' entered the area wearing a neatly-ironed, khaki outfit and some federal-issued boots, shined to perfection. It was as if Dolla and Savannah were staring in a mirror, looking at Dolla thirty years into the future. Dolla and Savannah both stood up and Dolla hugged his father and shook his hand.

"What's up, son?" Dante' asked Dolla.

"Nothin'. Just came up to see you, now that you can get visits again," Dolla replied.

"Ahh, and this young lady must be Savannah, my future daughter-in-law."

Savannah smiled and began to blush.

"Why hello, beautiful. It's nice to finally meet you," Dante' said, extending his hand.

"Likewise," Savannah said shaking his hand.

They sat down and talked, catching up on the time they hadn't seen or heard from each other, eating snacks and drinking sodas from the vending machines.

"So, you fuck with Gordo, huh?"

Dante's question caught Dolla off guard. He didn't know what to say. He just sat there, dumbfounded.

"Listen, Darin. Just because I'm locked up, don't think I don't know what's going on out there. Plus, it ain't hard to tell you out there hustling. The Rolex flooded with diamonds and the diamond ring are a dead giveaway too, son."

"Yeah," Dolla said holding his head down, sliding a small pebble around the floor with his foot.

"I created you, so I know what's in your blood. I just want you to be careful. Gordo's alright, but he's the type that will try to keep you owing him favors. Whatever you do, make sure you pay for your shit with your money and don't accept too many "blessings" or "gifts" from him. Ya dig? I don't want you to end up like me, rotting away in prison or dying from this drug shit. Be smarter than me. Plan ahead and save as much money as you can so you can walk away from this shit in one piece."

Dolla told his father about how he was going to open a few businesses in the next month or so. Dante' was impressed with his son's ambition and intentions, but he knew that the road to hell was paved with good intentions as well.

"That's what's up. Just make sure you execute your plans. Don't wait until it's too late, son. Learn from my mistakes. By me waiting too late and staying in the drug game, I was snatched away from you by these fuckin' feds and your mother."

Dante's words trailed off. He covered his face with his hands, trying to hide the shame and the grief.

"Just know that if you fuck up, not only does it affect you, it affects your loved ones as well. It's so many snitches out there nowadays, you GOTTA keep your circle small as possible and keep your grass cut low so you can see the snakes... So, tell me a little about yourself, Savannah. How did you and my knucklehead-ass son meet?"

Savannah told him how she and Dolla met and a little about her family history and how she was majoring in criminal law with the hopes of having her own law firm in the future.

"Wow. Beauty and brains. Boy, you better not mess this up with this young lady or we gonna fight. Ya hear me?" Dante' said, putting up his fists.

Dante' and Dolla looked like twins apart from the small patch of gray hair on the top of Dante's head and his massive frame. He was in better shape than most guys in their early twenties and had to smash a few young niggaz who thought they were tough throughout the years of his tour through the Federal Bureau of Prisons.

They sat and talked for about four hours. They talked about all types of things. Dante' had Savannah's full attention as he talked about his rise to power in the streets. Dolla was proud of his father, despite the fact that he had to spend the rest of his life in prison. When it was time to go, they embraced each other and Dolla promised he would visit more often.

On the way back to Lansing, Dolla let Savannah drive. He was deep in his own thoughts. He sat back and stared at her as she drove and sang along with the radio, completely unaware that he was watching her. Dolla cracked a smile. He thought about what his father had said, and he didn't want to do anything to hurt her. He knew what he had to do, and that was invest his money into some type of legitimate business. He was always gonna hustle, but he wanted to eventually fade into the background and only deal with the plug and let his niggaz run the streets. Dolla stayed in Lansing for the night and left early that next morning headed back to Detroit.

Over the next few weeks, everything moved like clockwork. Mettetal was doing good. In fact, the daily intake increased, bringing in an extra $500. Blackstone was killing 'em. That was the busiest spot of them all.

The neighborhood had finally cooled down. The murders on Burgess soon faded into a distant memory for most of the people in the community, but for the niggaz in the street, it was a constant reminder, just in case anybody thought about fucking with the team of niggaz on Blackstone.

The weed spot on Joy Road was almost running neck and neck with the one on Mettetal. Monster had a knack for dealing with the customers. The crack spot was doing numbers too. Bo and T-mac were running that bitch in a militant manner. They had the fiends in check and no one in that hood dared to oppose them. They brandished fully automatic assault rifles with thirty round clips, so everyone in that hood knew what time it was. Fuck with them niggaz in the apartments on Joy road and Greenfield if you want, you'll end up in the dirt...

After doing some consulting with Dennis, the boys were ready to open some legitimate business up. They were excited. It felt like nothing could stop them. The whole crew decided to celebrate, so they let Krissy, Dennis, and Bo hold down the spots and they drove downtown to Belle Isle, a public park where people from all over the city would come out to stunt, barbeque, drink, smoke, and just wild out.

They stopped at the liquor store and grabbed up boxes of blunts and a variety of different liquors, a few stacks of red cups, and a few bags of ice. When they crossed the Belle Isle bridge and hit the strip, bitches were all in, staring at the fleet of luxury vehicles and old schools on rims. Even the niggaz was staring too. Each of the boys had their sounds slapping, setting off car alarms left and right. It was as if the street was vibrating under them.

They found a space big enough for all of them to park alongside each other. Once parked, they popped their trunks and began opening bottles and rolling blunts. As expected, it didn't take long for girls to begin flocking towards where the crew was parked. Even a few stray niggaz made their way over to them. They were showing love, passing blunts left and right. Everybody had a cup with something in it.

The crew felt like they were on top of the world. They started from the ground up and built a strong team and empire. Now they were graduating to the next level; entrepreneurship.

They stayed at the park until the police closed it down around nine. From there, they headed to a club not too far from the park. Quick and Bruce met two young chicks and Rell followed them to a motel on Jefferson and booked a room for them. The rest of the crew hit the club and were dressed to the nines. Dolla, Hammer, Rell, and Rick were iced out. Their diamond chains, rings, and watches were flickering different colors, literally glowing in the dark.

Even though they still had unopened liquor in their cars, they bought enough bottles of champagne from the bar so everybody in the crew had one wrapped in their palms. They took pictures and each of the fellas had several different phone numbers from girls trying to put their bids in with the crew. It was as if the girls could smell the money, not to mention, the jewelry and the way they were dressed spoke for itself.

A month later Dolla, Rick, Hammer, and Rell opened up a barbershop named "Royal Cuts" and a clothing store called "Royal

Fashions". Three months after that, they opened a beauty and nail shop called "Royal Treatment", a car wash called "Royal Wash", and a penny candy store called "Sweet Dreams".

Rick's sister, Rita, ran the beauty salon, Rell ran the clothing store, Dolla ran the barbershop, and Hammer ran the car wash. Dennis helped run the candy store and he also helped oversee all of the businesses. In return, the boys gave him a small percentage from each of the businesses. They had a lot of love for Dennis, and they wanted him to be a part of whatever they had their hands in.

They also owned several homes that they rented out to Section 8, low-income families. The state paid the majority of the rent, and the tenants had to pay between fifty to $100 a month. They hired managers to help run the stores and people from the inner city to work for them.

They didn't quite realize it, but the boys were helping create an economy within some of the roughest neighborhoods on the west side of Detroit. They were giving people a chance to have something to look forward to other than food stamps and a welfare check once a month. They advertised their businesses through the radio and by passing out small flyers.

After a few months, they had a full return on the money they'd invested, and now, they were making all profit. Savannah was proud of Dolla. He kept his word about investing his money, and now he was making a contribution to changing the communities. She knew he would always have one foot in the streets, but at least he was doing something positive as well. She finally introduced him to her parents, and they were impressed that a young man such as Dolla was level-headed and business oriented.

The year was coming to an end, and winter was in full effect. During the annual clothing drive called Coats for Kids, Dolla, Hammer, Rell and Rick donated $15,000 to help needy kids. They felt good on the inside and knew how it was to struggle and how hard it was for single parent mothers to raise their children.

After a long day of checking the stores and the spots, Dolla headed home after stopping at the bank to deposit the store's take, when he got a call from Gordo.

"G! What up doe, baby?"

Dolla and Gordo had become close over time. They had earned each other's trust, not to mention millions of dollars. The crew was running through twenty bricks and damn near a hundred pounds a month.

"Come to the club. We need to talk," Gordo said.

"Everything straight?" Dolla asked.

"Just get here as soon as you can," Gordo said, then hung up the phone.

At the time, Dolla was pulling into his apartment complex, but after hearing the urgency in Gordo's voice, he turned around and headed to Southwest Detroit.

When Dolla got to the club, he walked in and saw Gordo sitting alone at a table, drinking Tequila. This was the first time he'd seen Gordo without men surrounding him, but he knew that someone was keeping an eye on him, even though Dolla didn't see anyone in sight.

The club was surprisingly slow. It wasn't as packed as usual.

"What's up? Is there a problem?" Dolla asked, taking a seat across from Gordo.

"Actually, there is a problem, and I need a favor from you," Gordo said, frowning his thick eyebrows.

"I'm here for you, Gordo. Just tell me what the deal is so we can handle the issue," Dolla said with concern.

"My brother, Ernesto, runs things in Arizona. He's the one who receives the product from our uncles in Mexico and is responsible for delivering the product to me. He has a problem with a man by the name of Phelipe'. Phelipe' operates in the Midwest as well, and he and my brother were once friends and associates. They ended up having a few differences and went their separate ways. Now Phelipe' feels like my brother owes him something and has made a few attempts on his life.

Phelipe' has gone into hiding, but we have someone in his organization on our payroll and is also in a compromising position with us."

"How y'all know he ain't playin' both sides of the fence?" Dolla asked.

"Because we have his daughter, and until Phelipe' is eliminated, he won't get her back," Gordo said without the slightest bit of emotion. He paused to see if Dolla had any more questions. After he saw Dolla had none, he continued.

"The person on the inside knows where Ernesto is located. The problem is, we can't send anyone from Arizona. It's too risky. Phelipe' knows everyone down there and is well connected, so by sending a stranger from out of town would be less suspicious. That's where you come in. We must seize the opportunity now, so I'm going to book you a first-class ticket to Phoenix. You will be leaving tomorrow morning. Upon your arrival, someone will be waiting for you and will take you to my brother."

"Alright. I got you," Dolla replied.

"Phelipe' must be terminated. I am counting on you, Dolla," Gordo said sternly.

Dolla poured a shot of Tequila and downed it.

"Say no more. I'll take care of him personally," Dolla said, looking Gordo straight in the eye.

The two shook hands firmly and Dolla left the club and headed back to the hood.

On the way back, he called Rell, Hammer, and Rick and told them to meet him at Dennis's house. As soon as Dolla turned on Mettetal, he saw their cars parked in front of Hammer's mother's house. When he entered Dennis's house, he damn near caught a contact high from all the weed smoke that was in the air.

He greeted everyone with daps then grabbed a lit blunt from Dennis and took a heavy drag and blew the smoke from his nostrils.

"That was right on time," Dolla said.

"What's up, bro? What's the sudden meeting about?" Rell asked.

Rell knew that whenever a meeting was called unexpectedly, it usually meant bodies were about to drop. Dolla told them about the meeting with Gordo and the fact that he had to leave on a plane to Phoenix the next morning. He gave them specific instructions on how to handle things in case something went wrong, and he didn't make it back.

"I think we should go with you on this one," Hammer suggested.

"Naw, I gotta take care of this on a solo," Dolla replied.

They all talked and smoked a few more blunts before Dolla left to go home.

"I gotta bounce, y'all. I wanna get some rest before I get on that plane. Thanks for coming."

"Thanks for coming? Nigga, we family. Ain't no need for all that extra shit," Rick said.

"Yeah, you right about that. Hey, can you swoop me up and take me to the airport?" Dolla asked Rick.

"Fa sho. I got you," Rick said.

Dolla left and made it to his apartment in less than fifteen minutes. He stuck his key in the door and turned the lock and walked into his apartment. He loved how quiet and peaceful his apartment complex was. He rarely ever saw his neighbors and whenever he did, they just spoke and kept it moving. He took a few shots of brandy and jumped in the shower. After that, he packed a suitcase with some clothes and hygiene products then climbed into bed. He had a light buzz from the blunts he'd smoked earlier, along with the four shots he just drank.

"Phoenix, here I come," he said then drifted off to sleep…

CHAPTER THIRTEEN

Terre Haute United States Penitentiary, located in Terre Haute, Indiana, housing some of the world's most dangerous criminals; a high-security level prison and where T-mac's brother, J-rock, had been locked up for the past eight and a half years. J-rock and his little brother damn near looked like twins, even though they had a fifteen-year age difference. He and J-rock were both small, except J-rock was about five feet eight, and weighed about 155 pounds.

J-rock wasn't able to sleep the night before, and that's because today would be his last day behind a barbed wire fence. He was ready to hit the streets and get back to the money. Most of his crew had caught cases and were in jail, so he would have to rebuild a team. Even though he'd lost contact with friends over time, his brother had been bringing him up to speed on what had been going on in the streets for the last two years.

When J-rock left the streets, his little brother was eight years old. Now, his brother was making a couple of dollars out there. He'd planned to take his brother under his wing and take control of the hood. Even though he had been gone for almost ten years, he was considered to be a living legend and niggaz in the streets still had love and respect for him.

It was four o' clock in the morning, and he was already dressed and packed up. He looked in the mirror and took his dreads down from a ponytail and let them hang down over his shoulders. The C.O. opened the cell doors at six in the morning and breakfast was served at the chow hall at six thirty. J-rock walked down to the chow hall, but he didn't eat. Instead, he kicked it with a few of his homies. After they closed the chow hall, he went back to his unit and watched some T.V.

"Ritz! 47344-039, report to R and D!" the C.O. announced over the intercom.

J-rock had been waiting to hear those words for the last eight and a half years, and now it was here. He jumped up and grabbed his prison I.D., dapped everybody in his unit, and walked out, headed to R and D. It took them about two and a half hours to process him. They gave him a bus ticket and $100. He didn't have to stay at a halfway house. He chose to max out his time so he wouldn't have to go through that for the first six months of his release.

"Ritz! The van is parked out front, let's go!" the white heavyset C.O. barked to J-rock.

He was dressed in blue jeans and a white polo shirt, and a tan colored jacket they provided him with, along with the gym shoes he'd bought from the commissary. The C.O. walked him to the front door and let J-rock out.

"Take care of yourself out there, Ritz," the C.O. said to J-rock, but he didn't respond.

He walked to the white van and climbed in.

"On your way home, huh?" the driver said.

He was an older inmate from the prison camp and had a job driving newly released inmates to the bus station. In order to have a job as a driver, you had to have two years or less and be at the prison camp.

"Yeah, I'm out this bitch," J-rock said.

J-rock and the driver made small talk until they reached the bus station. It took about thirty minutes to reach the terminal. Once they arrived, J-rock hopped out and walked into the station. He looked at his ticket and noticed that his bus wouldn't be departing for another forty-five minutes, so he decided to walk across the street to the liquor store. He purchased a pack of cigarettes and a half pint of vodka and a small bottle of orange juice. J-rock blessed the bottle then cracked it open. He poured out a small amount in memory of his dead homies and the ones on lockdown, then took a swallow of the vodka straight.

He swallowed the warm liquid, shaking his head from side to side. He'd forgotten how strong vodka was. He opened the orange juice and poured out a little over half of its contents, then added the vodka and shook it up. He opened the pack of cigarettes and put one in his mouth and lit it. He took a pull and inhaled and exhaled the nicotine smoke slowly through his nostrils. The robust menthol flavor gave him a head rush almost instantly. He'd only smoked in prison occasionally, so his lungs weren't quite used to tobacco smoke.

By the time the bus was ready to depart, he was buzzin' hard from the liquor. He boarded with the other passengers and found a seat in the back next to a skinny red head white girl who looked to be in her early twenties.

"Hey, my name is Brandy," the white girl said, extending her hand.

This bitch friendly than a muthafucka, J-rock thought to himself.

"I'm J-rock," he said and shook her hand.

"If you don't mind, can I get the window seat?'" J-rock asked.

"Sure!" Brandy said and got up and slid her slender frame across J-rock before he even thought about getting up from his seat.

She didn't have much of an ass, but she had a nice set of titties on her. J-rock's dick got hard instantly as she passed him, and her breast were merely inches from his face. If he would have as so much as sneezed, his face would have been buried in the crease of her cleavage. They switched seats and J-rock took another sip of the vodka and orange juice and stared out the window as the bus pulled out of the terminal.

"Can I have a sip of that, J-rock?" Brandy asked.

"Some of what?" J-rock asked confused.

"That," Brandy said, pointing to the bottle of orange juice.

J-rock shrugged his shoulders, "Sure," he said and handed her the bottle.

She took a large gulp and handed him the bottle back.

"Mmmm… Is that gin or vodka?" Brandy asked.

"Vodka," J-rock responded dryly.

"You're not from around here, are you?" Brandy continued.

"Naw, I just got out of prison," J-rock said and turned and looked at her dead in the face.

She was beginning to irritate him with all her questions, and he thought that if he mentioned that, it would scare the shit outta her and then maybe she would shut the fuck up.

"Oh my. How long were you locked up?"

"Almost ten years," J-rock answered.

"Wow, that's a long time… no freedom, no woman. My parents live in this town. I live in the next town over with my friend. I just came to visit for the weekend."

J-rock didn't respond. He just stared out the window.

Maybe if I just ignore this bitch, she'll get the message," he thought.

Brandy had never been this close to a black man before, not to mention, a black person period. There were no Blacks in her town or the town she was from. The only time she saw Blacks was on T.V. and porno flicks.

She was looking at him while he was looking out the window and wondered if he had a big dick like the black men she would masturbate to on the porno flicks. Her pussy was getting wet.

"J-rock," Brandy said in a husky voice and tapped his shoulder.

He turned and looked at her without saying a word.

"Thanks for giving me some of your drink. Now let me give you a little something," she said and placed her hand on his upper thigh right to his dick.

He looked down at her hand, then looked her in the face. He wanted to say something, but at the moment, he couldn't speak. It had been years since he had been this close to a woman. His heart was thumping in his chest like a drum. He quickly opened the orange juice bottle and took a huge swallow of the vodka. She put her coat over her head and placed her head in his lap. She then unzipped his pants and pulled his dick out.

Wow, it looks just like the ones on the porno flicks, she thought to herself.

J-rock was looking around to see if anybody was watching them, but no one was paying attention. All of a sudden, he felt the warmth and wetness from her mouth and leaned back and closed his eyes. Twenty minutes later, he was filling her mouth up with cum.

Brandy wished she could feel him on the inside of her and was tempted to ask him to come spend the night with her, but she knew that wouldn't be possible. The white men in her small town would have hung both J-rock and Brandy the minute they were spotted together. She put his dick back inside of his pants and lifted her head up.

"Did you like that?" Brandy asked him.

"Yeah, ma. That shit was straight," J-rock replied.

She literally sucked the energy out of him.

"Welcome home," Brandy said and cracked a smile.

Welcome home... Those words swirled around in his mind. He couldn't wait to get home. First thing he wanted to do was hug his mother and spend some time with her. Then he wanted to get some pussy. After that, he was gonna link up with his brother and start the beginning of the rebirth of his drug empire. He closed his eyes and fell asleep...

Rick dropped off Dolla at Metro Airport at about 6:45 a.m. They blew two blunts on the way to the airport, so Dolla was already in the clouds. Gordo told him to be there at least an hour before his flight left, just in case it was crowded, so Dolla made it about an hour and forty-five minutes early.

He waited in line and when he got to the counter, he told the attendant that he had a ticket reserved under the name of Darin Jones. The attendant asked him for his I.D. Once she had it, she typed something into the computer and printed out his ticket and handed it to him. After that, he had to stand in line and go through the security check. They took all of his hygiene products, so after he got through security, he grabbed up some travel size hygiene products, some gum, and a few other snacks.

This was his first time flying, and an older white man he was in line with suggested he buy some gum. He told Dolla it would help keep his ears from popping due to the rise in altitude. He sat in the boarding area until it was time for his plane to depart. Once they started boarding, they asked for all the first-class passengers to board first. People started getting up and passing the flight attendant after showing her their tickets.

"Mr. Darin Jones, please board the plane," he heard his name over the intercom.

Why are they calling me? Dolla thought, as he approached the attendant and handed her his ticket.

"You may board," the attendant said politely and handed him his ticket back.

The stewardess greeted him with a warm smile.

"Ummm, can you tell me where my seat is?" Dolla asked the stewardess.

"Let's see here," she said, looking at Dolla's ticket. "Oh, you're in our business first class area, Mr. Jones. Follow me," she said.

She was an older woman and to be a white lady, she had a fat-ass booty. Dolla was hypnotized. He couldn't take his eyes off her juicy backside. She walked him to the front of the plane. He damn near walked over her, running smack into her plump bottom.

"Sorry about that," Dolla said embarrassed.

"It's okay, Mr. Jones. Your seat is right here," the stewardess said.

He was in the first row next to a stuffy looking white man. He was reading a newspaper and when he tilted the paper and looked at Dolla, he did a double take. He was surprised to see a black man sitting next to him. Dolla being young, didn't make it any better.

Damn rappers, the man thought to himself and began reading his paper again.

Dolla put his suitcase in the overhead storage unit then had a seat. The chairs were plush, and he had plenty of space. He reclined his seat and buckled his belt and tried to relax. A few minutes later, a tall lanky brunette tapped him on his shoulder.

"Mr. Jones, can I see your ticket please?" she said sternly.

The way she asked, it sure didn't sound like a request. He pulled the ticket from out of his pocket and handed it to her. She snatched it from his hands and inspected it closely as if it was fake or something.

"I'll be right back," she said and walked away with his ticket.

A few minutes later, she returned and handed him his ticket and walked away.

"Dumb-ass bitch," Dolla mumbled under his breath.

It was finally time to take off. The plane took to the runway and lifted into the air. Dolla was nervous as hell. He stuffed about five sticks of gum in his mouth. He was glad he wasn't by the window seat. He would have probably thrown up in his lap.

The takeoff was a little rough, but once they reached the desired altitude, the plane was soaring through the air with grace.

"Is there anything I can get you?" the rude brunette asked Dolla.

He glanced at the menu earlier and noticed they had a small selection of alcoholic beverages. Before he had a chance to speak, she told him what they would be serving foodwise.

"Okay, thank you. How much do your shots of liquor cost?" Dolla asked.

"They're free of charge, sir," the stewardess replied rudely.

"Okay then. May I have a double shot of Jack Daniels please?" Dolla asked.

She walked away, and in less than a minute, she returned with a cup and two shots of Jack Daniels. Dolla unfolded his tray and swung it around until it was over his lap. The stewardess sat the cup on the tray and opened the shots and poured them for Dolla. He was about to take a swallow of the liquor when she asked him for his I.D.

Dolla was trying to remain calm, but now she had pissed him off. Even though he was too young, he decided to run game on her.

"Let me ask you something. Why the fuck do you keep fucking with me, lady? Where's your supervisor?"

Dolla was bombarding her with questions. He wasn't yelling, but he was speaking at a volume where people in the first few rows could hear him. The white man next to him was terrified. He knew how young black men could get when they became angry.

"Um, if I have offended you in any way, I apologize," the stewardess said.

Her cheeks were red, and she was embarrassed from the scene he was causing.

"If there's anything else you need, please let me know, Mr. Jones," she said and backed away.

"Yeah, I'll do that, "Dolla said, sarcasm dripping from his voice. He downed the shot of liquor with one large swallow.

"Matter of fact, I would like another double shot please," Dolla said before she left out of ear's reach.

"Yes sir, right away," she said and quickly brought him two shots and refilled his cup.

During the rest of the flight, she waited on him hand and foot and was courteous as if nothing had happened. When she brought him his food and he finished, she brought him a warm towel and wiped his hands for him.

It took a little over four and a half hours to arrive in Phoenix. Once he got off the plane and walked to the front of Sky Harbor Airport, the heat hit him instantly. It was December, but it was almost eighty degrees outside. He took off his coat and his skullcap and folded them under his arm. He sat his suitcase down and pulled his cell phone out his pocket and turned it on.

Now where the fuck is this ride at? Dolla thought to himself.

He was just getting ready to call Gordo when he looked up and saw a cab parked about four cars away with a man standing, holding a large sign that had "Darin Jones A.K.A. Dolla" written in black marker. He put his phone in his pocket and grabbed his suitcase and walked over to the cab.

"Are you Dolla, Señor?" the Spanish man asked.

"Yeah, that's me," Dolla said.

"Okay, then. Let's go," the cab driver said.

The driver opened the door for Dolla, and he got in the backseat. The driver closed the door then walked around the cab to the driver's seat and got in.

"Where we headed to?" Dolla asked.

"Tucson, my friend. It's about two hours away," the driver said.

He started up the car and they pulled off. The driver took Dolla to a motel on I-10 and Sixth Avenue. It was a seedy motel and the neighborhood didn't look so hot either.

Damn, this shit look like home a lil bit, Dolla thought to himself as he walked in the front door of the motel office. He paid for the room and the Indian man at the front desk gave him a room key.

Once Dolla got in the room, he sat his suitcase in a chair and plopped onto the bed. He arrived in Phoenix at 12:45 p.m. Detroit time, but in Arizona, the time was three hours ahead, so it was actually 3:45 p.m. By the time he made it to Tucson it was 6:00 p.m., and he was exhausted.

I'll get a few hours of sleep, then I'll call Gordo and see what's up, he thought to himself.

He fell asleep in ten minutes, but his phone was ringing off the hook five minutes later. He jumped up out of his sleep when he heard the ringing noise. At first, he thought it was just in his dream, but he looked over and saw he had a missed call. The number had an 870 area code.

Dolla was just getting ready to call the number back when his phone started ringing again. It was the same number on his screen.

"What up?" he said when he answered the phone.

"What's up, man? You alright? You straight, Dolla?" the Spanish-sounding man said. He was speaking fast… so fast, it was hard to understand him.

"Who dis?" Dolla asked.

"Ernesto. Ernesto! Gordo's brother!" the man said. "You at the room?"

"Yeah, I'm here," Dolla said.

"What's the room number?" Ernesto asked.

"Room 204," Dolla said.

"I'm on my way, see you in a minute," Ernesto said, then hung up the phone.

"Fuck!" Dolla was hoping he could have gotten a little rest, but that looked to be out of the question.

He got out of bed and walked over to the sink and splashed some cold water in his face. He grabbed the pack of cigarettes out of his coat pocket and stuck one in his mouth and lit it.

Boom! Boom! Boom!

Someone was banging on the door and at first, it scared the shit outta Dolla. He dropped his cigarette on the floor from the sudden noise and leaned down to pick it up.

Boom! Boom!

"Who the fuck is it?" Dolla yelled, slightly pissed off and paranoid at the same time.

"It's me, Ernesto! Open up!"

Dolla opened the door and Ernesto came flying though like a bat outta hell. Ernesto looked completely different than his brother, Gordo. Both of them were handsome, but Ernesto was very lean and trim. His hair was slicked back, and he was dressed to the ninnies in a white linen shirt and pants and what looked to be snakeskin belt. Dark designer glasses covered his eyes. He had an olive skin complexion, but the Arizona sun gave him a slight tan. He raised his sunglasses to the top of his head and scanned the room. His eyes were bloodshot red, and it looked like he had been staring into a pair of headlights for hours.

"What's up, bro?" He slapped hands with Dolla then pounded fists with him. "How was your flight?"

"Scary as fuck. I need to smoke something," Dolla said.

"Weed?" Ernesto asked, then reached into his shirt pocket and pulled out what looked like a quarter ounce and gave it to Dolla.

"You got a blunt?" Dolla asked.

"Blunt? No, no, I got papers," Ernesto said, and handed Dolla a pack of rolling papers.

Dolla walked over to the dresser and pulled out a chunk of weed from the plastic bag and began breaking it down while Ernesto sat at the table in the corner.

Sniff, Sniff, Sniff...

Dolla turned around and saw Ernesto snorting a line of cocaine he had laid on the table.

No wonder why this nigga runnin' around here so goddamn amped, Dolla thought to himself.

"Ernesto, ain't none of that shit in here, is it? 'Cause I don't fuck wit that," Dolla said, pointing to the weed.

"No. Of course not. I wouldn't do something like that. I smoke weed too," Ernesto said sincerely.

Dolla examined the weed closely. It looked just like the weed he copped from Gordo.

If I get to tweakin' off this shit, I'm gon' kill this nigga, Dolla said to himself, then rolled the joint and fired it up.

He looked over at Ernesto who looked like he was high out of his mind. Ernesto was more Americanized than his brother, Gordo. He was wild as hell while Gordo was calmer and more reserved.

"As you know, I have a problem with an old friend of mine, and I need you to get rid of him. His name is Phelipe', and we used to make a lot of money together. But he started getting too greedy and began to steal my clients from me. He would lie and tell them I got locked up or that I was being watched by the feds in an attempt to stop people from buying from me. The only problem is, he doesn't have the connections back in Mexico like me, so his resources are limited where on the other hand, my resources are unlimited. So, I just cut off all ties with him and started dealing on my own. It didn't take long for me to pass him up and he began to get jealous. We had a big argument and after that he had a few of my men killed. In return, I had a few of his men killed too. He's tried to kill me three different times, but never succeeded, however one of his men did hit me in the chest during the last assassination attempt," Ernesto said and lifted up his shirt and showing the gunshot wound to Dolla.

"Enough is enough. Now he must go. There is no other way. Can you help me with this?" Ernesto asked.

"Yeah, I got you. I just gotta know where he's at and I need a strap too," Dolla said.

"Yes, yes. I'm going to supply you with everything you need. Tomorrow I'll come pick you up and we'll go from there."

They smoked a few joints together and talked casually. Then Ernesto made his way to the door.

"Gotta go. Be ready for tomorrow, my man." Ernesto said, shaking Dolla's hand. He let Dolla keep the weed and once he walked out the door, Dolla laid down and fell asleep.

Dolla woke up early and decided to go out for a walk and find something to eat. He smoked two joints before he left and walked about four blocks until he came across a small restaurant. He had the munchies and needed something from the menu that didn't take long to cook.

"How may I help you, hunn?" a heavyset white woman asked Dolla, ready to take his order.

"Um, let me get a Mexican omelet and a grilled ham and cheese sandwich with some hash browns… and gimmie an orange juice to go," Dolla said.

"It's gonna be about ten minutes," the waitress said, and headed to the back to give the order slip to the cook.

Dolla stepped outside to smoke a cigarette. When he was finished, he paid for the food and the waitress handed him a greasy paper bag with his food inside and a foam cup filled with orange juice. He walked back to the room and as soon as he sat down at the table and had a spoonful of omelet to his mouth about to chow down, somebody knocked on the door.

"Goddammit!" He got up and walked to the door. "I don't feel like fuckin' wit this nigga right now. It's too early for that amped-up shit," Dolla grumbled to himself.

He swung the door open and expected to see Ernesto, but instead he saw a small, feeble, older man.

"Can I help you?" Dolla asked.

"Yes. Are you Dolla?" the man asked, fixing his glasses.

"Yeah, that's me," Dolla said.

"My name is Benny. I'm a friend of Ernesto's. May I come in?"

"Yeah, come on in," Dolla said, moving aside to let Benny in.

This guy looked like a nervous wreck. He lugged a large suitcase into the room with him. He sat down and took a second to catch his breath.

"I'm going to help you get close to Phelipe' so you can take care of him. I've worked for Phelipe' for about ten years, and I'm the one responsible for bringing new clients to him. He likes to sit down with his new clients and try to feel them out. He has a long reach in his business and knows just about all the major dealers in the Midwest.

You're going to tell him your name is 'Black' and you're from Columbus, Ohio. There's a major dealer from Columbus that deals with Phelipe' who goes by the name 'G'. He supplies everybody in Columbus, and Phelipe' is going to ask you if you know him. Of course, you will say that you do know G and that you are here to purchase fifty kilos of cocaine. G referred you and you're his bother-in-law. After that, Phelipe' will contact G by telephone to verify who you are. G has been paid a large amount of money to say that he knows you. After that, he'll be ready to do business with you, and that's when you must kill Phelipe'. He usually has two bodyguards with him at all times, but today only one will be with him. Kill the bodyguard first, then Phelipe' will be a sitting duck. We'll be meeting Phelipe' four hours from now. Inside this briefcase is $700,000, which will be the money for the fifty kilos. He charges seventeen thousand per kilo - a total of $678,000 for fifty. Do not let anything happen to this money. It must be returned to Ernesto. We have about four hours to spare, so just relax and then we'll be leaving. I'm just gonna sit here if that is okay with you," Benny said.

"That's cool," Dolla said.

Dolla's breakfast was now cold, but he still wolfed it down, then smoked two fat-ass joints. He was stretched out on the bed watching T.V. while Benny made phone calls to Ernesto and the dude named G from Ohio. Dolla ended up dozing off without even realizing it. He woke up to Benny tapping his shoulder and standing over him.

"Dolla, it's time to go. Are you ready?"

"Yeah, let's get this shit over wit," Dolla replied and got up from the bed and stretched.

They left the room and headed out to meet with Phelipe'. While on the way, Benny kept drilling the information into Dolla's mind. Over and over, they rehearsed who Dolla's character was supposed to be and what Dolla was supposed to say.

They pulled into the garage of a small ranch style house and knocked on the front door. A huge Mexican man came to the door and opened it. The man had on a shoulder holster, but it was empty. He was holding the large pistol in his hand.

This must be the bodyguard, Dolla thought to himself.

Benny slid past the man. Dolla attempted to walk behind Benny when the large man stuck his hand out, stopping him in his tracks.

"Wait a minute. Let me search you first," the man said and began patting Dolla down.

Once he was convinced Dolla didn't have any weapons on him, he stood to the side to let him in the house. Dolla walked past the bodyguard but didn't know which way to go.

"Straight ahead and to the left," he instructed.

He walked down the hallway and cut a sharp left and entered a large bedroom that had been converted into an office. A stocky built Mexican with a long ponytail sat behind a desk and was talking on the phone when Dolla and the bodyguard walked in. Benny was standing to the side against the wall. Looking up at Dolla, he ended his phone call. He stood up from his chair and introduced himself.

"My name is Phelipe', and yours?" he asked Dolla.

"Black," Dolla responded and shook hands firmly with Phelipe'.

"Have a seat," Phelipe' said, nodding towards the chair next to Dolla.

Dolla sat down and Phelipe' poured what looked to be brandy or Cognac from a funny shaped bottle.

"Would you like a drink, Black?" Phelipe' asked.

"Naw, I don't drink," Dolla said lying to Phelipe'. He wanted to avoid touching things as much as possible. He didn't want to leave any fingerprints.

"So, where you from?" Phelipe' asked, looking straight into Dolla's eyes. He had a knack for seeking out deception from another person.

"Columbus, Ohio," Dolla replied, meeting Phelipe's stare.

Phelipe' had an intimidating look, and the fact that he had a glass eye didn't help either.

"Columbus, Columbus…How is it down there?"

"Shit, it's straight, but it's nothin' compared to here," Dolla replied.

"I see... Do you know a man by the mane of G?" Phelipe' asked.

"Yeah, everybody knows G. That's my bother-in-law. He's the one who referred me to Benny and yourself," Dolla said.

For a few seconds Phelipe' didn't say anything, he just stared at Dolla.

"I don't mean to be rude, Black, but I must make a quick phone call," Phelipe' said, searching for the telephone.

He dialed a number and sat back in his chair, never taking his eyes off Dolla.

"G, what's happening?" Phelipe' said though the receiver. "I have someone sitting across from me right now that says he knows you and that you recommended him to me... goes by the name Black."

Phelipe' said nothing for a minute as if he was listening to the person on the other end of the phone.

"I see, I see. How does he look?" Phelipe' asked the person on the phone.

When Phelipe' asked how Dolla looked, Dolla instantly became nervous. Phelipe' was still staring at Dolla in the face, so he had to maintain a poker face, but on the inside, he was worried. He saw Benny out the corner of his eye standing next to the bodyguard. Both of them had stoic looks on their faces. What Dolla didn't know was that Benny had called G when they were still at the room and had described Dolla to a tee, all the way down to what Dolla was wearing.

Phelipe' grinned and chuckled lightly. "Yeah, that's him," Phelipe' said to the man on the phone. "Okay G, thanks and I look forward to seeing you soon, my friend," Phelipe' said then hung up the phone.

"My apologies for the delay. I have some enemies out to get me and I had to check you out to make sure you are who you say you are. Can't ever be too safe these days," Phelipe' said.

"No problem. I understand," Dolla said, lightly relieved.

"Okay, now we can get down to business. What can I do for you?" Phelipe' asked.

"I need fifty bricks," Dolla said.

"Fifty bricks…not a problem. My price is $678,000. Is that okay with you?" Phelipe' asked.

Phelipe' told Dolla $678,000 nonchalantly as if it was nothing… as if it were $678.

"That's fine. I have it in the car. If you'll excuse me, I'll go get it," Dolla said.

"No problem. While you do that, I'll have Renauldo grab the product for you," Phelipe' said, pointing to the bodyguard.

Dolla got up from the chair and walked down the hallway into the garage. He opened the trunk and quickly took off his shirt and put on a bulletproof vest, then he put his shirt on over the vest. He grabbed the 9 mm Beretta with a silencer attached to it and the extra clip and stuck it in the waistline of his pants.

Once he adjusted himself, he grabbed the suitcase and walked back into the house. The closer he got to the room, the more his palms began sweating. He wiped the free hand on his pants, then switched the suitcase to the dry hand and wiped the other one off.

When he got back to the room, the bodyguard was already back from retrieving the cocaine. He began placing the kilos on the desk where Phelipe' was sitting. Dolla sat the suitcase on the table and opened it and stood to the side. Neither Phelipe' or the bodyguard noticed the bulletproof vest under his shirt. Benny slid out of the bodyguard's space and stood in the corner. His adrenaline was at an all-time high. He couldn't wait for it to be all over.

Phelipe' was counting the money while the bodyguard put the last few bricks on the desk when Dolla quickly reached in his waistline and pulled out the 9mm Beretta. The bodyguard saw Dolla and yelled, "boss!"

He was a second quicker on the draw and let off a shot, hitting Dolla in the side. At the same time, Dolla let off two shots, striking the bodyguard once in the chest.

"What the!" Phelipe' shouted, then began fumbling in his desk drawer for something. Dolla was on the floor clutching his right side with his left hand, still holding the pistol in his right hand.

Fewp! Fewp!

He hit the bodyguard in the chest again, then in the face. The bodyguard laid on the floor completely motionless. Dolla reached over and pointed the gun at Phelipe' and fired a shot. Phelipe' had just found the .357 in his drawer but dropped it and ducked from the shot. He tried to make a run for the door and Dolla steadily fixed his aim on Phelipe' and let off two shots.

Fewp! Fewp!

One of the bullets struck Phelipe' in the back, knocking him to the ground halfway out the door. Benny got up from the corner of the room and quickly helped Dolla to his feet.

"Don't let him get away!" Benny yelled.

Dolla was in pain. It hurt every time he took a breath. It felt like the bullet went through his vest. Still clutching his side, he walked up behind Phelipe' who was crawling on his stomach and moaning from the pain.

Dolla released his hand from his side and flipped Phelipe' onto his back.

"Aww!" Phelipe' yelled from the pain. He was taking short but fast paced breaths, clenching his jaws.

"Now you see how it feels to be stabbed in the back!" Benny yelled from behind Dolla.

"Fuck you! You fuckin' traitor! You…"

Fewp! Fewp!

Two bullets ejected from the silenced 9 mm, hitting Phelipe' dead in the face. For a second, both Benny and Dolla just stood there staring at the dead drug lord, lost in their own individual thoughts.

"Hey! You've got to get outta here! Take the van in the garage, the keys should be on the bodyguard," Benny said.

Dolla searched the dead bodyguard's pockets and found a set of keys and headed for the garage.

"Wait!" Benny yelled.

Dolla stopped in his tracks and turned around.

"What now? Dolla asked. He did the job and now he was ready to get the fuck on.

"You gotta shoot me too." Benny said.

"What? What the fuck is you talkin' bout?" Dolla asked, confused as to what Benny was talking about.

"I need you to shoot me. That way Phelipe's men won't suspect I had something to do with it."

"Where you want me to hit you at?" Dolla asked.

"In the arm. C'mon, I'm ready." Benny said, bracing himself for the gunshot.

Dolla stood back and fired a shot into Benny's arm.

"Unngh!" Benny winced in pain and clutched his arm. "Okay, now get outta here. I'm gonna give you a little over an hour head start, then I'm gonna have to call Phelipe's men."

Dolla ran down the hallway and into the garage and climbed in the old van. He started it up then pulled out of the driveway. He remembered the way back to the motel. It was basically a straight shot once he made it to the main intersection. All he had to do was make a left turn and keep straight. Benny would give him an hour head start. It only took 30 minutes to make it back to the room so he wouldn't have to drive at breakneck speed.

Benny watched Dolla pull out onto the street and turn the corner. His arm hurt like hell, but he had a big smile on his face as he looked out of the living room window. Ernesto would give him his daughter back, now that the job was done. He'd kept Benny's daughter for insurance, just in case Benny tried to fuck him out of the $1 million he wired to his bank account a week prior to today. That way Benny wouldn't have gotten any bright ideas.

Benny was glad it was all over. He already had a fall guy to put the hit on, and he didn't give a fuck about the guy either. Benny was going to take his wife and daughter and move out to California and start a new life. He was tired of the drug game. He had seen it all in the ten years he was involved in the drug trade.

He pulled out his phone and called Ernesto.

"It's done," Benny said and hung up the phone and walked away from the window.

Dolla was watching his surroundings closely as he drove down Sixth Avenue. He had the pistol on the floor of the van and still had eight shots and an extra clip, just in case he ran into any trouble. He reached a red light and came to a stop.

Dolla's head was on swivel, looking in every direction. He just so happened to look in the back of the van when he noticed a green duffle bag sticking out from behind the seat. He leaned and got a better look and noticed it was two army duffle bags. He tugged on the zipper and opened one of the bags slightly and saw nothing but $100 bills.

"Damn!" Dolla said, caught off guard by the dead presidents staring him in the face.

He jumped a little when he heard a car horn blowing behind him. He looked up and noticed that the light had turned green. He pulled off and focused on getting to the motel.

He made it to the room in about 25 minutes, five minutes earlier than it took them to go see Phelipe'. He quickly got out of the van and opened the room door. Then he ran back to the van and grabbed the two bags and ran them into the room.

Dolla began to wonder how much money was in the bags. They were heavy as hell. He locked the room door and hopped back into the van. It was still running, so Dolla threw the gear into reverse and cut the wheel to the left. Once he was facing the exit to the motel, he put the gear into drive and pulled back onto Sixth Avenue.

He drove down about six blocks, then made a right turn onto the side street. The street was quiet, no one was outside. He drove down the first block when he noticed a vacant house three houses off the corner. He pulled into the driveway and parked the van on the grass in the backyard. He took and old oily rag he found on the floor of the van and wiped off the steering wheel, ignition, gear shift, and the inside and outside of the driver side door handles.

He took the keys from the ignition, then ran to the sliding door of the van and wiped the outside door handle clean as well. Finally, he walked back to the driver's side door, which he'd left open and grabbed the pistol. He turned and casually walked out of the backyard of the vacant house. Once he made it to Sixth Avenue, he came across a manhole cover and dropped the keys to the van down into the sewer and made his way back to the room.

Once back at the room, he took off the bulletproof vest and examined his side. The bullet didn't go through, but it did bruise his side badly. After counting his lucky stars, he sat on the bed and immediately began counting the money. It took him about four hours to count the two million dollars in all $100 bills.

Dolla's hands were sore and his dick was hard from counting all that money.

I can't get on the plane with this shit. How am I gonna get all this paper back to the D? Dolla thought to himself.

"I got it!" he said out loud and snapped his fingers.

The cab pulled up at the bus station and let Dolla out at the front entrance. Dolla got out and grabbed the large suitcase and a large black duffle bag and walked into the bus station. He bought a one-way ticket to Detroit then took a seat. He called Rell to let him know shit was straight and that he would be back in the city soon.

It was about four-thirty in the afternoon, and the bus didn't leave from the terminal until about seven, so he had about a two and a half hour wait.

"Man, I wish I had some time to check out this city," Dolla thought to himself as he stared out of the window at the moving cars and palm trees.

He had the pistol on him, just in case he ran into some trouble and shit got ugly. Dolla's bus was finally ready to depart. He could see people getting on the bus. He grabbed the suitcase and the duffle bag and got up and quickly walked to the bathroom. Once inside the bathroom, he stepped into one of the stalls and pulled out the gun and wiped his fingerprints off it as well as the extra clip. He then threw it in the trash.

Afterwards, he made his way to the bus and found a seat. He placed the suitcase and duffle bag in the overhead compartment and plopped into his seat. The bus wasn't that full, so he had a whole row to himself. Dolla was exhausted. He had $127,000 taped to his body, another $60,000 on the inside of his winter coat, and $20,000 in his pockets. The rest of the money was inside the long black duffle bag and the suitcase he had.

He was glad to be on the bus, but he knew that he wasn't out of the woods yet. There was a chance that the bus could be pulled over by the police and be subject to a routine search. If that happened and the police found all that money on him, he would go straight to jail. There was no way he could explain why he was coming from Arizona with $2 million in cash. He said a silent prayer to himself before the bus pulled off.

In route to Detroit, Dolla had to switch buses a few times and they made a few stops. It took two days for him to make it back to Detroit. He tried to call everybody out of the crew to pick him up, but the only one available was E-baby. The bus pulled into the terminal in Detroit on Howard and Sixth Street downtown. When Dolla got off the bus with his luggage, it was then that he couldn't stop smiling.

I made it, he thought to himself, thanking God.

As soon as he walked out the front door and onto Howard Street, he could see E-baby parked in his Impala and bobbing his head to the music blasting from his sound system. E-baby saw Dolla crossing the street with the heavy baggage and quickly started the car and drove over to where he was. E-baby parked and popped the trunk, helping Dolla with the bags.

They dapped each other then got in the car and pulled off. Dolla saw a blunt in the ashtray that hadn't been fired up yet.

"Let me blaze this shit, bro," Dolla said, reaching for the blunt.

"That's what it's there for, nigga! I figured you probably needed something to blow the second you touched down," E-baby said. "So how was your trip? Did you fuck wit some hoes down there?" E-baby asked.

"Naw, I didn't get a chance to do that shit for real, just took care of some business…. Speaking of business, how's everything going?" Dolla asked.

"Shit, man. Everything smooth. Blackstone steady killin' 'em, Joy Road movin'… I talked to Rick earlier and he said Mettetal still slappin'. He said somethin' about the hook been through the hood though, but they ain't fucked wit the spot though. Hammer and Rell over on Blackstone wit Gary, and I been on Joy Road wit Monster and Bo for the last two days," E-baby informed him.

"Where that nigga T-mac at?" Dolla asked.

"Shit, he ain't been around to the spot. He said something about his bother getting out the joint.

"Oh, okay, That's what's up. Did he say when he would be back through?" Dolla asked.

"Nope. He ain't said shit," E-baby said.

No one knew it, but E-baby didn't like T-mac one bit. He had gotten even more tight with Monster over the past two days, and he didn't like how T-mac treated his own childhood friend.

How can this nigga be one hundred and loyal if he can't even keep it one hundred wit his manz, Monster? E-baby asked himself. Truth be told, he hoped T-mac wouldn't come back at all…

T-mac left the spot and drove over to Terry Street, which was five blocks away, when his mom called and told him J-rock had made it home. J-rock was on the porch when he saw his brother pull up in an all-black 1999 Acura Legend.

Damn, my lil bro doin' it, J-rock said to himself. If T-mac was eating like that, then taking over the hood was gonna be easy.

T-mac got out the car with his chest poked out. He wanted his brother to see how he was living and be proud of him. T-mac never knew his father, so J-rock was the only real father figure he had ever known. After J-rock got indicted and sentenced to ten years, T-mac was left to fend for himself in the streets. He would talk to his brother on a regular basis and everybody in the hood would tell him different stories about his legendary bother during his reign in the late eighties into the early nineties.

J-rock and his team were some young niggaz at that time, but they were ruthless and dedicated to the game. He left the streets just before his twenty-fourth birthday, and now, he was back to pick up where he left off.

"What up, big bro?" T-mac said with open arms.

They hugged, and for a quick second, T-mac had a flashback of when they were younger.

"Look at you, nigga! You doin' it out here, huh?" J-rock asked.

"Yeah, remember my best friend, Monster?" T-mac asked his brother.

"You talkin' bout the lil ugly kid, Antonio?" J-rock asked.

"Yeah. He ain't little no more. We both rollin' for some niggaz out the apartments on Joy Road and Greenfield.

"Oh yeah? Who y'all workin' for?" J-rock asked.

"They from Schoolcraft," T-mac replied.

"Schoolcraft?! Since when did niggaz start letting dudes from other hoods just set up shop and roll? Tell me about these niggaz," J-rock said, frustrated that niggaz in the hood was getting soft.

In his day, if anybody tried some shit like that, him and his team would have flatlined them niggaz - no questions asked. T-mac told his brother everything he knew about Dolla and his crew, including the other spots they had, even though he didn't know exactly where the spots were located.

"I don't really kick it wit them niggaz like that. They just pick up the money and drop work off. The only one I kick it wit is that nigga, Hammer. He straight. He the one who helped me get this car," T-mac said.

"Listen to me, bro. You helpin' them out, not the other way around. They wouldn't be able to move over here without somebody from this hood to keep niggaz from comin' at 'em," J-rock said. "What they pushin' out the apartments?" he asked.

"Weed out of one apartment, and across the hall, they got the fiends in a trance off of dime rocks." T-mac said.

"Wait a minute… They got two spots in the apartments?" J-rock asked.

"Yep, and them bitches bang hard as fuck," T-mac said matter-of-factly.

"Starting today, lil bro, we gonna dead that shit. Them niggaz gotta go," J-rock said.

He was so angry on the inside, someone could have fried an egg on the top of his dreadlocks.

"You know I'm wit you, bro, but we gotta build ourselves up 'cause them niggaz got army guns and long money… ya feel me?" T-mac said.

"Yeah. We gonna do shit under the radar, and by the time they realize what's goin' on, it will be too late. They'll be dead," J-rock said, rubbing his hands together. "Let yo big bro teach you the art of war."

They went inside the house for a minute, and T-mac went into his room and pulled $2,000 from his stash. He walked out to the living room where J-rock and his mother were sitting on the couch.

"Here, bro," T-mac said, handing him the large roll of small bills.

"Damn. Good lookin'. My baby bro done blessed me," J-rock said, hugging his brother.

"Ma, I'm about to take J-rock to the mall. You need something?"

"No, baby. Y'all two just be careful," their mom said.

T-mac loved his brother and momma very much. There was nothing he wouldn't do for them.

Yeah, it's time for us to take what belongs to us, T-mac thought to himself. He used to dream about him and his brother getting money. Now the time was finally at hand.

They got in the car and pulled out the driveway, headed to the mall.

"I'm bout to take you shoppin'. Then I'm gon' pick you up the baddest bitch in the hood and drop y'all off at the room," T-mac said.

"Naw, bro. You gon' pick up the baddest bitch in the hood and we gonna get a room and fuck her together," J-rock said, looking at his little brother and smiling.

"Welcome back, baby bro. Welcome back," T-mac said as he turned up the music…

E-baby dropped Dolla off at his apartment and headed back to Joy Road. Once Dolla stepped in his apartment, he took the money off he had wrapped on his body and pulled a fresh bottle of Remy V.S.O.P. from his bar and poured a shot. After that, he stashed the money and took a shower. He had a lot of shit to take care of, so after he got dressed, he hit the streets.

He stopped at all the legit business locations and went over the numbers the stores made for the past three days with the managers. All the businesses were flourishing, growing more and more with each month that passed. Dolla was especially proud of Rick's sister, Rita. She had the salon booming, thanks to her business savvy and hard work. She was determined to make Royal Treatment Beauty and Nails the most successful salon in Detroit. She even talked to Dolla about possibly opening another location in Bloomfield Hills where all the rich people lived.

After that, Dolla drove from spot to spot, checking up on his team of street niggaz. He told everybody not to make any plans for the next day. He wanted to have an important meeting with all of them.

The next thing he did was make a phone call to Gordo, then stopped at the nightclub on the southwest side to meet with him and talk. He told Gordo how the play went down in Arizona. Gordo was extremely thankful for what Dolla did for him and his brother, Ernesto. Gordo didn't want anything to happen to his only brother. If Phelipe' would have killed Ernesto, it would have caused an avalanche of problems. Gordo would have had to end up relocating to Arizona to take over his brother's position, which would have jeopardized his operation in Detroit. It took years to build his empire and gain the power he had in there, and there was no one he could trust to leave as heir to the city. He amassed close to $ 1 billion in drug money from the streets of Detroit in a ten-year period. He came to the city as a young child, and once he was in his twenties, he began his rise to the top of Detroit. He'd made his uncles back home in Mexico filthy rich.

He showed his appreciation to Dolla by buying him drinks and paying for dances from the strippers. Gordo also told Dolla that he would go down an extra $1,000 per kilo on his future purchases of cocaine. Now Dolla would pay only $15,000 a brick.

After a few dances and a fifth of tequila, three dancers literally kidnapped Dolla and took him to a private room in the back of the club where only the elite clients were allowed to enter. The room had a king size bed and an open bar with exclusive top-shelf liquor and champagne that they didn't even sell at the club. That ended up being one of the best sexual encounters Dolla had ever experienced.

The next day, Dolla had the whole team meet up at the spot on Mettetal. Everybody in the crew told the custos that the spots would be closed between the hours of seven a.m. until nine a.m. The whole crew was on Mettetal by 6:30 a.m., so Dolla went on and started the meeting.

Everybody was in the living room and blunts were in rotation. Dolla began to speak in between hitting the blunt he had in his hand.

"Today, I called this meeting to speak on the importance of honor and loyalty. I know I've spoken on this subject before, and so far, everybody on the same page. Shit goin' good right now, but I need y'all to keep in mind that we in the game, and we in this shit deep. I have plans for us to span all over Michigan - Lansing, Jackson, Flint, Muskegon, Saginaw, Battle Creek... We gonna touch the whole muthafuckin' mitten. Y'all my top niggaz - the ones I count on if shit get thick, the ones I can trust with my life. We ARE a fuckin' family, and our blood mixes through this game we in. Some of y'all gonna have to relocate to the surrounding cities for a while to get shit established. Then, we'll all rotate from city to city. We will have niggaz rollin' under us. I'm gonna split the pie with niggaz. Everyone will have their own bricks and pounds once I set this operation off. I just gotta get shit straight for the plug and we gotta solidify our empire here within the city. We muthafuckin' royalty, the cream of the crop! Ain't nothin' or nobody gonna stop us! Even if some of us get knocked, we gon' make sure a nigga and his family straight. Ya feel me?" Dolla looked around at everyone to make sure his words were clear to everyone in the room.

T-mac was sick to his stomach. *Who the fuck do this nigga think he is?* he thought to himself. He cursed himself for even showing up to this bullshit-ass meeting, but J-rock told him to stay in the circle and find out as much as he could before they executed their plan.

Dolla walked down the hall to one of the bedrooms and opened up the duffle bag filled with $100 bills from Arizona. He had seven bundles of $15,000 stacks separated from the rest of the money in the bag. He put the seven bundles of money in a trash bag he'd left in the room before the crew got there and walked back to the front room.

The whole crew's morale was at an all-time high. Everyone was ready to step their game up so they could begin the takeover of the state. Everybody was talking and didn't even notice Dolla enter the living room with the bag in his hand.

"Dig, I got a lil somethin'-somethin' for y'all," Dolla said, reaching into the bag.

One by one, he called Bruce, Quick, Bo, Gary, E-baby, Monster and T-mac and hit them off with $15,000 each. It caught each of them off guard, Monster and E-aby looked like they were about to shed tears of joy, Gary, Bruce, Quick and Bo began dapping each other, and T-mac was just standing there with a strange expression on his face.

"As I say, *loyalty brings royalty*, and that's my gift to y'all for maintaining your loyalty," Dolla said.

He then motioned for Dennis, Rell, Rick, and Hammer to follow him to the bedroom. Once they were all in the room, Dolla shut the door behind them.

"Bro, what up?" Rell asked Dolla, wondering what was going on.

"I just wanna tell y'all that I love y'all niggaz to death. It ain't nothin' I wouldn't do for y'all. Whenever I eat, y'all niggaz gon' eat too," Dolla said, then he pulled the duffle bag full of money from under the bed and sat it down on top of the mattress.

"It's $300,000 in this bag right here. Y'all split this shit four ways," Dolla said.

They all dapped Dolla and thanked him.

"Where you get all this extra paper from?" Rick asked.

"I came up on a lil lick out there in Arizona, and this y'all cut," Dolla explained.

"Yo, we gettin' ready to make a serious power move soon. We'll all be multi-millionaires. The sky's the limit," Dolla said.

"Well, just know we ridin' wit ya, homie. All the way to the finish," Dennis said.

"Yo, D. You mind taking the bag to your house and keeping it there til y'all split that shit up??" Dolla asked.

"Yeah, I got it," Dennis said, stuffing the money into the bag and zipping it closed.

"I'll take it down there in a little bit." Hammer wanted to call Victoria to tell her to make sure she was at the crib tonight. He had to drop some work off over there, plus he planned on spending the night and dicking her down. That was his down-ass bitch, and he had love for her. He patted his pockets and realized he'd left his phone in the car. Dolla, Rick, Rell, Hammer, and Dennis all left out of the bedroom and Hammer headed for the front door.

"Where you goin', Ham?" Rell asked.

"I'll be right back. I gotta get my phone from the car," Hammer said, and walked out the door.

When he stepped outside, he saw T-mac on the phone, pacing up and down the sidewalk in front of the spot. It looked like he was upset about something.

"T-mac, what up? Everything straight?" Hammer asked, concerned about his little homie. He liked T-mac, and he could tell the boy had potential.

T-mac looked up and saw it was Hammer and told the person on the phone he would call them back.

"You good?" Hammer asked him again.

"Yeah, yeah… I'm straight. This lil bitch I be fuckin' wit getting' on my muthafuckin' nerves," T-mac lied. It was really his brother on the phone.

"Don't let these bitches see you mad. That's what they be wanting. You a made nigga. Hoes come a dime a dozen for niggaz like us," Hammer said, placing his hand on T-mac's shoulder.

Hammer's mother was leaving out the house and headed for the garage.

"Hey, baby," Karen said, waving at her son.

"Hey, Momma. Where you goin'?" Hammer asked.

"I'm just gonna go to the market to get something to cook and then I'm gonna probably go over to Shirley's house and play some cards," she said.

"Ok, be careful," Hammer said.

"I will. You too," she said, then walked into the garage to her car.

"That's yo O.G. right there?" T-mac asked.

"Yeah, she good people's," Hammer said, then ran across the street to his car.

He opened the side door and grabbed the phone from off the car seat and ran back across the street. He and T-mac both walked into the house together. The crew blew a few more blunts then everybody left, headed back to their posts.

T-mac blessed his brother with $5,000 and he immediately went and copped four and a half ounces of crack. He broke the ounces down to dime rocks and passed out a few testers to the fiends. He would make a few dollars, but that was only from his name in the hood and the fact that he intimidated the hell out of the fiends. J-rock would have to literally stalk the areas where the fiends hustled and made their money. He would stand at gas stations and count how much money fiends would make pumping gas and keeping the area free of debris. He was having to force the fiends to fuck with him and it was frustrating.

He was walking down Joy Road when he ran into a fiend named Ten Man. Ten Man had been in the hood forever, and he'd witnessed the rise and fall of J-rock's organization and he had a lot of love for the young hustler.

"Yo, Ten Man. Let me holla at you," J-rock said."

Ten Man already heard through the grapevine that J-rock was pressuring people into buying his product, but Ten Man wasn't going for that.

"What's up, youngster?" Ten Man asked.

"Dig, I got these ten-dolla boys on deck. You straight?" J-rock asked.

"Yeah, I'm straight. I just copped from yo brother's spot on Greenfield," Ten Man said.

"Damn! Look, let me give you a tester and smoke it right quick and tell me what you think," J-rock said, reaching into his pocket and pulling out a dime bag. He handed it to Ten Man.

Ten Man took the rock and opened the small baggie and put the rock into his glass stem. He lit that shit up right on Joy Road. He didn't have no shame in his game. It didn't take long for him to finish.

"Well, how is it?" J-rock asked, hoping that Ten Man told him something good.

"It's alright, but to keep it all the way real with you. It ain't fuckin' with the spot on Greenfield. They got the strongest shit in the hood."

"Fuck!" J-rock yelled. He'd just spent $2,500 on the work he'd just copped, and the guy he bought the dope from supposedly had the best shit around. The connects he had from the past were non-existent. One older guy he used to cop from named AC, ended up falling off and started smoking himself.

"I gotta get my hands on some better dope… I gotta think," J-rock said to himself. Then suddenly, he came up with an idea…

Dolla had been feeling like the walls were closing in on him in his two-bedroom apartment. He had a few extra dollars to kick around from the lick in Arizona a few weeks prior, so he decided that he would boss up and buy a new house. He had been looking at different houses and came across one house he liked in particular. It was a beautiful colonial-built brick house with four bedrooms and three bathrooms. It had a full living room and dining room, a den with a bar and library area, and huge kitchen with a breakfast nook. It also had a large backyard with a wooden deck and a small swimming pool with a beautiful view of a small lake, a huge finished basement and a three-car garage. The master bedroom had a fireplace, bathroom, and a walk-in closet the size of a small bedroom itself.

The seller was asking $350,000 for the house. After two days of negotiating, Dolla and the realtor shook hands and closed a deal for $250,000, a one-time cash payment. Dolla had no problem paying cash, and with the several businesses he owned, he didn't have to worry about raising any flags with the feds.

He met with the seller and real estate agent and paid for the house in cash. He also paid the taxes up on the house for the next five years in advance. He still wanted to do some customizing to the house, so he spent the next few days just walking through and making notes on what he wanted done. First, he ordered some nice furniture for the house. Then he placed big screen T.V.s throughout the house, bought some swimming pool cleaning equipment, a top-of-the-line BBQ grill, a riding lawnmower to cut the grass with, and a pull-away basketball rim for when the homies came through.

He ordered a custom-made aquarium that was installed into a wall in the living room, complete with exotic fish. In the basement, he bought a theater projection screen and had a pool table, dart board, ping pong table, even a pinball machine installed.

Dolla pulled out his cell phone and made a call to Les.

"Hello?" Les answered in the first two rings.

"Les. What up, doe? This Dolla. Let's make a deal…"

Dolla was excited. Everything was done with the house. The jacuzzi was installed in the master bedroom and the alarm system was installed for his and Savannah's safety. He had been talking to Savannah all week and had convinced her to come down to the city for the weekend. As soon as her last class let out, she headed to her dorm to pack and Dolla was already there waiting for her. She packed her things and they left the college, headed to Detroit.

Once they were in Detroit, Dolla got onto the I-696 freeway and headed to Sterling Heights.

"Where are we going?" Savannah asked Dolla.

"Ah, nowhere special," Dolla replied.

When they got to Oakwood Drive, he slowly drove down the street until they got to the house. Once they were at the house, he pulled into the driveway and shut the car off.

"Baby, whose house is this? I'm tired, and I don't really feel like meeting anyone right now," Savannah said.

It had been a busy week for her, and she was exhausted. She just wanted to relax and hide from the world. She didn't want to go out, shop, or anything else.

"C'mon. I promise you'll get some rest later," Dolla said, and got out of the car.

She reluctantly got out of the car behind him. Dolla quickly opened the front door and disarmed the alarm before Savannah made it to the porch. She was so busy pouting that she didn't even notice what he was doing. When she first walked into the house, she did like the layout of the place.

This is a nice place, she thought to herself. They both walked into the living room and Dolla turned around to face her and spread open his arms.

"Well, do you like it?" He asked with a huge grin on his face.

"Yes, Darin. I like it, but again, what are we doing here?" Savannah only called Dolla by his government name when she was pissed off at him.

"Shit, what you mean? We LIVIN' here, baby! This house belongs to us!" Dolla said proudly.

"Boy, don't play with me right now," Savannah said. Her mood was slightly changing for the better.

"I'm serious, this is our home."

"Ahhh!!" Savannah screamed and hopped into Dolla's arms. She wrapped her legs around his waist.

She planted a wet sloppy kiss on his lips.

"Ehhh," Dolla said, and wiped his mouth on the shoulder of his shirt, still cupping Savannah's ass with both his hands.

She gave him about five more quick pecks on the lips then brought her legs down to the floor.

"I wanna go check out the house!" she said, then took off running.

She ran in and out of each room, growing more and more elated by the minute. Dolla could barely keep up with her as she darted from one section of the house to the other. She fell in love with the basement and the theater projection screen.

"We ain't never gotta go to the movies again!" She was completely blown away.

By the time she got to the master bedroom, she was speechless. She turned to Dolla, who was standing in the doorway of the bedroom as tears filled her eyes and began to roll down her cheeks.

"Oh, Dolla. What have I done to deserve this? I'm so thankful to have a man like you in my life. You mean the world to me."

He walked up to her and held her tight in his arms.

"I'm glad to have someone like YOU. You're the only thing I have in this world that is pure, and I'll do anything I can to make you happy. You're my soul mate," Dolla said sincerely.

They stood silent, holding each other… temporarily frozen in time.

"I wanna go do some shopping for the house," Savannah said.

"What more do we need? We got everything!" Dolla said, laughing.

"Duh! We need some hygiene products, washcloths, towels, tissue…" Savannah said, running down a list of necessities.

"Damn, I didn't think about that," Dolla said, feeling a little stupid. "Alright, go ahead. I'm gonna stay here and play the game," Dolla said. He dug in his pocket and gave her about four hundred dollars in $20 bills.

"Ok. Well, give me the car keys," Savannah said.

"Oh no. You ain't drivin' my shit," Dolla said.

"Well, how am I gonna get to the store?" Savannah asked.

For a second, Dolla just stood there, staring at her. This was the moment he had been waiting for.

"C'mon then," Dolla said, pretending to be mad.

They walked out the side door towards the garage.

"We ain't gotta go if you don't want to," Savannah said. She felt kind of bad, after all he went through buying the house and furnishing it.

"Shit, I'm out here now. Fuck it, let's go," Dolla said.

He walked over to the garage and just stood there.

"Baby, the car is right there. You didn't park in the garage," Savannah said, pointing to his Benz parked at the front end of the driveway.

"You so worried about the store, you ain't even check out the garage," Dolla said.

She smacked her lips and walked over to the garage and just stood there with her arms folded. She was about two seconds from cursing his ass out.

"Open the door!" Dolla yelled.

She opened the garage door and what she saw made her stumble backwards. It was a rose-colored 2000 BMW Z3.

"This is mine?!" Savannah asked, grinning from ear to ear.

"What you think?" Dolla replied, laughing and dangling the keys in his hand.

She grabbed the keys and swung her arms around his neck and kissed him passionately.

"Thank you," she said in a hushed tone.

"You ain't gotta thank me. Just go get what we need from the store," Dolla said.

"Oh, I'm gonna thank you later. Trust and believe that," Savannah said and walked in the garage to check out the car.

Dolla walked into the garage behind her. "It's a thirty-day temporary tag in the back. You gotta go to the Secretary of State and put the car in your name and get a plate," Dolla said.

She started the car and was playing with the radio.

"Where's a store at around here?" Savannah asked.

"I don't know, but I'll bet you'll have fun looking though," Dolla said and cracked a grin.

"Let me pull my car out the driveway so you can leave," he said and walked to his car.

She stepped on the gas pedal while the car was still in park, and the roar of the foreign engine gave her an orgasmic feeling on the inside. *I'm gonna put it on his ass this weekend,* Savannah said to herself.

Once she saw Dolla pull out of the driveway, she threw the car in reverse and backed out onto the street. Dolla was parked in front of the house as he watched the love of his life back out the driveway and pull off. He enjoyed doing things to make his loved ones happy. Even after blessing his crew and buying the house and furnishing it along with paying the taxes up for five years and Savannah's car, he still had close to $1.2 million left from the hit in Arizona, not to mention what he'd saved from the streets and his legit business ventures.

At twenty years old, he was well off and more successful than any of the older adults he knew in his life. It was a very humbling feeling to say the least. He looked over at the house and smiled.

Thanks, Phelipe', he said to himself…

Savannah returned from the store and entered the house through the side door. She walked through the kitchen and saw Dolla sitting on the couch in the living room, playing video games and smoking a blunt.

"Dolla, come help me out with these bags."

"Ok. One second, baby," Dolla said. He paused the game and got up from the couch.

Savannah took the blunt from Dolla and he walked outside to get the grocery bags out the car. After he brought the bags into the house, Savannah put the food in the refrigerator. The products she bought for the house, she put them where they belonged. After that, she cooked spaghetti and breadsticks and they sat at the table and ate. They washed the food down with a bottle of champagne. Dolla was so full he could barely move.

"Baby, can we have a party tomorrow?" I want to invite some of my friends from school," Savannah asked.

Dolla thought it was a good idea. He would invite Hammer, Rick, Rell, and Dennis over and sic them on Savannah's friends.

"Bet. Put it together," Dolla said.

Savannah cleared the table and put the dishes in the dishwasher. She rolled up a blunt then went upstairs to the master bedroom and filled the tub with hot water and made a bubble bath. She took off her clothes and sat in the tub and lit the blunt. She soaked in the bath water and blew the blunt to the head then scrubbed her body with some scented soap. Once she was done, she lotioned her body and put on some tight-fitting boy shorts and a button up pajama shirt and headed downstairs.

Dolla had crept upstairs and peeked in on Savannah while she was bathing, so he grabbed some clothes and went to the downstairs bathroom and jumped in the shower. He got out and changed into a white beater and some hoop shorts, then he rolled up a few blunts and sat next to Savannah on the living room couch. She was playing the video game when Dolla lit up one of the blunts and handed it to her.

"Why don't we go down in the basement and have a few drinks from the bar?" Dolla asked.

Without saying a word, Savannah cut off the game and headed for the basement. Dolla got up and followed behind her, admiring her plump round backside. They poured a few shots then played a few games of darts. After that, they sat back and watched a movie on the theater screen and smoked a few blunts. Dolla was high as a kite and he began to doze off. Savannah looked over and saw him falling asleep.

"Uh-uh. Wake yo ass up, boy," she said, nudging him with her elbow.

"What? What up? I wasn't sleep," Dolla said, lying.

"C'mon, let's go upstairs and break the new bed in," Savannah said.

They both got up to head upstairs to the bedroom. They spent the rest of the night exploring each other's bodies.

The next morning, Savannah woke Dolla up to some of the bombest head he'd ever had. She had already cooked some pancakes, sausage links, eggs and some bacon. He tried to lift her head from between his legs, so he could enter inside her love box, but she buckled down and began bobbing up and down aggressively on his manhood. He couldn't take it, he released into her mouth.

She sat up and said, "Good morning, honey. Breakfast is downstairs," then walked into the bathroom.

Dolla got up from the bed and his legs felt like rubber as he made his way downstairs to fix a plate. After breakfast, they began making calls to friends to invite them to their house for a party. Savannah ran to the store to grab some plastic cups and plates and a case of blunts. Dolla opened the glass sliding door and stepped outside to smoke a cigarette. It was cold as hell outside, but he wanted to get some fresh air. It was snowing outside but it wasn't sticking to the ground just yet.

I gotta get a truck, Dolla thought to himself. He knew he couldn't drive the Benz in the snow and Savannah couldn't drive her BMW either. He made a mental note to call Les Monday morning.

He stepped back inside and rolled up a blunt and waited for Savannah to get back. Once she made it back, he sparked up a blunt and after they smoked, they began to prepare for the party. They had chips with dip, buffalo wings, and they had only the best beer, wine and liquor for the night.

By six 'o'clock, all the guests had arrived. Savannah invited her best friend, Carrie, and Carrie's baby daddy, Eddie, who was the quarterback for the college team at MSU. Carrie had just given birth to their son, Eddie Jr., so she was looking forward to the party. She wanted to unwind. She wasn't able to smoke during her pregnancy and she only drank wine occasionally. Savannah also invited her roommate, Mary, and her classmates, Ashley, Tonya, and Lisa.

Rick, Rell, Hammer, and Dennis were looking like new money. Savannah's friends were already choosing between the four of the guys themselves. Savannah took the girls for a tour of the house and the crew introduced themselves to Carrie's baby daddy, Eddie. It was a little awkward when Rell and Carrie first saw each other, but they kept their cool. Eddie didn't know the two had a past, and neither Carrie nor Rell was going to speak on it.

Once the girls were done checking out the house, Dolla went over to the stereo and cranked it up full blast. The fellas began rolling blunts and the ladies were popping bottles and pouring glass after glass of drinks. Dolla had a fifth of Remy clutched in his fist and a huge blunt in the other hand. They all went into the basement and the fellas were playing darts against the ladies. The ladies won the majority of the games and rubbed it in the guys' faces. Everybody was feeling good from the combination of the weed and the liquor.

They began dancing and grinding on each other to the music. Rick was dancing with Mary. He was feeling her creamy white petite frame. Hammer was paired up with Tonya, a sexy-ass, caramel-skinned chick who was a cheerleader for the college basketball team. Dennis was dancing with Lisa, who was a white girl with the ass of a black chick. Her body was well put together and from the moment she laid eyes on

Dennis, she fell in love with his grown-man swag. Rell was with Ashley, a cute mixed girl with long curly hair and a bangin' body.

Each of Savannah's friends liked Dolla's homies. They were much different from the stuffy, square guys at the college. These niggaz were certified gangsters, and Savannah's classmates had never come across these types of guys. They all came from suburban neighborhoods and the only time they saw a ghetto was on T.V.

Carrie and Eddie were hugged up dancing, but Carrie would glance over at Rell from time to time. Rell wasn't thinking about Carrie. He was too busy getting to know Ashley. As far as he was concerned, what they had was over with. At first, when he found out she ran off with Eddie, he was a little hurt, but he never told anyone or let it show. From that point on, he felt like all women were sneaky and not to be trusted. He vowed to never let a female into his heart again. He didn't have any ill feelings towards Carrie, he just accepted the way things were.

Everybody began sitting down to rest and more weed smoke filled the air and more bottles were turned up. All the fellas decided to have a dice game and began shooting in the middle of the basement floor. Eddie didn't know shit about dice, so the rest of the fellas were teaching him. Dolla, Rick, Rell, Dennis, and Hammer were making big bets and Eddie's money wasn't that long, so each of them gave him $100 to gamble with. Eddie was in awe at how they just handed him $500 without breaking a sweat, and they were betting between $20 to $500 dollars a pop.

When it was all over with, Hammer ended up walking away with an extra $4,500 in his pocket. He was feeling so good that he gave each of the ladies $200 each. He was proud of his friend, Dolla. Dolla truly bossed up and made shit happen for the crew. All of them were eating and they had legitimate investments. Because of Dolla, Hammer was able to provide for his mom and let her enjoy life, instead of worrying about bills and where their next meal was coming from. Hammer liked Savannah too. She and Dolla looked good together. He was thinking about buying a house like this for himself, Victoria, and his mother. The only problem was that his mom didn't want to move off the block. He made his mind up that he was gonna sit his mother down and convince her to move out the hood with him.

"Aye, Dolla. Where yo bathroom at?" Rell asked.

"Go upstairs and walk through the kitchen and living room and it's the first door to your right," Dolla said.

Rell headed upstairs and made it to the bathroom. He took a piss and washed his hands then opened the bathroom door.

"Oh, shit!" Rell reached on his waist for his pistol out of habit, even though he'd left his strap in the car.

It was Carrie standing in the doorway with her head tilted to the side and her hands on her hips. She was buzzin' good, and it wasn't hard to tell.

"Damn, girl. You scared the shit outta me!" Rell said with his hand over his heart. He tried to slide past her, but she had him blocked in.

"What you doin'? Watch out," Rell said, trying to squeeze past her.

"Oh. So, it's like that? You ain't even paying me no attention, as if I never meant anything to you," Carrie said.

"Carrie, you trippin'. You the one who wanted it this way. You the one who just took off and left me hangin'. You ain't even have the decency to get at me and let me know the deal. But I ain't mad at you though. And I spoke to you when I first saw you. What more do you want? Yo baby daddy here!" Rell exclaimed.

She knew everything Rell was saying was true, and she secretly hated herself for playing him like that. Eddie was a good guy with a promising future, and she wouldn't take back having her son for anything. But one thing about love, it's like a stray bullet, and it has no names on it. You can't force yourself to love someone, and that was exactly what she was trying to do with Eddie. She really loved Rell.

"Nigga, shut up. This my dick," Carrie said, reaching out and clutching his dick in her hand. "I'm the bitch who turned you out. There ain't no bitch you fuckin' with know how to work this muthafucka like me," she hissed.

"Girl, chill out. Yo baby daddy…" Rell couldn't even finish his sentence. She was on her knees and took him inside her mouth.

"Fuck," Rell mumbled. He knew that Carrie told the truth. He hadn't come across a woman yet that could match her sexually. He'd fucked strippers and some of the baddest bitches in the city, but it just seemed like him and Carrie connected sexually.

After she was done with Rell, she slipped back downstairs into the basement and Eddie didn't even have the slightest clue as to what had just taken place. Actually, no one noticed anything because they were too busy partying.

Five minutes later, Rell came walking down the stairs and into the basement. As he passed Carrie, she was sitting down next to Eddie. She looked at Rell and smirked a sly grin, then turned to Eddie and whispered something in his ear and patted his lap. For a hot second, Rell felt a twinge of jealousy, but quickly shook it off.

I'm trippin' like a muthafucka, Rell said to himself and made his way over to where Ashley was and picked up with her where they left off.

The party began to wind down and come to an end. Eddie and Carrie were the designated drivers, but they decided to spend the night at Dolla and Savannah's place and leave in the morning. Dennis invited Lisa to his place, and she accepted.

Rick ended up driving Savannah's roommate, Mary, back to Lansing, and they talked all the way back to the college. They were feeling each other, and Rick even stayed at the dorm with her for an extra hour or two, just kicking it. He didn't get the pussy that night, but he wasn't tripping.

Hammer and Tonya ended up fucking and passing out in one of the guest rooms. Tonya thought Hammer was a pretty-boy thug, and she liked his long hair. She thought the scar on his face looked sexy too. Rell and Ashley spent the night as well. It had been so long since she'd had as much fun as she did with a man, and Rell was the remedy to her boredom. She was able to have fun and let her hair down for a change, and she liked Rell's confidence and personality.

Oh, what the hell..., she thought to herself as they got to know each other a little better in the bedroom. Rell hit it good. Ashley was fast asleep within ten minutes with her thumb in her mouth after they fucked, curled up in bed like a baby. Rell sat up and smoked a cigarette, then he too became tired and fell asleep.

As he was sleeping, Rell felt like someone was pushing him, slightly waking him.

"What up, man?" Rell said, half asleep.

He thought it was Ashley trying to wake him up for another round. He felt a set of warm soft lips press up against his, and it was then that he woke up. Rell had never been the kissing type. When he opened his eyes and saw Carrie crouched down by his side of the bed, he thought he was dreaming. He rubbed his eyes and strained his vision in the darkness of the bedroom to focus as he realized that he wasn't dreaming. Carrie was really in his room. She tugged his arm, attempting to pull him out of the bed. He turned around to make sure Ashley was still asleep then, turned back around and faced Carrie.

"What the fuck!" he whispered as low as he possibly could.

"I want some now!" Carrie whispered back. She had a look in her eyes that gave off the impression that she wasn't taking no for an answer. That's how Carrie had always been, persistent until she got what she wanted. Rell leaned in close to Carrie's face so he could make sure she heard him.

"Girl, go take yo ass back to bed wit yo baby daddy!" he said sternly.

"If you don't get out this bed, I'm gonna start making noise and wake your little girlfriend up!" Carrie said, raising her voice slightly.

Rell knew how Carrie could get, he knew she wasn't bluffing.

"Carrie, this shit gotta stop, you..."

Smack!

Carrie smacked the shit outta him. Ashley moaned and moved a little, but she didn't wake up. Next thing Rell knew, it was as if he was watching himself get out of bed and chase Carrie out of the room. They made it into the hallway, and he caught up with her and grabbed her by the arms.

"What the fuck is wrong wit you? I outta knock yo ass out!" he said, still whispering.

Carrie didn't say anything. She just stood there, looking at Rell with a blank stare. She still had feelings for Rell, but today was the day she realized that she was in love him, and she wanted him to be in her life forever. She didn't know how to express her feelings to Rell in words, so she just caused a scene of confusion instead.

All of a sudden, Rell started kissing Carrie. He palmed her ass with both hands as she let a soft moan escape from her mouth. Rell picked her up and carried her down the hall to the bathroom and stepped inside. Rell turned around to close the door and Carrie snatched off her jogging pants and panties and grabbed a towel and sat on the edge of the sink. She opened her legs for Rell, giving him easy access to her love button.

Rell slid out of his boxers and entered inside her. *This is the last time,* Rell thought to himself, but deep down, he knew that there would never be a last time. He loved her and she loved him. They couldn't control the feelings they had for each other.

He was gripping her waist and sliding in and out of her wetness. Carrie was palming his head with both hands as they kissed each other passionately, breathing hard and gasping for air. She placed her hands on his chest and gently pushed him backwards. He stood back as Carrie slid off the sink and turned around to face the vanity mirror. She grabbed both ends of the sink and leaned forward, raising her juicy round ass in the air.

He slid in her from behind and she began moaning loudly as Rell maneuvered his way in and out of her. He slid his right hand over her mouth, attempting to muffle her voice and caressed her breast with his left hand. She began licking and sucking on the tip of one of his fingers then began to jerk violently.

"Ooohh Rell," she said as she came all over his manhood.

Rell noticed she was cumming and started stroking faster. Her ass was so soft and was rippling small waves as he pounded her from behind. Rell felt a tingling sensation at the tip of his dick.

"Shit, I'm bout to cum!" Rell said as he moved backward trying to pull out of her.

Carrie heard him, and when he took a step back, she leaned towards him. She was throwing her ass on him while at the same time clenching her pussy muscles on his dick.

"Ungghhh! Rell mumbled as he released inside of her.

They stayed in position for a minute breathing hard, trying to catch their breath.

"Damn, look at what you made me do," Rell said, easing out of her.

Carrie stood up and wiped the sweat from her forehead. She looked at Rell and winked.

"I told you, you're mine. Them other bitches might have you for a night or two, but you'll always be a part of me. Now get back down the hall to your little bitch. I gotta take a shower," Carrie said, and stepped to the side to let Rell pass.

As he walked past her, she smacked him on the ass. Rell just looked back at her and shook his head. He tiptoed down the hallway and back into the bedroom and slid back into the bed with Ashley. He reached on the nightstand and pulled out a cigarette from his pack and grabbed the lighter and lit it. He was lying on his back as he inhaled then exhaled menthol-flavored tobacco, blowing the smoke towards the ceiling. He was thinking about what had just taken place in the bathroom with him and Carrie.

"Man, I hope she don't get…" Rell quickly shook the thought from his mind.

As soon as he finished his cigarette, he closed his eyes and began to doze off. Ashley rolled over, still half asleep and threw her arm across Rell's body and lowered her hand down to his dick and began stroking slowly up and down the shaft. He began to feel his manhood rise and he reached down into his pants, which were next to the bed and pulled out a condom.

Here we go again, he thought to himself…

The next day, everybody got up early and showered and got dressed. The girls cooked some breakfast for Hammer, Rell, Dolla, and Eddie. They all sat at the table and ate their food. Then after that, they rotated four blunts between them. Afterwards, Dolla, Hammer, and Rell stepped outside on the back porch to talk business for a minute. Eddie just sat at the table by himself while the girls huddled on the living room couch and talked about what they did with the boys last night. Carrie just sat back and listened. She didn't speak a word about what she and Rell had done.

Dolla, Rell, and Hammer stepped in from the cold. Rell and Hammer were getting ready to leave and go check on the spots while Dolla and Savannah would swing by all the legit businesses to check on the numbers. Rell and Hammer exchanged numbers with Ashley and Tonya, then everyone began to say their goodbyes. Carrie and Rell didn't say a word to each other, but the looks they exchanged said it all. Savannah noticed the glare Rell and Carrie exchanged and just shook her head. Everyone parted ways, while Dolla set the alarm. Then he and Savannah took off, headed for Detroit.

This was the first time Savannah had seen the different stores Dolla, Rick, Rell, and Hammer owned, and she was impressed to say the least. She picked out an outfit when they stopped at Royal Fashions, and she got a manicure and pedicure at the Royal Treatment. She also got the chance to meet Rick's sister, Rita.

When they were done checking the stores, the two headed back home and enjoyed the last day Savannah was going to be in the city before going back to Lansing. Rell, Hammer, and Rick rode together as they made their rounds, checking one spot after the next. Quick and Bruce were holding shit down on Mettetal, and everyone had love for the two young soldiers on the come up. Even though they were still young, they were dedicated and focused, and they were looking forward to the expansion of the business in hopes of getting a spot of their own someday.

E-baby and Gary had Blackstone banging. All the fiends were coming through the spot and they even had a few custos from Redford, which was a nearby suburban community. Hammer, Rell, and Rick pulled up behind the apartments on Greenfield and Joy Road and walked through the back door and up the hallway stairs to the top floor. Rell and Rick checked on the weed spot and Hammer checked on the dope spot. When Rick and Rell got to the front door, there were two female custos coming out.

"What up, ladies?" Rell said, watching them walk down the stairs.

Him and Rick walked in and dapped Monster who was counting a large amount of small bills.

"What's the word?" Monster asked.

"Shit, just came to see what's goin on," Rick replied.

Rell grabbed some loose weed that was on the table and broke it down, then split a blunt open and began rolling up.

"This y'all right here," Monster said, handing Rick two huge knots of cash.

Rick counted the money and it was $3,500 in five and ten-dollar bills.

"Damn, Monster! They comin' like that?" Rick asked.

"Yeah, this bitch done picked up. $500 of that is from today though. I'm down to about $600 in bags, so I'm gon' need y'all to hit me off today," Monster said.

"We got you. Soon as I leave from here, I'm gonna put you a sack together and drop it off to you," Rell said, handing him the blunt.

Hammer lit up a cigarette and kicked it with Bo while T-mac was getting the money together from yesterday's take.

"How slow has it been?" Hammer asked Bo when he told him custos wasn't coming through.

Before Bo got a chance to answer Hammer's question, T-mac walked over and handed him $600 in small bills.

"What the fuck is this?" Hammer asked T-mac.

Hammer was pissed off, but he tried to keep cool until he heard T-mac's explanation.

"It's been slow," T-mac said, shrugging his shoulders.

His head was to the floor, not even looking at Hammer in the face.

"Somebody tell me somethin' that make sense. Just the other day, we bringin' in thousands. Now all of a sudden, only $600 come through this bitch yesterday? That shit don't add up. Either somebody in this hood just copped some better dope, which I highly doubt, or somebody t-rollin' 'round this bitch, flat out. Y'all niggaz been keeping an eye out for niggaz lurkin' around the building?" Hammer asked.

"I was outside off and on yesterday and I ain't see nobody suspicious around," Bo said.

"We got some of the best shit on the westside. Ain't no way we should have only $600 here from yesterday," Hammer said.

Hammer took the $600 and headed for the door. He went across the hall to the weed spot where Rick, Monster, and Rell was at.

"Yo, we gotta talk," Hammer said to Rick and Rell.

"What up?" Rell asked Hammer.

"Matter of fact, let's hit some corners and I'll tell y'all what's goin' on," Hammer suggested.

"Everything straight?" Monster asked.

"Yeah, just keep doin' what you do, big fella," Rick said, patting him on the back.

The three of them dapped Monster, and Rell reminded him that he would be back with a sack in a little while. Once they all got in Hammer's truck, he told them about the numbers the dope spot did the night before.

"Wait a minute. How the fuck we got some of the best dope out here and we only did $600 yesterday?" Rell asked.

"Yeah, something ain't right. The muthafuckin' weed spot did $3,000 yesterday. How the fuck the weed sellin' more than the crack?" Rick asked.

Hammer had a headache. He didn't like when there was a question he couldn't answer. He knew there was a reason for everything, and he planned to find out the reason for the spot being so slow the night before. He pulled in the gas station on the corner of Joy Road and Greenfield. He walked in and gave the cashier a $50 bill.

"Put that on number four!" he yelled through the bulletproof glass and walked out.

He popped the gas tank open and was about to pump the gas when Mike, a neighborhood fiend and also one of their custos, asked to pump the gas for Hammer. Hammer was about to tell him to get the fuck on, but he decided to go ahead and let him pump the gas while he picked the dope fiend's brain for information.

"What up, man? You ain't been up the way?" Hammer asked.

"Naw. Not today, nephew. Why? Y'all got some of that shit y'all used to have before yesterday?" Mike asked.

"What?!" Hammer asked, confused from what the fiend just told him. "Our shit been the same since day one, nigga."

"Naw, nephew. That shit y'all had the other day was weak as hell. That shit ain't do nothin' but clog my stem up," Mike said.

Hammer was pissed. That would mean either T-mac or Bo switched up the product and that was a no-no.

"You gon' be up here for a while?" Hammer asked the fiend.

"Yeah, I'll be up here all day," Mike said, knowing he couldn't really guarantee it. Wherever the money was, Mike was going right along with it.

"Alright, bet. I gotta shoot a move right quick and I'm gonna come back up here and bless you wit something," Hammer said.

"How long you gonna be?" Mike asked.

"Gimme about twenty minutes," Hammer said and gave him a $5 bill then hopped in the truck and pulled off.

"Y'all niggaz ain't gonna believe this shit," Hammer said to Rick and Rell.

"What up?" Rell asked.

"Man, I asked the fiend when the last time he been through the spot, and he turned around and asked me did we have some of the same shit we *used* to have before yesterday!"

"We always got the same shit. We ain't never switched up," Rick said matter-of-factly.

"Yeah, I know. That's what I told him, but he swears that shit ain't our regular product." Hammer said.

"That mean one of them niggaz on some bullshit over there," Rell said, referring to T-mac and Bo.

"Right. Whenever I drop the shit off, I only put it in T-mac's hands, that way Bo don't get too tempted and smoke that shit up," Hammer said.

"If that's the case then, that little nigga T-mac been…"

"I know, Rick. But before we get to accusing niggaz, I'm gonna hit that fiend Mike off wit a lil something and after he smoke it then see what he say," Hammer said, cutting Rick off.

Hammer didn't want to believe that T-mac would do some shit like that. He stopped on Mettetal and dropped Rick and Rell off.

"Call us when you find out what's goin' on," Rell said. Then he swung over on Fenkell and Westbrook to Victoria's house and put together a $7,000 sack in dime rocks and headed back to Joy Road.

Once he pulled into the gas station, he saw dope fiend Mike, sweeping up the lot. Hammer blew the horn to get Mike's attention and when Mike saw him, he walked over to the truck. Hammer rolled down the window and told Mike to get in. Mike walked around to the passenger side and climbed in.

"What up?" Mike asked Hammer.

"Look, I need you to go over to my spot and get a dime."

"I ain't got no money," Mike responded. Even if he did, he wouldn't go over to the apartments and spend it on that bullshit dope they had.

Hammer reached in his pocket and pulled out a knot full of $100 bills in his lap. Mike damn near drooled on himself when he saw all those bills in Hammer's lap. His dope fiend instinct kicked in and he thought about snatching as much money as he could and hopping out of the truck and taking off on foot, but he quickly changed his mind when he saw the butt of Hammer's pistol on his waist.

"Here," Hammer said and gave Mike a $20 bill.

"Go ahead and run over there right quick an come straight back here. I'll be waiting for you. Don't say I sent you though. And when you get back, I got something else for you," Hammer said and reached under the seat and showed him a fat sack full of rocks.

"You got it! I'll be right back, champ," Mike said, thanking God for his luck so far today.

"Make sure you bring me back my muthafuckin' change too, nigga!" Hammer said as Mike got out of the truck and closed the door.

Mike just threw a thumbs up and kept walking towards the spot.

Five minutes later, Mike came strolling down Greenfield and into the gas station where Hammer was parked waiting. Mike opened the door and got in the truck.

"Let me get that change," Hammer said flatly. Mike frowned and handed him the $10 bill.

"This look like the same shit as yesterday," Mike said, holding his hand out, showing Hammer the small piece of crack rock.

Hammer glanced at the $10 rock, but he couldn't tell the difference.

"What you want me to do with it?" Mike asked.

"Smoke it, muthafucka!" Hammer yelled, throwing his hands in the air.

"Alright," Mike said and pulled out his stem.

"Not in here, nigga! Go in the alley behind the station!" Hammer barked.

"Oh, my bad," Mike said and got out of the truck and walked behind the gas station and into the alley.

A few minutes later, Mike emerged from the alley and got back in the truck with Hammer. Hammer was trying to see if Mike was high, but from the looks of it, he looked about the same as he did before he went to smoke.

"Well?" Hammer asked.

"Man, that shit some trash y'all got over there. I felt a lil something when I first hit it, but when I was done, the high was gone before I even got back here. It's like you gotta be still when you smoke that shit or else you'll lose the high."

"Hmmph. Okay then. Do me a favor and go smoke this right quick and tell me what you think," Hammer said and gave Mike a dime rock he got from the stash at Victoria's house.

Mike got out the truck and walked back into the alley and did his thing. When he came out from behind the gas station, his eyes were wide open like he'd seen a ghost and it also looked like he was struggling to keep his balance.

When he got back in the truck, he turned to Hammer and asked. "You got some more of that shit?"

The proof was right in front of Hammer. There was no denying the fact that T-mac was switching up the sacks and pushing bullshit dope out of the spot.

"Now that's the shit y'all had on deck the day before yesterday," Mike said, snapping Hammer out of deep thought.

Hammer gave Mike the $10 bill that he had brought back to him from the spot and gave him another dime rock.

"Good lookin', but I just need one more thing from you," Hammer said.

"What can I do for you?" Mike asked.

"I need you to spread the word to all the custos that the good shit back at the spot on Greenfield. If you can do that for me, I got five more stones for you once shit pick up," Hammer said.

"That's it? Sheiiit, I'll have everybody that smoke bangin' the door down in the next fifteen minutes! That's gon' be easy 'cause ain't nothin' hittin' like this shit around here!" Mike said.

He got out the truck and headed down Joy Road and Hammer pulled off, headed to the spot up the street. When Hammer pulled up in front of the apartments, he saw people coming from the weed spot, but when he looked in the direction of the dope spot, it looked as if it was deserted. This pissed Hammer off even more as he got out the truck and made his way up the stairs. When he turned the key and let himself in, T-mac and Bo was smoking a blunt and watching T.V.

"What up, bro? You brought some more work with you?" T-mac asked.

This little nigga think he got all the sense, Hammer thought to himself.

"Shit, you ain't finished wit the shit you got, is you?" Hammer asked.

"Naw, ain't nobody else been through yet," T-mac said, not knowing his little scheme had been exposed.

Hammer was done playing games with T-mac. He whipped out his 9 mm Sig Sauer and put it up to T-mac's head.

"That's how you gon' play, niggaz? Huh?" Hammer asked through clenched teeth.

"I…I…what you talkin' bout?" T-mac asked. He sounded like a child. That tough shit he always used to be on went right out the window as he stared into the barrel of the gun. He knew how Hammer got down. He just prayed that he let him live.

"Lil nigga, if you lie to me again, I'm gon' blow yo muthafuckin' brains out. Now tell me, why the fuck you try to play me and my niggaz?" Hammer asked, pressing the gun into T-mac's head harder.

T-mac took a deep breath then said, "I'm just tryin' to eat, dawg."

"Just tryin' to eat? Nigga, you been eatin' good! Me and my niggaz blessed you! You had money in yo muthafuckin' pocket and I helped you get that muthafuckin' Acura you got!" Hammer yelled.

Hammer was hurt. He couldn't understand why T-mac would betray him like that. Bo was stunned. He was somewhat pissed at T-mac too because of his sneaky actions that could have ended up getting both of them killed.

Hammer's finger was twitching as it was wrapped around the trigger. He was on fire as he looked T-mac dead in his eyes.

Smack!

Smack!

Smack!

Hammer hit him across the face with the pistol, dropping T-mac with the first blow. He stood over him and hit him twice more and reached at T-mac's waist and snatched the .357 Magnum that he gave him a while back.

"It's yo lucky day, 'cause if my niggaz was here right now, they would have deaded yo ass. Now get yo lil bitch-ass outta here before I kill you, nigga! Be thankful I spared yo life," Hammer said and turned his back on him.

T-mac got up and was holding his jaw. His mouth was split open and bleeding and it felt like his jaw was broken. He walked out the door, humiliated, and crawled into his car and pulled off.

"Bo, hold shit down until Rell get here," Hammer said and tossed the new sack to Bo.

"I got you. Don't trip," Bo said after clearing his throat. *These niggaz playin' fo keeps,* he thought to himself.

He'd just seen first-hand, how shit could get ugly for someone if they ever thought of crossing Hammer and his crew. There was nothing else to be said. Bo wasn't stupid. He knew if he tried some dumb shit, niggaz was gonna paint the walls with his brains. Plus, he liked the niggaz and the money he was making with them, so crossing them never entered his mind.

Hammer left and walked across the hall to the weed spot and let himself in with the spare key. Monster was sitting on the couch chilling, watching a movie on T.V.

"What up, fam?" Monster said, giving Hammer dap.

Hammer sat on the couch next to Monster and told him what happened across the hall.

"Damn, I can't believe that nigga. I bet you his brother put him up to that shit."

"His brother?" Hammer asked.

"Yeah, his brother just got out of the feds. He used to be the man back in the day when me and T-mac were kids. We gotta keep our eyes open cuz them niggaz might want some get-back behind this shit," Monster said.

"Shit, if them niggaz come through here wantin' some smoke, they gon' get they asses capped, straight up. Hammer knew that T-mac and Monster were best friends, so he had to see where Monster stood with the situation.

"You wit us?" Hammer asked.

"Ain't no secret. I ain't goin' nowhere. Like you, Rell, Dolla, and Rick said... we family. Y'all niggaz put me on my feet. I would probably be a bum if it wasn't fa y'all. I still got love for T-mac though, but shit was getting to his head, for real. Sometimes he would talk like him and his brother was gonna take over and roll over me too," Monster said.

"We'll see about that. Them niggaz betta stay in they place," Hammer said. "I'm bout to buss up. Rell gonna be here in a lil bit. He gonna post up with Bo and hold shit down over there. You good?" Hammer asked.

"Yeah, I'm straight. Tell Rell to come holla at me when he touch down," Monster said.

"No doubt," Hammer said, then walked out the door.

Hammer called Rell and told him what happened and asked him to come through.

"I'll be there in about twenty minutes," Rell said and hung up the phone.

Damn, you can't trust nobody nowadays, Hammer said to himself then started up the truck and pulled off.

CHAPTER FIFTEEN

T-mac was driving down Joy Road in a daze. He was hurt. More so his pride than physically. He had grown kind of close to Hammer, and he didn't want shit to go down like that.

"Fuck that shit! That nigga pulled a muthafuckin' pistol on me!" he screamed, punching the steering wheel. "I kill niggaz too. He gon' get his, I'll make sure of that."

He pulled into the liquor store on Joy and Schafer and went inside. He bought a pack of squares and a half pint of vodka and headed back to the car. As soon as he was about to pull out of the parking lot, he saw his brother walking up the street with his friend. He blew his horn to get his brother's attention and once J-rock saw him, he jogged over to the car. When he first saw his brother in the parking lot, the first thing that came to mind was, *Damn, he ran through that bullshit already?* It wasn't until he got in on the passenger side that he saw his brother's face.

"What the fuck happened to you?" J-rock asked his brother with concern.

"Them niggaz caught on to that shit," T-mac said.

"Oh, them niggaz rushed you? They dead!" J-rock said, pounding his fist on the dashboard.

"Naw, I ain't get rushed. That nigga Hammer pistol whipped me."

J-rock was heated. He was ready to murc some shit. But he was mad at himself even more. His greed took over and he ended up putting his brother's life in danger. His greed and self-centeredness almost got T-mac killed.

"I'm sorry, bro. I shouldn't have put you in a position like that. This shit is my fault," J-rock said and dropped his head to his chest.

"Don't even trip, bro. I want them niggaz out the picture just as much as you do," T-mac said.

"Listen, I need you to tell me everything you know about them niggaz," J-rock said…

Christmas came and went and now the new year was approaching. The crew had plans to have a party on Mettetal. Krissy and her boyfriend, Keith, would hold the spot down on Blackstone and the crew would still serve custos that came through for weed on Mettetal. Everything was going good for the crew. After getting rid of T-mac, the dope spot on Joy Road was doing over $5,000 a day easily, and on the first of the month it would do damn near double the daily take. They could barely keep up with the business coming through. It wasn't doing as good as the spot on Blackstone, but it was damn sure holding its own.

Maine from Joy Road and Evergreen was still copping bricks and a few pounds here and there from the crew, thanks to Monster. Everybody had a lot of love for Monster. He showed his loyalty to the crew time and time again, and he and E-baby had grown close like brothers - close like Monster and T-mac used to be.

Monster tried reaching out to T-mac by calling him, but T-mac wouldn't answer his phone. Monster got pissed off one day and started blowing T-mac's phone. T-mac finally answered, but he didn't even give Monster a chance to speak.

"Nigga, fuck you! You one of them now," T-mac said, and hung up the phone.

That broke Monster's heart. Even though he was still getting money with the crew, that didn't mean he lost love for T-mac. He just wanted to check on his friend to make sure he was ok. Monster knew it had to be J-rock that put him up to switching the sacks like that, and Monster lost all the respect he had for J-rock behind that shit. As far as Monster was concerned, J-rock was a hoe-ass nigga for putting his own blood brother on front like that for a few dollars. Real niggaz don't do shit like that. Monster felt like J-rock was bad news for T-mac, even though they were brothers. *He gonna fuck around and get my nigga smoked out here,* Monster said to himself, shaking his head.

New Year's Eve finally came, and all the spots were doing record numbers. It was as if everybody and they momma on the westside wanted to get high off something. Dolla, Rell, Rick, and Hammer were scrambling, trying to keep the spots filled up with product.

The Royal Fashions clothing store was banging, and the Royal Treatment Beauty Shop was off the hook. Everybody wanted to be fly on the last day of the year. Business hours flew by and the managers closed up the stores and headed home to their families.

By ten o'clock, the whole crew was on Mettetal. Everybody was celebrating as the music played in the background. There was a dice game going on in front of the house, and there were ladies everywhere. Dennis had invited a few female friends, and they cooked a boatload of wing dings and french fries, so people had something to put on their stomachs while they were drinking. There was every type of liquor, beer, and wine a person could imagine.

The crew pitched in and spent damn near $10,000 on drinking alone. There was more than enough to go around, and there was sure to be plenty left over. Earlier that day, Dennis went to the gun store and bought an assortment of bullets to shoot off at midnight. Dennis had even invited Lisa, the big-booty white girl he'd met at Dolla and Savannah's house. Dennis was a player. The two females that he invited to cook were also romantically involved with him. When Lisa arrived, the two women didn't reveal that they were fucking with him, nor did they act funny towards her. They played their positions well.

Rick invited Mary, Savannah's college roommate. The two of them had grown pretty close to each other, and Rick would spend the weekend in Lansing at the college while Savannah would spend the weekend at her home with Dolla. Savannah didn't want to come to the party. She stayed at the house instead. She didn't care too much for guns, and she didn't want the risk of getting hit by a stray bullet either. Every year since she could remember, she either spent New Year's Eve at church or at home in the basement.

Hammer brought Victoria along with him, and they were enjoying themselves. He even took her across the street and introduced her to his mother. The two of them hit it off and when Victoria was out of ear's reach, Hammer's mother whispered, "She's a keeper, honey. Hang on to this one. Trust your mother." Hammer nodded his head and smiled.

E-baby, Gary, Monster, Bo, Rell, Quick, and Bruce were running wild, trying to pull every female at the party. Even Rick's sister, Rita, came to the party. At fifteen minutes to midnight, E-baby, Monster, and Gary used their cars to block traffic from turning on the block and the crew started getting guns together to shoot off. Everybody gathered around outside on the corner, and all cups were filled with liquor. Everybody out the crew had some type of automatic rifle.

As the countdown to midnight began, Dolla faced the guests and his crew and held his cup high.

"We gon' bring this new year in the same way we ended this one…Getting muthafuckin' money! Y'all know what time it is."

"Loyalty brings royalty!" the crew yelled out in unison.

The guests yelled the same thing, and everyone slammed their cups of liquor in one swallow.

"Five! Four! Three! Two!…"

Pop!

Pop!

Pop!

Rat tat tat tat tat!

The crew had their guns raised to the sky and emptied clip after clip in the street. After they were done shooting, it took them about half an hour to clean up all the empty gun shells.

The party lasted until about three in the morning, and everyone said their separate goodbyes and went their separate ways. Gary and E-baby went back to Blackstone. Monster, Bo, and Rell headed back to the apartments on Joy Road, and Hammer went to Victoria's house on Westbrook.

Rick took Mary to his crib for the night and Lisa stayed at Dennis's house. Both Mary and Lisa had a ball. They had never been to the hood, and that was their first time chilling at the spot. Everybody at the party showed them love and didn't act funny towards them because they weren't from the ghetto. Quick and Bruce stayed on Mettetal and ended up passing out shortly after everybody left. Dolla drove home and crawled in the bed with Savannah.

The next day, a snowstorm hit the city. Traffic was backed up on highways and city streets. The news said to expect at least twelve inches of snow by nightfall. The snow was coming down in flurries, making it difficult for drivers to see the road in front of them.

Even in the midst of the blizzard, the spots were still doing numbers. The spot on Mettetal and the weed spot in the apartments on Joy Road had an early morning and afternoon rush but slowed down during the middle of the day. But the crack spots were booming like clockwork.

All businesses, schools, and just about everything else was closed for New Year's Day, so Dolla didn't have to worry about opening up any of the stores. The banks were closed as well, so Dolla had to wait until the next day to deposit the money from the stores into his business account. He decided to just stop by the stash house in the apartments on Greenfield and Eaton and count the money. He was glad that he hooked up with Les before Christmas and bought a Ford Expedition. He'd bought Savannah a Ford Explorer too. He didn't want to be driving around in the blizzard in his Benz or his old school.

He got up and hopped in the shower then got dressed.

"Baby, where you going?" Savannah asked, still half asleep in the bed.

"I gotta shoot some moves right quick. I won't be gone too long," Dolla said.

"But the weather is bad out there. Come back to bed with me."

"That's why I got us some trucks, so whenever days like this come around, we can roll right through that shit," Dolla said.

He walked over to Savannah and kissed her on the forehead.

"Be careful," Savannah said as Dolla grabbed his pistol and walked out the door.

Dolla drove to the stash house on Greenfield and Eaton. When he pulled in the back of the apartments, he noticed that Rell's car was gone, but Rick's car was there. He walked up the stairs and knocked on Rick's door.

"Who dat?" Rick yelled from the other side of the door.

"It's me, bro. Use yo peephole, nigga!" Dolla said.

A few seconds later, the sounds of locks began clicking and the door opened. Rick was in his robe with his pistol in his hand. He shivered from the burst of air that was coming from outside as he unlocked the security gate. Dolla stepped in and dapped Rick.

"What up doe, nigga? Everything straight?" Rick asked.

"Yeah. I was just gonna swing by the stash house and see what I'm lookin' like and I noticed you was at home, so I stopped by to kick it for a minute," Dolla said.

"Wanna blow one?" Rick asked.

"We can do that."

"Bet. I wanna kick it wit you about some shit anyways," Rick said, then walked into the bedroom and grabbed up some weed and some blunts.

Mary was still asleep from the pounding he'd put on her. Rick was the first black man Mary had ever fucked, and once she got a taste, she couldn't get enough. Rick was the perfect gentleman and he was a good lover in the bedroom too.

Rick came from out of the bedroom and tossed the two blunts to Dolla.

"Split those open while I break down the weed," Rick said.

After rolling up, Dolla lit the first blunt.

"Yo, I was kickin' it wit baby girl, and she was tellin' me it's some money out there in Lansing," Rick said.

"Who you talkin' bout, Mary?" Dolla asked, handing Rick the blunt.

"Yeah. She say she got peoples on the east and west side and basically gave me the whole spill on how the areas are. Her friend's cousins be hustling on the east and west, and Mary's friend always be tellin' her about how it ain't shit but fiends around the way. We already been talkin' bout settin' up shop out there. Why not put the plan together now?" Rick asked.

"Shit, I don't see why not. We got the plug behind us. All we gotta do is get some workers from out there, then we can send somebody from the crew down there to keep an eye on things. See if you can hook up with the friend's cousins and then we can take it from there," Dolla said.

They chopped it up for a little while longer then Dolla got up to leave.

"I'm a get at you, dawg," Dolla said, dapping up Rick.

"Alright, bet. I'll hit you up later," Rick said.

He got up and let Dolla out the door. Once he locked the door, he walked back to the bedroom. He lifted up the covers on the bed and admired Mary's body as she laid there, stark naked. *Time for round two,* Rick said to himself and took off his robe and slid into bed.

Dolla opened the door to the stash house across the hall from Rell and stepped inside. He quickly disarmed the alarm and headed to the bedroom. He pushed the king size bed from the spot it was sitting in and reached down with a flathead screwdriver and began lightly prying up the floorboards. Once he had them all pulled up, he opened the large safe that was installed in the floor with the customized combination that Dolla, Hammer, Rell, and Rick came up with.

The safe was stuffed with cash, small and large bills. The four of them would fill the safe up, then pick up their cuts every week. Every week, the spots would clock in as follows: Blackstone generated $105,000, Mettetal $24,000, the weed spot on Joy Road did $21,000, and the dope spot on Joy Road would bring in a little over $60,000 a week. That wasn't including the kilos and pounds they were serving to the niggaz in Brightmoor and to Maine on Joy Road. They split that down the middle immediately after making the sales. In total, every week, the spots brought about $210,000, sometimes more during the first week of the month, but the number never went lower.

After separating his cut, which was $51,625, he put it inside of a black trash bag then locked it back up in the safe. That way when the bank opened tomorrow, he would have the money already separated and wouldn't have to recount it.

He put the floorboards back in place over the safe and it didn't look like a safe even existed. Then he put the bed back in place over the safe and set the alarm and walked out the door.

Leaving from the stash house, he drove over to the spot on Mettetal and checked on Bruce and Quick to make sure they were straight. He stayed for about a half hour then left and headed over to Joy Road to holla at Rell. Once he got over there, he checked on Monster then walked across the hall to holla at Rell.

Bo was sitting at the table counting money and Rell was on the couch watching T.V., smoking a blunt.

"What up, nigga?" Rell said and stood up to dap Dolla.

Dolla dapped Bo and grabbed the blunt from Rell.

"What's crackin'?" Dolla asked.

"Shit, just chillin' wit this nigga, Bo… reminiscing about last night. The spot back doin' numbers like it was before T-mac pulled that nickel-slick shit," Rell said.

"Yeah, I see," Dolla said. When he was coming from across the hall, he saw three fiends being served at the door,

"Bo, you wanna tell Dolla the good news or you want me to tell 'em?" Rell asked.

"What news?" Dolla asked.

"That nigga been clean for almost a week now," Rell said.

"I'm thru smokin' yae. I only fuck wit the weed," Bo said with confidence.

"That's what's up, bro. You don't need that shit no way. You got too much potential," Dolla said, handing Bo the blunt.

"No doubt. And it's thanks to y'all that I realized my potential and now it's time to put that shit to use," Bo said, taking a pull from the blunt.

Rell reached and grabbed the half-full fifth of Hennessey and poured a shot.

"Get a cup and drink wit me," Rell said.

"Shit I'm straight, it's too early," Dolla said.

"Nigga, it ain't never too early to have a drink. Get some of this shit up in you. It's cold as fuck out there. A few shots 'a warm you up," Rell said.

"You right," Dolla said and grabbed a plastic cup from the kitchen and poured a shot.

Dolla told Rell about what Rick said earlier about setting up shop in Lansing.

"Yeah, bro. We need to jump on that. I think we should send them lil niggaz, Quick and Bruce, out there to run shit."

"Yeah, I was thinkin' the same shit," Dolla said.

After talking for a while and drinking a few more shots, Dolla was ready to go. He dapped Rell and Bo before leaving. It had gotten even colder, and it was still snowing hard outside.

I'm glad I didn't drink those shots before I left, Dolla said to himself and lit a cigarette.

He got in his truck and pulled off. He wanted to stop by the spot on Blackstone and kick it with Hammer, E-baby, and Gary, but the weather was too bad, so he decided to head home.

"Let me call this nigga," Dolla said referring to Hammer and pulled out his phone.

Hammer didn't answer so he called E-baby.

"What up, doe?" E-baby answered the phone in two rings.

"Shit, chillin'. Where dat nigga Hammer at?" Dolla asked.

"Man, dat nigga came over this morning and dropped something on me and Gary then went back to Victoria's house. Nigga was all hung over and shit… said he had to get some sleep," E-baby said.

"Damn, bro. I would come over there and kick it wit y'all, but this weather is fucked up. I just left from Joy Road, but I'm gonna go back to the crib," Dolla said.

"Go ahead. We ain't on shit over here. That nigga Gary said what up," E-baby said.

"Tell my nigga I said what up," Dolla said.

"Alright, then. I'mma get off this phone and holla at y'all later."

"Alright, be easy," E-baby said then hung up.

Dolla hung up the phone and stuck it in his pocket. He took his eyes off the road for a second while putting the phone in his pocket and when he looked up, he was reaching the stop light on Greenfield and Chicago Avenue. The light was yellow and was about to turn red, but Dolla was already too close. The road was too slippery to try to stop so he just kept going.

The light turned red before he crossed the intersection, and there was no way he could have stopped in time to catch the light. He didn't notice the police that was four cars behind him. As he crossed the intersection, his phone rang.

"Shit!" Dolla yelled, fumbling in his pocket to get his phone, trying to stay focused on the road at the same time.

"Hello?"

"Aye, I think you left something at my crib," Rick said.

"What is it?" Dolla asked.

"It's a key. I know it ain't mine and Mary say it ain't hers either. Plus, I found it by where you was sitting at when you came over, so it's gotta be yours."

Dolla remembered that he had taken the spare house key when he left from home in the morning and he didn't attach it to his key ring with his truck key.

"Damn, good lookin', I'll be over there to…" Dolla stopped mid-sentence when he saw the blue and red lights flashing behind him.

"Fuck!" Dolla yelled.

"What's wrong, bro?" Rick asked.

"The fuckin' hook flickin' me," Dolla said.

"You straight?" Rick asked.

"Yeah, I got my L's on me, so I'm good. Don't hang up though," Dolla said.

The two officers got out the police car and one approached the driver's side while the other approached the passenger side. They didn't have their guns drawn, but they did have their hands on their weapons while they were still in the holsters. Dolla already had his window rolled down halfway by the time they got to the truck.

"License and registration," the officer who was on the driver's side said to Dolla.

The officer on the passenger side of the truck was looking inside the truck to see if he could spot something illegal.

"Here you go, sir," Dolla said and handed the officer the information.

When Dolla spoke, the officer could smell the liquor on his breath from the shots he'd taken before he left the spot on Joy Road.

"Sir, have you been drinking?" the officer asked Dolla.

"Not really. I just had a few…"

"Step out of the vehicle, sir," the officer said, cutting Dolla off.

Dolla clenched his teeth and shook his head. He knew this wasn't gonna turn out good. He had shut the engine off when they pulled him over, so there was no way he could try to flee. He opened the door and got out of the truck. Once he was outside, he sat the phone in the driver's seat. Rick was still on the phone, so he could hear everything that was going on.

"Any weapons or drugs on you, sir?" the officer asked.

Dolla ignored the officer as he began to search him. The officer drew his weapon once he ran his hands across Dolla's waist.

"He's got a gun!" the officer yelled, keeping his aim steady on Dolla.

The other officer came from the passenger side with his gun drawn and handcuffed Dolla, then grabbed Dolla's Glock .40 with a thirty round extended clip and handed it to his partner who placed the gun on the hood of the police car. The officer who cuffed Dolla did a more thorough search and found an ounce of weed in his coat pocket.

"Oh, you sell drugs too?" the officer asked Dolla.

Dolla didn't say a word, but he cursed himself for forgetting about grabbing the weed from the stash house earlier that day. They also found about $1,200 in cash and confiscated that as well. They put Dolla in the back of the police car and began searching the truck. The first thing they came across was Dolla's cell phone. The officer noticed it was on and shut it off.

CHAPTER SIXTEEN

Mary had a great weekend with Rick. The two of them had grown fond of each other in a short amount of time. She really liked Rick. In fact, she wanted to take things further and be in a relationship with him.

Don't rush it. He'll be your man in due time, Mary told herself as she stepped out of the shower. She grabbed her towel and dried off her body. Then she dried her hair and wrapped her towel around her body and stepped out of the bathroom into Rick's bedroom. She noticed Rick was sitting on the edge of the bed with a blank look on his face.

"Ricky, what's wrong?" she asked.

"I need you to call Savannah for me and tell her Dolla's in jail," Rick said without even looking in Mary's direction.

"Oh my God!" Mary screamed and ran to her purse and pulled out her phone.

"Hello," Savannah said softly as she picked up the phone.

"Savannah, this is Mary. I hate to be the one to tell you this, but Dolla just got arrested."

"What! What the hell happened?!"

Mary explained to her how Rick was on the phone with him and heard everything.

"I told his ass not to go out today!" Savannah said. She was angry at Dolla, even though she knew he was a businessman and hustler. This type of stuff came along with the game. The game never sleeps or stops. The only way to stay on top is to supply the demands and you must be available at all times.

"Where is he at?" Savannah asked.

"Rick said most likely they took him to the second precinct on Grand River and Schafer," Mary said.

"I gotta get down there," Savannah said as she got out of bed and started getting dressed.

She forgot that the weather was fucked up, and she didn't know how to drive in the snow, not to mention, in a blizzard.

Damn, I can't drive in this shit, Savannah said, remembering how bad the weather was.

"Hold on, girl. Let me see if Rick can pick you up," Mary said.

Rick didn't mind going to pick her up, but he also knew that it was a chance that he could get stuck trying to reach her. He quickly came up with an idea.

"Let me call Hammer and see if he can pick her up in his truck. If he don't wanna come out there, then I'll pick her up." Rick said to Mary, picking up his phone to call Hammer.

Hammer answered the phone, still hung over from the New Year's party the night before.

"That nigga Dolla locked up," Rick said to Hammer.

"What the fuck happened?" Hammer asked.

When Rick told him about what happened, his hangover seemed to leave him immediately.

"Savannah needs a ride to the police station. You know how fucked up the weather is, and she can't drive in that shit. Can you pick her up?" Rick asked.

"Yeah, I'll scoop her up. I just need her address and phone number," Hammer said.

Rick told Mary to get Savannah's phone number and address, so Hammer could pick her up. Mary was still on the phone with Savannah and she scrambled to find a pen and a piece of paper. She wrote the information down and handed it to Rick, who in return, gave Hammer the information.

"I'm 'bout to call her and let her know I'm on my way," Hammer said.

"My girl on the phone wit her right now. I'll have her let Savannah know you about to head that way," Rick said.

"Alright, bet. I'm 'bout to throw some clothes on and be out." Hammer said.

"After you pick her up, swing over here and scoop me up," Rick said.

"I got you," Hammer said and hung up the phone.

After getting off the phone with Hammer, Rick called Rell and let him know what happened to Dolla. Rell wanted to meet them at the police station, but Rick told him he should stay posted at the spot. That way if E-baby or Gary needed a sack or the spot on Mettetal ran out, Rell could go hit them off.

Hammer was driving like a bat outta hell on his way to pick Savannah up. He weaved in and out of the freeway lanes, passing the slow drivers in his luxury SUV. He made it to Savannah's house in an hour. Had he been driving at the pace of the other drivers, it would have taken him twice as long to get there. Once he pulled into the driveway, he called Savannah and let her know that he was outside. While waiting for her to come outside, he looked at their house in admiration.

"Fuck that. I'm gonna get a house like this and move Victoria and Mamma out the hood."

He already tried to move his mother to a better neighborhood, but she refused. Hammer decided that he was gonna move her off the block whether she wanted to or not. He would burn down the house on Mettetal if that's what it took.

Savannah came outside, clutching her coat, trying to shield herself from the brisk wind that was blowing. Hammer reached over and opened the passenger door and Savannah climbed in the truck.

"Whew!" she said, shivering from the cold air.

Hammer had the heat on blast, so it didn't take long for her to warm up.

"Thanks for coming to get me," Savannah said.

"Ain't no thang, we family," Hammer said.

"You got here quick. I didn't expect you to make it here so fast."

"There wasn't much traffic on the freeway," Hammer lied.

They made small talk while driving from Sterling Heights to Detroit. Hammer drove with caution on the way back. He didn't want to freak Savannah out by driving crazy like he did on the way to pick her up. It took them about an hour and a half to make it to Detroit.

They stopped to pick Rick up, and from there, they headed to the second precinct. Rick had already gotten in touch with a lawyer and they met up at the police station. The lawyer introduced himself as Otis Woods to the three of them.

"Can you get him out today, Mr. Woods?" Savannah asked.

"Please, call me Otis. I don't know if that's possible, but I'll try my best to make it happen," Otis said sincerely.

Otis spoke with an officer at the front desk in the lobby. A few minutes later, he came walking back to Hammer, Rick, and Savannah.

"I'm sorry, but I won't be able to get him out today. By it being a holiday, there was no court in session to give him a bond, but he will have video arraignment tomorrow morning and the judge will give him a bond then. Darin is being charged with the intent to deliver marijuana and carrying a concealed weapon with obliterated serial numbers," Otis told the three of them.

Savannah just shook her head and Rick and Hammer let out a flurry of curse words.

"What time should we be up here in the morning?" Rick asked the lawyer.

"I'll be up here before the video arraignment begins and once I find out how much the bond is, I'll call you and then you can come up here with the money," Otis informed Rick.

"Alright then. We'll be waiting for your call tomorrow," Rick said.

"Do you think we can see him?" Hammer asked.

"I asked the officer at the desk if it was possible for the three of you to speak with him, but unfortunately, there are no visits today due to the holiday," Otis said.

The lawyer shook hands with the three of them, and they all left out of the police station. Hammer, Savannah, and Rick went back to Rick's apartment to chill for a while. Savannah and Mary stayed in the bedroom and talked, smoking a blunt while Rick and Hammer stayed in the living room. They all agreed it would be best for Savannah to stay the night at Rick's apartment, that way, they would be able to go straight to the police station once the lawyer called. It wouldn't make sense to take her all the way back to Sterling Heights, only to turn around and have to pick her up in the morning. Plus, the weather was still terrible.

Rick and Hammer were smoking a blunt when Rell called Rick's phone to check on Dolla. Rick told him they would be bonding him out in the morning. Hammer's phone started ringing and when he answered, it was E-baby.

"E. What up, nigga?" Hammer asked.

"Shit, what happened wit that nigga, Dolla?"

"We gonna get him out in the morning," Hammer informed E-baby.

"Yo, I need you to swing thru and hit me and G wit something. We bout to be done over here," E-baby said.

"I'm on my way. I'll be there in a lil bit," Hammer said and hung up the phone.

"I gotta buss up. E-baby and Gary need another sack," Hammer said to Rick.

"Damn! That's a million-dollar spot we got over there," Rick said laughing.

"Oh, yeah. I almost forgot to tell you. We bout to get shit crackin' in Lansing, my nigga."

"Straight up?" Hammer asked.

He knew they were making plans to expand, and he wouldn't mind having a change of scenery.

"Yeah. I gotta go down there and holla at some of Mary's people. Then we gon' bust shit open down there. Me, you, Rell, and Dolla gonna have to sit at the table and put this shit together." Rick said.

"Fa sho. You know I'm wit it," Hammer said.

Hammer got up and walked to the bedroom door and knocked. The door was open, and Mary and Savannah looked up to see Hammer standing in the doorway.

"I'll be over here in the morning to pick you up and take you to bond Dolla out," Hammer said to Savannah.

"Okay, thank you."

"You alright?" Hammer asked her.

"Yeah, I'm fine," Savannah said.

"Alright then, tomorrow," Hammer said and headed for the door.

"Hit me up as soon as you hear from the lawyer." Hammer said.

He dapped Rick then left. He was on his way to Blackstone. Rick decided to go over on Mettetal and chop it up with Quick and Bruce. He called Dennis and told him he was coming through and Dennis told him that he would meet him at the spot. Rick wanted to give Savannah and Mary a little space and he also wanted to kick it with Dennis and let him know what was going on with Dolla. He grabbed the keys and told Mary where he was going. He kissed her lightly on the cheek and left.

By the time Rick made it to Mettetal, Dennis was already at the spot with Quick and Bruce. Rick told them what was going on with Dolla while Bruce rolled up a few blunts.

"Yo, we out of blunts. Can you go get some?" Bruce asked Rick.

"I just rolled up two and I know that ain't gon' be enough for us."

"I got you, my nigga. Y'all need anything else?" Rick asked.

"Yeah, grab up some cigarettes and something to sip on," Quick said.

"Alright, I'll be back in a minute," Rick said.

"I'll ride wit you," Dennis said, and they left out the door.

They got in the minivan and took the alley to the liquor store on Grand River and Grandmont.

"We bout to open up in Lansing. If you interested, let us know," Rick said.

Dolla, Rell, Hammer, and Rick were always trying to pull Dennis in on the money they were making. Dennis rubbed his chin as if he was in deep thought about the offer. He had a few dollars saved, but he knew that eventually it would run out. He actually had been contemplating talking to the boys about possibly opening up a spot, so maybe now was the time to invest with them.

"Tell you what, let me know what I need and when y'all ready, get wit me," Dennis said.

"Hell yeah! We got the O.G. on the team now!" Rick said, happy that Dennis was jumping in the game with them.

"Shit, nigga. Y'all been had a O.G. on y'all team the whole muthafuckin' time! And y'all niggaz ain't babies no mo' either, while you talkin' that O.G. shit!" Dennis was laughing.

"True dat," Rick said, laughing with him.

They bought two packs of squares, two packs of blunts and a fifth of Hennessey and went back to the spot.

As the day turned into night, it stopped snowing and business began to pick up. They smoked a few blunts and ran through the fifth of Hennessey while shooting dice. Dennis ended up walking away from the dice game $500 richer.

"I'll break y'all niggaz every time. I told y'all, I do this for bread and meat!" Dennis said, straightening out the crumbled bills.

Rick ended up leaving the spot around 11:00. He pulled up in the back of the apartment and parked the minivan next to his BMW and stumbled up the stairs and let himself in. Mary and Savannah were in the bedroom smoking a blunt. Weed smoke and the smell of chicken invaded Rick's nostrils.

"Hey, boo. You hungry?" Mary asked, hugging Rick.

"Yeah," Rick said. His speech was slurred from the liquor he was drinking earlier.

"Ricky! You fucked up?!" Mary asked, smacking him on the ass. "Go sit down while I fix your plate."

Savannah walked from the bedroom to the living room and handed Rick the blunt. Rick was already on cloud nine, but he took the blunt from her anyway.

"Thanks. You alright, sis?" Rick asked Savannah.

Savannah liked everybody in the crew, especially Rick. She could tell he had a good heart and felt the vibe of loyalty from him.

"Yeah, I'm straight. I just can't wait to pick this boy up tomorrow and take his ass home," she said.

Mary brought Rick his plate and a glass of ice water to wash the food down with.

"Thanks, baby," Rick said and smashed the plate of food within minutes.

After eating, Rick ended up passing out on the couch with a full stomach, and Mary and Savannah fell asleep in the bedroom.

Rick woke up to the sound of his phone ringing. It was Hammer on the phone.

"You heard from the lawyer yet?" Hammer asked.

"Naw, ain't called yet. What time is it?" Rick asked.

"It's eight o'clock, my nigga. Get up and get dressed, I'm on my way. I might as well post up over there wit y'all and wait for the lawyer to call. That way, all we gotta do is grab the money and shoot right to the precinct," Hammer said.

"Alright, come on through," Rick said and hung up.

Rick hopped in the shower and was out, fully dressed in ten minutes. Mary and Savannah were still sleeping, so he woke them up and told them to get ready.

Hammer made it to Rick's place and once the girls were out the shower and fully dressed, Rick rolled up a blunt and the four of them had an early morning session.

"Darin Jones, step in front of the camera!" the fat turnkey yelled.

Dolla walked towards the small T.V. screen and stood directly in front of it. He had on a black hoodie, black jeans, and a pair of black Timberland boots. The old white man who was the judge read off Dolla's charges and set the bail at $50,000, ten percent which was $5,000.

After the other inmates saw the judge, the turnkey returned them to their cells. After video court, the lawyer found out how much Dolla's bail was and immediately called Rick and told him to bring $5,000.

Once Rick got the call from the lawyer, him and Hammer went to the stash house, which was a few doors down, and grabbed the money. Rick, Hammer, Rell, and Dolla had put up $500,000 just for times like this. If anyone caught a case in the crew, they would be able to bond them out right way.

Rick, Hammer, and Savannah drove up to the second precinct to bail Dolla out. As soon as they walked In, they saw the lawyer sitting down waiting for them.

"Otis!" Rick called out to the lawyer. The lawyer got up and walked over to them and shook their hands. Rick handed Otis the $5,000 to get Dolla out.

"Please have a seat while I get your friend released from custody," the lawyer said and walked to the front desk.

The three of them sat down and talked amongst themselves while they waited for Dolla. About fifteen minutes later, Dolla emerged from the back and gathered his property from the officer at the front desk. The three of them stood up and Savannah took off running towards

Dolla. She dove into his arms and was squeezing him so tight he could hardly breathe.

"So, you missed me, huh?" Dolla said with a sideways grin on his face.

Savannah began kissing him all over his face.

"They didn't hurt you back there, did they baby?" Savannah asked.

"Naw, I'm good, boo. It was only for a day," Dolla said.

Hammer and Rick walked over and dapped Dolla. Rick then turned to the lawyer and shook his hand and thanked him. He had already given the lawyer $2,500 as a retainer fee. He was one of the best criminal defense lawyers in the city.

"Mr. Jones, you'll most likely have your court date set about thirty days from today. I'll be your lawyer on this case, and by it being your first offense, you will most likely receive probation." The lawyer reached in his pocket and handed Dolla his business card.

"Feel free to call me if you have any questions or concerns. I'll get in contact with you before your court date and let you know exactly what's going to take place."

"Thanks," Dolla said and shook his hand.

"You're welcome, Mr. Jones. Be safe and try to stay out of trouble until we meet again," the lawyer said and walked out the police station.

"Where they got your truck at?" Hammer asked.

"The hook told me it's at the impound yard on Trumbull Avenue," Dolla said.

"Alright, then. Let's go pick yo shit up then," Hammer said about to walk out the door.

"Before we do that, I gotta get something to eat. I'm hungry than a muthafucka. I ain't ate shit but a hoe-ass bologna sandwich," Dolla said.

They left the police station and drove across the street to the Coney Island restaurant and ordered some breakfast. The cashier was a custo who copped weed from the spot on Mettetal. She was good peoples and she hooked the four of them up for half price.

"Good lookin'. We'll remember that next time you come thru," Rick said, winking at her.

"Just take me out on a date and we can call it even," the young cashier said with a seductive look on her face.

Rick was blushing. No one could tell because he was dark-skinned. Rick could feel Savannah's eyes on him. She was standing right behind him along with Dolla and Hammer. Rick just smiled uncomfortably and paid for the food. He turned around and just as he suspected, all eyes were on him.

"What?!" he said when they sat in the booth.

"Don't make my girl have to come over on Mettetal and cut a bitch," Savannah said, pointing her finger at Rick.

"Naw. I ain't gonna play Mary like that," Rick said, holding his hands up in front of him.

"You better not," Savannah said.

Hammer and Dolla were both cracking up.

"What the fuck is so funny?" Rick asked.

They both ignored him and continued laughing. They sat inside Coney Island and ate their food, then left, headed to the impound yard.

Before leaving the Coney Island parking lot, they rolled up two blunts. Dolla felt relieved as he took a pull from the blunt and let the weed smoke dance around in his lungs.

"Call that nigga Rell and let him know you straight," Hammer said to Dolla.

"You right. Let me do that," Dolla said, pulling his cell phone out of his hoodie pocket.

He called Rell and let him know that he made bail. He also called Monster, E-baby, Gary, and Dennis to let them know that he was back on the streets too.

Rick was on the phone with Quick and Bruce. They were running low and needed another sack. Rick told them that they'd just picked up Dolla and he would be that way in about an hour.

"Y'all got enough to hold y'all until then?" Rick asked Bruce.

"Yeah, we should be straight. Tell that nigga, Dolla, me and Quick said what up."

"Will do, my nigga," Rick said and hung up the phone.

They arrived at the impound yard, and Dolla went inside and paid the fee and they retrieved his truck for him. He didn't have any money on him since the police sized what he had on him the day he was arrested. The police said it was drug money because they found the ounce of weed Dolla had on him. Hammer gave him some money to pay the impound yard. Once the worker brought Dolla's truck from the yard, he got out and handed Dolla the keys. Dolla inspected it for damage then got in and pulled out of the lot.

Hammer, Rick, and Savannah were parked on the side of the impound yard, waiting for Dolla. Dolla pulled up behind them and got out the truck. He thanked Hammer and Rick for their help.

"What you bout to do?" Hammer asked Dolla.

"I'm gonna shoot to the stash house and grab something to smoke, then I'm goin' home and chill out for the day," Dolla said.

"Alright, then. Be safe, my nigga," Hammer said.

"If y'all need me, hit me up," Dolla said and dapped Rick and Hammer.

Both Dolla and Savannah jumped in the truck and took off. Dolla pulled up at the apartments on Greenfield and Eaton and ran upstairs to the stash house. Once inside, he grabbed $3,000 out of his cut that he put to the side the day he was arrested. Then he grabbed an ounce of weed and a nine-millimeter Ruger and stuck it in his waistline.

I'd rather be judged by twelve than carried by six, Dolla said to himself, setting the alarm and walking out of the apartment.

The weather was a lot better than the day before. The city had sent out plow trucks to clear excess snow from the roads and freeways, so the ride to Sterling Heights was pretty smooth for Dolla and Savannah. Once they made it home, Dolla took a long hot shower and Savannah cooked something to eat.

Once he got out the shower the two of them sat down, ate, then smoked a few blunts while watching a movie. After the movie went off, Dolla went upstairs to the bedroom and took a nap. He didn't get much sleep at the police station, so he was in need of some good rest. Savannah didn't get much sleep the night before either. She had sat up talking with Mary and she was worried about Dolla. She ended up crawling in the bed next to him and falling asleep too...

Monster had the time of his life last night. He'd spent the night at the motel room drinking, smoking, and fucking. He had two females with him that were custos from the weed spot. That was his first threesome and the two girls wore him out. It was $200 well spent as far as he was concerned. And the crazy thing about it was that the two girls didn't even ask for money. He just gave them $75 a piece anyway. He didn't mind looking out for them. They were good peoples.

Monster pulled into the back of the apartments and headed upstairs. Bo held down the weed spot for him while Rell stayed across on the couch watching T.V.

"So, what happened last night wit them two hoes you had?" Bo asked.

Monster filled Bo in on the details while they smoked a blunt. After the blunt was gone, Bo stood up and was getting ready to shoot across the hall to the dope spot.

"I'm bout to go across the hall. That nigga Rell tryin' to dip out for a little while," Bo said to Monster.

"Alright, good lookin' out on holdin' shit down for me last night," Monster said.

"Fa sho. It ain't shit. Oh, I almost forgot to tell you… That nigga T-mac came thru lookin' for you last night. Twice. I didn't tell him you was gone for the night. I just said you was out takin' care of some shit," Bo informed Monster.

Nigga done finally came to his senses, Monster thought to himself. He still had love for T-mac, even after he made that comment about him being on the "other side". He didn't care if they weren't getting money together anymore. They were still friends. They grew up together and nothing could break the bond they had. As far as Monster was concerned, it was T-mac who let all this shit go to his head, then he turned around and let his brother, J-rock, send him on a dummy mission by having him switch sacks at the dope spot. He should have known it would only be a matter of time before Hammer and the rest of the crew found out. T-mac was lucky Hammer spared his life the day he found out the grimy shit he was up to.

Monster was tired, but he knew he had to stay up. It was the middle of the afternoon, and custos were coming left and right. After he would serve a custo, he would sit on the couch and begin to doze off. It seemed like as soon as he would close his eyes, somebody would knock on the door. He kept going to the bathroom and splashing cold water on his face. He even turned on the radio to try to keep him awake, but every once in a while, he would drop his head and doze off.

A knock on the door woke him up from his temporary nap he was taking.

"Shit!" Monster cursed out loud and shook his head from side to side, trying to wake up.

He got up from the couch and opened the door and saw T-mac standing on the other side of the security gate.

"I need to holla at you," T-mac said.

The burst of cold air that was coming from outside woke Monster up. He just stood there for a moment, staring at T-mac. He didn't say a word. He just unlocked the security door and let T-mac in. Once T-mac entered the apartment, Monster locked the security door and locked the double deadbolt on the apartment door and left the key inside the lock. T-mac had a seat on the couch while Monster sat at the dining room table.

"I just came by to apologize for what I said to you. You my nigga. I just felt like you choose these niggaz over me. Me and my brother tryin' to put some shit together right now, and I want you to be part of it. This our muthafuckin' hood!" T-mac said, raising his voice and pounding his chest.

At first, Monster didn't respond. He just looked a T-mac with a blank expression on his face.

"Mac, I never chose anyone over you. I felt as if you choose your brother over everything and everyone else. You used to always talk about how y'all was gonna be shittin' on niggaz, and never once did you include me in y'all plans. Yo brother using you, bro. Think about it. He put you in a situation where you could have been killed… and for what? A couple thousand? And why would you wanna fuck over Hammer and the rest of the crew anyway? If anything, you should have introduced your bother to them so he could have copped his own dope from them. You and your brother went about shit the wrong way. These niggaz got the best work in the hood! You know Dolla would have looked out for you and your brother. If it wasn't for Hammer, Rick, Dolla, and Rell, neither one of us would have shit. And that nigga Hammer had a lot of love for you. You wrong for that shit you did. I can respect the fact that you and J-rock wanna put some shit down. This is our hood, and y'all have the right to have a spot of y'all own, but you shouldn't have played them niggaz like that. Real recognize real, no matter where you from and them niggaz kept it real wit you. I got nothin' but love for you and I wish you the best, but as far as shit goes wit me, I'm gonna chill where I'm at. Just be careful because yo brother ain't goin' about things the right way to get back in the game," Monster said.

On the inside, T-mac was burning up. *Who the fuck this nigga think he is, speaking on my brother like that? That's alright, just do what you came here to do,"* T-mac said to himself.

"You right, fam. You right. Feel like rollin' something up? I wanna smoke one wit you right quick before I leave," T-mac said, reaching into his pocket and pulling out a $10 bill.

"C'mon man. Don't insult me like that," Monster said, referring to T-mac trying to give him some money.

"I'm tryin' to grab a bag so I can have a lil something for later," T-mac said.

"Man put that shit back in yo pocket. I got you," Monster said.

"Good lookin'. You got some blunts?" T-mac asked.

He knew Monster always kept some blunts in the bedroom dresser drawer, and he was hoping that was still the case since he had left.

"Yeah, let me go get 'em," Monster said, then walked into the bedroom.

T-mac quickly got up from the couch and turned the radio up full blast. Monster walked back out to the front to find T-mac standing by the radio with his right hand in the front pocket of his hoodie.

"Yo, turn that shit down!" Monster yelled, trying to talk over the loud music blasting through the speakers.

"I can't hear the door if…"

In one swift motion, T-mac pulled the .380 pistol from the pocket of his hoodie and fired two shots.

Pop!

Pop!

One of the bullets missed Monster but the other bullet struck him in between his shoulder and his neck. Monster winced in pain from the burning sensation of the bullet and stumbled backwards, tripping over the dining room chair and falling to the floor. T-mac walked over to Monster and stood over him.

"Like I said before, you one of them now, nigga."

Monster was stunned T-mac had shot him and was now standing over him, about to take his life. The sight of that alone hurt more than the bullet that was lodged inside his body.

"Fuck you!" Monster yelled, clutching his gunshot wound.

"No, nigga. Fuck *you*!" T-mac said, pulling the trigger.

Monster closed his eyes and braced himself for the end, but he didn't hear a sound.

"Fuck!" T-mac said and took a step backwards.

He was struggling, trying to cock the weapon, but the gun had jammed on him. Monster opened his eyes and saw T-mac trying to eject the jammed bullet from the chamber and suddenly felt his adrenaline begin to rush throughout his body. He got up and staggered toward T-Mac.

"You muthafucka!" Monster yelled as he reached forward, trying to grab T-mac. T-mac couldn't free the bullet that was jammed in the chamber and he saw Monster charging after him. T-mac knew Monster was strong and even with him being shot, he didn't want Monster getting ahold to him. He turned and ran to the door, quickly unlocking it. Then he unlocked the security door and took off running down the stairs and around the side of the building.

Monster was losing a lot of blood and the sudden burst of energy he had quickly faded. He stumbled across the hallway and banged on the door to the dope spot three times as hard as he could.

"Who the fuck is knocking on the door like that?" Bo yelled, grabbing the 12 gauge. He looked out the peephole but didn't see anybody. He unlocked the door and opened it, only to find Monster passed out on the ground, completely covered in blood.

"Oh shit, Monster! Monster!" Bo yelled before running back into the apartment and grabbing his cell phone.

CHAPTER SEVENTEEN

The evening was approaching and Dolla was stretched out on the couch, smoking a blunt with his head in Savannah's lap. The two of them were discussing Savannah's future as a lawyer and starting her own law firm when Dolla's phone started ringing. His phone was on the coffee table and he reached over and picked it up.

"What up, doe?" Dolla said when he answered the phone.

"Bro, we need you over on Joy Road ASAP," Rell said to Dolla.

From the noise in the background, it sounded like Rell was in traffic.

"What's goin' on?" Dolla asked. He was now sitting upright on the couch. He could tell from the urgency in Rell's voice that something was wrong.

The crew was always careful about talking business over the phone, so Rell didn't give any specific details.

"Some shit popped off. Meet me on Joy Road," Rell said, then hung up the phone.

Dolla hung up the phone and massaged his temples. Savannah could tell something was wrong. She constantly had to remind herself of the nature of the business Dolla was in and to remain calm and supportive instead of acting hysterical and nagging him to death about quitting the game like most wifeys did. She loved Dolla unconditionally, and whatever Dolla chose to do, she would stand by him in right or wrong.

"Baby, I gotta go," Dolla said to Savannah, looking at the floor as if it would give him the answers as to how to handle the current situation.

"Is everything alright?" Savannah asked.

"I don't know. You know we don't be talkin' on the phone about that kind of shit," Dolla said.

"Just be careful. You just got out of jail this morning. Try to keep in mind that you're out on bond, honey," Savannah said, placing her hand over his.

"I know, I know. I'll be careful. Whatever the problem is, I'll take care of it as quickly as I can then come straight back here."

"You betta," Savannah said playfully, pushing his forehead with her index finger.

"I love you, baby," Dolla said and kissed her softly on the lips.

"I love you too, baby," Savannah said, looking into his eyes sincerely.

Dolla got up from the couch and quickly got dressed, then grabbed his pistol and left out the door. When he pulled up behind the apartments on Joy Road, he noticed that Rell, Rick, and Hammer were parked next to each other.

Damn, one of the spots must have got raided, Dolla said to himself as he got out the car and walked up the stairs.

He noticed the door to the weed spot was cracked open and he could hear someone talking, so he walked over to the door then opened it and stepped inside. He saw Rick, Hammer, Rell, and Bo standing in a circle talking.

"What happened?" Dolla asked calmly.

"Somebody shot Monster," Bo said.

Dolla could hear the anger in Bo's voice.

"What? Who?" Dolla asked. He wasn't calm now. He was yelling damn near at the top of his lungs.

Bo ran the story down to Dolla, telling him about how Monster came across the hall and banged on the door and how he found him lying on the ground in a pool of blood. They took him to Henry Ford Hospital in Dearborn, right down the street from the mall.

"Ain't nobody been up there to see him?" Dolla asked.

"No not yet. The paramedics said that it didn't look to be a fatal wound. They said he still had a pulse, but they had to try to stop the bleeding. I called Rell, then cleaned up all the blood that was in the hallway and inside the apartment and held down both of the spots until y'all started showing up," Bo said.

"Whoever shot him did it inside the apartment," Rick said to Dolla, pointing at the bullet hole in the wall behind them.

"One thing I know for a fact about Monster is that he only let females inside the spot during the day, and at night, he wouldn't let nobody inside the spot," Hammer said, referring to the custos.

"Whoever it was had intentions on trying to shoot him because the music was turned all the way up. You could hear it from outside the apartment. Monster never liked to have the music turned up too loud because he wouldn't be able to hear the custos at the door," Bo said.

"A bitch must have set him up," Rell suggested, trying to put the pieces of the puzzle together.

"The crazy thing about it is that nothing was missing from the apartment. The sack and the money was still in the bedroom and the place wasn't ransacked either." Bo said.

Dolla scratched his head then rubbed his chin, looking up at the ceiling.

"Tell me everything that happened earlier today that you can remember," Dolla said to Bo.

"Well, I held the spot down for Monster the night before. He took two bitches to the room for the night."

"Did you recognize them?" Rick said, cutting Bo off.

"Yeah, they some regular custos who come by just about every day. Everything was going normal while he was at the room wit the hoes.

The same custos who come by every day were coming thru and…wait a minute!" Bo yelled.

"What?" Hammer asked.

"Come to think about it, that nigga T-mac came thru twice while Monster was at the room wit the hoes last night."

"T-mac?" Dolla asked as if he didn't hear Bo when he said it the first time.

"Yeah, he came thru lookin' for him twice. I told him he was takin' care of some business."

Now everything started to make sense.

"It had to be that nigga T-mac that shot Monster like that," Rell said, slamming his fist into his hand.

"Oh, that nigga dead. I'm gon blow his muthafuckin' brains out his head," Hammer said.

"Hold on a minute. Before we do anything, we gonna holla at Monster first and make sure it was T-mac before we move," Dolla said.

"Are you serious? It ain't hard to tell, bro. This T-mac's work right here," Rick said.

"That may be the case, but we gotta be sure that it was him first," Dolla said.

"Well, what we wastin' time here for? Let's go to the hospital and holla at Monster," Rell said.

"Bo, can you hold both of the spots down while we go holla at Monster?" Hammer asked.

"Go ahead. I got this over here," Bo said.

"Dig, we gotta leave our straps here though. The hook be flickin' muthafuckas left and right in Dearborn. Y'all already know they don't like niggaz," Rick said.

The four of them left the spot and drove to the hospital in Dolla's truck. By the time they made it to the hospital, it was ten o'clock at night.

"Um, my brother got shot earlier today and I was told the ambulance brought him here," Hammer said to the nurse at the front desk.

"What's your brother's name?" the nurse asked Hammer.

She was typing something in the computer when she asked for the name of the patient. When she looked up and saw Hammer, his rugged appearance and the long scar down the side of his face made her uncomfortable and she couldn't hide it.

"His name is Antonio Reynolds," Hammer said, noticing the white nurse's discomfort.

"Hang on a second," she said and typed the name into the computer. "Yes, your brother is here, but you won't be able to see him tonight. Visiting hours are from eight a.m. until five p.m."

"Damn. Is there any way you can check on him for me and let me know how he's doin'?" Hammer asked.

"Sure," the nurse said and picked up the phone sitting next to her and dialed a number.

Hammer walked over to Dolla, Rick, and Rell who were standing back a distance from the desk and told them what the nurse said.

"Excuse me, sir," the nurse called to Hammer.

Hammer walked back over to the desk. "Is he okay?" Hammer asked.

"Yes, he's in stable condition at the moment. He lost a lot of blood, so he's gonna have to stay here a few days and rest before he can be released," the nurse said.

"Okay, thank you," Hammer said and walked back over the where the crew was standing and told them what the nurse said.

"At least he's alright," Dolla said.

They left the hospital and drove back over to the spot on Joy Road. When they got back, they walked up the apartment stairs and saw Bo running back and forth between the weed spot and the dope spot. Custos were waiting at both of the spots to be served. One of the custos from the weed spot noticed Rell and spoke. Rell walked into the apartment and grabbed a handful of bags and served the custos who were waiting.

Bo came back to the door of the dope spot and served the fiends. It was then he noticed Rell and the rest of the crew had made it back from the hospital. He locked the door to the dope spot behind him and walked over to the weed spot where the rest of the crew was at.

"How that nigga doin'?" Bo asked.

"He straight, but we couldn't see him. They told us to come back in the morning," Rick said.

"I might as well post up for the night. It wouldn't make sense to drive back home then drive all the way back in a few hours," Dolla said. He pulled out his cell phone and called Savannah.

"Hello?" Savannah answered the phone on the second ring.

Dolla could tell from the tone of her voice that she was worried.

"Hey, baby. I'm not gonna make it home tonight. I got some shit I gotta take care of in the morning, so I'll see you tomorrow afternoon sometime."

"Is everything alright?" Savannah asked.

"Yeah, everything straight. I just wanted to call you to let you know I'm okay."

"Okay then, see you tomorrow and please be safe. I love you," Savannah said.

"I love you too," Dolla said and hung up the phone.

"I need a drink," Dolla said and plopped down on the couch.

"Somebody walk to the store with me. I'll grab a bottle," Hammer said.

"C'mon, I'll go wit you. I need a little fresh air anyway," Bo said and the two of them walked out the door.

Dolla lit up a cigarette and inhaled the menthol-flavored nicotine and blew the smoke out of his nostrils. He was in deep thought, trying to assess the situation. Looking at the facts and how it just so happened that T-mac popped up the night before, looking for Monster was a red flag. The new year was already starting off fucked up.

Bo and Hammer came back with a fifth of Hennessey and a twelve pack of beers. They blessed the bottle and filled their red plastic cups to the brim with Cognac.

"This fo my nigga, Monster," Rell said and poured out a little bit of liquor.

"Shit, he ain't dead yet," Rick said.

"Yeah, we should be thankful we haven't lost anybody from our crew," Hammer said.

"You right. Instead, let's celebrate for Monster still being alive," Bo said.

They rolled up a box of blunts and started up a dice game. Custos were coming to the dope spot constantly. They had to keep stopping the dice game while Bo ran across the hall to serve the fiends.

"This shit fuckin' my roll up," Rick complained, shaking the dice that were clutched in his fist.

He was getting tore out of frame. Custos were coming to buy weed too. A few of them noticed Monster wasn't there and they asked about him.

"Monster straight. He chillin'," Dolla would say.

Bo ended up winning the dice game between the five of them. He sorted out the $1,200 in small bills before folding them and putting them in his pocket.

"Lucky-ass nigga was hittin' the whole time," Hammer said.

"It was his time. Plus, he been workin' a double shift today. He deserves it," Dolla said with a smile on his face.

At about two-thirty in the morning Hammer and Rick left. Hammer went back to Victoria's house and Rick went back to his apartment with Mary. Dolla decided to post up at the weed spot. He didn't want Bo by himself, just in case whoever shot Monster wanted to try to creep through in the middle of the night…

"Man, I'm tellin' y'all, I don't know who the fuck shot me," Monster said to the two police officers who were standing in his room.

Monster was irritated. It was early in the morning and he had a pounding headache. Meanwhile, the hook was bombarding him with questions.

"The neighborhood you're from has a lot of drug activity. Were you shot as a result of drug beef?" one of the officers asked.

"Man, I don't sell no muthafuckin' drugs. I work for a living."

"What do you do for a living, Antonio?" the other officer asked.

They were taking turns asking him one question after another.

"Landscaping," Monster replied dryly.

"What's the name of the company you work for?" Monster ignored the question and closed his eyes tight then opened them and stared at the ceiling. If he had the strength and energy, he would have jumped out of the hospital bed and beat the shit out of the two officers.

"Listen, I'm done talking. I ain't answering no more muthafuckin' questions. Now do me a favor and get the fuck outta my room. I got a headache and I'm tired," Monster said and closed his eyes.

That pissed the officers off. "Look, I'm only trying to help you. We were hoping you could give us some information that could lead to the arrest and prosecution of the person who shot you. Fuck this shit, let's go. You know how these kind do. He's gonna handle it himself in the streets. To tell you the truth, I don't give a fuck what happens. We'll be scraping him up off the sidewalk or booking him for murder. It makes no difference to me," the tall lanky officer said.

Monster opened his eyes and ice-grilled the officers. If looks could kill, the two officers would have dropped dead from the murderous stare Monster gave them.

"Listen, we'll leave you to rest, but if you ever want to get in touch with me, here's my card," the well-built short officer said and sat his business card on the nightstand next to Monster.

Once they left the room, Monster began thinking about T-mac. He was feeling all types of different emotions at once. He was hurt, mad, and disappointed at the same time. He felt like T-mac's brother, J-rock, had him blinded and was taking him down the wrong path. One thing was for certain, T-mac definitely tried to kill him last night, so that was the end of their friendship. T-mac had to die for that.

There was a knock at the door and the nurse entered the room.

"You have a visitor, Mr. Reynolds," the nurse said.

Who the fuck is it now? he thought to himself.

"It ain't the hook is it?" he asked the nurse.

"The hook?" the nurse repeated what Monster said, not knowing what the hook was.

"The police," Monster said slightly chuckling.

"Oh, it's not the police. It's your bothers. I know you've had a long morning already. I could send them away if you want."

That's gotta be Dolla and 'em, he thought to himself. "Naw, you can send them in," Monster said to the nurse.

She nodded and walked out of the door. She walked into the waiting area, which was close by Monster's room where Dolla, Rell, Rick, and Hammer were waiting.

"Your brother is in room 509. You all may see him now," the nurse said with a pleasant smile on her face and walked away.

They walked down the hall and knocked on the door before entering Monster's room.

"What up doe, my niggaz?" Monster said, trying to sit up. He became dizzy. The whole left side of his body was in pain. He felt like he had been run over by a truck. He fell back onto the bed and shook his head. He hated the feeling of being immobilized, but he was glad to see his homies standing around him.

"How you feelin', bro?" Dolla asked.

I'm a little better. They took the bullet out of me last night, but that shit got the whole left side of my body hurtin'.""

"So, tell us. Do you know who shot you?" Rick asked.

"Yeah, it was that hoe-ass nigga, T-mac. He would have killed me too if the gun didn't jam up on him." Monster said.

"I knew it! I told y'all niggaz it had to be T-mac! Once Bo said he came thru lookin' for him the night before, I knew then and there it was him," Rell said.

"What happened the night he shot you?" Hammer asked.

Monster told them how T-mac came through to the spot acting like he wanted to apologize and how he shot him and tried to finish the job, but the gun jammed.

"We gotta get to him and his brother," Dolla said.

"Oh, yeah. Somebody wanna holla at you," Hammer said and pulled out his phone. He dialed a number.

"Yeah, I'm at the hospital wit him now, hold on one minute," Hammer said and handed Monster the phone.

"What up, my nigga? How you feelin'?" It was E-baby.

They talked on the phone for about ten minutes before hanging up.

"If I can, I'm gon' come up to the hospital and holla at you once I get the time. If not, I'll see you when you come back to the crib. I always knew ya manz was a snake-ass nigga, but just know, we all got love for you and we here for you. We gonna straighten this shit out, you can believe that," E-baby said.

"Fa sho, fam. I'll holla at you," Monster said and hung up the phone.

"I see the hook came to holla at you," Rick said, noticing the business card with the officer's name and number on the nightstand next to the hospital bed.

"Yeah, the hook came to holla at me. I went the fuck off and told 'em to get the fuck outta my room."

They stayed for another half hour before they were ready to leave.

"Get some rest, my nigga," Rell said and walked over to the bed and dapped him.

The rest of the crew dapped him and headed for the door. "Oh yeah, before we go, we gonna need to know where them niggaz stay at," Dolla said...

Every Wednesday, T-mac and J-rock's mother would go to Bible study at the church around the corner from their house. Ms. Rita would leave the house in the morning and would stay at church all day and wouldn't make it home until the evening. An angel must have placed its wings around her. Little did she know shit was about to get ugly moments after leaving her house.

E-baby pulled all the way up in the driveway and into the backyard as Hammer, Dolla, and Rick got out of the van. E-baby and Rell were the only two in the van as they quickly pulled out of the driveway and drove to the corner of Coyle and Mackenzie and parked on Mackenzie at an angle where they could see T-mac's house. Monster had told them who all stayed in the house and the plan was to kick in the door and hold T-mac's momma hostage until T-mac and his brother came home. They were going to have Ms. Rita call them and tell them to come home where Rick, Hammer, and Dolla would be waiting.

"Don't hurt her," Monster told the crew.

Ms. Rita was good peoples. She'd helped raise a lot of young boys from that hood, including Monster. It wasn't her fault that her sons were some grimy niggaz.

The three of them slid the ski masks they had down over their faces and Dolla kicked in the side door. Rick and Hammer stormed inside the house. Dolla went inside behind them and shut the door then began searching the house with Rick and Hammer.

"Fuck! Ain't nobody here!" Hammer yelled and kicked over the glass coffee table, causing it to shatter on the hard wood floor.

"Chill out, bro. Don't even trip. Somebody bound to show up," Rick said.

"So, what we supposed to do until then?" Hammer asked. He was in murder mode, ready to straight up kill shit.

"We wait," Dolla said calmly.

Rick pulled out his cell phone and called E-baby.

"Yeah, what up?" E-baby answered.

"Ain't nobody here. We gon' post up and wait til' somebody show up. If you see anybody pull up or the hook, call me," Rick said.

"Bet. We on it," E-baby said and hung up the phone.

Two hours had passed and still no sign of T-mac, his brother, or their mother, Ms. Rita. E-baby and Rell were sitting in the car with the windows cracked, sharing a cigarette. They had the music turned down low and their heads stayed on swivel, looking for T-mac's car.

"Man, we might as well dip out. These niggaz ain't comin' back no time soon," E-baby said, frustrated.

"Ain't no turnin' back now. If we leave, them niggaz gonna know we came through, and that would give them the ups," Rell said, tossing the cigarette butt out the window.

"True, true. I just wonder how much longer…Oh shit!" E-baby yelled and began fumbling in his coat pocket…

J-rock and T-mac had a spot on Hubbell and Joy Road right behind the gas station. It wasn't like the spot Dolla and the crew had on Joy Road and Greenfield, but it was staying afloat. A lot of fiends would post up at the gas station and try to pump gas for change and clean the parking lot. Next door was a Coney Island restaurant and every day in the morning, all the fiends in that area would be up there, smoking cigarettes and drinking coffee.

J-rock came across a plug on Joy Road and Wyoming. The dope was good, but it was nothing compared to the dope Dolla and the crew had. They had a worker at the spot named Tez. He was twenty years old and worshipped the ground J-rock walked on. The spot was running low on product, so T-mac and J-rock left Tez at the spot and went to pick up a sack.

After the attempted murder of Monster, the two of them were on alert. They knew that Dolla and the rest of the crew would try to retaliate sooner or later. It was just a matter of when they would strike. Wherever they went, they went together. They turned off Joy Road onto Coyle Street and pulled up into the driveway of their mother's house.

"Let me run in here and grab the sack, I'll be right back," J-rock said.

He opened the car door and stepped out. T-mac just so happened to look up at the house and he immediately saw something was out of place. Ms. Rita never, ever liked for her curtains in the front window to be pulled open. She would complain whenever T-mac would look out the front window and walk away without straightening them.

"Boy, fix my curtains. I don't want people to be able to see all up in the house," she would say.

"Bro, hold on! Somebody in the house!" T-mac yelled to J-rock who was about to close the door and walk up the driveway to the side door. T-mac pulled his pistol from his waist and took the safety off.

Rick's cell phone rang, and he picked it up on the first ring.

"They in the driveway! Get ready!" E-baby yelled through the receiver.

Rick was already standing by the window with the curtain slightly cracked open. When Rick hung up the phone and yelled to Hammer and Dolla, telling them to get ready, and he inadvertently cracked the curtains apart a little more to get a better view of T-mac and J-rock. Then, out of nowhere, J-rock froze in his tracks and began walking backwards to the car.

"Somethin' wrong. They gettin' ready to try and buss up. We gotta take 'em in the driveway!" Rick yelled.

Hammer was the first to the side door and swung it open. He stuck the AK-47 out and started letting off rounds.

"Oh shit!" J-rock yelled, caught off guard, quickly making it to the car door. As he was getting back in the car, a bullet went through the passenger door, hitting J-rock in the leg.

"I'm hit, bro! Get us outta here!" J-rock yelled.

T-mac already had the car in reverse and stomped on the gas pedal. The car quickly shot backwards out of the driveway and into the street. Seeing T-mac reversing out of the driveway, Rick and Dolla started shooting out of the front windows of the house at the car. T-mac and J-rock were ducked low in the car as bullets were hitting the hood of the car and penetrating through the windshield of T-mac's Acura.

Everything seemed to be moving in slow motion as T-mac put the car in drive and pulled off, headed for Joy Road. When E-baby and Rell saw T-mac and J-rock trying to get away, they started up the stolen van and turned onto Coyle Street, headed in their direction.

Bullets coming from Dolla, Rick, and Hammer were hitting the driver's side of T-mac's car as they pulled off.

"Damn! They gettin' away!" Rell said as he rolled down the window and started shooting, hitting the back window of T-mac's car.

T-mac made it to the corner and made a sharp right turn, running the traffic light. They got away.

"Fuck!" E-baby yelled, punching the steering wheel.

He pulled into the driveway of Ms. Rita's house and Dolla, Rick, and Hammer jumped in the van and E-baby pulled out the driveway and flew down Coyle to Mackenzie and turned right.

"Oh, these niggaz wanna fuck around wit mamma's house?! It's on and poppin' now!" T-mac said, looking through the rearview mirror to make sure Dolla and his crew wasn't on their tail.

T-mac looked over at his brother who was rocking back and forth in the passenger seat, clutching his right upper thigh. Blood was leaking out of his leg like a faucet, and J-rock was squeezing tight, trying to slow down the bleeding.

T-mac made a right on Lauder Street and pulled over. He quickly took off his jacket and removed his long sleeve thermal shirt and began wrapping it around J-rock's leg, using it as a tourniquet to slow down the bleeding.

"Gimmie your gun," T-mac said, reaching into J-rock's waist and pulling out the .45 Desert Eagle.

He jumped out of the car and ran into the alley behind the auto shop and hid the two pistols and jumped back in the car. His car was in bad shape. It was riddled with bullet holes and it was leaking what looked to be anti-freeze. It was surprisingly still running.

"We bout to go to the hospital," T-mac said and pulled off, headed for the hospital in Dearborn.

E-baby made a right on Mackenzie and Prest and the five of them jumped out of the stolen van. They left the weapons in the van as Rell poured gasoline from the gas can on the floor of the van and Dolla threw a lit cigarette into it. After making sure the van caught fire, they ran on foot to Mackenzie and made a right, then another sharp right into the alley and ran to the back of the apartments on Joy Road and Greenfield up the stairs and into the weed spot.

Even though it was broad daylight, they had on ski masks, so if anyone was watching, they wouldn't be able to see their faces.

"Everything straight?" Bo asked as the five of them crashed through the front door.

"We missed them niggaz," Hammer said to Bo, trying to catch his breath.

"We gotta shut down. Shit about to get nasty over here," Rick said.

Minutes later, the whole hood was on fire. Police cars were flying up and down Greenfield. E-baby and Hammer stood in the window as they watched the hook make a right turn on Mackenzie. There was an unsettling silence between the six of them.

"I personally don't think they'll be comin' back today," Dolla said, breaking the silence.

"Oh yeah? What makes you so sure of that?" Rell asked.

"Well for one, they gotta regroup and come up with a plan. They know if they come over here that we'll be ready and waitin' for 'em. I'm sure T-mac told his brother about the type of firepower we have. They would be some fools to try to come over here," Dolla said matter-of-factly.

What Dolla said made perfect sense. They wouldn't be coming back today, but they would try to strike again sometime soon.

That night, the five of them posted up at the apartments with Bo and kept their eyes open, just in case T-mac or his brother wanted to try some dumb shit. Just as Dolla predicted, nothing happened that night, but they decided to switch things up a bit. Rick, Rell, and E-baby would post up at the apartments, and Hammer would be on Blackstone with

Gary. Quick and Bruce were doing a good job holding down the spot on Mettetal, so they really didn't need any more help. And if they did, Dennis was right down the street. Dolla would be on call if someone needed a rest or if a sack needed to be dropped off. Dolla would handle it.

They also beefed up on firepower and had two M-16s and two AR-15s, all of them fully automatic. If need be, they would be able to spit thirty out of a clip in a little over three seconds.

CHAPTER EIGHTEEN

Dolla had been so busy with maintaining the spots, he had very little time to spend with Savannah. Her winter break was coming to an end, and she would have to be leaving in a few days to return to the college campus. The legit stores they had open were now basically running themselves. The managers were able to handle mostly all of the day-to-day affairs, so Dolla wanted to spend some time with Savannah while he had the opportunity to do so. They spent the day shopping at Somerset Mall, then stopped at a restaurant and grabbed a bite to eat. After that, they went back home and smoked a few blunts and made love all night.

For the next few days, Dolla handled his business and went straight home to spend time with Savannah before she had to go back to school. The day came for Savannah to head back to Lansing. First, she had to swing by Rick's apartment to pick up Mary. Before leaving the house, she hugged Dolla and gave him a kiss that would have made a person think they weren't going to see each other again.

"Be safe and call me as soon as you get there," Dolla told Savannah.

The hospital was finally ready to release Monster after keeping him for a week. Dolla picked him up bright and early in the morning. No one was expecting him, so it would catch everybody by surprise when they saw him walk through the doors of the apartments. He was still recovering and wasn't at a hundred percent yet, so he couldn't post up at the spot.

As soon as they got on the freeway, Dolla lit up a blunt and handed it to Monster. It had been over a week since he had smoked, and he was already buzzing off the first five hits he took from the blunt. While driving to the apartments on Joy Road and Greenfield, Dolla told Monster about the botched hit on T-mac and his brother J-rock.

"We gotta put our ears to the street and find out where them niggaz be at. We don't wanna give them the time to grow in strength and numbers," Dolla said.

"I'm gonna put the word out, but it's a lot of people that got love for J-rock in this hood, so I doubt if anything will come out of it," Monster said.

The hood had love for Monster just as much as J-rock, which meant all the street niggaz and hustlers would stay neutral on the beef between them and just let them war between each other.

They pulled into the back of the apartment and they both got out the truck and walked upstairs to the weed spot. There were two female custos at the door waiting to be served when they looked up and saw Dolla and Monster approaching.

"There's my teddy bear! Where you been hiding at, baby?" one of the girls said and hugged Monster tight.

"Shit!" Monster winced from the pain of the gunshot wound.

"I'm so sorry. What happened to you?" she asked, pulling her arms back from Monster.

"It's alright. I just had a little accident, that's all," Monster replied.

"Well, the next time I come thru and you're here, I'll see what I can do to make you feel better," the girl said, winking at Monster.

The two girls walked down the stairs and Dolla walked into the apartment first and Monster followed behind him. The crew went crazy when Monster came through the door. Everybody was dapping him and Rell immediately poured him a drink.

"Welcome back," Rell said and handed him a plastic red cup full of Hennessey.

E-baby was glad Monster was out of the hospital and back with the team.

"I'm gonna post up with you over here, bro. Let one of them niggaz show they face around here and I'm gon' scatter they brains all across this bitch," E-baby said sincerely.

They all sat around and talked while rolling up blunt after blunt. Everybody could tell Monster was in a lot of pain and still needed a little time to rest up before coming back to the spot.

"I want you to stay at my crib until you get better," Rell said to Monster.

"You sure?" Monster asked.

"Man, what type of question is that? You family. Plus, I'm gonna be posted up over here most of the time. While you on vacation, I'm gonna send you a bad-ass stripper bitch over there to speed up the healin' process, ya feel me?" Rell said and looked over at Monster with a grin on his face.

Everybody in the crew knew Rell was a lady's man, so Monster knew he wasn't bullshitting. Monster spent the rest of the day getting drunk and high, kicking it with the crew. He even served a few custos too.

"Monster, what you doin'? You off the clock, nigga. Kick back and relax, bro," Hammer said to Monster, who would take off towards the door every time a custo came knocking.

"We the Royal Family. Ain't no days off!" Monster said and raised his cup in the air.

"You muthafuckin' right. Royalty brings loyalty," Rick yelled and held his cup to the ceiling.

"Royalty brings loyalty!" the rest of the crew yelled, raising their cups.

By the time the sun went down, Monster had a buzz so good he felt numb. He almost forgot that he'd gotten shot a week ago almost.

A few hours later, his left collar bone and neck began to ache. His left collar bone had been broken from the gunshot. The bullet had snapped his collar bone and lodged itself in the trap between his shoulder and neck. He had been drinking and smoking heavily, so he couldn't take any pain killers the doctor prescribed him.

"Yo, Rell. Can you shoot me to yo crib? I need to lay it down," Monster said.

Monster dapped everybody in the crew and was getting ready to walk out the door behind Rell when Dolla called his name. He stopped and turned sideways so he could see Dolla.

"You still get yo cut while you restin' up," Dolla said.

"Fo sho. Good lookin', fam," Monster replied.

He caught up with Rell who was already waiting by Monster's Range Rover that was parked behind the apartments. The alley was filthy. Dope fiends got high, fucked, slept, and did God-knows-what-else behind the building. Everyone in the neighborhood called it "crack alley," and Monster, Bo, and the rest of the crew parked their luxury vehicles in the alley, and no one dared to try to steal or vandalize their cars. They exercised the right to bear arms and best believe, they showed off numerous automatic rifles and pistols of all kinds. Every dope fiend and hood nigga knew better than to take their chances to fuck with their cars or even try to rob them.

"You want me to drive?" Rell asked.

"Yeah. I'm fucked up, bro," Monster said, walking over to the passenger side of the SUV.

The two of them got in the truck and headed towards Rell's crib. Monster had the seat reclined and was nodding off within minutes of pulling out of the alley and onto Greenfield.

"Damn, Monster. This bitch feel like we floating on air," Rell said.

"Yo, you think that nigga can…" Rell looked over at Monster and he was out cold.

Rell just smiled and shook his head as they made their way to his apartment. Once at Rell's, he woke Monster up and handed him the key.

"Apartment number 204. The alarm code is 1218. There's weed, and some blunts in the nightstand next to the bed and the liquor is on top of the refrigerator. Ain't no food in the house, so you gonna have to get a pizza delivered or something. Call me if you need anything."

"Good lookin', fam. 204, right?" Monster asked.

Rell nodded. Monster shut the door and walked up the stairs and into the apartment, disarmed the alarm and passed out on the bed with his clothes and coat still on…

Dolla got a phone call from his lawyer. He said that he wanted Dolla to stop by his office so they could talk in person.

"Is everything okay?" Dolla asked.

"We'll talk about it when you get here," the lawyer said.

Most of his clients were drug dealers, so he never liked to discuss anything over the phone in fear his client's phone may be tapped by the FBI or some other government agency. If anything about the case was discussed on a tapped line, it could crumble his defense and even possibly be removed from representing the client altogether.

"Do you have the address?" the lawyer asked.

"Yeah, it's on the business card you gave me," Dolla replied.

"Okay, then. See you soon," the lawyer said, then hung up the phone.

Dolla had spent the night on Joy Road with Rick, E-baby, Hammer, Rell, and Bo. After getting the call from his lawyer, he pulled himself together and got in the shower. He was still drunk and high from the night before, but the hot water spraying down his body refreshed him.

He got out of the shower and put on the same outfit he had on the day before. E-baby was the only one awake besides Dolla. He was standing in the window looking at the traffic on Greenfield, smoking a cigarette. He let E-baby know where he was going, then left out the door and headed downtown.

The law office was on Woodward and Jefferson inside a large building that rented office space to different companies. Dolla pulled into the parking garage across the street and parked. Then he ran across the street to the building. Once inside, he stepped into the elevator and got off on the fourth floor.

The law office was the first door to the right and Dolla knocked before entering.

"Hello! How can I help you?" the receptionist asked Dolla.

She was a white woman with blonde hair and with what looked to be breast implants. She was extremely upbeat, as if she'd done a few lines of cocaine and drank a few cups of coffee.

"Yeah. Is Otis Jackson here?"

"Yes, he is. If you'll give me a moment, I'll let him know you're out here to see him." She picked up the phone on her desk and pressed a number.

"Mr. Jackson, you have a young man out here who would like to see you. His name is… I'm sorry, I didn't get your name," the receptionist said to Dolla. When she looked up and asked Dolla for his name, she caught him staring right into her cleavage.

"Oh, um, Darin Jones," Dolla said, knowing that he had been caught red handed. *I'll fuck the shit outta this bitch,* Dolla thought to himself.

"He'll be with you in a moment. You may have a seat if you like while you wait," she said.

"Okay, thank you," Dolla said, then walked over to a chair and sat down.

What Dolla didn't know was that the receptionist was checking him out too. She was fucking Dolla's lawyer who was somewhere in his fifties, but she would sometimes fantasize about having sex with some of Mr. Jackson's younger drug dealing clients.

I wonder if he has a big cock, she thought to herself as her pussy began to get moist.

A few minutes later, a young brother who had a dope boy swag, stepped out of the door behind the receptionist. As he walked past, the receptionist spoke to him.

"See ya, gangster. Be careful," she said to the young hustler.

"You know it," he replied and walked out the front door.

Immediately after that, the phone rang on the receptionist's desk.

"Ok," she said and hung up the phone. "Mr. Jackson will see you now," she said to Dolla.

"Good lookin'," Dolla said as he got up from the chair and walked through the door.

Mr. Jackson was standing in front of his desk when Dolla walked into his office.

"Mr. Jones," he said to Dolla with his hand extended.

The two exchanged firm handshakes, and Dolla had a seat. Mr. Jackson sat down behind his desk. Mr. Jackson was in excellent shape and one wouldn't know he was in his fifties, except for the fact that he had a head full of grey hair and a grey goatee. If he was to dye his hair black, he could easily pass for thirty.

"What's up?" Dolla asked, wanting to know what this meeting was all about.

"Mr. Jones, I'm going to be frank with you. There has been a change in your case regarding your charges."

"Like what?" Dolla asked.

"Well, your case is no longer a state case. The FBI has decided to pick it up."

"The FBI? What the fuck the feds want wit me?" Dolla asked, completely taken off guard from the news.

"The serial numbers on the firearm were obliterated, which is a federal crime. Also, the fact that you had an ounce of marijuana didn't make things better. They're trying to convince the judge that you were protecting the drugs with the firearm you had in your possession."

"That's bullshit! I was gonna smoke that weed they caught me with!" Dolla exclaimed.

"Yes, I agree, but that's how the feds operate," Mr. Jackson said.

Dolla took a deep breath and calmed himself down.

"Ok, so what am I looking at?" Dolla asked.

"Well, as of now, the charges carry a maximum of ten years in a federal prison, but..."

"Ten muthafuckin' years for a pistol and some weed?! I know niggaz who done got caught wit a pistol and some dope and only got two years in the state prison!" Dolla yelled, cutting the lawyer off.

"Before you cut me off, I was going to tell you that I should be able to get them to drop the drug charge and get them to offer a plea deal for possession of an illegal firearm with obliterated serial numbers," the lawyer told Dolla.

"How much time would I have to do if you was able to make that happen?" Dolla asked.

"No more than three years. And the feds have good time and six months early release into a halfway house, so you'd do around two years," the lawyer said.

"If you can do that, there's an extra $5,000 in it for you." Dolla said.

"Don't worry. I can assure you, I'll do my best to get you the least amount of time possible. I handle state cases, but I also specialize in criminal cases as well. I'm going to get in touch with the prosecutor and offer a deal and set a court date. After that, I'll call you with your court date." The lawyer stood up and held his hand out.

"Sounds good," Dolla said, shaking his hand.

Dolla then turned and walked out the door.

"Have a nice day, Mr. Jones," the receptionist said when Dolla walked past her desk.

Dolla ignored her and walked out the front door.

The receptionist didn't cop an attitude when Dolla didn't speak to her. She got that a lot from Mr. Jackson's drug dealing clients.

"Such a same," she said, shaking her head. Then she got up from her desk and hung up the out-to-lunch sign on the front door. She walked to Mr. Jackson's office door, unbuttoning her blouse.

As Dolla stepped in the elevator, he was in a daze. *These muthafuckas wanna try to give me ten years? The feds play dirty as hell,* he said to himself as the elevator began to slowly descend to the first floor.

J-Rock was pissed off as he sat in the recliner inside the spot on Joy Road and Hubbell. T-mac was at the side door serving a custo and Tez was out on the street networking, trying to push fiends to the spot.

When their mother returned from church, she was extremely upset when she saw the bullet holes in her front window and shell casings all in the driveway. They tried their best to explain the situation, but the truth was, there wasn't an explanation, other than their greed caused this to happen. She had just recently paid off the house. This was the place where she raised her sons and she didn't want to give that up, but she knew it wouldn't be safe to stay.

They convinced her to temporarily move in with her sister until things calmed down.

"We need to go to them niggaz spot on Greenfield and blow that bitch up," T-mac said.

J-Rock didn't respond. He grabbed his crutches and stood up and went into the bathroom to take a piss. The AK bullet went in and out of his thigh and luckily didn't hit a major artery, so it wouldn't take too long for the wound to heal. T-mac had rushed him to Henry Ford Hospital in Dearborn, the same hospital where Monster was. Ironically, both of their rooms were on top of each other. Monster was in room number 504, and J-rock was in 409. J-rock only had to stay one night to let the doctor clean his wound to prevent it from getting infected.

J-rock plopped back into the recliner and lit a cigarette, blowing the smoke straight up towards the ceiling. T-mac wasn't feeling his brother's carefree attitude towards the situation.

"Bro, what the fuck we gonna do?" T-mac said with his hands in the air.

J-rock threw the half-smoked cigarette on the floor and stomped it out. He looked at his brother and just when he was about to open his mouth and speak, Tez came walking in through the side door.

"What up, doe? They been coming thru?" Tez asked.

"Yeah, a few here and there," J-rock said.

Out the corner of his eye, he could see T-mac was waiting on J-rock to give him an answer.

"Listen. Here's what I need y'all to do," J-rock said with a sinister sneer on his face…

The sun was shining early in the morning, even though it was still cold outside. Hammer's mother, Ms. Scott, wanted to do a little shopping and treat herself to something nice. She decided to go to the mall and stop at a few shoe and women's clothing stores. She bundled up and left out the front door, locking it behind her.

She walked into the alley and opened the garage door. When she pulled her car keys from her purse, she heard a noise coming from behind her car. When she looked up, there were two men who seemed to come from out of nowhere and both had guns pointed at her face.

"Bitch, don't move," one of the men said, stepping in closer to her.

"Here, there's some money in my purse," Ms. Scott said, trying to hand over her purse without making eye contact with the two men. She was so nervous that she was shaking. She wanted to scream in hopes of getting someone's attention, but she didn't want the men to shoot her for yelling. She was hoping they would just take her purse and leave.

"Bitch, we don't want yo money," the gunman closest to her said and snatched the purse from her hand, throwing it to the ground.

The other gunman moved quickly towards her, pulling some zip ties from his pockets and began to tie her hands together.

"No, please! What are you…"?

Smack!

"Bitch, shut the fuck up fo I kill you where you stand!" the gunman said after smacking her across the face with his pistol.

He hit her so hard that it slightly blurred her vision. The other gunman stepped behind her and wrapped a bandana around her mouth, jerking her head back violently as he tied it up. Then he pushed her on the ground and put zip ties on her ankles to prevent her from trying to run. They opened the trunk of her car and the two of them picked her up by the waist and feet and tossed her inside, slamming the trunk shut.

Bruce was standing on the side of the spot smoking a cigarette. He'd just got finished serving a custo and wanted to get a little fresh air. Quick had the heat on hell, so it was stuffy in the house. He saw Hammer's mom pull out of her garage and fly down the alley, making a left on Asbury Park. It looked like there was someone on the passenger side, but the car was moving so fast, he couldn't tell for sure.

She must be in a rush, Bruce thought to himself before flicking the cigarette and going back into the house.

Once the two men who snatched up Hammer's mother made it out of the alley, they turned on Asbury Park and the driver pulled over and let the other gunman out who ran to a car that was parked and got in. He started it up, then the two pulled off simultaneously…

J-rock had fallen asleep waiting on his brother and Tez to get back. When the side door flew open, it slammed against the wall, waking J-rock up. It was so loud, he thought it was the police raiding the spot or some stuck up niggaz. He had a pistol in his hand and damn near shot himself when he jumped from the loud noise.

"Who dat?" he yelled, still sitting in the chair.

He heard what sounded like a woman moaning and a smile immediately spread across his face. T-mac and Tez carried Hammer's mother into the basement and threw her on an old couch that sat in the corner. J-rock grabbed his crutches and made his way to the basement stairs.

"Help me out, bro!" J-rock yelled to his brother from the top of the stairs.

T-mac ran up the stairs and J-rock leaned his weight on T-mac's shoulder and hopped down the steps on his good leg. He leaned up against the wall while T-mac ran back up the stairs and grabbed his brother's crutches. Once he had his crutches, he made his way over to the couch where Hammer's mother was sitting.

Tears were streaming down her face as she wondered what was going on and why did these men kidnap her. She looked around the basement and noticed all the windows were covered. The basement smelled like mold and mildew and was extremely cold. One of the guys did look vaguely familiar, but she couldn't put a finger on where she had seen him before. She turned her head and closed her eyes as J-rock loomed over her.

"So, this is his momma, huh? J-rock said, not really asking anyone.

He grabbed her chin and forced her to make eye contact. He could look in her eyes and tell she was terrified.

"Your son has caused a lot of trouble for me and my brother. Now it will be up to him to save your life. In the end, he will have to pay with his," J-rock said.

Looking at Hammer's features in her face, he almost instantly went from calm to a state of rage.

Smack!

Ms. Scott was crying as blood began leaking from her mouth and nose.

"Yo bitch-ass son kicked in the door of my momma's house and tried to kill me and my brother!" J-rock said, leaning in so close he was spitting on her as he talked.

T-mac walked over and stood next to his brother. Ms. Scott was in pain, and it was only the beginning of her misfortunate ordeal. T-mac grew angrier as he looked at her, just like his brother, and smacked her a few times. Then he pulled out his pistol and put it to her head. She was screaming and crying, but her sounds were muffled because of the gag that was in her mouth.

"We might as well kill this bitch right now!" T-mac said with a look of murder in his eyes.

J-rock placed his hand on top of T-mac's gun and slowly began to lower the gun from her face. He felt his little brother's pain, but the plan wasn't to kill her. They needed her alive so they could have control over Hammer.

"Not yet, bro. We need her breathing. Plus, we gonna have a little fun first," J-rock said.

He could tell that Hammer got his pretty-boy looks from his mother. Even though she was older, she still was beautiful. Long curly hair, light-skinned complexion, and her body was in near perfect shape. J-rock's dick was getting hard as he looked her over as she lay on her side, still crying out of fear. Out of nowhere, he lifted her sweater as high as it would go, exposing her bra. Then he began caressing her soft breasts.

He pulled out one of her titties and began rubbing her nipple in a circular motion with his thumb.

"Yeah, we gonna have some fun wit you," J-rock said in a husky tone.

Man, these niggaz some gangsters fo real. They kidnappin' niggaz mommas, Tez said to himself.

He was glad to be on a team with niggaz who were as ruthless like J-rock and T-mac. *After this, ain't nobody gonna want to fuck with us.*

He heard a knock at the side door, and it snapped him out of his thoughts as he ran up the stairs to get the door. He shut the basement door behind him so the custo couldn't see what was going on.

"Let me get two of them," the older man said and handed Tez some folded bills.

Tez counted the money and saw only eight dollars.

"Next time you want something and you short, let me know before handin' me the muthafuckin' money, you hear me?"

Tez didn't like the fact that the fiend had just tried to finesse him. He wanted to just keep the money and tell him to get the fuck on, but he knew that wouldn't be a smart move. J-rock had said to take shorts for now because they were trying to build the spot up, so Tez ran into the living room and searched though the sack and pulled out two nickel rocks, but one of the stones was smashed into crumbs.

He ran back to the side door and placed the two stones in the fiend's hand.

"There you go," Tez said and watched as the fiend examined the one bag that was crushed.

"Hey, can I get a different one?" the fiend said.

"That's what you get when you short, fam," Tez said to the fiend.

The fiend didn't even respond. He just balled his hand in a fist, clutching the stones, and walked off.

"Damn, I can't even get a 'good lookin' out' for takin' yo shorts?" Tez said laughing.

He closed the door and went back down in the basement where T-mac and J-rock were. When he got down there, what he saw made him sick to his stomach. Hammer's mother's sweater was ripped off her, and her breasts were exposed. T-mac was pulling down her pants while J-rock was standing by, watching with his pants down and his dick in his hand. Ms. Scott was squirming and screaming until T-mac punched her in the face a few times. After that, she lay still as if she was already dead.

Tez was down for kidnapping, but he wasn't feeling that rape shit.

"Yo Tez, you want a shot of this pussy?" J-rock said, sticking his finger inside of Ms. Scott.

Neither he nor his brother heard Tez go upstairs and slam the basement door shut about five minutes prior. J-rock looked around and Tez was nowhere to be found.

"Oh well. More for us, bro," J-rock said…

After they were finished with Ms. Scott, they both got dressed and T-mac lit up a cigarette. For the next few minutes, there was complete silence between the three of them. Karen had never felt so violated in her life. Even back when her husband was alive, she never thought things could be worse than what she went through with him. After Hammer had killed him, things had been better for her. She couldn't remember the last time she had a peace of mind and freedom like she had for the last six years.

Now, she was laying in a cold basement, tied up by the wrists and ankles… naked and raped by two young men who had beef with her son.

Lord, what is it that I've done in this life to deserve this? she said to herself.

"Huahhhh!" she screamed out in pain. She was snapped out of her thoughts as J-rock put out a cigarette on the side of her face.

"What we gonna do now?" T-mac asked his brother.

J-rock spit in her face, then told T-mac to run upstairs and get the polaroid camera…

Tez was told to look for a new Lexus truck when T-mac and J-rock sent him to make a special delivery. They told him to check in the alley behind the apartments on Joy and Greenfield and if it wasn't there, then he was told to go back to the house that him and T-mac kidnapped the woman and it would be parked there.

He really didn't want to go back on Mettetal where they'd snatched the woman, but he didn't want to show any weakness. He let out a sigh of relief when he saw the silver Lexus truck sitting in the alley behind the apartments on Greenfield and Joy Road. He pulled into the alley behind the truck and threw his car in park. He pulled his pistol from his waist and jumped out the car with it still running. He didn't know how the owner of the truck looked and judging from the beef he had with T-mac and J-rock, he had to be a killer too. He quickly slid the envelope under the windshield wiper then jumped in his car and sped off.

After getting the news from his lawyer that he would have to do some time in prison, Dolla called Savannah and told her to come home.

The next day, she didn't go to class. Instead, she drove to Detroit to meet up with Dolla at their home in Sterling Heights.

When she pulled up, she saw Dolla's Expedition parked in the driveway, which meant he was at home. She parked and got out the car then entered the house through the back door. It was quiet inside the house. Savannah thought Dolla was upstairs asleep. She walked through the kitchen and was startled when she saw him sitting on the couch. He had on a white beater and some jogging pants as he sat on the couch, smoking a blunt so fat it looked like he stuffed a quarter ounce inside of it. In his other hand, he had a fifth of Remy V.S.O.P., hitting it straight from the neck. It was clear to see that Dolla was stressing.

"You okay, baby?" Savannah asked him, placing both her hands on his broad shoulders.

He looked up at her through his bloodshot red eyes.

"Here, gimmie this," Savannah said, taking the bottle from his hand.

She sat it on the coffee table and picked up the ashtray and sat on the couch next to Dolla. He had ashes on his shirt and in his lap. Savannah brushed him off and he handed her the blunt. She took a pull and started coughing as soon as the large cloud of weed smoke entered her lungs. Dolla patted her on the back as she gagged from the smoke.

"Whew! I pulled a little too hard that time," she said, wiping the tears that formed in her eyes.

"Okay, so tell me exactly what's going on," Savannah said to Dolla.

Dolla explained to her exactly what the lawyer told him, and the time he could possibly be looking at.

"Ten years for a goddamn gun and an ounce of weed? That's insane! There's no way possible they can do that," Savannah yelled.

Tears began rolling down her checks. Ten years was a long time to be away from her man. She knew that the game he was in could land him in prison for a long time, maybe even for the rest of his life, if that day was ever to come. But she was completely caught off guard when Dolla told her how much time he could be facing. She never would have thought the feds would pick up such a petty case. She thought he would get probation or would have to sit in Wayne County jail for a few months at the most. She was devastated.

"The good thing is that the lawyer said that he could guarantee that I won't get sentenced to more than three years, and he said that the feds have good time where you only do about eighty-five percent of your time, so it might be less than that."

Three years or less sounded a lot better than ten, but she was still crying because she knew that sooner or later, she would wake up one day and he wouldn't be laying next to her side...

Hammer was at the spot on Joy Road with E-baby and Bo, Rick was on Mettetal, Quick and Bruce wanted to do some shopping and they had some females they were gonna hook up with for the day. The two of them deserved some time off. They rarely ever left the spot and because of that, they were able to save up a lot of money.

Rell left to pick up some girls he'd met at a strip club on Six Mile and Woodward and took them back to his apartment where Monster was chilling at. Hammer's phone rang, and he picked it up.

"What up, doe?" he said, answering the phone.

"Shit. What up, bro?" the caller said.

He was speaking very fast and Hammer didn't recognize his voice.

"Who dis?" Hammer asked. He could barely hear because the music was on and Bo and E-baby were shooting dice, so he opened up the door and security gate and stepped outside.

"Don't worry about who I am, my nigga. I need you to go to yo truck and get that message that I left for you."

"What message?" Hammer asked.

"Nigga, go to your truck that's parked in the back and find out," the caller said.

Hammer walked down the back hallway stairs and into the alley where his truck was parked.

"What muthafuckin' message?" Hammer asked.

He was about ready to hang up on the person on his phone, thinking it was some type of joke.

"Look in the windshield, my dawg," the caller said.

Hammer looked on his windshield and sure enough, there was an envelope under his windshield wiper.

"What the fuck is this?" Hammer asked, reaching for the envelope.

"Open it and find out," the caller said.

Hammer finally had the envelope in his hand and when he opened it what he saw made him sick to his stomach. He immediately grabbed his stomach and bent over and began throwing up on the side of his truck. In the process of doing so, he dropped his phone and the caller could hear Hammer puking his guts out. He quickly picked up the phone and yelled into the receiver.

"What type of sick fuckin' joke is this?! Don't play wit me!"

Hammer was in tears and snot was running from his nose. Inside of the envelope was a picture of what looked like Hammer's mother. She was badly beaten, her breasts were exposed, and her pants and underwear were down to her ankles as if she had been sexually assaulted. She had a gag in her mouth and dried up blood was in the corners of her mouth and around her nose. She had a purple bruise on the right side of her face and what looked to be a burn on the side of her cheek. At the bottom of the picture it read, "missing you" with a smiley face drawn next to it.

"Naw, nigga. Dis shit ain't a game. Now listen to me. These niggaz is not playin'. If you don't do what I tell you, I can guarantee that you'll never see yo momma again. These niggaz want the top guys in your crew dead. Dolla, Rick, and your homeboy, Rell. They want them dead, and you have to be the one who does it. They want proof, so grab a camera and take pictures of each of them after you kill them. You have six hours to kill them. If you're one minute past the six-hour limit, yo mamma is dead."

"I don't believe you. Give me proof that you got my momma," Hammer managed to say between sobs and the tears falling down his face.

"You want proof, muthafucka?! You want proof?!" Hammer could hear the caller running down some stairs then he heard him say to someone, "put the bitch on."

"Michael, please help me! They say they gonna…"

The caller snatched the phone away from his mother. "Now you think it's a game?"

Hammer knew it was his mother. Hearing her voice hurt him even more. He had a feeling who it was, and he was ready to kill.

"How I know y'all ain't gonna kill her anyway?" Hammer asked.

His voice was weak. He wasn't speaking in the tough guy tone like he was earlier. He sounded like a helpless little boy, like he used to sound when his father used to beat his mother and he was too little to do anything about it. The caller could hear the defeat in his voice.

"This is what's gonna go down. You gonna kill yo homies, take the pictures of them after you kill 'em, then I will call you exactly six hours from when I hang up. I'm only gonna call once, so if you don't answer the phone, I'll take it that you didn't do the job and that will be the death of your momma. If you do answer the phone, I'll take it that you handled yo business and then I will give you directions to meet me somewhere. Bring the photos with you. Once I see them and I know they're official, I'll make a phone call and they will let your momma go. She will have a phone with her and once they release her, she will call you herself and let you know she's safe. If I think the pictures are fake, or if I even see a police car while meeting with you, she's dead. Don't think about doing anything crazy. You'll be in my territory and I will be closely guarded by niggaz. Do the right thing, Michael. You only get one mother. Niggaz come and go. You have six hours starting now."

Hammer heard the click and the line went dead. He got in his truck and started punching the steering wheel. He was yelling so loud, it almost sounded like a wolf howling in the night. He was completely hysterical. He was in a terrible predicament. He had a choice to make. Either he kills his best friends, street brothers… the niggaz who held him down his whole life and his mother when he was locked up for killing his father or let his mother die at the hands of his enemies for something that he got himself into on the streets.

Hammer looked at his Rolex watch. It was 3:13 p.m., which meant he had to do what he had to do by 9:00 p.m. *This shit ain't for her, man. This shit ain't for her,* Hammer said shaking his head.

Tears were pouring down his face like water running from a faucet. He checked his waist to make sure he had his seventeen shot 9 mm Glock with him. Once he felt it, he opened the glove box and made sure the extra clip was in there where he left it. Once he stuck his hand in the compartment and felt the clip, he closed it shut. He started up his truck and pulled out of the alley.

He was flying down Greenfield Road, but he was keeping his eye in the rearview mirror on the lookout for the hook. He pulled into the drug store parking lot on West Chicago and Greenfield and shut the engine off and ran into the store. The drug store also developed film and sold different types of cameras. Hammer flew down the aisle where they sold cameras and grabbed a Polaroid camera and a box of film and ran towards the front counter. The place was crowded, and shoppers were looking at Hammer like he was crazy. He had dried up tears on his face, his eyes were bloodshot red, and his nose had dried up snot around it. Hammer looked like a maniac. The line was long, so Hammer went to the front of the line cutting in front of everyone else.

"Hey!" a shopper yelled at Hammer, but he ignored the woman as he dug inside his pocket to get some money.

At first, the security guard by the front door thought Hammer was trying to run out with the camera. He was just getting ready to approach Hammer until the guard saw him pull out a $100 bill and slam it on the counter. The camera and film cost about $50 altogether.

"Keep the change," Hammer said, and flew out the door.

That security guard just didn't realize how much God was on his side at that moment. If he would have attempted to stop Hammer when he thought he was trying to steal the camera, Hammer would have shot him dead in front of all those customers without any hesitation.

Hammer quickly jumped in the truck and started it up. He pulled out his phone and called Rell.

CHAPTER NINETEEN

Monster and Rell were enjoying themselves with the two women that were dancing in front of them to the music. They both were sitting on the couch with a blunt in rotation and a stack of $1 bills that they were throwing at the girls. Monster and Rell both had cups filled to the rim with Hennessey. Being a drug dealer wasn't an easy occupation. There was a lot that came with being deep in the game, but it was times like this that made it all seem worthwhile.

Rell's cell phone was ringing as he was stuffing a few bills in one of the girls' thongs.

"Man, who the fuck is this?" Rell said, slightly irritated. "Yeah?" he answered.

"Bro, what you got goin' on?" Hammer asked.

"I'm kinda in the middle of something. What's up?" Rell asked.

"Shit. I need you to roll wit me right quick. It's a house in Brightmoor I wanna check out. It got the potential to bring us in some serious paper," Hammer said.

"That shit can't wait til later? I got some hoes on the floor right now," Rell responded.

"Naw, the owner waitin' for me right now. We gotta make this shit happen now or we might not have another chance. I got all this money on me and I want you to roll, just in case this nigga tryin' to set me up or something," Hammer said.

Hammer knew that Rell wouldn't leave him hanging when he mentioned that he didn't' want to risk going alone to do business with a stranger.

"Damn, Hammer! C'mon. Come swoop me up. How long you gonna be?" Rell asked.

"I'll be pulling up in a few minutes, so be ready," Hammer said and hung up the phone.

About four minutes later, Rell's phone was ringing.

"You outside?" Rell asked, knowing it was Hammer on the phone.

"Yeah, I'm parked out back," Hammer said.

"I'll be out in a minute," Rell said, then hung up the phone. *That nigga gone have to wait a few more minutes*, Rell thought to himself as one of the girls put her face back in his lap and went back to servicing him with her mouth.

Rell had to place one of his hands behind the girl's head and began pumping in and out of her mouth as hard and fast as he could to speed up the process. Almost ten minutes later, he bust in her mouth and got up and pulled his pants up. He walked over to the bedroom door and knocked before opening it. When he swung open the door, he saw the girl with Monster bent over with her elbows on the bed and Monster was behind her. He was crushing the big-booty red bone chick from the back. He was trying to take it easy because the left side of his body was sore, but the weed and liquor and plus the fact that the girl had some good-ass pussy, made him temporarily block out the pain.

"Yo, I gotta shoot a move wit Hammer right quick. Something about checkin' out a new spot in the Mo' or something. Y'all keep ol' girl company until I get back. This shouldn't take long." Rell smacked the tall thick brown skinned girl on the ass and her ass cheek jiggled like a bowl of Jell-O.

The brown-skinned girl walked into the bedroom and climbed onto the bed and opened her legs wide directly in front of the redbone who was getting hit from the back by Monster. The redbone chick began using her tongue to please the brown-skinned girl who threw herself back in pleasure.

"Y'all be careful," Monster managed to say between thrusts.

"Naw, nigga. You be careful," Rell said, laughing as he picked up his coat and pistol off the living room couch and walked out the door.

As Rell was walking down the stairs, Hammer was calling him again. He could hear him blowing the horn too. He opened the door and walked over to Hammer's truck and got in.

"My fault. I was…"

"Damn, nigga! What the fuck took you so long?!" Hammer yelled, cutting Rell off.

"Aye, calm yo muthafuckin' ass down wit that shit, fo real! You the one that caught me off guard with this shit, nigga," Rell snapped at Hammer.

Hammer didn't say a word. He just pulled out the lot and onto Greenfield.

"What's up wit you? You been drinkin' or something? Yo eyes red as hell and yo face look swollen," Rell said, noticing Hammer's appearance.

"Yeah, I been drinkin' a lil bit," Hammer replied dryly.

"So, what up wit this new spot? Dolla know about it?" Rell asked.

"Uh-uh, not yet," Hammer said and turned up the radio.

He wasn't in the mood to be answering a lot of questions or having small talk. He felt like the scum of the earth, the grimiest nigga living. They weaved in and out of traffic until they crossed Fenkell and Burt Road and entered the heart of the Brightmoor community.

"What block is it on?" Rell said, trying to yell over the radio.

"Not too much further. A couple more blocks down," Hammer yelled.

Hammer had no idea where he was taking Rell. He was making up everything on the go. They crossed Fenkel and Lahser. Now Hammer's time was limited, and he had to pick a street quickly. There were only about thirteen blocks left and they would be in Redford, which was the suburbs.

Hammer made a left turn on Decosta. He drove through the first block and felt like it was too close to Fenkell, so he crossed over to the second block.

This is it, Hammer said to himself.

The block looked just like Blackstone, full of vacant and burned down houses with only a few people living on the block.

"Here we go right here," Hammer said, pulling into the driveway.

There was trash littered everywhere. Clothes, broken bottles, shoes, wood and scraps… you name it, it was around the house. The houses on each side were burnt up, only a portion of the houses remained.

"C'mon, let's go," Hammer said, shutting off the engine and stepping out of the truck.

"Where the fuck the owner at?" Rell asked, noticing they were the only ones there.

"Shit, he probably thought we was bullshitting and left. It took you about twenty minutes to come outside," Hammer said. "Let's just go inside and see what it's lookin' like. I'll call the owner back in a minute."

There weren't any doors on the house, so they walked in through what would be considered the side door. The inside of the place was trashed, and it felt colder in the house than it did outside. They carefully walked through the kitchen and into the living room, which was probably the most decent part of the house. The front windows were boarded up, which made it slightly dim in the living room. Only a few streaks of light shined through the cracks of the plywood that covered the windows.

"How much this nigga want? He can't be askin' for no more than a few thousand for this bitch," Rell said.

His back was turned to Hammer as he was looking down the hallway which led to the bedrooms. Hammer quickly pulled his Glock from his waistline and pointed it at Rell.

Rell was like his big brother. It was gonna be hard to shoot him but Hammer definitely wasn't gonna shoot him in the back. Rell didn't deserve to go out like that.

"I love you, bro. Don't ever forget that," Hammer said, focusing his aim.

"What the fuck is you – "

Pop! Pop!

Pop! Pop!

Pop! Pop! Pop!

Rell turned around to face Hammer, only to be gunned down in a hail of bullets by his best friend.

After the first shot, Rell died instantly. The next two bullets struck him directly in the heart, while the rest of the bullets entered different parts of his body. Hammer didn't want to hit him in the head. He wanted Grandma Cill to be able to give him a traditional open casket funeral. Rell was dead, but his eyes were wide open.

Hammer kneeled next to Rell and ran his hand down his face, closing his eyes shut forever.

"God bless you, bro," Hammer said and kissed Rell on the forehead.

He grabbed Rell's pistol from his waist and stuck it inside his inner coat pocket. He figured it might come in handy later. He quickly ran outside to the truck and grabbed the camera he got from the drug store and ran back inside the house. While he was waiting for Rell outside of his apartment, he had loaded the film into the camera. He took a picture and before he left, he shook the picture dry and examined it to make sure Rell's dead body could be seen clearly on the picture. Once he saw the picture was good, he left the abandoned house and jumped in his truck.

Next stop, Mettetal, Hammer said to himself.

Hammer flew down Fenkell Avenue until he reached the Southfield Freeway service drive. It was there that Fenkell and Grand River crossed each other, so a person that was driving would have the option to cross over to Grand River or stay on Fenkell. Hammer merged over onto Grand River and pressed the gas pedal to the floor. He would be on Mettetal in a few minutes.

Rick served the two young custos at the side door.

"Yo, where Quick and Bruce at?" one of the young dudes asked Rick.

"They out fuckin' wit some hoes right now, my dawg," Rick said. He handed them two dime bags and closed the door.

He watched the two boys leave and smiled to himself. It seemed like only yesterday he was the same age as the two boys who'd just left, running around, trying to come up on something. He liked posting up on the block hustling. It reminded him of when he first hooked up with Dolla and Rell. Even though he got shot in the alley directly across the street from the spot, he liked this spot the most. It wasn't as much drama like the other three spots. Rick could feel the love on Mettetal. Custos felt more like family, where at the other spots, the only reason custos came was because they had the best dope and weed in those neighborhoods.

Rick plopped on the couch and lit up a cigarette. He began to reminisce and look back on how the last five and a half years had been good to him. Now he owned spots, had a partnership in legit business investments. Yes, life was good. He had to lay down a few sucka-ass niggaz, but it was well worth the reward.

There was a knock at the door and Rick didn't feel like getting up, but he knew he had to get that money. *Every muthafuckin' dollar counts*, Rick said to himself as he got up from the couch.

When he got to the side door and opened it, he was surprised to see Hammer.

"What up, bro? Why ain't you just use your key?" Rick asked.

Hammer's mind was moving a hundred miles per hour in a hundred different directions. Dolla, Rell, Hammer, and Rick had spare keys to every spot, including Dennis's.

"Damn, I wasn't even thinking. I'm trippin' like a muthafucka. I came through because I ain't got shit to smoke on and me and my girl tryin' to blow something," Hammer said.

"What you need?" Rick asked with his hand out.

"Um, let me get – "

"Man, would you knock that shit off? C'mon in and get whatever the fuck you want! This our spot, remember?" Rick said, cutting Hammer off.

Hammer walked in and shut the door behind him. He needed to get Rick outta the way quick. Time was passing, and he still had to go see Dolla. He yanked his pistol from his waistline and called Rick's name. As soon as Rick turned around, he froze. He was stunned to see Hammer pointing his gun at him.

"Aye, bro! What the fuck you doin'?! Put that shit up and stop playin'!" Rick said. He was completely baffled as to why Hammer had his gun pointed at him.

"I'm sorry, Rick," Hammer said and pulled the trigger.

Tat! Tat!

Tat! Tat! Tat!

All five bullets struck Rick, sending him crashing to the kitchen floor. He hit him the same way he hit Rell, with all the shots hitting him in the upper body. No head shots. He quickly ran outside to his truck. It was parked in the alley. He grabbed the camera and dashed back into the house. He snapped the picture and waved it dry. Once he saw it was a clear shot, he took off out the door. He locked the side door behind him and got in the truck. He opened the glove compartment and began searching through it frantically.

"Where the fuck is it?" he said out loud. "I got it!" It was the directions to Dolla's house in Sterling Heights.

He ejected the almost empty clip from his Glock, then grabbed the extra clip from the glove compartment and stuck it in his gun.

Two down, one to go. Don't worry, Momma. I'm coming to save you! Hammer said to himself and started up the truck and pulled off.

He was in so much of a rush that he didn't realize that when he'd shot Rick, he landed on his back. By the time Hammer ran to the truck to get the camera and came back inside the house to take the picture, Rick was laying on his stomach.

Hammer was waiting at a red light on Grand River and checked the time on his Rolex. It was 6:13 p.m., which meant he had about three hours left. It would take him an hour to reach Dolla's crib, which meant he was making good time.

Dolla was pissed. Gary had called him and said they were out of dope on Blackstone.

"Did you try calling Rell or Hammer?" Dolla asked. He knew Rick was posted on Mettetal, so he wouldn't be able to go and make the drop, so he didn't even mention his name.

"Yeah, I tried callin' both of 'em and I ain't getting no answer," Gary said.

He wanted to send Gary over to Victoria's house on Westbrook, but he knew Victoria wouldn't give him shit. Plus, he didn't know her phone number and wasn't no tellin' if she was home or not.

"Alright, I'm on my way," Dolla said and hung up the phone.

"I gotta run this sack over to Blackstone right quick," Dolla said to Savannah.

"Why can't nobody else do it?" Savannah asked.

"Cause ain't nobody else available. Niggaz ain't answering they phones," Dolla said.

"Well, let the spot be without a sack until somebody else can do it then."

"Now, you know I can't do that," Dolla said.

"What you mean, you can't do that? You the one that run shit!" Savannah exploded. "You had me stop what I was doing and drive here in this cold-ass weather, only for you to take off and leave me here by myself for God knows how long."

"I told you, I'll be right back, Dolla said.

"Nigga, you said that shit the week before I left, and you didn't come back for damn near two days!"

"But that was different," Dolla said.

"You know what? Fuck it. Gone ahead and do whatever it is you gotta do, I don't care. You out on bond and you running around like you got a license to do what it is you doing. If you don't give a fuck, neither do I," Savannah said.

"You can come with me if you want," Dolla said. He knew everything she was saying was the truth, but the game never sleeps. He had to handle his business.

"Boy, I just got out the shower. I ain't about to go out in the cold and get sick. You got me fucked up."

Whenever Savannah talked like that, it meant she was mad. She usually kept calm even when she was irritated.

"Like I said, I'll be right back," Dolla said and got up to get dressed.

He was in a rush, so he just threw on a sweatshirt and grabbed his coat and skull cap. He grabbed his pistol and his pack of cigarettes and headed for the door. He stood in the doorway and yelled "I love you" to Savannah. She mumbled some type of smart remark Dolla couldn't understand, and he slammed the door behind him.

While on the road, Dolla tried to call both Rell and Hammer, but he didn't get an answer. He made it to Detroit and parked on Westbrook in front of Victoria's house and got out the truck. Victoria was in the bathroom when she heard a knock on the front door. For the last three and a half weeks, she had been sick, throwing up early in the morning and late at night. She had also missed her period as well and as she stood in the bathroom and held a pregnancy test to the light, she wasn't surprised when the results were positive. She was pregnant with Hammer's baby.

Right on time, she thought to herself as she walked to the front door. She thought it was Hammer, but when she looked through the peephole and saw Dolla, she became worried. She quickly opened the door and let Dolla in.

"Is everything alright?" she asked Dolla.

"Have you seen Hammer?" Dolla asked Victoria.

"No, not today. He said he would be on Joy Road."

"Hmmm… Well, him or Rell ain't answerin' they phones right now and Blackstone outta dope, so I had to drive all the way from my house to come out here and grab a sack to take over to the spot."

"Do you think they're okay?" Victoria said.

"Yeah. They probably shooting dice and got the music turned up or something, Dolla said."

"Right, well the sacks are in the basement, under the dryer," Victoria said.

"Good lookin'," Dolla said and went downstairs to the basement and grabbed a $15,000 sack, already cut up into rocks from under the dryer and ran back upstairs.

"Thanks, Victoria. I'mma get this over to Blackstone. You alright? You look kind of sick," Dolla asked.

"Actually, I just found out I'm pregnant," Victoria said with a smile spread across her face.

"Straight up? Damn, I'm about to be an uncle!" Dolla grinned.

"Make sure you tell Hammer to come straight home when you talk to him, but don't tell him the good news," Victoria said.

"I won't. And congratulations," Dolla said and gave her a hug.

"Thanks. Make sure you tell Savannah I said hello," Victoria said to Dolla, who was already off the front porch and almost near his truck.

"I will," Dolla said and climbed into the truck.

He pulled up in front of Blackstone and got out the truck and used his spare key to get in the front door. Gary, Krissy, and Keith were sitting in the dining room talking when Dolla walked in.

"Yo, I'm glad you got here when you did. Custos been comin' left and right. I been tellin' em to come back in thirty minutes," Gary said.

Dolla pulled out the sack from his coat and tossed it on the dining room table.

"Roll something up, G. I'm tryin' to smoke before I get back on the highway," Dolla said.

His nerves were bad, and he wanted to be relaxed by the time he got back home so he could straighten things out with Savannah. Gary pulled a half ounce out of his pocket and began breaking down a large chunk of weed. Dolla grabbed a blunt from off the table and split it open.

CHAPTER TWENTY

Hammer pulled in the driveway of Dolla's house and threw his truck into park. He quickly realized Dolla's truck wasn't in the driveway, but Savannah's explorer was parked near the garage.

"Fuck! This nigga ain't even here!" Hammer yelled as he punched the roof of his truck.

He started to pull out of the driveway and head back to the city to try to find him, but he knew he was running out of time. He couldn't waste precious time going on a wild goose chase. Then he came up wit an idea. It was a shot in the dark, but he had to take a chance. He got out of the truck and walked up to the front door. He rang the doorbell and knocked as hard as he could.

Savannah was on the couch when she heard the doorbell ring and someone knock.

I wonder who this is? she said to herself as she got up from the couch and walked to the front door.

She thought it may have been one of the neighbors, but when she saw Hammer on the porch, a chill shot down her spine. She opened the door and looked him over.

"Hammer, what you doing out here?" she asked.

"Some shit done went down. I need you to call Dolla for me," Hammer said.

"Okay, come in," Savannah said, unlocking the security gate.

Yes! She fell for it! Hammer thought to himself. He needed her to open the security door before he could make his way into the house.

As soon as he stepped across the threshold, he pulled out his gun and shoved it into her ribs. Savannah gasped. She tried to scream but nothing came out. She was in shock to say the least. She couldn't believe Hammer just pulled a gun on her.

"Listen up. I don't want to hurt you, but I need you to get Dolla on the phone right now!" Hammer said, raising his voice.

Savannah nodded her head. She was scared. She walked over to the couch and grabbed her phone and Hammer was on her heels every step of the way.

"Sit down," Hammer commanded with the gun still pointed at her.

Her hands were shaking violently, but she still managed to dial Dolla's phone number. Dolla was hitting the blunt when his cell phone rang.

"Hello?" Dolla said, picking up the phone.

"Baby, come home quick. Hammer over here and he got a gun," Savannah said. Her voice was trembling, and it sounded like she was about to cry.

"Hey! Don't play like that, I ain't got no time – "

"Dolla, I'm tellin' you now. You got exactly one hour to make it over here. If you don't, I'm gonna kill yo girl," Hammer said, cutting Dolla off.

"Nigga. what the fuck is you talkin' about?" Dolla yelled into the phone.

"Nigga, you heard me. One hour or she's dead," Hammer said and hung up the phone.

Dolla's ears were ringing. He couldn't believe what he'd just heard.

"Is everything straight?" Gary asked.

Dolla instantly became hot and started sweating.

"Yeah, shit smooth. My girl just trippin', that's all. Look, I gotta dip. I'll holla at y'all," Dolla said and headed for the door.

Once he got outside, his stomach felt queasy on the inside. He went to open the door and climb into the truck and outta nowhere, he began throwing up. Dolla forgot to lock the front door, so Krissy followed behind him to lock it. She went outside and began rubbing Dolla's back.

"Baby? You alright?" she asked him…

Dolla made it back to the house in under forty-five minutes. By the grace of God, there wasn't a lot of traffic on the roads and there wasn't a police car in sight. He pulled up in front of the house and got out the truck, leaving the driver side door wide open. He wanted Hammer to see that he came alone. Dolla came rushing through the front door to find Hammer standing over Savannah with his gun pointed at her.

"Hammer! Put that muthafuckin' gun down, right now!" Dolla yelled.

Hammer yanked Savannah off the couch and stood behind her with the gun to her head.

"What the fuck is wrong wit you, nigga? Have you lost your goddamn mind?" Dolla asked Hammer.

They got her, bro. They got her. I gotta do this shit," Hammer said.

"Who got what? What the hell is you talkin' about?"

"T-mac and his brother. They got my momma! They say they gonna kill her if I don't kill you, Rick, and Rell. I already got Rell and Rick…"

"Hold up. You killed Rell and Rick? Hammer, how could you?" Tears began to fall from Dolla's eyes. "You didn't have to do that! We could have done something…"

"Nigga, I ain't got a choice! They told me I got six hours, now I only have less than an hour and a half! I had to do it! This shit ain't for her, man," Hammer yelled.

He was now crying too.

"It kills me that I had to kill my own brothers, you just don't know. But I gotta get my momma back, no matter what," Hammer said.

He was crying like a baby.

"I'm sorry, bro. I'm sooo sorry. May God forgive me," Hammer said and raised his gun and pointed it at Dolla, still holding Savannah in his grasp.

"Hammer, wait!" Dolla yelled.

Boom!

Pop!

Two shots went off and Dolla fell to the ground.

"Ahhhhhhh!" Savannah screamed.

She was completely covered in blood, but it wasn't hers. It was Hammer's. Savannah ran over to Dolla and cradled him in her arms. She was hysterical.

"Are you okay, baby?" Savannah asked Dolla.

"Yeah, I'm straight. Help me up," Dolla said to Savannah.

He stood up and took his hand and examined his shoulder. He had only been grazed by Hammer's bullet, but Hammer wasn't so lucky. Krissy had blown his head clean off his shoulders with a 33 revolver, the same kind of gun he used to kill his dad when he was a kid.

Hammer didn't even hear Krissy creep in the side door. She'd made it just in time. Dolla had let her out of the truck at the corner of his street. He gave her the spare key to the side door and told her to sneak in and if necessary, shoot Hammer. When she made it into the house, it was evident that it was necessary to kill him. It was a blessing that Krissy stepped outside and saw Dolla throwing up next to his truck. At that moment, Dolla was in a state of shock and told Krissy what was going on.

"What?! Hold on. Let me go get my shit," and she had run back into the spot.

"What's going on?" Keith had asked as Krissy darted past him and picked up her purse.

"I gotta drive Dolla somewhere," was all she'd said before leaving out the front door.

Dolla was in no condition to drive, so he had given Krissy directions to get to his house. She'd hit the freeway and driven to Sterling Heights at top speed. Once they'd gotten close to Dolla's street, she pulled over and they switched seats. Dolla ended up taking the wheel and let her out on the corner. When she'd gotten out the truck, she opened her purse and made sure her gun was loaded before walking down the street to Dolla's house.

Dolla stepped outside on the front porch. He wanted to see if any neighbors had heard the gunshots. The block was quiet. Then he thought about it. This was the suburbs. If somebody heard the shooting, the police would have already had his house surrounded by now. He walked back in the house and shut the front door behind him.

He walked over to Hammer who lay on the ground with a large chunk of his head missing. Savannah went upstairs and got in the shower and Krissy was in the kitchen smoking a cigarette.

"Damn, bro," Dolla said, shaking his head.

He leaned down and searched him, finding another pistol in his jacket and about $6,000 in one of his pants pockets. In the other pocket, he found a picture of Hammer's mom. She was beaten and bloody, naked and tied up by the hands and ankles. "He wasn't lying," Dolla mumbled to himself as more tears fell from his face.

Dolla walked over to Krissy and hugged her.

"Thanks for being there for me," Dolla said.

"I told you, I love you like a son. Ever since I can remember, you always treated me like a human being, not a piece of meat or a dope fiend. You treated me with respect at times when I didn't treat myself with respect. I'll always love you for that," Krissy said.

"They really did kidnap his momma," Dolla said, showing Krissy the picture.

"Damn, they had that boy in a fucked-up position," Krissy said looking at the picture.

Dolla looked over his shoulder at Hammer's lifeless body.

"Krissy, I'm gonna need you to follow me in my truck. I gotta clean this shit up," Dolla said, motioning towards Hammer's dead body…

"Where the fuck these niggaz at?!" Dennis said, hanging up his phone.

It had been almost three hours since he'd found Rick laying on the floor in the hallway, shot up in the spot on Mettetal. Dennis had just finished having lunch with one of his girlfriends downtown, when he turned on Mettetal. He noticed there were four people standing outside in the front of the spot. The scene just didn't look right. Custos never just hung out in front of the spot.

Damn, they must have got hit, Dennis said to himself, thinking the police raided the spot.

He decided to pull over and see what was going on. He parked and got out his car and walked across the street.

"Ain't nobody here," the female custo said to Dennis.

"You sure about that?" Dennis asked.

"Yeah, I been here twice already. This the first time I never got an answer since I been coming over here," she said.

Dennis walked over to the side door and pulled out his keys and found the spare to the spot and stuck it in the security door. He opened the security door and the side door and stepped inside.

"Rick!" he yelled.

He knew Rick was there by himself. He thought he was asleep or something. When he got in the kitchen, he saw Rick laid out in a pool of blood.

"Oh, shit! Rick!" Dennis yelled, pulling his pistol from his waist.

He stepped over Rick's body, almost slipping in his blood and did a quick search of the house. He wanted to make sure nobody else was hiding inside. After checking the house, he ran over to Rick's body and grabbed his wrist an checked his pulse. His pulse was still beating, but very slow and faint. Rick was still alive, but he was quickly dying.

Dennis pulled out his cell phone and dialed 911. He told the operator how he found his nephew and the directions to the spot.

Moving quickly, he grabbed the two AK's and wrapped them inside a cover and grabbed the sack from the living room. When he got to the side door, the female custo was standing there.

"What's going on?" she asked.

He stepped out of the house and pulled the side door up behind him.

"Wait right here," he said to her, then he ran to his car and popped his trunk and tossed the rifles and the weed inside then slammed it shut.

The other three custos that were outside when Dennis pulled up were gone.

"I need you to tell me exactly what you saw when you came over here the first time," Dennis said to the girl.

"Nothing. Nobody was around. I knocked on the door, but I didn't get an answer, so I left. Then, I came back about an hour later and still got no answer, and that's just before you pulled up," she said.

"Okay, listen. I'm gonna need you to leave. The police and the paramedics on the way," Dennis said.

"What happened?" she asked.

"Somebody shot my nephew," Dennis said.

"Oh my God! Is he gonna be okay?"

"I don't know. Now go ahead and get up outta here before the hook pull up. They gonna have a lot of questions and I don't want you around," Dennis said politely but sternly. "The spot won't be back open until tomorrow morning."

She nodded and got in her car and pulled off.

Something wasn't right with this picture. Rick was in the house shot up but, yet the place wasn't ransacked. The sack was still there, and money was still in Rick's pockets, so it wasn't a robbery. Also, the side door's security gate was locked, which meant either somebody took Rick's keys, or somebody had keys of their own. Only himself, Rick, Rell, Hammer and Dolla had keys to the spots, which meant somebody had to force their way inside. The whole situation just seemed sour. Nothing made sense.

A few minutes later, the ambulance arrived, and the police came immediately behind the EMS. They put Rick on a gurney and placed him in the ambulance and rushed him to Sinai Grace Hospital. The police questioned Dennis for about an hour and a half before letting him leave. They were all inside the spot, searching everything. They found six gun shells in the kitchen and Dennis also noticed one of the officers taking a set of keys from the lock on the inside of the door. That was a serious red flag and Dennis made a mental note of that.

After leaving the spot, he drove down to his house and dropped off the sack and the rifles and left headed for Sinai Grace Hospital on Schafer and Outer Drive. When he got there, the doctors were still operating on Rick, trying to save his life. He tried calling Rell, Hammer, and Dolla, but he couldn't get in touch with anybody. Something wasn't right…

Krissy followed Dolla all the way back to Detroit. She was driving Dolla's truck and Dolla was driving Hammer's truck with Hammer in the back. They exited off the freeway on Seven Mile Road, then made another right on Rosemont Street and drove to Pembroke and made a right. This was also a crime-infested area with a lot of abandoned houses. Dolla used to fuck with a chick from this hood a long time ago.

He pulled up in the driveway of an abandoned house and Krissy pulled up a few houses down. Dolla pulled up in the garage and grabbed the gas can next to Hammer and got out. He poured gasoline on the inside of the truck and on the inside of the garage. He stuck his head inside the truck and took one last look at Hammer.

"I still love you, bro. I always will," Dolla said.

He walked out of the garage and lit two cigarettes and tossed one of them inside the garage then walked off smoking the other cigarette.

He dropped Krissy off at the spot on Blackstone, thanked her and told her to keep what happened to herself until he decided on what to tell the crew.

He was on his way back home and he wanted to call Savannah to let her know. He didn't have his cell phone on him. He'd left it in the trunk, and it had been there since he had rushed home earlier when Hammer had Savannah at gunpoint.

He reached and grabbed his phone from the passenger seat. As soon as he started to dial Savannah's number, his phone rang.

"What up, doe?" Dolla said when he answered the phone.

"We got a problem. I'm at the hospital with Rick. Somebody shot him up," Dennis said.

"Which one you at?" Dolla asked.

"Saini on Outer Drive and Schafer," Dennis said.

"I'm on my way right now," Dolla said and hung up the phone.

Dolla made a U-turn and headed to the hospital. Once he got there, he found Dennis sitting in the corner of the lobby with his head down, massaging his temples.

"How's he doing?" Dolla asked, sitting down next to Dennis.

Dennis looked up and saw Dolla and dapped him.

"I don't know. Doctors operating on him now. When I found him, he barely had a pulse. Somebody tried to kill that boy," Dennis said.

"I already know. It was Hammer," Dolla said calmly.

"Hammer?" Dennis asked.

"Yeah, you heard right."

"Dolla told Dennis everything that happened and how Hammer said he killed Rell.

"Damn! Have you found Rell?" Dennis asked.

"Nope, not yet. I can tell you this, that Nigga T-mac and his brother gonna pay. I'm gonna personally make sure they suffer," Dolla said.

They talked for a few hours and a doctor came into the lobby and told Dennis and Dolla he had some good news.

"Well, we've been able to stabilize your nephew, but right now he's in a comatose state."

"How long will he be in a coma?" Dennis asked.

"Can't say. Could be a few days, a few months… I don't know when he'll wake up," the doctor said.

"Damn. Okay. Thank you, doctor," Dennis said.

The doctor told him and Dolla the visiting hours and excused himself. Dolla and Dennis agreed to hook up the next day to tell everybody else the news. They dapped each other and left the hospital.

Dolla went home and took a long hot shower. As he showered, he cried like a baby as images of his best friends flashed through his mind. That night, he fell asleep in Savannah's arms as she comforted him.

The next morning, Savannah left to go back to school, but before she left, Dolla made her swear to keep her mouth closed and not to speak on what happened the night before.

"But what about Mary? She's gonna wonder where Rick is," Savannah said.

Dolla hadn't thought about that. "Don't tell her today. Wait until tomorrow. I'm already gonna have enough on my plate today," he said.

He left the house and met up with Dennis on Mettetal. From there, Dennis got in the truck with Dolla and they went to pick up Monster form Rell's apartment. They got to Rell's place and told Monster to get dressed.

"What's going on?" Monster asked.

"We'll tell you everything once we meet up with the rest of the crew," Dolla said.

They drove over to the spot on Blackstone and picked Gary up. Krissy and Keith agreed to hold the spot down until they got back.

On the way to Joy Road, Dolla called Quick and Bruce, who were still at a motel room with some girls and told them to meet them at the spot on Joy Road. Dolla told them it was a mandatory meeting.

They pulled up behind the apartments and got out the truck and walked up the stairs. Both spots were bangin' when they got upstairs.

There were custos at the dope spot and the weed spot. Dolla signaled for Bo and they all walked inside the weed spot.

While the crew was talking amongst themselves, Dennis and Dolla stood outside and shared a cigarette and talked as they waited for Quick and Bruce. They pulled up about five minutes later and once they made it upstairs, Dolla and Dennis followed them into the apartment.

"Ok, everybody. Listen up. I got some things I wanna talk to y'all about and it ain't good. Hammer and Rell are both dead and Rick is in the hospital in a coma, right now as we speak," Dolla explained. Questions along with a bunch of crying erupted from the crew.

"What happened?"

"Who did it?"

"Were they all together when they got shot up?"

Dolla told them of how T-mac and J-rock kidnapped Hammer's mother and how he killed Rell and tried to kill Rick in exchange for getting his mother back.

"Them niggaz is dead! I'mma torture them hoe-ass niggaz!" E-baby yelled. Tears were welling up in his eyes.

"Don't trip. We gonna take care of em, but first there's gonna be some changes. Dennis and I will be overseeing things until we know what's gonna happen with Rick. If I can't be reached, this is the person who will be around to handle things. Make sure y'all get wit him and get his number," Dolla said, placing his hand on Dennis's shoulder.

"E-baby, I want you here on Joy Road for now. Monster, once you get better, you'll be on Blackstone wit Gary for a while. We gonna have to shut these two spots down and relocate. It's too dangerous to remain here and keep hustling. We sittin' ducks. Also, I want y'all niggaz to be strapped at all times. Ain't no tellin' who them niggaz got watching us. Make sure all of you stop by the collision shop on West Chicago and Greenfield and get stash spots installed in y'all cars. Do it before the week is out. Y'all gotta watch y'all surroundings. These niggaz playin' dirty. I suggest relocating y'all loved ones somewhere safe. Y'all makin' enough money to move y'all peoples around. I don't want a repeat of what happened yesterday. This shit is real and right now, we at war! Don't get caught slippin'! All that hangin' out and partying and fuckin' hoes gotta cease for now. Until we can get to these niggaz, I want y'all to invest in some hoopties to ride around in. All the whips on rims gotta be put up. They stick out too much. That nigga T-mac know what most of y'all drivin' so the hoopties will help niggaz fall under the radar. For now, this meeting is over. By the end of the week, I don't want to see y'all driving y'all whips. I want everybody to head back to their spots and resume business. Quick and Bruce, be careful. If y'all see any police, shut down the spot and call Dennis. Remember, tough times don't last. Tough niggaz last. Ain't nobody gonna break us or destroy us! Royal Family until the casket drop! Let's smarten up and handle business in honor of Rell, Hammer, and Rick!" Dolla yelled.

The rest of the crew yelled, "Royal Family!" and began dapping each other.

"Yo, E-baby. Let me holla at you," Dolla said.

"What up, doe?" E-baby asked. He was the smallest of the crew, but he was definitely one of the strongest, a straight up soldier.

"Send some niggaz over on Coyle to burn down them niggaz momma's house. I want it done tonight," Dolla said.

"It's done," E-baby said, looking Dolla in the eyes.

Everybody began leaving, heading for their posts. Dolla dropped Gary off on Blackstone. Monster stayed behind with E-baby and Bo. His truck was parked behind the apartments, so he could leave when he was ready. Dolla dropped Dennis off on the block and left to check on the legit store.

Later that night on the news, the reporter said the owner of an auto shop on Joy Road and Wyoming found a woman in her forties, beaten to death and naked behind his shop. They didn't know who the woman was at the moment. They also said a homeless man found a young man shot to death in an abandoned house on Detroit's northwest side, on Fenkell and Decosta.

That's gotta be Rell and Ms. Scott, Dolla thought to himself.

The news didn't say anything about finding a body on Pembroke Avenue where Hammer was.

The next day, Dolla stopped by Victoria's house and told her that Hammer was missing, and he couldn't find his mother either. He told her that he feared something was wrong and told her he had beef with some nigga on Joy Road. He wanted her to file a missing person's report for Hammer and his mother.

"Oh God!" She placed her hand over her stomach. "I'm gonna get dressed and go to the police station," she said.

From there, Dolla drove over on Mettetal and pulled up in front of Grandma Cill's house. He knocked on the door and a few minutes later, she unlocked the door and let him in. She was glad to see Dolla, but when he told here about the body that was found on Dadosta and that it was a possibility it might be Rell, she busted out in tears.

"Lord, no! Please don't let that be my grandson!" she screamed.

She got dressed and her and Dolla drove to the morgue downtown. When she went in the room to see if the man they found in the house was Rell, her heart dropped when she saw it was her grandson laying on the slab with a tag that read "John Doe".

"Oh my God. That's my grandbaby!" she wailed. She felt light-headed and would have fallen if it wasn't for the medical examiners that caught her. One of the examiners called Dolla in the back to help with Grandma Cill. He helped her sit in a chair and got her a glass of water. She was sweating and complaining about the left side of her body feeling numb, so Dolla called 911 and Grandma Cill was rushed to a hospital. She ended up having a stroke and passing away before she made it to the hospital.

Dolla was tore up behind that. Grandma Cill was like a grandmother to him. He knew deep down she didn't die from a stroke. It was from a broken heart.

T-mac and J-rock were laying low. They were staying away from Joy Road. They were staying with J-rock's girlfriend on Six Mile and Sunderland. They would meet up with Tez in the parking lot of a phone store on Plymouth and Schafer to pick up the money from the sales of the spot on Joy Road and Hubbell and give him sacks to flip at the spot. They let Tez bring his best friend Ray to the spot to give him a hand.

"So, what's been going on at the spot?" J-rock asked.

Tez let him know that it was starting to pick up. It was doing about $1,300 a day.

"Oh yeah. I rode past y'all momma house on Coyle and somebody burnt that bitch down," Tez said.

"What?" J-rock asked. He knew his momma was gonna be upset with him and his brother behind this.

"That was Dolla and the rest of them niggaz! Let's go chop they spot up," T-mac said.

He'd had enough and was ready to kill all them Royal Family niggaz.

"We gotta lay low for a while longer. They want us to come lookin' for 'em," J-rock said.

"How much longer we gonna wait?" T-mac asked.

"Until we got the money, firepower, and manpower to knock them niggaz off. Our little plan with Hammer didn't work, so we gonna have to handle that shit ourselves. Don't worry, bro. Our time will come. And when it does, we gonna end this shit once and for all," J-rock assured T-mac. "We just gotta be patient."

A week later, funeral services were held for Jerell Thomas and his grandmother, Pricilla Gaines. Dolla and Dennis temporarily shut down the spots for half a day and the whole crew attended. There were a lot of people from Mettetal and the hood that came to pay their respects as well. They decided to combine Rell and his grandmother's funerals. Their caskets were set up in a way where Rell and his grandmother were facing each other. Everyone walked up to the caskets and put flowers in them while saying their final goodbyes.

Everyone at the funeral was crying. It was truly a devastating loss for the community. The funeral was held in the hood at the church on the corner of Grand River and St. Mary's. After the funeral, everybody drove behind the hearse to the cemetery where the preacher said a few last words before Rell and his grandmother were lowered into the ground.

After the burial, the crew met up on Mettetal and had a barbeque. They ordered cases of liquor and smoked about four ounces of weed. Tears were shed and even laughter as they reminisced, remembering the good times they had with their brothers. At about six in the evening, the party came to an end and everyone returned to their posts and opened up shop.

Two days later Victoria received a phone call from the police department. Dental records had come back from two different murder victims and they matched those of Michael Scott and Karen Scott, Hammer and his mother. Victoria was devastated. She was two months pregnant with Hammer's baby and she didn't even get the chance to tell him or his mother. She called Dolla and told him the news about Hammer and his mother.

"I'm pregnant with his child and he's dead. I don't know what to do," Victoria said to Dolla over the phone, crying.

"Don't worry. You and the baby won't need for anything. I'm going to move you to a better neighborhood. I just want you to relax and try not to stress out. I know you got a lot of love for my nigga, Hammer. It's gonna be hard, but we'll make it through this together. We family. I gotta make funeral arrangements. Don't hesitate to call me if you need anything, no matter the time of day," Dolla said.

A week later, they had another double funeral. This one was for Hammer and his mother. They had it at the same church in the hood and the whole crew was there along with the entire neighborhood. People were angry and filled with rage behind Karen's death. She was the victim of a violent and brutal murder and the community wanted justice. Some wanted justice from the police department, but most wanted street justice. They wanted the animals who did this to her to suffer just like she did.

The hood was hurt behind Hammer's death as well, but everyone knew that Hammer was in the streets and death or jail was almost always the end results of being in the dope game.

After the funeral and the burial, the crew had another cookout on Mettetal. Grandma Cill and Ms. Scott's houses were covered with stuffed animals, balloons, cards, and empty liquor bottles. The crew shut down shop for half a day, the same way they did for Rell and his grandmother. The hood lost four good people and one was clinging on for dear life in the hospital. It was a very stressful time for the crew as well as their families.

Just as the party was beginning to come to an end, Dennis got a phone call. It was the doctor from Sinai Grace hospital. He had good news. Miraculously, Rick came out of his coma. It had been almost three weeks since the shooting, and things weren't lookin' good for him, but he pulled through - clearly a blessing from God. The doctor also said that he should make a full recovery.

After Dennis got off the phone with the doctor, he told Dolla the good news. Dolla was elated that Rick was going to make it. He made an announcement to the crew about Rick's status and everybody yelled and screamed joyfully. The crew returned to the spots with their spirits and heads held high, for that was a sign of things getting better.

Dennis and Dolla rushed to the hospital to see their friend. Rick's mother and his sister Rita were already there. They were happy and giving God the glory for sparing Rick. The four of them hugged and embraced each other. Rick was awake, but he was still very weak. He had lost a lot of weight and still needed his rest. He didn't have the strength to talk, but when he saw his mother, sister, Dennis, and Dolla, a smile came across his face. He was happy to be alive, and from that day forward, he vowed to live life to the fullest and never take anything for granted.

Rick was discharged from the hospital a month later. He moved his family out to Sterling Heights, a few minutes away from Dolla's house. Dolla appeared in court and six months later. He plead guilty and was sentenced to thirty-six months in federal prison. He is currently in McKean FCI, located in Bedford PA.

Dennis and Rick continue to oversee the day-to-day operations of The Royal Family.

Just like Dolla said, "this shit don't stop until the casket drop."

ABOUT THE AUTHOR

Don Michael was born and raised in Detroit, MI where he still resides. He is currently working on a sequel to this book and various other titles.